Time & Again

Ruby Killingsworth

Volume 2

Amanda Cherry

ISBN-13: 978-1-948280-39-6

Other Ruby Killingsworth Stories

Rites & Desires (DefCon One Publishing, 2018)
"Facing the Music," *Cobalt City Dragonstorm* (DefCon One Publishing, 2021)
Femmes Fatale, with Erik Scott de Bie (DefCon One Publishing, 2022)
Bad Intentions (Femmes Fatale 2), with Erik Scott de Bie (DefCon One Publishing, 2023)
"Villian Origin Story," *99 Fleeting Fantasies* (Pulse Publishing, 2024)

CONTENTS

To everyone who's making the most of a second chance

ACKNOWLEDGEMENTS

This book was one of those books. Every author has them, you hear about them in your early career, but until you have one, you don't know exactly what it means. Now I've had one, and I have been humbled by it. And even though my name is the one on the cover, this book was absolutely a group effort.

My loudest, most profound thanks to Erik Scott de Bie for talking me down off the ledge multiple times, for reminding me that I actually do know how to write a book, and for not letting me make major career decisions while running a fever. Every author needs someone like you, and I am so glad you continue to put up with me.

Giant thanks to Dawn and Jeremy, without whom I would never have dared attempt writing a book in the first place, and to Nate Crowder for creating this amazing universe we all get to play in. I know a lot of words, but none of them are strong enough to express my gratitude to the three of you.

Shout out to Rosemary, Gabrielle, and the rest of the Writing Church family; Jennifer Brozek and the Wit 'n Word crew; Laura Anne Gilman, Emily Skaftun, and the Brewery Patio league; Seanan McGuire, Crystal Frazier, and the We Blend adventuring party; Elsa Sjunneson, Scott James Magner, Lindsey Johnson, Erin Wilcox, Ben Gorman, Sarah Gulde, Kelsey Dawn Scott, Cherie Priest, Joseph Brassey, Tom Hoeler, and all my amazing friends across sci-fi and fantasy publishing who keep us excited about what we do and the future of this business.

Thanks to the Dungeon Scrawlers—Allie, Erin, and Yang especially—for making space for me to live out yet another dream. And to Tom, Scott, Tami, Karen, Lance, Kelli, and the rest of the Random Rockers for giving me the chance to feel like an actual rock star. You all keep my creative well filled so I can continue to pour feelings onto the page.

Thanks to Jet City Roller Derby for a dozen years of badass athletes to watch and learn from. Your grit, enthusiasm, and generosity are admirable, important, and greatly appreciated.

Thanks to the Batteys for being amazing friends to our whole family, incredible supporters of my work and my ambitions, and A+ Disney companions.

Thanks to Mac for being my biggest fan, my most enthusiastic cheerleader, my helper, my skating buddy, and my favorite fellow Swiftie. You are awesome.

And finally: a million and more thanks to my husband, Andrew, for dealing with crises and deadlines and how very Extra I get around book launches, convention readings, podcasts, and band jobs. Without you, I would definitely not be where I am. Thank you for being my shoulder to lean on and my partner in snark, my favorite sailing partner, and the best dad our human kid and perfect pups could possibly have.

CHAPTER ONE

Ruby Killingsworth did not make a habit of going to meetings.

Not that meetings weren't a fixture of her life; she attended plenty, several per week on average. She sat in on some, presided over most, and had even been known to call into a few from her limousine or bathtub. What she did not do, what she had not done more than a handful of times in the past twenty years, was *go* to meetings. Since her very first foray into the Goblin Records C-suite as a fresh-faced twenty-two-year-old, meetings, for the most part, came to her.

But not this morning.

Not this meeting.

It had taken a lie to get this meeting on her books to begin with, and this conversation was too important to risk not being the one to do the traveling.

As she dashed across the street with just enough magic in effect to keep passers-by from recognizing her, she had to hope it would be worth the trouble. The late July morning was muggy and warm, making Ruby thankful for the breeze off the plaza, even if it did mean she'd need a minute to magically repair her appearance once she was finally back in the air conditioning.

She paced herself as she rounded the corner, taking care not to let herself perspire. The plaza side door opened automatically as she approached, a touch of tech that felt enough like magic to make her smile.

A quick whiff of actual magic meant the receptionist waved her past without either woman having to speak. And another made the three young men she found waiting for the elevator choose not to board the car when it arrived. Finding herself alone in the elevator as the doors slid shut, Ruby took a deep breath to center herself before working the magic necessary to assure her face, hair, clothing, and accessories would appear fresh, flawless, and unmussed by the time the lift reached its destination.

She wasn't looking forward to what she was here to do, and she wasn't about to go into this meeting feeling anything short of her best.

The elevator was fast, shooting upward with enough speed Ruby felt her stomach drop a little. Or maybe that was just the reality of being here setting in. Either way, it was unpleasant. Mere moments later, an automated voice announced the car's arrival as it slowed to a stop near the top of Starcom Tower. As the doors began to slide open, Ruby slipped a swirl of magic into the air to compel the staff in the outer office away from their posts.

That should be enough.

In case this meeting didn't go as she intended, she wouldn't be leaving witnesses.

The doors came fully open, and Ruby stepped out of the elevator, looking as polished and put together as any human possibly could. It was a pain in her ass to have come here today, but she knew better than to let that show. She'd come to ask a favor, not a position she found comfortable; she'd set her life up in such a way as to generally be the one *granting* the favors, rarely requiring such consideration for herself.

This was new territory, and she did not like it. She armored herself mentally for the conversation she had come here to have. It wasn't going to be pretty. And she'd use magic if she needed to. Because *not* getting her way this morning would be unacceptable. She hoped she wouldn't have to, though. She hoped that logic and reason would be enough.

But hope was not a plan. And Ruby Killingsworth had plans.

She clutched her handbag a little tighter and started across the lobby. Her heels sank into the oddly high-pile carpet, giving her steps a quietude she found unsettling. The door was closed as she approached, with nary a sign of either of the two assistants who usually staffed the desks in this office. Good. Her magic had done its job, then.

She considered for one moment the possibility of changing her mind. Surely there was some other way to attack this problem. But no. She'd exhausted every means she had to resolve this trouble on her own, and she'd gotten all the help she could from friendly quarters. She was out of options, and she knew it—otherwise, she wouldn't be here.

Annoyed with this sudden bout of second guessing herself, Ruby shook her head and set her jaw. She looked down at her wristwatch, the delicate diamonds sparkling brilliantly under the high-efficiency lights. 12:11.

It was now or never.

~

Jaccob Stevens had never cared for publicists.

He understood their utility, of course. He'd never been great at talking to the press himself, and between his position at Starcom and his career as a hero, he'd had plenty of occasions to prove that. So keeping a professional on retainer who could handle those things in his stead made all the sense in the world.

It was just that those people made him uncomfortable. Facility with words and comfort while in the public eye felt to him like untrustworthy traits in a person. Every word out of the mouth of a media professional seemed to Jaccob to be disingenuous.

Maybe Lyle Prather had gotten to him a little more than he'd like to admit. But no matter its genesis, Jaccob's distrust for media relations people remained.

At least he was sure Mike's publicist meant well. The way she'd handled things after the White House bombing had been enough to prove that point. Still, Jaccob wasn't looking forward to talking with her. And he also wasn't sure why this meeting couldn't have been a phone call.

Despite his best efforts, and those of Elizabeth and their respective legal teams, word of their recent divorce had hit the news just this week, and no amount of avoiding his rock star son's spokesperson was going to change that. Best to get through with this and on with his life.

He'd glanced at his StarPhone where it sat on his desk. 12:11. He wasn't sure when or how come he'd taken to setting meetings in twelve-minute increments, but that had been the way of things for long enough, it just felt natural at this point. He could only hope his appointment would show up on time. He was due in the lab at 12:36, and he patently refused to waste his technical staff's time by making them wait while he talked to a media specialist—even if the point of the meeting was to support Mike.

He'd always been better behind a work bench than behind a desk, and he knew his best utility to his company lay in his technical prowess. There had been a lot of very vocal doubt as to his ability to run the company since Elizabeth's departure from the C-suite to run their charitable foundation, and it had gotten louder as rumors of their separation had wound their way through the halls of Starcom. If he could have his next piece of wearable tech ready to announce at the next shareholder meeting, that would do a lot to assuage concerns.

The new generation of Starbands were small enough to pass for a fashionable bracelet (or so said the women in his R&D department); they contained the self-same shielding technology Jaccob always had on his person and an emitter that allowed them to fire a single stun blast if the need arose. In Jaccob's estimation, this was the generation they'd be able to release onto the consumer electronics market.

He was close. He knew he was close; this iteration was the best yet, but the prototype still needed some bugs worked out of it. He was more than ready to get through with this meeting and onto the next thing.

Just as the clock on his StarPhone changed over from 12:11 to 12:12, the door to Jaccob's office blew open, seemingly all on its own. He snapped his head upward at the sound of the door hitting the stop. His breath caught in his throat when he realized who was walking through it.

He'd been prepared for a media rep. He'd even been prepared to field questions related to his recent divorce, his ex-wife, his grown children, and his personal life. He had not, by any stretch of the imagination, been prepared for *her*.

Jaccob's past had come calling, and not a piece of his past he was strong enough to deal with at the moment.

"I can't see you now, Ruby," Jaccob said, his voice breaking a little. Ruby didn't so much as slow her walk. The office door closed itself softly behind her. Jaccob swallowed hard. "I have a noon appointment." He was proud of how normal he'd managed to sound.

"The appointment's at twelve-twelve," she corrected him. "And I'm it."

Jaccob took a deep breath, stroking his beard in a vain attempt to soothe his nerves as he tried to figure out someplace—anyplace—appropriate to look that wasn't back at Ruby. Finding none in evidence, Jaccob finally met her gaze just as the silence was beginning to grow awkward.

Ruby had stopped a little more than halfway to his desk from the doorway. She stood stock still, looking back at him with a hint of a smile on her face. Was she giving him a moment to gather himself, or keeping her distance for her own reasons?

Jaccob breathed in deep again, realizing as he did that he could smell the familiar floral note of her perfume. That ... did not help.

Her crimson-colored blouse was all but see-through, and her black skirt hugged her hips perfectly. Her hair was down, falling onto her shoulders in loose waves that turned under at the ends. Her lips were as red as her top, and her tiny diamond earrings set off the sparkle in her eyes. She looked flawless. And he couldn't stand it.

Jaccob had never been much for reading noir novels, but in this moment, he suddenly felt like he was living inside of one. *She walked into my office like a blast from a furnace on the coldest day of the leanest year* ... He had half a mind to adjust his air conditioning.

He'd seen Ruby precious few times in the two years since he'd abruptly ended their romance on the heels of learning she'd kept the secret of her magic from him. They'd even worked together briefly not long after their breakup when, desperate and out of options, she'd called him for help exorcising a demon that had taken up residence both in her building and in the person of his former flame, Vivienne "Lady Vengeance" Cain.

That moment, when he'd watched Ruby save Vivienne, and almost die trying ... It was a lot. He'd walked away from that encounter with his heart mostly intact, and with every intention of continuing to stay the hell away from all things magical—especially those involving Ruby Killingsworth.

So much for good intentions.

"But—" Jaccob could barely form words. His head was spinning. Why was she here? Had she seen the news of his divorce? And how come the pretense?

Just looking at her was making him dizzy. She was a thousand might-have-beens in a low-cut blouse—and today, of all days, he wasn't sure his heart could take it.

"Yes, yes, Jaccob," Ruby said back, having no patience for his slack-jawed need to process what was happening. "You've been lied to. I'll thank you to save the outrage for some other audience. I don't have the time. You thought you'd be meeting with Mike's publicist because that was a meeting request I could be reasonably sure you'd accept. Which you did. Meaning I was right."

Jaccob sighed and hung his head. "I took your call. Last time."

"That you did. And you even agreed to help. And then you stationed an obsessed madman on your roof who nearly put a bullet through my skull."

"You know I didn't mean—"

"I know you didn't."

"It was an emergency."

"The hell, Jaccob," she snapped. "What do you think this is, a social call? I'll have you know I don't like this any more than you do."

"So you need my help? Again?" he asked, rolling his chair back from his desk and crossing his arms over his chest. She didn't strike him as the kind of person who regularly needed help; she'd only come to him last time because she was desperate. And because the situation involved Vivienne.

He was suddenly more curious than he wanted to be as to what she was doing here.

~

Ruby felt the bile rising in her gut. She did need his help, and she hated it. But she'd come this far; there was no way she was going to leave here without his agreement. Time to get to the point.

"Listen to this."

Ruby pulled her StarPhone from her handbag as she took a few steps forward. She pressed a button on the device and then set it on the edge of Jaccob's desk, careful to keep plenty of distance between them. He was afraid of her, she could tell, and although she wasn't sure how she felt about that, she did know she didn't want to scare him off.

Music began to play from the phone on Jaccob's desk.

"That's Mike," he said, when the singing began.

"Indeed." Ruby stepped forward again to pick up her device. "That audio was taken last month in my office. They've only just finalized the lyrics and the arrangement. Mike and his producer are scheduled to go into the studio with it beginning tomorrow. But then this showed up in my email last week."

She poked at the phone's screen until music started playing again. She set it down and watched as the wheels in Jaccob's mind began to turn.

"That's ... that's the same song," he said.

Ruby nodded but didn't speak.

"But that's not Mike."

"And we have a winner!" Ruby snarked, frowning at Jaccob. "It is the same song: a song that Mike has written but has not yet begun to record. And I know he wrote it himself, because I've been in on the process since it was nothing more than four catchy lines and a somewhat clever hook—that's what you heard in the first recording."

"So you have a leak?" Jaccob asked, unimpressed.

"I do not have a leak!" Ruby snatched her phone off his desk and slid it back into her clutch. "First off, security in my building is airtight. Hell, you ought to know that. You're the one who designed and built it. And anyway, I don't expect you to know anything about how the music business works, but it takes longer than just one night to go from what you heard of Mike with his guitar to this fully produced—" She paused for a moment, fuming, looking for the right word to describe what she'd heard. "—ripoff."

Jaccob frowned. "So what are you saying?"

"I'm saying it's time travel," she declared. "I'm saying someone is using *time travel* to steal creative properties, either to profit off the work directly, or as part of some elaborate blackmail scheme against me, and Mike, and Lord knows who else. Whichever it is, I have a problem with a time traveler, and so does your son. And that's why I'm here."

Jaccob shook his head. "Time travel is impossible. If this is happening—which I'm not saying I believe it is—but *if* someone has managed to steal music from the future, it's probably some sort of magical precognition-divination-runecasting-crystal ball hocus pocus, which you know is not my specialty. Maybe," he suggested, shrugging, "you should get Loki to help you."

That was a dig. They both knew it. She'd occasionally let herself wonder over the past couple of years how Jaccob was feeling about the way things had ended between them. That comment made it pretty clear he was still angry, and he was still hurt. Ruby begrudged him those feelings a little, as he'd been the one to walk away from her, not the other way around. If he hadn't healed from his own choices by now, he really oughtn't be making it her problem.

She didn't care. Not even a little bit.

"Do you really think I hadn't thought of that already?" Ruby couldn't help but throw her hands up in frustration. "The trouble is there is no sign of anything magical going on. That kind of stuff leaves traces. And I *did* ask Loki. All he's been able to tell me is he's sure it's coming from somewhere on this plane, and it doesn't involve anyone immortal. Believe me, Jaccob. I *wish* this was something magical, because I'd have dispatched with the son of a bitch already and been on with my life. But it isn't. It's not magic. Which means it must be tech. And if it is tech, then you're the best man for the job, and that's just that. Never mind that it's your son's career possibly hanging in the balance; there's a thief out there with the ability to travel through time without using magic, and we could very much use your help in doing away with him. Or her. Or them."

She paused, hands on her hips, and looked down at Jaccob expectantly. Before he could speak up, though, she reiterated the point, just to forestall his stubborn objections.

"If it was magic, I'd have handled it already. I've spent the last week and change trying to do just that. But it's not magic. It's not anything I'm able to handle on my own. And I wouldn't have come to you if I had any other choice. So please. Do what heroes do. Help us out here."

"So you have powers?" Jaccob asked her then, his voice suddenly softer.

He knew the answer. He had to. He'd stood not fifteen feet away from her and watched her astrally project her way into Vivienne's consciousness to wrest her mind from the clutches of a demon. There was no way Jaccob didn't know she had powers.

But she'd never told him directly. Not then, not before. *Never.*

Ruby suppressed a wince. He just wanted to hear her own up to things. And if making that admission was what it was going to take to get Jaccob to agree to help, then it was a price Ruby was glad to pay.

Ruby took a deep breath and let out a heavy sigh. "I have powers," she replied with a tiny nod of her head.

Jaccob set his jaw and frowned. "And how many of them are you using on me just now?" he asked wryly. "Because I can feel myself beginning to be convinced."

Ruby let herself smile, just a little. "I promised I'd never use magic on you."

She had made that hollow promise to him when, in truth, she was using magic to make him believe it. And he had believed it then; she'd been sure. She wasn't so sure he still did. Either way, she hadn't used any magic on him today. Not yet. Oh, she'd resort to magic if she had to, but appealing to Jaccob honestly seemed to be doing the trick.

When Jaccob looked back at her, there was something heartbreakingly familiar in his expression. He'd trusted her once, and she'd betrayed that trust by keeping her magic a secret from him. This time, at least, things were all out on the table. If they could just be goddamn adults about this, they should be able to work together just fine.

"Have you told Mike about this yet?" he asked, switching the conversation back to the topic at hand.

Ruby shook her head. "No. Not yet. I was hoping to get to the bottom of it fast enough I wouldn't have to. Once I was sure I couldn't, I thought I should speak with you before I spoke to him. If whoever's behind this is after money, there was no telling whether or not you'd been similarly targeted. Also." She shrugged to accentuate the point. "I'd like to be able to temper the news by telling him we'll have your help to resolve it."

Jaccob took a deep breath and ran his hands over his beard. "I'd like to be there when you tell him."

"All right." Ruby was sure she wore her surprise all over her face, but she couldn't be fussed to care.

"Look, there's been some tension between Mike and me ever since you and I—" Jaccob frowned, but Ruby nodded. He didn't need to finish that sentence. "I think he thinks I was only supportive of the whole music thing because you and I were seeing each other."

"Music *thing*—"

Ruby had to rein in her reaction to that. She just about had him on the hook here, and she'd be damned if she let her anger get the better of her and blow the whole thing. But she also couldn't let Jaccob get away with what he'd just said.

"You do realize your son is very talented? You are aware that even though you and I were ... involved, we wouldn't have offered him a contract if I hadn't seen legitimate potential? And I hope you at least understand that his freshman album went double platinum and spent three weeks at number one, and his follow-up is poised to do even better." She crossed her arms over her chest, glowering as to scold him as she continued. "Mike's career has nothing to do with *us*. He's an excellent musician, and I don't want to see his hard work compromised by some mad damned scientist out to steal his future."

"I didn't mean it like that." Jaccob sighed. "I didn't mean any offense, I just ... I don't have the vocabulary not to sound like a damn fool trying to talk about it." He placed his forearms on his desk as he shook his head. "I didn't mean any insult."

He looked up at Ruby, sadness and regret splayed across his features as clearly as the green of his eyes.

"None taken. But I'll thank you to remember it's *Mike's* profession. He's not just a kid with a hobby anymore. We're talking about a promising career—one that's being threatened by some force you may be better equipped to stop than anyone else on the planet."

"Yeah, I get it."

"Good."

"Look," he said then, still staring at his desk. He didn't need to say anything else, but if he was going to explain himself, Ruby would listen. "I felt like I needed to keep my distance—especially at the beginning. Especially while Liz and I were trying to make things work. And I think Mike got the impression my keeping my distance from you was really keeping my distance from *him*. And I just—" He blew out a heavy breath. "I don't know, Ruby ... I just think it's about time I showed him that you can be in his corner and I can be in his corner, even if we're not standing there together. I think it's probably about damned time I stopped being afraid of you and did better by my son."

"So you're in?"

It wasn't really a question. She'd process Jaccob's having admitted to fearing her later. Normally, she liked that in a person.

But coming from someone with whom she'd been so intimate, it struck her as a little bit sad.

Jaccob nodded. "I'll put a team together. Some other capes, tech people, younger people, people who understand music better than I do. I can't promise a result; I'm not the greatest investigator, and I don't know what we'll be able to do. There's no guarantee we can find this guy, much less catch him, but I'll make some calls. I'll see what I can do."

"Thank you." Ruby tucked her bag under her arm. "Mike is scheduled to be in the studio tomorrow, and I intend to put the kibosh on that until we know what we're working with. If you'd like, I can have my assistant send over his schedule. You can meet us in the morning, and you can be there when I break the news."

"Yeah, okay." Jaccob nodded. "I'll try to get the ball rolling tonight, so we have a direction—something we can tell him other than he has to stop working."

"Excellent." Ruby tried to keep her tone all business and her face unreadable. "I'll have someone get you the schedule, and I'll see you in the morning. I can show myself out."

She took a tiny step backward before pivoting on the spot and starting toward the exit.

"Ruby," Jaccob called, just as her gloved fingers reached for the doorknob. She glanced back at him over her shoulder but didn't turn around. "You look good."

"I am aware," she replied, allowing herself the tiniest hint of a smile, "and so do you."

Jaccob didn't say anything else.

CHAPTER TWO

When his office door finally closed, the first thing Jaccob Stevens did was to take a very slow, very deep breath.

Had that really just happened?

Focus. His feelings for Ruby Killingsworth were complicated—far too complicated to let them invade his thinking right now. If there really was someone with the ability to travel through time, and that person really had set their sights on fouling things up for Mike, then Jaccob wasn't about to let himself get distracted.

He also wasn't about to let himself take this thing on alone. He'd said he'd assemble a team, and he'd meant it. Working with ... or for ... his ex-lover would be awkward enough; working with her one-on-one was an absolute non-starter.

That way could only lead to trouble.

And besides, he had no actual experience with machines that did the kinds of impossible-sounding things Ruby was so convinced were going on. But he knew someone who might. And the more minds at work on this, the faster it might get resolved.

As far as Jaccob was concerned, the sooner the better. Every moment saved was one less moment of upset for Mike. And the faster this was over, the faster Jaccob could once again be done with Ruby Killingsworth.

Not that all the other people he was about to be dealing with would be a proverbial walk in the park, but at least none of them had ever broken his heart.

So the second thing he did was to get on the phone.

His first call was to Kara Sparx. The cyan-haired millennial techno-prodigy had never particularly cared for him, and Jaccob had never understood why. Keeping with the old adage "another person's opinion of you is none of your business," he'd made little effort to find out. The one thing he knew for sure about her, other than the fact that she was no fan of Stardust, was that she was a mechanical whiz the likes of which he'd never encountered elsewhere. She might even be better at robotics and engineering than he was—it was hard to compare such things when one of the people in question was a billionaire with a tech empire at his disposal and the other one ... wasn't.

What Kara was, without question, was someone better versed in unusual and esoteric uses of technology than anyone Jaccob had ever met. If there was a genuine possibility of a time machine, she was the most likely person on the planet to understand how such a thing might work, and therefore what to do to try and track it down.

To be honest, he'd kind of hoped she would laugh in his face, tell him time travel was impossible, inform him in the most colorful language available that Ruby was putting him on in some elaborate ruse to get close to him again, and that would be that.

Instead, she reserved the colorful language for exclamations of wonder and awe and made no effort to mask her excitement over the possibility of a working time machine. As expected, she wasn't thrilled to be working with Stardust, but between the interesting assignment and his offer of putting unlimited funds at her disposal for the duration of the job, she agreed to a meeting.

That was something.

But he also knew it wasn't *everything*. Between the two of them, he and Kara would have the technical side of things well in hand, but he'd learned from experience there were more bases to cover when investigating something as bizarre and impossible sounding as time travel.

And then there was the matter of having to dispatch with the trouble once they uncovered it. If the perpetrator turned out to be a tech genius from the future, there was every chance they'd be more than capable of defeating even the best Jaccob and Kara could come up with. Better to have some more traditional heroes on the team ... just in case.

His next call, therefore, was to Friday Jones.

There had been a time when Jaccob "Stardust" Stevens had known absolutely everything about everyone engaged in the hero business in Cobalt City and environs. But things changed, heroes came and went, and over the years, he'd allowed that near-encyclopedic knowledge to dwindle to the contents of a single spreadsheet. As best he could tell, Friday, heroic identity Dulcamara, was the organizer of Justice or Something: the confederation of young capes on and around the campus of the University of Cobalt City.

Not as good a name as The Protectorate, but identifiable enough to be at the top of the spreadsheet.

Friday sounded very surprised to be hearing from him and was initially hesitant to agree to a meeting. But there had been chatter in the background of the call. Jaccob's best guess was that Friday's teammates were nearby, because by the time he hung up the phone, he'd agreed to meeting with as many members of Justice or Something as cared to show up.

Which had been no problem at all. The more the merrier, as far as Jaccob was concerned.

His final call was to a super he knew even less about than the members of Justice or Something. The one thing he did know about Cassidy Sweet was that she had a history as a pop performer and recording artist. She understood music, and the music business, better than any other cape in town and he wanted someone in the room *who wasn't Ruby Killingsworth* to demystify things of that order.

With Cassidy, as well as with Friday and her teammates, he'd conveniently neglected to mention who'd brought this problem to his attention in the first place. Kara having a positive reaction to the time-travel angle was a lucky fluke—he knew for sure that Cassidy would have an issue with Ruby's involvement, and he decided to be safe with the kids. He figured they'd have a harder time saying no if they had to look him in the eye.

All five of them agreed to meeting as soon as possible, which, with Jaccob's calendar being what it was, meant seven o'clock that night. It was mildly inconvenient to be scheduling things in what he liked to think of as his off-hours, but this was more hero-business than business-business, and heroes didn't exactly get nights and weekends off.

What was missing dinner in the grand scheme of things?

It came as no surprise to Jaccob that getting the young supers to show up for a meeting was the easy part. Getting them to take on the job, however, was proving a challenge. He'd been prepared for a bit of resistance, but not for the degree to which he was hearing it.

He used to have more pull in this town.

"You do know she's evil?" Cassidy asked him plainly. She was the eldest of the assembled heroes by a decade at least; she wore her intentionally gray hair shorn in back with chin-length layers in front, and her pale face was made up with a gentle goth sensibility. Sitting quietly, she seemed mild mannered and unassuming, but when she spoke, her voice commanded the room in a way that made Jaccob uneasy. He wondered if that was how some of her powers worked.

"No, she's not," Jaccob countered.

"I don't know about *evil*," Friday said then, "but I do know she hangs out with Loki." Friday Jones was as serious a young woman as Jaccob had ever met. A stern-faced Latina who wore her honey-highlighted hair in a thick braid, she had an air of authority about her even in a tee shirt and jeans, and even when addressing heroes more than twice her age.

Friday's two teammates, a pair of young Japanese women with brightly colored hair, nodded knowingly. Jaccob almost asked how Friday knew that, but decided this was neither the time nor the place.

"I promise you," Cassidy said, "she's evil."

Jaccob looked around the room for an ally, someone who might be receptive to moving this conversation away from his ex-lover and back to the work he was hoping to engage them for. His gaze finally settled on Kara, who had disengaged from the conversation a little when the subject had turned to whether or not Ruby Killingsworth might be evil.

"She may very well be evil," Kara said with a shrug, when she noticed Jaccob's attention, "but that doesn't mean that whoever's targeting her isn't also evil."

Although not the eldest of Jaccob's invited guests, it had been clear from the moment they'd all sat down that Kara was absolutely The Adult in the room. No more enthralled by Stardust than she was averse to Ruby, she was interested only in the problem at hand. She'd come dressed for business, in pressed trousers and a striped button-down, with her aqua blue hair pulled back in a clip.

Jaccob could tell she was interested in what was going on. Having her on board would probably be enough to help him get to the bottom of this, but he still hoped she'd talk the rest of them into signing on. Because as much as he didn't think Ruby was actually evil, he did want to put as many people between himself and his former sweetheart as possible.

"So an enemy of my enemy kind of thing?" Lisa offered. She was drumming her fingers on the conference table in a way that made her rainbow-colored hair dance on her shoulders. Jaccob narrowed his eyes but nodded.

Lisa Yamamoto had been a surprise to him—almost as big a surprise as learning the group had ceased calling itself "Justice or Something" late last year. He had no record of Lisa and no idea as to what her power set entailed. But her teammates obviously respected her, which was enough to satisfy him for the moment.

He'd get to updating his spreadsheet after he talked them into signing on to the mission.

Kara shook her head.

So did Friday. "That doesn't so much work with supervillains. Everybody could be everybody's enemy. Doesn't make any one of them into somebody I want to work with."

"She's not a—" Jaccob started to protest, but the conversation was moving on without him, so he stopped short.

"I still do not like the idea of helping her," Cassidy stated.

"Weren't you the one who rescued her from that alien abduction a few years back?" Jaccob asked. He was pretty sure he had that right. In fact, he was almost certain that was how he'd first heard of Cassidy's super alter-ego Gray Dawn.

Cassidy shook her head. "Well," she answered, her voice thick with hesitation, "technically ... yes. But there were extenuating circumstances, okay? And anyway," she added, glowering squarely at Jaccob, "you saved Lyle Prather on live TV. Are you trying to tell me you don't think he's evil?"

Jaccob's face screwed itself into a frown. He had no idea what to say to that.

"Yumi," Lisa said as the silence between Jaccob and Cassidy started to feel awkward, turning to the red-eyed young woman sitting beside her, "you're being uncharacteristically quiet. What's up?"

Yumi Kujikawa was a diminutive girl who wore her jet-black hair streaked with a red that matched the unusual color of her irises. Jaccob knew her primarily as a swordswoman, although he was sure his information on her was as incomplete as the rest of his Justice or Something spreadsheet tab. She'd been looking down at her phone and absently swiveling her chair back and forth for the last few minutes.

At the sound of her name, Yumi stopped moving and sat up straight, gathering her feet into the chair lotus-style. She looked at Lisa before shrugging, leaning forward, and flattening her elbows on the tabletop.

"I think I'm going to have to go with Stardust on this one," Yumi said. "I'm not sure she's evil."

"Yumi," Friday addressed her sternly, "when I tell you she's friends with Loki, you know how I know that ... right?"

Jaccob, who absolutely did not know that, stood up a little straighter.

"Yeah, I do," Yumi replied. "And I get wanting to judge people by the company they keep. But I'm on the fencing team with Allory Greene, actual Nazi. And like Cassidy just said: Stardust himself saved Lyle Prather's worthless life a couple of years ago. So maybe there's more to Ruby Killingsworth than your source knows. I've been looking her up." Yumi reached into her lap for her phone. "And, like, I'm sure she has a whole ass PR team to scrub her image online and all, but it really seems like she's not a bad boss, at least. She pays people well. And since she took over, Goblin Entertainment employee retention is actual best in the business—and that includes in all the businesses they keep acquiring. We're not talking about trying to be her friends, we're talking about maybe taking a job. And from what I've been able to find, nobody who works for her hates her. In fact, most of them like her a lot."

"And that includes my son," Jaccob asserted, "which is the whole reason I agreed to take this on."

"Yeah, okay. You have a point. And I don't know how I feel about judging someone's whole character when we don't really know her." Lisa leaned back in her chair and nodded. "Sometimes the impression you get from afar isn't really the right impression."

"Sometimes, maybe," Cassidy said. "But I will remind you that my impression is not from afar. I actually do know her. I've known her for over twenty years. I assure you that *not* everyone who works for her thinks she's swell, or even completely human. She's the absolute poster witch for everything that is wrong with late-stage capitalism. And it remains my position that she's evil."

"You worked with her twenty years *ago*," Jaccob said. "I can assure you I know her better than you do."

"Yeah, I bet you do," Yumi mumbled under her breath, eliciting giggles from both Friday and Lisa.

Jaccob pretended not to notice and continued speaking. "She's a friend of mine, and she's asked for my help. And I'm asking for your help."

"She is not your friend," Kara countered.

"That woman is nobody's friend," Cassidy said flatly.

Kara nodded in agreement and then turned back to Jaccob.

"Um," Friday interjected, "she's Loki's friend. That's the whole problem I'm having."

"She's someone from your past," Kara said, paying no mind to Friday's comment about Ruby's friendship with the Norse god of mischief. "I'm guessing she's someone you have a lot of guilt over. You feel bad about how things ended, or maybe you feel bad the whole thing happened at all. And I think I speak for all of us here when I say I don't care. I just do not care about that. I'm not sure I could possibly care less that you had an affair with this woman, or that you broke her heart, or that she broke your heart, or whatever pitiful end the whole sad episode came to. But I do care, and maybe I'm the only one besides you who does, that there's someone in town who might have developed a time machine and could be using it for nefarious purposes—blackmailing your rock star son or whatever."

The overall reaction in the room suggested some level of agreement. "So," Kara began again, "can we maybe all agree to take this on? *Not* to help Ruby Killingsworth, who everyone except Stardust agrees might be evil, but because a bad guy with a time machine could do all sorts of damage that none of us wants to see?"

"I hate to be the one to say this," Cassidy said, seeming to somehow shrink in her chair. "But I think Kara has a point. The possibility of a time machine is absolutely worth looking into. But if I can, I'd prefer to work from a distance. I'm a little close to the evil in question, and I'm just not ready to out myself and my powers to my former employer."

"Oh, hey, that's fair," Friday said.

"Anybody else concerned about their secret identity?" Jaccob asked, finally taking a seat in the chair he'd been standing in front of for the past twenty minutes. "Because I'll admit that's a thing I forget about."

"Not really," Friday replied.

"Don't have one," Kara said wryly.

"I mean ... a little—?" Yumi said. "But, like, you all know already, so mostly it's just whether Miss Killingsworth, who—for the record—I also don't think is evil—"

"I said 'might'," Kara said back to her.

"Okay, fair," Yumi replied. "Might. Meaning also might not. And I'm in the 'might not' camp. And since I don't think she's evil, and I do think she probably keeps bigger secrets than mine all the time, I'm not going to let myself sweat the fact she might find out."

"I don't have a secret identity, either," Lisa added. "So ... as long as they don't care—"

"So can we agree then?" Jaccob asked the group. He looked down at his phone, at an hours-old message he hadn't let himself dismiss. "Just as a preliminary, can we agree? Ruby wants a meeting tomorrow morning at ten. She'll tell us what she knows and what she's already done to rule things out. You'll get the whole story, you can ask whatever questions you need to. And after that, if you want to walk away, I won't hold it against you. Can we all, with the exception of Cassidy, just agree to show up tomorrow morning and hear her out? And Cassidy, will you agree to listen to one of these ladies if they decide it's worth it to go forward?"

"I'll be there," Kara said.

"Yeah, me too," Yumi added quickly.

"If you're going, I'm going." Lisa reached over to take Yumi's hand. "Maybe I can help somehow."

"Of course you can, babe."

"Yeah, I'll go, too," Friday said then, "if for no other reason than to keep you two from getting too excited and jumping into something without thinking it through."

"I think I can work with that," Cassidy agreed after a moment. "If you all think this is worth pursuing, then I'm happy to help out, as long as *she* doesn't find out I'm helping."

"Good," Jaccob said, once again standing from the chair he'd only just sat in. "Good. I'll see you tomorrow, then. Ten a.m. in the Goblin C-suite conference room. Civilian clothes."

There was a chorus of nods as Jaccob pushed his chair back from the table. He was disappointed it had taken Kara's level head to convince the others they should go after whoever was behind this thing, but he was satisfied enough to have them on board. He saw his guests out of the conference room and into the elevator back to the plaza side lobby before taking the stairs down to the lab.

He'd spend some time wrapping his head around how little sway he had with Gen Z heroes later.

But it wasn't like they didn't have a point. He did have trouble thinking clearly where Ruby Killingsworth was concerned—he always had. He probably always would. But he refused to believe she was evil. Not really. Not completely.

The lab was dark when he arrived—shut down for the night—but the lights and HVAC sprung to life when the building's AI registered Jaccob's presence in the space. He knew better than to think he'd be getting any real sleep tonight. He had a hard time not thinking about Ruby in the middle of the night when he *didn't* have plans to meet with her first thing in the morning.

If he could spend a few hours head-down on the Starband project, he could probably tire himself out thoroughly enough to catch a few winks before time to head across the street. And if that didn't happen, at least he'd be getting work done.

CHAPTER THREE

The meeting was scheduled for ten o'clock, and as best Jaccob could tell from the morning's text exchanges, none of the young heroes he'd tapped for this assignment had decided to back out. That was good. But he had a piece of business to handle before their meeting, which meant showing up half an hour earlier than everyone else.

He spent his morning shower doing his best to calm his nerves, and to convince himself those nerves were solely attributable to Mike's situation. Breaking the news to his son that someone possibly meant him harm—and that someone could very well have access to time travel—would have been stressful enough no matter whose company he'd be in when doing so.

But Jaccob had just enough self-awareness to know that wasn't entirely it.

And it wasn't the fact he'd been up until the wee hours tinkering in his lab, either. This wasn't what sleep deprivation usually did to him, and he hadn't had nearly enough coffee for that to account for his jitters.

Jaccob couldn't help but feel a little foolish as he stared blankly into his closet. There was something in him that had to look just *so* to see Ruby this morning. For whatever reason—one he had no interest at all in interrogating—he needed to prove he could put on a fresh suit, throw his shoulders back, and stride into her office just as cool, calm, and unaffected as she'd strode into his. He didn't know why he needed this—needed to somehow show her just how completely he could have his act together around her—but he really, really did.

It was windy out, threatening rain, and as soon as he was out his door, Jaccob felt silly for having spent so much time on his tie and his hair. There was no denying he'd be a mess by the time he made it across the street. He supposed that was his comeuppance for suddenly deciding to care so much about his appearance. At least his cologne wouldn't be affected by the weather.

The morning's fixation on his appearance had cost him time. As he dashed across the narrow lane between his building and Ruby's, his StarWatch alarm was already buzzing to tell him he was late. The problem, he realized as he stepped onto the curb on Ruby's side of the street, was that she'd told him exactly when she expected him in her office but had left him on his own to figure out how to get there.

The Ruby Tower had a total of eleven doors on the ground floor—Jaccob knew the location and design of all of them, owing to his having overseen the installation of the doors themselves and their attendant security measures during the Tower's construction.

Not every door led to someplace with access to elevators that served the Goblin Entertainment offices on the forty-seventh floor. This morning, Jaccob couldn't seem to remember which were which. He didn't like the idea of having to use the door he had gotten used to when he and Ruby had been a couple, but that was the one he knew for sure would get him where he was going.

Worst case scenario, the doorman would be rude. But one way or another, he'd probably get directions.

He approached the brass and glass door beneath the small green awning on the Starcom side of the building and did what he thought was a passable job at containing his surprise when the doorman let him in without comment. Jaccob nodded his thanks and tried his best to appear calm and collected while passing through the brief lobby and into one of the two elevators.

There were only two possible explanations for that reception. Either Ruby had expected him to come this way and had gone to the trouble to inform the doorman, or she'd never rescinded her directive from two years ago that he be allowed anywhere in the building at any time. He wondered which it was as he waited for the elevator doors to close.

He'd chosen the executive guest elevator instead of Ruby's personal car. It had appeared he had a choice, but there was something about boarding the lift that would give him possible access to Ruby's inner office and the private floors of her residence that felt like overstepping. From here, he could only reach the corporate suite, the outer lobby of Ruby's fiftieth-floor penthouse, or the helipad on the building's roof. Those were the only floors a casual guest of Ruby Killingsworth needed access to without an escort.

Jaccob was being sent up unescorted.

But he was probably under surveillance. And he was definitely behind schedule.

He pushed the button for the forty-seventh floor.

The elevator opened again to reveal Ruby's outer office, where her second assistant was standing on the wrong side of his desk, fiddling with some papers. The assistant looked up at the open elevator and greeted Jaccob with a cheerful, "Good morning, Mr. Stevens!"

"Good ... um ... morning, Ethan," he replied, trying not to trip over his tongue too badly as he struggled to recall the young man's name.

"Jaccob, good, you're here." Ruby's voice startled him. Somehow between his curiosity as to the doorman situation and his desire to not be rude to a twenty-year-old office assistant, he hadn't yet managed to notice the door to her inner office was standing open.

Ruby blew into the room then—a force of nature in an ivory dress suit and nude pumps. He'd known her to prefer a more vintage fashion sensibility, even in the office. But today was something entirely different. She looked sleek, modern, *dangerous.*

"I ... um ... I hope I'm not late," he said, as she walked past. She hadn't so much as looked up at him; her attention was fixed on the tablet in her hand. Jaccob had no idea what to do. Was she being rude, or was she just busy?

"You're not *too* late," she replied, still not looking up. "Mike should be just about to get started. I warned the producers I'd be coming in. They'll be waiting on us."

She hadn't stopped walking; by the time she finished her sentence, the heavy double doors from her suite into the hallway were swinging open.

Jaccob didn't remember those doors being wired to open automatically. Either that was an upgrade he hadn't been told about—possibly installed after the demon occupation had smashed the place up—or she was using magic. He wasn't sure which thought made him more uncomfortable. He'd probably be looking up the work orders when he got back to the office.

The double doors had come open just enough for Ruby to pass through them without breaking her stride. She was several paces down the hall by the time it occurred to Jaccob he was probably expected to follow. He scrambled after her then, barely making it through the doors before they began to close again.

She was halfway down the hall by the time he caught up.

"I'll get the staff out of the room," she said, as he fell into step beside her right shoulder. She still wasn't looking up from the tablet she'd brought with her from her inner office.

It was driving him a little mad.

"Okay," he said, hoping that maybe a two-way conversation would get her to look at him.

"Once the room is clear," she continued, as though he hadn't said anything at all, "and it's just us and Mike, I'll play him the track from my email and explain what's going on."

"Okay," Jaccob said again.

"Then you can get us both up to speed on your plan and on these capes you found, who I'm about to pay two grand a week to handle this bullshit."

"Yeah, okay." Jaccob felt a little flustered. He was sure he had more to say, he just couldn't think of what or how.

"Then," she went on, still without pause, "once we've got Mike squared away and feeling all right, you'll come with me to the conference room where we'll get your little minions under contract and on task."

Jaccob stopped himself from saying "okay" again. He just nodded and continued following her as she turned a corner and then paused in front of a door with a red light above it. Ruby glanced over at Jaccob, frowning.

"Capiche?" she asked. "Any questions?"

"No, um ... we're good."

The door swung open then, and Jaccob was once again left to wonder whether automation or magic was behind it.

The room beyond was painted dark red, filled to brimming with machines Jaccob didn't recognize, and so dimly lit he couldn't quite fathom how anyone got any work done in here. A young Black woman sat before a large console; she wore silver headphones over her purple braids and appeared to be paying rapt attention to the knobs and sliders in front of her. Just on the other side of the console, an older Latino man with a close-cropped salt-and-pepper beard was fiddling with a handful of cables. And at the far end of the room, in a glassed-in booth, wearing headphones and adjusting a microphone on its stand, was Mike.

Jaccob felt entirely out of place. He couldn't remember the last time he'd been in a room full of machinery and had no idea what any of it was for. He realized in that moment just how little he knew about how Ruby's—and Mike's—business worked. Maybe he could use this opportunity to learn a few things.

Mike looked up then, a huge smile coming to his face when he spotted Ruby in the doorway. He slipped off his headphones and hung them hastily over the microphone stand before bounding out of the booth toward where she and Jaccob were standing.

"Hey there, Miss K!" Mike greeted her as soon as he was clear of the glass door.

"Hello, dear," Ruby said, reaching out her hand to take Mike's for a moment.

"Um ... Dad," Mike said when he saw Jaccob standing behind Ruby. He stood up a little straighter, looking something between concerned and confused.

Jaccob felt sheepish. That wasn't the greeting he'd been hoping for, but it was pretty much the one he'd expected.

"If you'll excuse us," Ruby said to the two producers before Jaccob had the chance to say anything back to Mike.

"Oh, yes, ma'am," the young woman replied, pulling off her headphones as she stood from her seat. The bearded man nodded and followed her swiftly out the door.

"Is ... um ... is everything ok?" Mike asked, as his producers pulled the door closed behind them. He looked back and forth between his dad and his boss, eyes getting wider as he did.

"I'm afraid not," Ruby answered. "You'd best have a seat."

Mike did as she suggested, stepping past both of them and taking a seat behind the control console as Ruby pulled her phone from her jacket pocket and set it on the desk in front of him.

Jaccob did his best not to fidget, or to otherwise let on how awkward he felt, as Ruby played the clip she'd shared with him the day before. He listened to her explain the situation to Mike—leaving out certain salient details, but all-in-all telling him most of the truth as Jaccob understood it.

Jaccob didn't like it, but she probably knew Mike's limits better than he did.

But wasn't that the point of having agreed to do this work? The whole reason he'd said yes to helping track down whoever was behind this attack was to get closer to his son. When he'd called it quits with Ruby, he'd inadvertently dropped out of Mike's life as well, owing to the fact that his son was an up-and-coming solo musician signed to Ruby's marquee label. Jaccob had been a mess in those days, and he hadn't meant to put so much distance between himself and his son. And he'd come here with Ruby today to start making things right between them.

Ruby outlined what she hoped to do, what she'd brought Jaccob in to manage, and what she wanted from Mike in the meantime. The recording was on hold, but she'd pay everyone to be on standby so they could get back to work the moment the issue was resolved. And Mike was grounded; just in case the perpetrators meant him harm, he'd need to move into one of the artist condos in the Ruby Tower, and he wouldn't be allowed to leave until things were handled.

Jaccob thought the restrictions were a little much, but Mike didn't seem to.

"You'll have your choice of floorplan," she told him, handing over the tablet she'd had her eye on the whole walk over. "Have a look and take your pick. Get the key from the front desk. Once you tell them which unit, someone will go in and stock the refrigerator. Run any specific requests through Ethan or Lillia. And yes, that includes booze. Anything stronger, I don't want to know about."

"Yes, ma'am," Mike responded, picking up the tablet off the desk.

"Oh," Ruby added, "and no visitors. Not even Katy."

Mike shook his head and frowned. "Really?"

"Really."

"But you don't think Katy—?"

"Of course not," Ruby replied in a tone that Jaccob thought sounded more like she was humoring him than like she actually agreed. "But until we are absolutely sure what we're dealing with here, we can't know that anyone showing up to talk to either one of us is really who they say they are. So, just in case some time-traveling ne'er-do-well can make themselves look like Katy, we can't even let her in."

"Okay," Mike said. "Yeah, I get it. Dad's got a device that can do that, there's no reason to think a bad guy who can build a time machine won't. I think I'd know within a few seconds if Katy was an impostor, but I can see how that impostor getting in the building and close to people and stuff is enough to worry about. Having a superhero for a dad sort of teaches you that seconds can be plenty long enough for a bad guy with a plan. You'll let me call her, though, right? Like ... we can still talk?"

"Talk to her all you want. Call, text, video chat, whatever you need. Just no in-person socializing and no sharing the details of why that is until we can be sure no one's going to use her—or the ability to look like her—to get to you."

"Yes, ma'am," Mike said back.

"We have a meeting with these other capes in a minute," Ruby said. "After that, your dad can go with you to get anything you need from home. We'll try and have the condo ready by the time you get back."

"Yes, ma'am," Mike said again.

Ruby's phone sounded then, startling the three of them when it suddenly vibrated against the wood-grain desk where it lay. Her eyes got wide as she snatched up the device and took a step back, away from Jaccob and Mike.

"I have to take this," she said, clutching the phone to her chest as she reached behind her for the door handle. "You two work out your afternoon plans." Then, to Jaccob, she directed, "I'll see you down the hall in a minute."

Jaccob nodded as Ruby turned and left, putting the phone to her ear as she pulled open the studio door. His mind was reeling. He knew Ruby had three phones: one for business, one for very specific business, and one for personal use. The phone that just rang—the same one she'd put on his desk yesterday—was her personal phone. When the two of them were a couple, he'd been the only person with the number. There was a little knot in his stomach when he let himself wonder who might be calling.

And also, who the hell was *Katy*?

He hated how much better Ruby knew his son than he did.

"Hey, Dad," Mike said, as the studio door closed behind Ruby. "I think it's pretty cool you're doing this. I know you and Miss K have history, and I can tell it's kind of awkward for you being around her right now. So ... like ... I really appreciate your help."

"Ruby and I are both adults," Jaccob said, in an odd echo of a conversation he'd recently had with Chuck concerning his ex-wife. "And we both care about what happens to you. So whatever else is between us, we're willing and able to work together on this one."

"Yeah, well," Mike replied with a shrug, "I just want you to know I appreciate it."

"Any time, son," Jaccob told him, finally managing a smile. "I'm going to get down the hall to this meeting. Then I'll come find you and we'll head over to pick up whatever you need from your place. And you can tell me all about Katy."

Mike chuckled as he looked back down at the tablet Ruby had handed him. "Yeah, okay."

Jaccob nodded. He patted his son on the shoulder before turning to go. He left the recording studio relieved to know Mike was happy to have him around.

It took him a minute to remember the way to the conference room. He'd never been to a meeting in the Goblin Media C-suite before. In fact, he hadn't been in this part of the building in a professional capacity since before the flooring was installed. Visits for personal and superhero reasons hadn't required a trip to Ruby's conference room. He was glad when he managed to find it on his own without having to stop and ask for directions.

As he approached the glass-walled room, Jaccob could see the rest of the team had already arrived. The four of them sat around the glass-and-chrome conference table while an assistant Jaccob didn't recognize stood in the corner holding a stack of file folders. There was no sign of Ruby, which made Jaccob hesitate, unsure whether he should wait for her or go inside.

After a moment, he felt like a fool standing out in the hallway where everyone could see him. The door was standing open, and he decided he'd feel at least a little less foolish sitting at the table with everyone else than he did standing all alone out in the hall.

But he hadn't made it all the way to the table when Ruby brushed past him on the way to the far end of the room. Once again, she didn't so much as turn her head to look at him. She did, however, give a nod to the young South Asian woman in the corner, who then proceeded to make her way around the table, passing folders and pens out to the four young women who were seated there.

The assistant departed when she was through. As the door came closed behind her, the glass walls of the conference room frosted and darkened. Ruby took her place at the head of the table, so Jaccob decided to take the seat at the far end.

"Good morning, and thank you all for coming." Ruby addressed the group as though she was beginning any run-of-the-mill meeting. "Before we get started with any substantive conversation, I'm going to need some signatures. Open the folder, pick up the pen. The first two pages are a standard NDA. Read it if you want, but no matter, I'm going to need you to sign it before I say anything more. It's the same form everyone who sets foot in this room has to sign with one very special addition. If you'll look on the second page, there's a rider I'd like to draw your attention to. I know you all are capes. I know a lot of things. And over the course of this endeavor, I'm likely to learn more. Dates of birth, home addresses, secret identities ... so on and so forth. This clause holds me liable if I divulge your secrets same as it keeps you from spilling mine."

Jaccob looked around the table. Kara was frowning but nodding. Yumi and Lisa exchanged a smile. Jaccob looked at Ruby then, watching her watch the others and trying to suss out what she was thinking as she sized up the team he'd gathered. Her gaze narrowed just enough for Jaccob to notice as she waited for Friday, the last of the four, to sign the NDA. If Friday bailed at this point, he was sure he'd never hear the end of it, so he was probably as relieved as Ruby was when the document was finally executed.

"Okay, good," Ruby said once the last of the folders were closed and the pens were down. "Now that we've gotten that handled: first things first. Some of you may suspect this already, as I am well aware of the circulating rumors. I am, in fact, a sorceress. A magic user—and a terrifyingly powerful one at that. Those signatures ... they aren't just *legally* binding. Violate my confidence, and you will live to regret it."

Jaccob looked around the table. None of the young women he'd recruited seemed rattled by that declaration. Good. What Ruby didn't know was how much time he and Cassidy had spent informing them of Ruby's magical ability. They had both wanted the others to know what they might be walking into, even if they'd disagreed on whether or not there was evil behind it. Honestly, Jaccob was a little stunned at how quickly Ruby had come forward with that information. After the way she'd kept her magical abilities from him for so long, he hadn't been prepared for her to admit things to the other capes so soon.

He tried not to let it hurt his feelings.

"The rest of the pages lay out my expectations," Ruby continued. "The tl;dr version is that someone appears to be using time travel to fuck with me and with one of my artists. So far it appears to be contained to just the two of us, but there's no telling what else is happening. What I can tell is that all this is being done in a way that is not at all magically detectable, and that's after consulting with an immortal on the matter."

Friday shot the others a clear look of "I told you so". Jaccob had neither confirmed nor denied Ruby's association with the Norse god of mischief during their meeting the day before. And he still wasn't sure exactly how Friday knew about that. Mostly he was surprised at how forthcoming Ruby was being with this information. She was telling these four things she'd never said out loud to him in the entire time they'd known each other. But, then again, she had just gotten their signatures on a magically binding non-disclosure agreement.

Jaccob found it curious she hadn't asked him to sign one, too.

"Your job," she went on, "will be to track this person or persons down and to stop them—trapping them in the here and now so they cannot return from whence they came and have another go. And I'll expect you to be on this full-time. I understand Miss Sparx to be a freelancer and the rest of you to be on summer break from the University. I presume this means that, outside of hero work, you aren't currently otherwise engaged. But if any of you are ... if you have day jobs, survival jobs, side hustles, what have you, I'm going to need you to take a leave of absence. And if you happen to have the kind of job that doesn't allow you to take a leave of absence, then I implore you to quit. You deserve better. And I promise you a glowing letter of recommendation in my very own handwriting when this whole episode is behind us. Take that to mean what you will."

"What if we want to work for you when this is over?" Lisa asked.

Ruby cocked her head to the side and steepled her fingers at her waist. "This business burns through junior executives at a ludicrous pace. We work hard, we think harder, and we don't get weekends off. If after you've seen our operation up close for a little while, you still think you've got what it takes to make it here, I'll gladly give you the same ninety days I give every college graduate who thinks the same."

"Even though I don't graduate for another year?"

"Even so," Ruby answered her. "For the record, I never bothered with college at all, and you see where I wound up. An incomplete education is only a liability in this business if you decide you're actually done learning."

Friday pushed her chair back from the table and crossed her arms over her chest almost before Ruby was done speaking. "In the meantime, you're over here telling us to quit our jobs to do this for you—how do you expect us to pay our bills?"

"Compensation is clearly outlined. It should be on page three of the main section."

The group of them turned their attention to the contracts on the table, paging through until they found the section on compensation.

"Mine has a typo," Friday said, pointing at a spot on the contract in front of her.

"No, it doesn't," Ruby snapped. "Jaccob—?"

Taking his cue from her, Jaccob stood and moved to look at the contract over Friday's shoulder.

"No. That's right," he said when he saw the number on the contract matched what Ruby had said out in the hallway earlier.

"Oh." Friday blinked. "*Oh*."

Yumi seemed less impressed. "This is the total?" she asked, still looking down at the page. "Not that we're used to getting paid for hero stuff, but I'm just trying to figure out how this is going to work."

"That's per person," Ruby replied. "Per week. Plus expenses. And lodging. I'll expect you to stay here in the Tower while you work on this. We keep two full floors available for artists and guests. I've promised Mike first choice, but once he's settled, you all can take your pick. As soon as these are signed, I'll have cards made to access your expense account. You can pick those up at the same time as your condo keys. And don't be shy about expensing things. Abuse the hell out of it, I don't care. You all decide you need shiny new super suits at my expense, as long as you solve my problem while you're wearing them, then have at it."

"What's this bit about a bonus?" Kara asked then, turning the page as she carefully examined the text of the contract.

"That," Ruby replied, "is to incentivize you all to get to the bottom of this as quickly as possible. I don't want anyone getting any bright ideas about drawing out the investigation for an extra few weeks' pay. So there's a bonus attached if we resolve this in under a month. And it goes down rather substantially with every additional week before I am rid of this pestilence. You won't do better by dragging your feet."

"Holy shit," Lisa said.

"What?" Friday asked.

"Turn the page," Lisa replied. "Look at the number."

"Holy shit," Friday echoed when she, too, saw the amount of the proposed bonus written on the next page.

Yumi nodded matter-of-factly.

"If we're all in agreement then," Ruby said, paying absolutely no heed to the chorus of swears. "Take a moment with the contract if you wish. Look it over, and sign if you agree. Aishwarya will be in to collect them shortly. I'll have her bring the tablet with the lodging information when she comes. You'll have the rest of the day to tie up loose ends elsewhere. I expect to see you all this evening at six in my sitting room. Fiftieth floor. Security will let you up."

With that, Ruby was clearly finished. She looked around the table once, nodded, and was out the door before Jaccob had fully realized the meeting was over.

The others read over their contracts, some of them more carefully than others. Jaccob realized he still didn't know what was going to be expected of him in this whole undertaking.

But he did know he needed to run an errand with Mike, so he figured he'd start with that.

CHAPTER FOUR

"Did it have to start raining?" Friday asked, as she pulled her car to a stop at the last light before the turn into the Ruby Tower. "That building was creepy enough in the sunshine."

Clearly, Ruby Killingsworth had no desire to make others comfortable in her spaces.

But the building's architects and designers had done a reasonable job making sure the building's other tenants could be comfortable in their own. The key cards the newly hired capes had been given gave them access not only to their own temporary accommodations, but also to several floors worth of amenities. Considering the weather, the most useful of these might have been the underground parking garage complete with assigned parking spaces for each of them.

While Kara had headed off on her own to pack up gear and other necessities, Friday had volunteered to drive Yumi and Lisa to their dorm to gather their things. At least the weather had held until they were on their way back to the Tower.

"I don't think this is right," Friday said, as the light turned green. The GPS was telling her the entrance to the parking garage was ahead on the left, but all Friday could see was a solid brick wall.

"Why not?" Yumi asked, adjusting the potted alocasia on her lap.

"Because it's on the opposite side from where we parked this morning."

"Well, the lady at the desk did say the residential side had a different address from the business entrance," Lisa reminded them.

"Yeah, I guess," Friday said, poking at her phone to enlarge the onscreen map. "But this is telling me to turn directly into the side of the building. Like ... it's a wall."

"Okay, that's—" Yumi began, but her words froze in her throat when what had just a moment ago looked like solid brick began to rearrange itself into the shape of a doorway. "Damn."

The curb transformed itself from a raised yellow barrier into a gently sloped driveway just in time for Friday to turn the car into it.

"Damn is right," Friday said, as she drove slowly through the newly opened garage door. "And I repeat: this place is creepy."

"I think it's kind of cool," Yumi said.

"Look," Lisa said then, pointing out the window, "there are little LED lights leading you to your assigned space."

"Neat," Yumi said.

"Freaky," Friday said. "The building just ... knew my car. That doesn't freak you out at all?"

"Nah," Yumi replied. "Think about it. Think about who lives here. Think about who their usual guests are. If I was some super famous rock star, I sure wouldn't want to have to stop to badge my way into a garage when there's every chance the paparazzi is hanging around outside. It totally makes sense for the garage to know who's supposed to be here and just let you in."

"Maybe," Friday allowed, "but it's still creepy." She turned the car to the right to follow the trail of flashing LED lights down the ramp toward her intended parking space.

"You really need to get used to the idea of all this automation," Yumi told Friday. "I've been looking at the realtor's website, and from the looks of it, this building is kind of next level when it comes to smart home stuff."

"I'm sure it is," Friday replied. "But after being introduced to our employer—the terrifyingly powerful sorceress—anything that feels like magic is going to give me the willies, at least for a little while."

"I mean," Lisa said, as Friday pulled the car into a parking place that was lit up green on all sides, "if it bugs you that much, I'm sure there's a way to turn it off. And I bet Kara could turn it off for you even if there isn't really supposed to be a way to."

"Yeah, maybe," Friday said, as she turned off the car. She got out from the driver's seat and went immediately to open the trunk.

She was still in the process of unfolding a collapsible wagon when Yumi and Lisa joined her behind the car.

"Wow," Yumi said, when she got a good look at the trunk's contents. "Friday, how many plants did you bring?"

Friday had filled all her vehicle's available space with potted plants; the cabin and the laps of her passengers had spent the ride over filled to the brim with greenery, and the trunk of the little sedan was pretty well stuffed to capacity.

Friday paused, frowning for a minute before reaching into the trunk to begin moving plants into the wagon for transport. "Thirty-two," she said after a moment. "This trip I brought thirty-two."

"Why?" Lisa asked, setting the begonia she'd carried in Friday's wagon. "Friday, why do you have thirty-two plants in the car right now?"

"Because that's all that would fit," Friday answered plainly.

"Because that's—"

"Oh, make no mistake," Friday said, continuing to unload plants from her trunk, "this is just the first trip. I'll go back as many times as I need to. Because I'm bringing *all* my plants."

"All of them?" Yumi asked her.

"Every last one," Friday answered.

Lisa chuckled. "Meanwhile, Yumi didn't even bring toothpaste."

"What?" Friday asked.

"Expense account," Yumi answered.

"Expense account?" Friday echoed.

"Look." Yumi shrugged before reaching into the trunk to help with the unloading. "I don't regret walking away from my dad and his money, but I do sometimes miss it. So yeah, I'm gonna buy toothpaste—like, really nice toothpaste. And probably an extra tube. Or two. And I'm gonna buy soap, and shampoo, and lotion and nail polish and ... and name brand salad dressing."

"Go off, I guess," Friday said, shaking her head as she contemplated a particularly colorful makoyana in a purple pot.

"For the next couple of weeks, or whatever," Yumi said, "we get to live like rock stars. Fancy condo, expense account, someone else to do the laundry and clean the bathroom. Now, I'm going to do the best job I can on this, even though I know that as soon as the job is done, all that evaporates. So yeah, I'm going to enjoy it all while I have the chance."

"I totally see your point." Lisa scooped up two trays of tiny succulents and turned to look at Friday. "But I'm not sure I really get yours," she said. "I just can't see what's not to love about this building, and I haven't even looked at the realtor's website."

"Like I said," Friday answered, "it gives me the creeps."

"I mean," Yumi said, "the outside is a little bit 'scenes from Orson Welles' but the inside ... Wait until you see the pools. *Pools*, Friday. There are three of them."

"I guess—"

"And it's not like we'll be locked in over here," Lisa reminded them. "Stardust said Mike isn't allowed to leave or to have visitors, but there's nothing stopping us from going out."

"Right," Friday said. "And my first order of business is going to be to get the rest of my plants over here."

"That's an awful lot of plants to move," Lisa said. "Especially when you could just go over and water them every couple of days."

"No way," Friday said. She pulled the last of the plants out of her trunk and moved to pull the wagon alongside the front passenger door, inside of which stood a four-foot-tall Ficus tree. "Some of these plants are my research. And some of them are like my children. I'm not going to leave them all alone for however long this is going to take."

"I don't know," Yumi said, "it just seems impractical, especially considering we may only be here a week or two."

"Look," Friday said, scooping up the Ficus tree and shutting the door behind her, "I don't like this building and I don't like having to move into it. But if I have to stay here, which apparently I do, I draw the line at living without my plants. When we had to pick out condos this morning, I found a three bedroom with a southern exposure. Two of those bedrooms are for plants. Possibly also the third. I can sleep on the sofa."

"I think there will be room for you and all the plants you want," Lisa said. "Heck, you probably could ask for a whole other condo just to put your plants in it if you want."

"No thanks," Friday said. "Not worth it."

"You're just saying that because you hate Miss Killingsworth," Yumi asserted.

"There's no 'just' about it," Friday said back. "I don't like her, and I don't trust her, and I'm not real happy about working for her." Friday shrugged and started toward the clearly marked doors to the residential elevators, pulling the wagon full of plants behind her.

"But you took the job," Yumi reminded her, pulling her key card from her pocket as she dashed ahead. "So you might as well do your best to enjoy the perks. Including getting to live for a few weeks in an amazing building. I, for one, am not mad to have concierge and maid service at my disposal for a while."

"The concierge and the maid service does sound kind of cool," Friday agreed, "but even with all that stuff, this building gives me the creeps in a major way. There's just something off about it. Like ... metaphysically. I feel like ... it feels like Freya doesn't want me to be here."

"Why'd you take the job, then?" Yumi pulled the door open and held it for Lisa and Friday to pass through.

"Because of you guys," Friday said. "I didn't like the idea of you two jumping headfirst into bed with an evil sorceress."

"Phrasing," Yumi said, and Lisa elbowed her in the side. "Ow."

Friday sighed. "I figured if I didn't come with you, I might not get you back."

"You really think we're that susceptible?" Lisa asked her.

"I think you asked about a job when this is all finished."

"Okay, I did do that." Lisa admitted. "But wanting an office job and wanting to join some magical circle of evil are not the same thing. And anyway, I'm still not convinced she's evil."

"Right?" Yumi asked. She pressed the elevator call button and turned to look at Friday.

"Right," Friday said. "Because someone who introduces herself as 'terrifyingly powerful' and makes people sign a magical NDA under penalty of pain and death couldn't possibly be evil."

"Nobody's saying it's not possible," Yumi told her. "Just that we don't know for sure. And even if she *is* evil, the time-travel thing seems cool, and it's not like there's any ethical consumption under capitalism, right?"

"Yumi makes a good point," Lisa said. "We could have plenty of less interesting, lower-paying jobs and still be working for somebody super evil. So we might as well take advantage of the fact that she's paying us way too much money and giving us a cool mystery to solve."

"Plus, we're only kind of working for her." Yumi shook her head and shrugged. "I mean ... we are, technically, in that she's the one paying us. But what I'm saying is that she's not the only one who stands to benefit. Jaccob and Mike Stevens are, as best anyone can tell, pretty good guys. And we're doing this for them as much as we are for Miss Killingsworth."

"I guess that's true," Friday replied as the elevator doors came open.

"It is true," Yumi assured her, gesturing for Friday to get aboard the lift first. "And you know what else is true? It wasn't all that long ago we were each, separately, looking at having to fight a dragon and kind of grumpy about the fact that we didn't think Stardust would pick up the phone if we called asking for help. Now *he* is the one calling *us* for help—for a problem affecting his very own family. That's kind of a major glow-up, don't you think?"

"I mean," Lisa said, "that is kind of badass." Lisa took hold of Yumi's hand as the two of them joined Friday aboard the elevator.

"Yeah," Friday replied, as the doors slid shut. "I get that. And also the part about it being a ridiculous amount of money. I'm not sad to spend a little while away from either my waitress job or my barista job. And now Yumi's got me thinking about what kinds of expensive plants I may be able to buy with this expense account. I'll be all right." The elevator took off upward, with no intervention from its occupants. "But I maintain," Friday added, frowning at her teammates, "this building creeps me the fuck out."

A concierge was waiting for the three young heroes when they arrived on the twenty-seventh floor. He offered to take the Ficus tree or pull the wagon, a pair of offers Friday quickly and pointedly declined. As he led the three of them to their temporary lodgings, he let them know Kara had already arrived, and gave them all a brief rundown on the building and its amenities. There were three pools, all salt water, and each kept at a different temperature and intended for different uses. The building also offered three hot tubs, a sauna/steam room/spa area, and a fitness center all at their disposal in addition to the features of their individual temporary accommodations—which would have been more than adequate all on their own.

Having found the only one-bedroom condo in the bunch already claimed by Mike Stevens for the duration of their employment, Yumi and Lisa had chosen a two-bedroom unit, while Kara and Friday had each decided on a three-bedroom, with room for machinery and plants respectively. The three of them agreed (although not in earshot of the concierge) that any one of the three units would probably cost more to rent per month than they paid for an average year.

The residences were plush, modern, and inviting—even if the building in which they were situated was exactly the opposite. The fixtures and finishes were luxe without being showy, and the mostly white base units had all clearly gotten attention from at least one decorating professional. Each was furnished in an attractive amalgam of neutrals with pops of color in cushions, rugs, lamps, and window treatments, all seemingly chosen to coordinate with the exquisite art pieces hung on the walls.

Everything, from the lights to the built-in surround sound and beyond, were controlled by a series of touch screens installed in nearly every room. Even the bathrooms came equipped with copious charging ports for mobile and other electronic devices, and in each unit, a tablet had been left on the kitchen counter for the express purpose of putting in a grocery order.

These were definitely digs meant for rock stars. Even Friday had to admit the condo was nice—especially after she learned the bedrooms came equipped with individual climate control, including built-in humidifiers. She'd be able to keep her plant babies as warm and happy as possible. It was never going to feel like home, but the three of them agreed they'd be plenty comfortable for the time being.

CHAPTER FIVE

Finding a way to make themselves at home in rock star accommodations was one sort of a challenge. Working with Ruby Killingsworth was liable to prove a more difficult one. This morning's meeting had been a flurry of new information, official paperwork, and logistics. There was no telling what this evening's meeting was going to be like.

So there was a bit of relief from all involved when Yumi, Lisa, and Friday headed for the elevator bank and found Kara already there.

"Oh, good," Kara said, when she spotted the other three. "I was trying to decide whether being a minute late or possibly the only one there would be the more uncomfortable situation. Now I don't have to worry about it."

"Looks like you'd already picked not late," Lisa said.

Kara nodded as she leaned forward to push the elevator call button. "Yeah. It being the first day and all, I didn't want to give the client a bad impression. Still, I'm glad we're all here so there's no chance I'll wind up alone with her."

"She gives you the creeps, too?" Friday asked.

"Not the creeps so much," Kara said. "I just ... I don't like talking to rich people. It's like they live on a completely different planet. Breaks my brain."

Yumi snickered. It was a little ironic, considering how wealthy she'd been until very recently.

Lisa, who definitely caught Yumi's meaning, shook her head. "We should start a group chat. That way we can all keep in touch and make sure that no one has to go around by themself if they don't want to."

"Good idea." Kara slipped her phone from the back pocket of her trousers and handed it to Lisa. "Put your number in. I'll text you so you have mine, then you can put the group together. I'll loop Cassidy in later. I already talked to her, and she's on board for behind-the-scenes stuff. I think mostly she's kind of keen on spying on our employer, but I think her music skill in particular could come in really handy. So there's that."

"Good," Friday said.

"I'm surprised you don't have a StarPhone," Lisa said, as she took hold of Kara's unfamiliar device.

"Meh," Kara replied, "I have a complicated relationship with Starcom tech. I avoid it when I can."

Lisa was still typing in her number when the elevator doors opened, and the four of them stepped inside.

"Anybody else think it's weird that we have to take three elevators to get to this meeting?" Friday asked, as the doors closed behind them.

"Nah." Yumi pressed the button for the second floor. "It makes sense. The residential elevators are separate from the business elevators, and Miss Killingsworth's private elevators are separate from all of them. Look, magic or no, if I was a single woman living alone in the city, I wouldn't want just anyone off the street to have a way into my place, either."

"Still," Friday said. "Three elevators seems excessive."

"And anyway," Lisa said, "at least this time we had to push a button to tell it where to go. That's got to be better than the one from the garage that just knew where to take us all on its own."

"Still excessive," Friday said.

"Have you seen anything about this woman that isn't excessive?" Yumi grinned, at least until Lisa gave her a look.

"Could have been only two," Kara reminded them. "We could take this one all the way down to the ground floor, then head outside and around to the private entrance. But it's raining a damn nor'easter out there, and I'd rather not show up to a meeting with my billionaire new employer soaking wet. So we take this one to the second floor, then we get on the corporate one to bring us back up to the office where we were this morning, and then security will put us on the other one."

The other three nodded. Kara made a good point. If there hadn't been a full-on squall outside, they could have gotten where they were going with a little less rigmarole.

At least the elevators were quick and smooth. The residential elevator gave them the option of opening a back door, which let them out onto the mezzanine gallery of the Goblin Records retail space. The elevators directly opposite were guarded by an attendant who gave the young women a single nod as they crossed the lobby and boarded the express car that carried them up to the forty-seventh-floor offices where they'd been this morning. They were met at the top by an older woman who introduced herself as Bridget, and whom none of them would have taken for the kind of person to be employed by the likes of Ruby Killingsworth.

Bridget was definitely surprising, but the elevator to the penthouse was not at all. It was all glass and chrome, with only four buttons and more reflective surfaces than the average disco ball.

That elevator then carried them to the fiftieth-floor elevator lobby, where a uniformed butler stood waiting beside a large marble-topped entryway table replete with an enormous arrangement of fresh flowers. The butler gestured for the four of them to follow, and they did—across the opulent vestibule and through what they had to guess was Miss Killingsworth's front door.

"Holy—" Lisa managed to swallow the swear word, but the sentiment was clear. "Is this place for real?"

"I don't know what I expected a billionaire's penthouse to look like," Kara said quietly. "But I'm pretty sure this isn't it."

Friday was just looking around wide-eyed. Even Yumi seemed impressed.

The entire room was gleaming white—from sparkling floor to twelve-foot ceiling—save for the intricate brass and wrought iron railing around a staircase leading down.

"Should we be taking our shoes off?" Lisa asked the butler, who seemed to be paying her no mind at all as the four women moved farther from the door and into the cavernous room ahead.

"No need for that," Ruby called from someplace off to their right. "Come in."

The four of them did as instructed, creeping farther into the whiteness like the cast of the *Wizard of Oz* in fear of lions and tigers and bears.

"This is the shiniest floor I've ever seen in my life," Yumi said. "I feel like I'm gonna scuff it."

"Yeah," Friday agreed. "I don't know what this floor is made out of, but it's kind of weirding me out."

"Maybe I'm just Japanese," Lisa said, "but I feel very uncomfortable walking on it with my shoes on."

"It's quartz terrazzo," Ruby called out again, though there was no way she should have heard them. "It's shiny and white, but it's also the floor, so I assure you, you should walk on it."

They kept walking—carefully—toward the sound of their employer's voice. The room beyond the doorway was just as unreal as the one they'd just left. The quartz-terrazzo floor went on for what seemed like forever, due in part to its own reflection in the glass that made up the walls on two sides. The room was too big. And it was almost empty. A few white leather sofas were clustered around a television against the left-hand wall and what looked like a small wet bar stood on the spit of wall separating the glass from the doorway they'd just passed through, but other than that, it was just a huge, open cavern of a space. It certainly didn't feel like it belonged in anybody's home.

Ruby was sitting on a white leather stool that could not possibly have been comfortable, leaning against the bar, with her StarPhone in one hand and a shockingly red drink in the other.

"Oh, good. It's everyone. Well, not *everyone* everyone. Jaccob has many truly excellent qualities; punctuality, however, has never been among them. Come have a seat," Ruby instructed, gesturing with her drink hand to the three sofas in the distance before sliding off the barstool and heading that direction herself. "Can I offer anyone a drink?"

"Do you mean, like, a drink-drink?" Yumi asked. "Or, like, water?"

"Anything you'd like," Ruby replied. "I am a stern taskmaster, but I'm not a tyrant. I trust you all to be adults. If you choose to engage in a little recreational substance use, I could not give a tenth of a damn, provided you're not regularly getting yourselves so inebriated it starts affecting your work."

"I'm the only one here besides Kara who's old enough to drink," Friday informed her coolly.

"I don't recall having asked anyone's age," Ruby replied.

"Sure, then," Yumi said. "I'll have a ... I mean ... what have you got?"

"A full bar and a licensed mixologist."

"Oh."

"I'll have whatever you're having," Lisa said.

"Um ... Long Island?" Yumi said, trying to remember the name of literally any alcoholic drink she'd ever heard was good.

"She said not to get inebriated," Lisa reminded her.

"Right." Yumi nodded at Lisa, then at Ruby. "I'll do the same as you and Lisa."

"I'll have an Aviation," Kara said. "Hendricks if you've got it."

"Of course I do. Life's too short for subpar gin. Miss Jones?" Ruby looked to Friday, finger hovering over the screen of her phone.

"Naw, I'm good," Friday replied.

"Suit yourself."

Ruby swiped at the screen of her phone for a moment and then slipped it back into her coat pocket before sitting down on the one piece of furniture none of the others had chosen to sit on.

"There are limits to my hospitality, but I don't ID heroes at the door, and I don't tell anyone what they can and can't do with their own bodies—and that includes my employees. Use whatever substances suit you, have as much sex as you want. As long as you're getting the job done, I don't give a damn what else you may happen to be up to. I will ask you to keep visitors to a minimum, mostly for Mike's sake. Since we're not sure whether it's him or me these bastards are really after, I've got him on a bit of a lockdown for the moment." Ruby took a sip of her drink and shook her head. "But I'm getting ahead of myself, I'll go over all of this properly once my esteemed neighbor finally decides to grace us with his presence."

"I hope he's all right," Yumi said, turning her head toward the glass wall on the other side of the room.

The storm outside was intense, a very rare occurrence for Cobalt City in late July. Raindrops were blowing sideways into the glass, and the wind howled through the space between Ruby's and

Starcom's Towers. It was a freak summertime nor'easter according to the news, and if Stardust was out flying in it, that could spell trouble.

"If he'd crashed his damn super suit," Ruby answered, "I'd know. I have an alert set up on my phone."

Yumi and Lisa exchanged a glance. The whole city knew that Jaccob and Ruby had had an affair a couple of years back, and there was something interesting about hearing she had an automatic alert set to go off if something were to happen to him.

They'd likely be up half the night postulating as to just what that meant in broader terms.

"You think maybe he's stuck somewhere?" Lisa asked. "Like, maybe he went out before the weather turned, and now it's not safe to fly, so he's got to find another way back home or something?"

Ruby shook her head. "Something you should know about me is that I'm one of those people for whom on time is late. Time is money and I prefer to waste neither. Your arrival five minutes ahead of our scheduled start time bodes well for our ability to work together. Mr. Stevens, who knows this about me, by the way, is as of this moment, officially late. And he has not yet bothered to send a message as to why. Sadly, he is not on my payroll and therefore not subject to consequence beyond my personal wrath. I'll give him until the drinks arrive, and then we'll just start without him. I don't care to waste your time any more than I'd appreciate your wasting mine."

"I really do wonder if it's the weather that's keeping him," Yumi said.

"I don't," Ruby replied. "In fact, I don't give a tenth of a damn why he's late. It only matters to me *that* he's late. The least he could have done is send me a text. Which he has not done."

"Well, I'm sure he has a good reason," Lisa said.

Before anyone could say anything further, Ruby rolled her eyes and shook her head. She rose abruptly and headed toward a barely discernable door built into the glass wall not far from the bar where she'd been sitting when they'd all arrived.

"What the—?" Friday said softly.

"Listen," Kara told the others, shaking her head.

It took a moment for it to be fully audible, but there it was—growing louder and louder as it closed on their position—the unmistakable droning of the Stardust suit in flight.

The glass door opened as Ruby approached it, and she leaned against the doorframe, arms crossed at her waist as she waited for Stardust to come in for a landing.

The four women watched from the sofas as Stardust approached from the city side of the building and landed gently on the balcony beyond the glass wall. The wind and rain appeared to be having little effect on his ability to fly. But what was really strange was the way the wind and the rain seemed to have no effect on Ruby at all. She was standing in the open doorway, fully exposed to the weather, with rain landing on the floor all around her. The others could feel the wind from where they were sitting, but Ruby didn't look to have so much as a hair out of place or a drop on her patent pumps.

"That's creepy as fuck," Friday mumbled.

"I think it's amazing," Lisa said back.

"And super useful," Yumi added. "If I could do magic like that, I would definitely use it to keep myself dry in a rainstorm. Also, this explains why her hair is always so perfect."

"I guess that's one way to make an entrance," Ruby said to Stardust when he flipped open the visor on his helmet.

"Sorry I'm late," he said. "I know how much you hate that."

"And yet," Ruby replied, gesturing for him to come inside.

At her invitation, he walked past her into the room, waving at the others once he spotted them. He was dripping wet, leaving little puddles on the ground at his feet. For the young women who'd been nervous even to walk on this pristine floor, it was a little disconcerting to see how little Ruby and Jaccob seemed to care.

"We've already made a drink order," Ruby told him. "So if you want a cocktail, you'll have to wait. But you know where I keep the Scotch, and you're welcome to help yourself."

"I'll just get a water for now," he answered.

"You know where I keep that, too."

Stardust opened a pair of panels on the forearms of his armored suit and flipped a switch beneath each one. The women watched in awe as the suit removed itself from Jaccob Stevens, sections sliding and folding themselves until the whole thing appeared as an unassuming, albeit dripping wet, suitcase beside the door, which had closed itself sometime when nobody was watching. Jaccob, now dressed in a tee shirt, shorts, and leather topsiders with no socks, went around to the back of the little bar and pulled a bottle of water from a half-height fridge built into the back counter.

As he shut the refrigerator and came to join the others, a very young man in a starched black uniform entered the room from the vestibule carrying a tray full of glasses. Ruby, Jaccob, and the newcomer all reached the seating area at the same time.

Ruby seated herself back in the place she'd been sitting earlier, and Jaccob plopped himself down on the opposite end of the same sofa. He cracked open his bottle of water as the fellow with the tray passed out the cocktails. The young man then scooped up Ruby's empty glass from the end table beside her before silently making his exit.

"Is it me, or was that creepy, too?" Friday asked quietly. She glowered at Yumi and Lisa as they examined the bright red drinks they'd been handed. It was enough to make Yumi set hers down without taking a sip.

"Because I have help?" Ruby asked her, again demonstrating her ability to hear even the faintest whispers.

"Because he didn't say anything," Friday replied. "You got some kind of magic silencing curse on him or something?"

Ruby chuckled. "Oh, I do enjoy your imagination, Miss Jones. But no. His English isn't the best. And he's hard of hearing. But he's excellent at his job, and I pay him well for it. He doesn't have to speak when he doesn't want to, and he certainly can't sign with a tray of glasses in his hand. Any more questions?"

"Nah," Friday replied, sliding back in her seat.

"Well, good," Ruby said. "Now we can get down to the business at hand. I'm not sure how much Jaccob has told you already, so I'd appreciate it if someone would please catch me up."

"We understand you got an email," Lisa replied. "And there was a song in it—like, a fully produced, but kind of bad version of a song that Mike just now finished writing and hadn't even started recording. And that you did everything you could do on your own to figure out where it came from and who could have sent it."

"And after yesterday," Friday added, "we understand that to include some seriously powerful and possibly questionable magical shit."

"I suppose I'll leave the definition of 'questionable' up to personal interpretation," Ruby said. "But yes. That's the long and the short of it. The message came in. I found it singularly disturbing. I did everything within my power and the powers of a certain immortal gentleman of my acquaintance—"

"You can say Loki," Friday said. "We know it's Loki."

"They know it's Loki," Jaccob added for emphasis.

"Indeed," Ruby answered, taking a tiny sip from her cocktail. "And I can tell from your collective looks of disdain that you both disapprove of my association with the god of mischief and also understand the amount of power wielded by such."

"Oh yeah," Friday replied. "We definitely do."

"You're the avatar, then," Ruby said to Friday.

"I ... yes," Friday answered after a moment.

"And you're the mechanical genius," Ruby said to Kara.

"Yep, that's me," Kara replied, raising her glass a little as she did.

"Which makes you," Ruby said, turning to Yumi, "the legacy hero with the bloodthirsty sword and all the fencing medals."

"One of those is even from the Olympics," Friday added.

"Should have been a gold," Lisa said.

Yumi shook her head. "More likely the silver. But yeah."

"And you," Ruby continued, inclining her head toward Lisa, "support and coordinate. Not really a hero, not exactly a sidekick—more like hero management from what I've been able to gather."

"Something like that," Lisa agreed.

"All right, good. Now that we've got that all out in the open," Ruby shrugged as she sipped her martini, and looked at Friday. "I respect your discomfort when it comes to my friendship with the Norse god of mischief, and I promise I shan't be involving them further in this undertaking. I can say with all certainty that they and I have, by our powers combined, exhausted all arcane avenues of investigation into what I found in my inbox and have reached the conclusion there's no magic behind it. And if it isn't magical, that means it's technical. I know exactly one technical genius. He just so happens to be my neighbor, as well as the father of the musician whose work appears to have been stolen. I took the issue to Jaccob, and he brought it to you. And now here we are."

"Time travel is intriguing." Kara took a sip of her drink and gave it a nod of approval before continuing. "But it's also supposed to be impossible."

"Hence everyone's initial presumption there must have been magic behind it," Ruby replied, also sipping at her own cocktail.

"I'll want a look at your email," Jaccob said, turning his whole body to face her.

"Oh, I bet you would," Ruby snapped, frowning at him over the rim of her glass.

"Look," he said, his voice sounding a bit apologetic. "It's not like I want to read your private messages. But there may be some data about the sender in there. Depending on how much care they took, I may be able to trace the email back to the machine that sent it. I may even be able to find the sender using that data."

"How about I forward it to you instead?" Ruby suggested.

"I guess that might work?" Jaccob replied.

"Then let's just start with that," Ruby said. "If you can't get what you need from a forwarded message, then maybe I'll let you have a look at my inbox. I'd rather we exhaust all other options before handing over my device."

"You do remember I set up your device?" Jaccob asked. "In fact, I set up your whole network. If I really wanted to get into your email, you know I wouldn't need to wait until you handed me your phone."

"Oh, I am well aware it's your aversion to all things sneaky and underhanded and not any function of my cybersecurity that keeps my private messages private. Let this be a lesson," Ruby said pointedly to the others. "Whenever possible, hire a Good Guy."

"So noted," Kara replied.

"So we're just going to have to work from the presumption that time travel isn't just possible but is actually happening?" Lisa half asked, as she sipped at her pomegranate martini.

"I think that makes the most sense," Kara said. "We presume the what, and we try to chase down the who and the how."

"I'm honestly not that interested in how," Ruby said. "I don't give a damn how they're doing it; I only care that they stop. So if figuring out how this thing is happening is going to help you stop it, then fine. Otherwise, please remember you're being hired to stop the time travelers, not to unearth all their secrets."

"Yes, ma'am," Kara replied. "I was only working to that end. Knowing how they're doing it may be the only way to know how to stop them."

"Agreed," Jaccob said. "We should probably be on the lookout for any reports of similar kinds of strangeness in the media. There's a chance that whoever is doing this isn't going to stop at one artist."

"Especially if they're in this for blackmail," Ruby added.

"I can put Lumien on that, if you're all right with it," Kara offered.

"That's your ... automaton?" Ruby asked.

"He's ... yeah." Kara answered. "I'm sure Jaccob could program some internet bots to do the crawling for us, but why not use a resource we already have? I can just ask him to comb the internet for anything suspicious and forward anything he finds to me for follow-up. It should get us what we need without costing us the time to write and debug a program. And since Lumien doesn't need to eat or sleep, he can be at it twenty-four-seven. Plus, doing it on my home machines means nobody should be able to track the searches—and if they've got some sort of next-level, future tech that means they do manage track the searches, they're unlikely to trace Lumien's internet activity back to you, which gives us extra time to figure them out before they have a chance to figure us out."

"Yes," Ruby said. "Good."

"As for the local angle," Kara continued, "We'll get ears to the ground in all the usual places. You think the heroes in this town are in cahoots, you should see the villains. We've got three hot young coeds here. We might as well use that to our advantage."

"What do you mean by that?" Yumi asked. "Please be as specific as possible."

Lisa blushed a little.

"I mean the last I checked, The Hollows was full of hipster hangouts where the wannabe wicked congregate in hopes of getting picked up for a freelance crime gig," Kara replied. "And if there's one thing I know about those kinds of posers, it's that they talk. A lot. If there's been so much as a whiff of a time-traveling techno-villain in town, it's going to be the hot gossip at Macky's."

"Macky's is a bar, isn't it?" Friday asked. "Are they even going to let these two in?"

"It is a bar," Kara replied. "But it's not the kind of place where you're going to get asked for ID. In fact, most of the people in there are either intentionally anonymous or pretending to be. A bunch of young, pretty women aren't going to have any trouble getting in there."

"Yeah," Jaccob concurred. "You'll be fine. Macky's is one of those places the city's worst people tend to congregate, and most of those guys aren't really into carrying government ID. I think Kara's right that we ought to see what we can find out by eavesdropping."

"That was a royal 'we', wasn't it Jaccob?" Ruby asked, turning in her seat to look Jaccob in the eye. "Some of your compatriots have secret identities. You ... do not. I doubt anyone in all of The Hollows is going to say anything about anything with Mr. Stardust in the room."

"Yeah," he said back. "No. I meant 'we' the team. Not we-including-me. I'm way too old and way too famous to do that kind of thing anymore."

"All right," Ruby said. "Just making sure it wasn't one of those recently single midlife crisis things."

Jaccob blanched. It was pretty obvious to everyone he hadn't expected his divorce to come up in this meeting.

"Nothing like that," he replied. "And anyway, I'll be busy on the tech side of things. If there's a way to get to the bottom of that email you got, I'm going to find it."

"The email is a good lead," Kara said, taking back control of the conversation. "But that's not the only tech angle we should be chasing."

"It isn't?" Jaccob seemed intrigued.

"I don't think so, no," Kara answered. "If somebody has really traveled back in time to the here and now, then that activity has also got to have left a trace—seismic, radioactive, atmospheric ... something. I think we should be looking into that too."

Ruby cocked her head to the side. "Go on."

"It stands to reason," Kara replied, "that people or machinery traveling through time would create enough of a disruption in at least some of the measurable, observable qualities of spacetime that a person with the right equipment should, theoretically, be able to detect it."

"Theoretically?" Ruby repeated.

"I'm just saying—" Kara shook her head and shrugged. "This is all theoretical at this point. But if—and I maintain that's a pretty big 'if'—but if someone is traveling through time then there will be ways for us to pick up on that. Maybe even trace it."

"With the right equipment," Jaccob added.

"Yeah," Kara said. "That part."

"I'm guessing from your tone of voice that you're not currently in possession of said equipment." Ruby drummed her nails against the stem of her glass, clearly displeased with the current tack of the conversation.

"Yeah, no," Kara replied. "It's never been my area of interest before now."

"Well, that doesn't really help us, does it?"

The question was probably rhetorical, but Kara answered anyway. "It doesn't."

"Could you build it?" Ruby asked her then.

"Maybe—?" Kara answered. "With enough time and money and the right tools, probably. But there's also a chance we don't have to."

"Go on."

"The kind of equipment I'm talking about already exists."

"It does?" Yumi asked.

"I thought you just said it was all theoretical," Lisa added, frowning at Kara over her martini.

"It is," Kara replied. "But theoretical doesn't mean impossible, it just means unproven. And there are people all over the world who study this stuff. In fact, there's a professor right here at the university who's done some really promising work on understanding disruptions in spacetime. He's supposed to have a lab full of exactly the kinds of machines we'd want for this investigation."

"There is?" Lisa was a Poli Sci major but spent plenty of her elective hours in the sciences. "Wait, do you mean—?"

"Yep." Kara sipped her cocktail as she nodded.

"Do you think he'd let you use his lab?" Lisa seemed doubtful. "Or look at his research?"

"Oh, he'll do better than that," Ruby asserted.

"He will?" Kara asked.

"You just get me his name and his department, and let me handle the rest," Ruby replied. "If this equipment exists, it'll be at our disposal soon enough."

"Almost ... like magic?" Lisa dared ask.

"Gold star, Miss Yamamoto," Ruby answered, lifting her glass toward Lisa in a toasting gesture. "Exactly like that."

CHAPTER SIX

Having never bothered to attend college herself, Ruby Killingsworth hadn't much experience with campus life. But she'd hired enough fresh graduates over the years to know that parking on the University of Cobalt City campus was perpetually inadequate. Normally she'd have driven herself on an errand of this variety, but she no more cared to walk from whatever far-off parking spot she'd inevitably get stuck with than she trusted her little Porsche two-seater to an overcrowded lot full of hungover teens.

By the time the limo pulled up in front of the newly constructed experimental wing of the Podmajersky Sciences Building, Ruby was sure she'd made the right decision not to drive. Not only was the tiny parking lot absolute bedlam, the "Re-elect Prather" propaganda was in full swing; she appreciated not having to look up and see it. As it was, she'd had to turn the radio off to avoid his commercials.

Lyle Prather was a pernicious narcissist, and the fact he'd managed to get elected in the first place was little more than proof of the collective gullibility of the American public. He'd been mostly out of her hair since she'd so abruptly ordered him off the stairs of her aircraft on the heels of the bombing of the White House concert. But emails from her legal department had been trickling in over the past several weeks that pointed to Prather's once again becoming a very present fly in her ointment.

But Prather was a problem for another day. This morning's self-important misogynist was one Professor William Kummerfeldt. Kara had given Ruby only the most basic rundown on the man—his areas of expertise and his general attitude toward people outside the sciences. Lisa had contributed a few anecdotes to illustrate his very well-known attitude toward women. He did not sound like the kind of person Ruby made a habit of conversing with.

This meeting was likely to stretch her patience thin, and possibly push her to use her powers in a way she rarely needed to these days.

She'd realized during the brief period in which she'd been missing her magic just how little she currently needed it. It was possible all the years of arcane influence had made an indelible mark on her closest associates, but the fact remained that people genuinely feared and respected her. Whatever was behind it, the revelation that her directives alone, without their magical component, were enough to see her will enacted had been an interesting one.

So today's meeting was likely to see her flex a muscle she hadn't needed in a while. If the reason for the meeting were any less dire, she might even have looked forward to it. As it was, Ruby was unlikely to enjoy the process, but she'd get the work done, nonetheless.

With magic or without, she was going to get what she was after this day.

The limo pulled into a loading zone alongside the newly refurbished J. Stevens Experimental Sciences Wing, and Ruby took a moment to let herself grimace as the driver got out. Funny how she'd never noticed how many things in this damn city were named after Jaccob or his ex-wife until after he'd made his unceremonious exit from her life a couple of years back.

Ruby watched her driver try the unassuming metal door before coming back to let her out of the car. Lisa had told her this side door was likely to be unlocked, and that it opened to a utility stairwell with access to the lower floor. Coming in this way meant Ruby could get where she was going without being forced to choose between traversing a busy staircase and waiting for a slow and possibly crowded elevator. Hers wasn't the most recognizable face in Cobalt City, but she wasn't exactly an unknown, either. She was likely much safer from unsolicited musical numbers in the sciences building than she'd have been in most other places on this campus, but she still preferred not to be accosted at all if possible.

She was hoping to avoid not only the attentions of campus wannabes, but also any questions as to what she was doing in the sciences building.

Lisa and Kara had done good work preparing her. Ruby was in the door and down the stairs within moments, and without encountering another living soul save for her own driver. Where the staircase ended, a matching door opened into the lower-level lobby. It was a dim cavern of a space with polished concrete floors, exposed ductwork, and walls that were bare save for the occasional poorly painted mural. Ruby supposed it was designed to look spartan, industrial, and cool, but in reality, it looked unfinished and uninviting, right down to the portable chalkboard painted with the Cup-O-Chino logo, sporting an arrow pointing to the nearby stairs and advertising a "Stardust Latte" in flowy script.

Ruby did not want to know the ingredients in that drink.

There was a bustle and din in this place, a chaos of students rushing from lectures and labs. She'd been warned the schedules in this building were wild and weird, and there was little chance of finding the place any less busy than it was at this moment. Ruby had contemplated trying anyway, but Lisa had made it clear that any time the student traffic went down, the chances for the professor to be out of the building went up.

And she was not about to make a second trip.

Ruby crossed the lobby, passed the offensive chalkboard, and rounded the corner toward the hall she'd been told housed the professor and the equipment she'd come seeking. She was proud of herself for swallowing the curse word that came to her lips when she nearly ran headlong into a twelve-foot-tall statue of her ex-lover in the center of the wide hallway. Seeing as one of her motivations for taking the basement route had been to avoid the much taller one in the building's main lobby, being surprised by this one was a particular upset. If she ever found out the identity of the artist, they would be in for a whole world of hurt.

The oversized stone-and-metal edifice would have been offensive enough in any case, but the choice of the artist to depict the man half in and half out of the Stardust suit might as well have been made to attack her personally. The bronze Jaccob was shirtless, with one hand on his hip and the other pointing at some unknown thing in the distance, and Ruby couldn't decide whether the sculptor had exaggerated the definition of his biceps ... and his abs. It was too much in every dimension. She brushed her fingers across the smooth metal of the statue's thigh as she passed, putting just enough intention into the exchange of energies to assure the thing would start to crack a few days from now and wind up a pile of dust and bolts by the end of the month.

It might have been more satisfying to watch it crumble right there at her feet, but the need to be sure no one could tie her visit to the statue's demise won out over her desire to watch it fall in real time. She'd have to check with Kara and see about tapping into any security cameras this building might have; watching from afar wouldn't be quite as satisfying, but she'd probably enjoy it.

She found the room where she understood her professorial quarry would be teaching and peeked in through the narrow window built into the door. It was one of those large lecture halls with seats arranged amphitheater style in a steep slope leading to another set of doors to the room from the floor above.

The classroom was packed. Rows upon rows of fresh-faced undergrads and serious older scholars stared at a smart board at the front of the room as their fingers poked frantically at laptops, tablets, and tiny keyboards set on the narrow tables in front of them. Normally Ruby wouldn't mind a room full of witnesses, but today's conversation was around a strange and sensitive enough subject that the lecture hall full of eager learners just wouldn't do.

This seemed like as good a way as any to warm up her magic muscles.

Getting Professor Kummerfeldt to look at her was easy enough. Their eyes met for barely a moment before he turned back to his class, shut down the computer he'd been using to project onto the smart board, and told the students they were dismissed.

Ruby couldn't help but snicker as the throng of visibly confused coeds packed up their things to leave. She took a moment to marvel at how quickly that had all transpired. Sometimes men were too damn easy. Probably why she hadn't bothered with any since being through with Jaccob. Women were always far more interesting.

And any hankering for male anatomy was easily enough satisfied by her increasingly frequent dalliances with Loki. Sure, it had taken some time and a pretty big favor for them to get back in her good graces after the business with Vivienne and the demon Ramisiel, but they'd practically bent over backward in their attempts to garner her forgiveness. Eventually, she'd melted, but only after Vivienne had declared she'd forgiven them already.

Gods were complicated. Mortal men, much less so.

Professor Kummerfeldt was shooing his students out of the room with the urgency of a manager about to run afoul of union overtime. Once Ruby was sure the last of the students was headed out the upstairs door and that none of them were about to try and exit through the door she intended to use, she let herself into the lecture hall proper and approached the professor.

This really was going to be too easy. She'd seen the look he wore on plenty of men before today. She'd barely had the chance to apply any magic at all and he was already putty in her hands; this fellow was going to be no trouble at all.

"Professor," she greeted him as she approached.

He opened his mouth to reply, but no sound came out.

"My card," she said, popping open her clutch and handing over the tiny item. The only card she used these days was blank: a slip of polished metal with an NFC chip embedded and a QR code only visible to infrared cameras. She didn't remember where the idea had originally come from, but it was a flex she enjoyed and a sure-fire way to keep her personal info from getting out courtesy of some paparazzi's telephoto lens.

Professor Kummerfeldt fumbled with the card before sliding it into the pocket of the shabby chambray shirt he wore unbuttoned in lieu of a jacket. There were cartoons on the tee shirt he wore underneath it and enough wear in his khaki pants to make Ruby wonder just how well this institution did or did not pay its employees.

"What can I do for you?" he asked, his voice cracking like he was a twelve-year-old schoolboy instead of a professor well into his fifties.

"I need a favor," Ruby replied, tempted to leave the magic out of her statement but deciding it wasn't worth the extra time. She hadn't come here to play with this man, she'd come to get things done.

"A ... a favor?" he asked, still stumbling over his words. He shoved his hands into his pockets for a moment then extended his right toward her. "I'm um ... I'm Bill Kummerfeldt."

Ruby stepped forward just enough to shake the man's hand. "Charmed, I'm sure.

"What is it—?" the professor asked. "What can I do for you?"

The hardest part of the conversation turned out to be pretending to give a damn about all the things Professor Kummerfeldt wanted to tell her. Ruby sat through diatribes on his work and his expertise and very detailed histories of the theory and operations of the equipment he was more than happy to lend.

More than happy, of course, was almost surely a function of her magical influence and not of any genuine desire on the part of the professor to share his instruments or work. By the time she was in the car and on her way back to the office, Ruby knew more about scientific theories surrounding time travel than she ever would have cared to. But she'd done what she'd come to do, and that was the thing that mattered.

Kara would have her gear, and that would put them one step closer to figuring this whole mess out. Whatever nonconsensual scientific education Ruby had to endure to make that happen was entirely beside the point.

CHAPTER SEVEN

Anyone who worked for Goblin Entertainment long enough got to know when and when not to call the boss.

Ruby had long ago empowered her best and highest-ranking employees to make decisions without the need to consult her. Most of the time, even when decisions had to travel up the corporate ladder, they stopped a rung or two below Miss Killingsworth's office. And on those rare occasions when that didn't happen, those with the means to contact Ruby directly had a complex matrix by which to judge just when and how to go about that. The farther from the middle of her day an issue came up, the more urgent it needed to be for it to be brought to her immediate attention.

No one reached the point in their career where they had access to Miss Killingsworth's direct email or priority phone number without knowing better than to use it in off hours barring an actual emergency.

So when her phone rang before she'd finished her coffee that Thursday morning, Ruby was as surprised as she was displeased. And when she saw the call was coming from Arsho Barsamian, she was downright disturbed. Arsho had been the building manager since the Ruby Tower was little more than a set of sketches and a pile of permits. They had supervised every brick laid, every wire run, and every finish as it was installed—both during the initial construction and the recent refurbishment after the demon occupation. And they'd done all of that without ever having disturbed Ruby outside of office hours.

All signs pointed to something unpleasantly urgent. That the call was coming in on her priority phone meant Arsho wasn't taking any chances with the possibility of Ruby not answering. The scant handful of people who had that number knew she'd answer it any day, any time. If there had been any way this issue could wait, the call would have come in on the standard business phone, or it would have been an email.

"Yes?" Ruby tried not to sound too gruff as she flipped on the speaker and set the device down on her vanity. She may have to take this call, but she was going to finish her face while she did.

"I'm sorry to bother you so early, Miss Killingsworth," Arsho began.

"Yes, yes," Ruby replied, cutting them off with a wave of her hand she didn't much care Arsho couldn't see. "Don't waste my time with apologies; I know you wouldn't have called if it wasn't important. What is it?"

"I just got summoned to the loading dock," Arsho replied. "And I've got two trucks here that say they're from the university marching band. The one driver says there's equipment they're supposed to unload, but I don't have any paperwork on this, and Special Projects isn't answering the phone."

"No one's answering the phone," Ruby reminded them, "because it's eight o'clock in the morning, and nobody is expected in the office until after nine. But I don't think this is a bit for Special Projects anyway."

"You don't?"

"I don't." Ruby finished with the eyeliner pen and set it back on the vanity. Picking up her mascara, she continued, "Have one of the drivers open the back of his truck. I'm pretty sure I know what's in there, and it won't be band equipment."

Ruby took the moment to apply her mascara. She hadn't given a whole lot of thought to what Professor Kummerfeldt's machinery was going to look like, nor how he was expected to get it to her. All she knew was he'd agreed to lend her the lot of it and that it would be delivered to the Tower as soon as possible. Two giant trucks borrowed from the marching band arriving at her loading dock less than eighteen hours later wasn't necessarily what she'd been expecting, but if that's what was going on, she wasn't going to be mad about it.

"Oh, yes, ma'am." Arsho's voice startled Ruby enough she was glad to be through with the mascara wand. It wouldn't do to poke herself in the eye this morning. The whole reason she was up and primping this early was that Vivienne had agreed to a quick visit and would be arriving sometime before lunch. Ruby's plan was to take the entire afternoon off.

"Yes?" Ruby asked.

"I don't know what any of it is, but it definitely isn't band equipment."

"Oh, good," Ruby replied. "I hadn't expected this delivery to arrive so quickly. Two trucks full, you say?"

"Yes, ma'am," Arsho replied. "An eighteen-wheeler and a standard box truck."

"Oh my." Ruby bit her lip and frowned. She'd pictured a few small devices, bits and bots that would sit on a counter or plug in to a laptop. She'd thought to have it all delivered straight to the condo Kara had chosen for the duration of the job. It sounded like she instead had an entire arcade's worth of cabinets and consoles on her hands. And that much gear would definitely not fit in Kara's spare room.

"Ma'am?" Arsho said.

"Wasn't expecting quite this volume," Ruby admitted.

"It's a lot."

"Indeed."

"Is it studio equipment?" Arsho asked. "Because, again, I don't have paperwork, and—"

"No." Ruby tried not to take umbrage at Arsho's repeated grouse at not having the proper documents to receive this delivery. They were a fastidious manager—a fact which had proven useful time and again over the course of their employment—but they'd never been particularly good at taking things as they come or going with the flow. "No," she repeated after a moment. "These machines are for a personal concern. Have them brought up to the party room. And don't let the drivers leave until every piece of that machinery is plugged in, switched on, and appears to be working."

"Yes, ma'am," Arsho replied. The phone went silent.

Ruby nodded and checked to make sure the call had fully ended. Arsho had never been one for superfluous conversation; once they knew what they needed to do, they were done asking questions. Ruby appreciated that. What she did not appreciate was the fact she was going to need to let Kara, and maybe the others, use a room in her penthouse as a workspace while Vivienne was in town. Even limiting the times of day when they were welcome in the penthouse could possibly curtail certain activities, and imposing limits might mean stymieing their ability to get to the bottom of things.

This was going to be a pain in her ass either way.

She figured she'd find a way to make the best of it and make it up to Vivienne later if her trip wasn't all she'd hoped for. It had taken a bit of convincing to get her to fly out here for such a short visit, and she'd only agreed to it on the promise she would be back in Seattle in time to be at work on Friday night. As much as it annoyed Ruby sometimes how devoted Vivienne was to that dive she managed, she had to admire a woman's dedication to her business.

Still, it was frustrating.

She supposed if she could run a multi-billion-dollar corporation, she could figure this out.

~

The rest of the morning turned out to be little more than one problem after another. Vivienne had already been upstairs to have a look for herself by the time Arsho sent a text to tell Ruby the machinery was in and running. Ruby could tell Vivienne was trying not to laugh at her level of frustration with the situation, and she appreciated not being mocked. But she wasn't enjoying herself.

They agreed to go out for dinner—Vivienne forever in her quest to see Ruby eat food in any appreciable quantity. Ruby figured she had just enough time between the end of her workday and their reservation to change her clothes and offer Kara and the others an introduction to their new headquarters. She called down to security and then texted the young women to come up as quickly as possible.

When it took them nearly ten minutes to make the trip up, Ruby also shot off a text to Jaccob. The hired capes needed penthouse access without having to walk around the building or wait for security to badge them into the private elevator. Any member of her security staff could have made the change, but there was something satisfying about making this Jaccob's problem.

Dressed to the nines for her dinner reservation, Ruby greeted her four employees at the elevator.

"You look amazing," Yumi blurted.

"Thank you. I have a dinner. But I have something to show you first." Ruby stepped out of the way of the others and gestured for them to follow her.

"There ... was a ... wall there," Lisa said quietly, pointing directly across the lobby to the space that had been home to the penthouse's front door when they'd visited just two days ago. "Right? There was a wall. Over there?"

"Yeah," Friday said. "There was."

Ruby ignored their comments. She gestured for the four of them to follow her around to their right and past the end of the elevator bank.

Something to show them indeed.

The wall to the right of the elevator bank, a wall that had been smooth and solid the last time they'd visited, had also gone entirely missing. In its place was a wide opening leading to a space they would never have guessed was there.

It was a huge room, larger even than the sitting room on the other side, and the floor was raised by several inches, with a gentle incline leading up from the lobby. The left-hand wall was draped floor-to-ceiling with ivory velvet curtains, and the wood-plank floor shone like it had been recently polished.

Rows of machines were laid out banquet-hall style, with the largest equipment on the far right-hand side of the room and additional consoles stretching out in rows perpendicular to those. Even Ruby had to admit it was pretty impressive. And she could tell from the looks on her hired capes' faces that they were, in fact, impressed.

"This—" Lisa looked at Ruby in confusion and awe. "This was not here before. There was a wall here," she said, pointing into the gear-filled room. "And also over there."

"Indeed." Ruby was coming to like Lisa in particular. She noticed details and she wasn't afraid to speak up.

"What—" Kara asked, her voice dripping with wonder as she continued to look around the room. "What is this?"

"I believe you ordered a university's worth of scientific apparatus," Ruby replied.

"Wow," Kara said. "I knew you said you'd get Kummerfeldt to hand over his gear, but—"

"How long did it take to load all this stuff in here?" Yumi asked, breaking off from the rest of the group to get a closer look at a nearby machine.

"All damn day," Ruby answered tersely. "They got here at eight this morning, and the whole production has been fouling my schedule ever since. I am on my way out. Feel free to poke around, get the lay of the land. But be out of here before eleven or else I'll be displeased."

"So this room," Lisa said, "and over there—"

"It's your temporary war room," Ruby replied. "Normally this side's a party room. I let musicians put on showcases in here, among other things. And after a few interesting electrical situations at my house in Regency Heights, I had this space designed with extra capacity. I can plug in a whole entire rock band, someone's ultra-elaborate EDM setup, all the lighting either one of them could ask for, and all the control apparatus that makes it all work together without overloading the circuit breakers. Initially I thought we'd be having Dr. Kummerfeldt's equipment installed in Miss Sparx's condo, but when I got a good look at it all, I realized this to be the necessary approach. I usually only pull the other wall for very large gatherings, but Jaccob may want to come and go from the balcony, and I've got a fridge full of water behind the bar you'll likely want access to, so I figured it's just easier to make it one big space for the time being."

"Yeah," Kara said. "This is—"

"You know what all this stuff is?" Friday asked her. "How to use it?"

"I can't say I do," Kara replied. "Yet. I should be able to figure it out, though. Might take me a couple of days, but—"

"There are manuals." Ruby pointed out a stack of bankers' boxes on the floor at the far end of the room. "The professor sent a very nice letter along with the shipment. He said these machines will need to be individually calibrated and then networked together for maximum efficacy. He also left his number and said you're welcome to give him a call."

Yumi smiled. "*We* are welcome to give him a call, or *you* are?"

Ruby waved away the clarification.

"Probably won't be necessary," Kara said. "But that's good to know in case I get stuck."

"Quite," Ruby agreed. "It's all at your disposal for as long as you need, Miss Sparx. And you're welcome to teach the other three how to use it all—or not—as you see fit. Either way, as soon as Jaccob gets here, you'll all have—"

She was cut off by the sound of knocking on glass coming from the next room.

"Well, well. Speak of the devil." Ruby shrugged as she left the others, following the sound of the knock into the other room. Jaccob was standing on the patio, a StarBoard beside him on the flagstones.

Ruby stopped short of her approach. It only took a tiny gesture on her part for the door to swing open.

"I got your message," Jaccob said.

"You know you don't need to knock," was all she said in reply, turning her back on him as she headed back into the other room.

"I don't?"

"Jaccob," Ruby answered, looking over her shoulder just long enough to be sure he could see her frown. "I wouldn't even have a lock on that door if you hadn't made me let you put one on it. I don't lock it; I'm not even completely sure I know *how* to lock it. For the duration of this undertaking, if I ask you to come by for something, please do me the favor of not making me have to walk all the way over there to let you in."

Her rebuke had the desired effect of flustering Jaccob a little. Ruby could tell he'd been on the verge of saying something about how good she looked in her wine-colored cocktail dress, but she already knew that, and didn't want to sidetrack things. Nor did she want to give the impression his opinion on her appearance mattered in the slightest.

"The, um, the walls are down," he said, trying his best to make casual conversation and failing as surely as he ever had at anything.

"You'll see why." Ruby gestured for him to follow her. "This is all the equipment from the University," she said, as the two of them passed through the penthouse vestibule and into the room where Kara and the others were getting acquainted with the machinery.

"Wow," Jaccob said. "Damn."

"My sentiments exactly," she replied. "I will admit it's nothing like what I pictured. Needless to say, there was no way this was all going to fit down in Miss Sparx's condo, so I had it all set up in here. Which would be fine, except they can't get in here without getting security to badge them in, and I can tell you right now the time is going to come when that turns into a pain in my ass. Arsho and my security team have a job to do that isn't just looking after my personal charges. So in the interest of stopping the headaches all around, I'd like you to get into my system and do what you do to make their faces work to get up the guest elevator and onto these floors—same as mine does ... or yours."

"Just blanket access?" he asked. "To anywhere in the building?"

"If that's easier," she replied with a shrug. "I don't care. The thing that matters is that they can come and go from up here as they please. If they want to come in early or stay here late, they shouldn't have to call security."

"Yeah. Yeah, I can do that."

"Good," Ruby said. "I have to go now. I have reservations. Feel free to stick around and learn this machinery or not. Ladies, stay late if you want to—again, though, be gone by eleven or else. Staff knows to check on you in an hour. They'll bring up dinner if you get hungry. I'll see the four of you tomorrow."

~

Jaccob couldn't help but to watch Ruby walk away, and not just because she looked so good in that red dress.

He didn't like the way she could walk past him without seeming to notice he was there, but even more than that, he didn't like how much he didn't like it. He had no right to want her to be nicer to him; he was the one who caused the rift between them to begin with. It was just odd for him to be around someone who seemed to have no interest in being friendly or pleasant—doubly so when the other person in question was someone he'd once been intimate with.

Not that he had much experience with exes and breakups. He'd met Liz in his teens, married her in his twenties, and been faithful to her until the day she'd walked out—both times. So maybe this was normal. Maybe the awkwardness and the chill between him and Ruby was par for the course. Maybe it would always be there.

But he hoped not.

He'd gotten it in his head this might be his chance to do better by her, to make things more amiable between them going forward. And he figured, if he wanted that, the first thing he could do was what she'd asked of him.

Yumi and Lisa were staring at him thoughtfully, having watched that whole interaction with rapt interest. Lisa had the decency to look away, pretending not to have noticed, but Yumi just nodded knowingly.

"All right," he said, eager to get past it. "Let's get these scans handled. Who wants to go first?"

CHAPTER EIGHT

Ruby's phone ringing before office hours the morning of Vivienne's arrival had been an annoyance. It happening again the next morning was a full-on upset.

Vivienne had only just gotten to sleep, her penchant for pulling all-nighters and the three-hour time difference conspiring to keep her up most of the night, which meant Ruby had also slept very little.

Losing sleep on a lover's visit was oftentimes worth it, but not when the cause was a blaring telephone at ten past eight in the morning. If it hadn't been for the fact of Vivienne laying on her arm, there was a real chance Ruby would have blasted the phone with magic to the point of shattering the infernal device. But when she finally got a look at the screen and saw it was Bridget calling, she knew better than to ignore it.

Bridget had run the CEO's office since long before Ruby was its occupant. She'd started out as a receptionist around the time Ruby was born and had managed the executive offices for the past three CEOs. And she absolutely would not be calling if it wasn't urgent.

"Yes?" Ruby grumbled into the phone as she pulled herself up to sit on the side of the bed.

"Miss Killingsworth," Bridget said, her voice with a sharpness to it that Ruby recognized as her being quite near the end of her proverbial rope. "I do hate to bother you this early. But I've got the President of the United States here in your outer office along with a couple of lawyers, and I figure you'll probably want to come down and deal with them."

"Lawyers?" Ruby asked, rubbing her eyes with the back of her hand as she slid off the edge of the bed. "His or ours?"

"Looks to be one of each," Bridget replied.

"Well, damn."

"Yes, ma'am."

"All right, Bridget," Ruby replied, sliding her slippers on and reaching for the dressing gown she'd left draped across the foot of the bed. "Have some coffee brought over; leave mine on my desk. Then tell them to hold their horses, and I'll be down as soon as I can."

"Yes, ma'am," Bridget repeated as Ruby hung up her phone. She scowled down at the darkening screen before heading toward her bathroom.

"Hey," Vivienne called after her as she reached the foot of the bed.

"Didn't mean to wake you," Ruby replied.

"I heard the word 'lawyers'. Everything okay?"

"Wait 'til you hear whose lawyers."

"Yeah?"

"Mmh," Ruby yawned as she looked back at Vivienne, still sprawled across the bed, tangled in her blankets. She would have Prather's ass for dragging her out of here.

"Lay it on me," Vivienne said then.

Ruby shook her head. Boils, maybe, or gangrene. Prather was going to pay for this.

"Lyle Prather," she replied, combing through her hair with her fingers.

"Damn."

"My sentiments exactly."

"That sad sack of fascism really sent his lawyers to your office at eight o'clock in the morning?"

"Not sent," Ruby corrected her. "Brought."

"Wait." Vivienne propped herself up on her elbow so she could see Ruby better. "Are you telling me that the President of the United States is downstairs in your office right now?"

"With his lawyer."

"That sucks." Vivienne flopped back down onto the pillows.

"Yes, it does."

"And on the one night I get to sleep over," Vivienne whined, pulling the covers back up over her shoulders.

"I know," Ruby agreed. "It's not fair."

"Want me to come down there and beat the snot out of him?" Vivienne asked. "I've always wanted to punch the President, and this one deserves it more than most."

"No, darling," Ruby said. "That won't be necessary. Plus, it would wind up involving the authorities and likely end up keeping him here longer."

"If you're sure."

"I am. But don't worry. It might not be a literal punch to his face, but I do intend to make him pay for this little transgression. Go back to sleep if you can. I'm going to do my best to get rid of him as quickly as possible."

"You know," Vivienne said, burrowing deeper into the disheveled pile of down comforters and satin sheets, "sometimes I think your life seems so glamorous and so fantastic. But then there are times like this when I wouldn't trade places with you for anything."

"Oh yes," Ruby said. "It's all fun and games until I have to smack down a sitting president over my morning coffee."

Vivienne giggled at that, and it was all Ruby could do not to climb back in the bed and tease her for it. As it was, she shook her head and let herself smile.

"I mean it," Ruby said. "Try and get some more sleep. I'll see what I can do to get rid of him, but he could very well draw this out long enough to run into my regular workday. There's no guarantee I'll get back up here before you have to leave."

Vivienne nodded as Ruby turned and headed into her bathroom. She made quick work of brushing her teeth, then stepped into the closet where she pulled on a simple black cap-sleeve dress and fastened its rhinestone belt buckle at her waist. She slipped on a pair of black round-toe pumps and pulled her hair into a clip at the nape of her neck. She then plied her face with enough magic to take care of any dark circles left behind from not having slept enough, and a little more just for good measure.

Normally she preferred a meticulous hand-application of high-end cosmetics, but she'd learned to fix her face with magic as a teenager, and it was a skill that had proven itself worth being kept up. Less than five minutes had passed between hanging up the phone and heading out the door to the elevator.

"Tell that asshole I'm voting for the other guy," Vivienne called after her.

"I'll try to work it into the conversation," Ruby said back over her shoulder.

The elevator ride down one floor was almost too quick. Ruby was only just getting her perturbed expression under control when the door opened to her inner office. An assistant whose name she wasn't sure she'd ever heard was setting a tall mug of coffee on her desk. He seemed startled to see her, the tray of drinks in his hand almost falling victim to his surprise. Quietly, Ruby cast an enchantment to keep them from spilling. There were very few ways this morning could get worse, but that much coffee pooled on her floor was one of them.

"Oh, Miss Killingsworth," the young man said. "Your coffee is on your desk."

"I saw. Thank you." She couldn't help but appreciate the assistant's choice to leave her coffee on her desk even in her absence before handing drinks over to the President or his retinue. He nodded once, smiling nervously, before turning to deliver the rest of the drinks. Ruby let him get out the door far enough ahead of her that it fully closed before she cast it open again.

She strode out of her office and looked straight at the President, her eyes narrowed and her hands on her hips.

Prather took his coffee and then a step in Ruby's direction.

"You know," she said, as he sipped his drink, "I don't usually see people without an appointment."

"Yes," he said, "but I'm—"

"Standing in my outer office uninvited, bothering my staff before business hours," she interrupted him before he had a chance to declare himself "special" or "a VIP". "So I'm going to presume this is urgent."

"It is," Prather said back to her. "It is."

"All right. Bridget," she said, turning to her receptionist with an expression that clearly communicated what she was about to say was not a suggestion. "If you could have these two fine legal professionals seen to the conference room. Mr. President, you and I can step into my office."

"But I need my lawyer!" Prather whined, waving a manilla envelope he'd been holding vaguely in her direction.

"I don't think you will," she told him frankly. "And even if I'm wrong, he's not going anywhere. He'll be right down the hall with Miss Milan. They can drink their coffee and speak legalese at each other while you and I talk turkey. If you really need him, we can have him here in a moment. But again, I tell you, you won't."

Prather frowned but relented—a good thing as far as Ruby was concerned. She was far from alert enough to have reliably used magic to make him agreeable. But she'd have tried if it had come to that. In her estimation, anyone who dared demand her attention at such an hour as to have gotten her out of bed deserved whatever they got. And that included any possibly botched magical influence.

"Look at this!" Prather demanded, shoving his envelope toward Ruby as soon as the door was closed behind them.

"We're in my office, Prather," Ruby scolded. "You don't get to make demands in here."

Prather scrunched his face into a wholly unattractive frown. But Ruby was sure he understood her meaning. Ever since it had come to light that she was the only sure way to communicate with Loki he had left, after his immortal patron had so unceremoniously ghosted him upon his inauguration, he'd done his best to mind his Ps and Qs around Miss Killingsworth.

Not that it had done him a whole lot of good.

"Look at this, please," he said.

Ruby inclined her head toward her desk in a gesture she was sure he'd understand as an invitation to set the thing down. She took her time getting behind her desk and took a moment to enjoy a first sip of coffee—that is, as much as a person can enjoy a first sip of coffee when in the presence of a pernicious gnat of a politician whose unexpected presence had roused her from her bed and the arms of a lover. It was only after she was settled in her chair and satisfied with the preparation of her coffee that she reached across the desk to pick up Prather's parcel.

She'd barely gotten the pages out of the envelope when she set it back down. "It's a standard C&D, Prather. What do you want?"

"What do you think I want?" he asked, flopping down in one of the Moroccan leather chairs facing her desk. "I want you to cancel it."

"No," she replied. "Now, if that will be all—"

"What do you mean, 'no'?"

"I mean, no," she replied. "I mean I won't do it."

"Well why not?"

"Because MerMeg Gilal has every right to tell you not to use her music."

"But can't you override that?" he asked. "Don't you own her—?"

"Newsflash, Mr. President," Ruby interrupted him. "It hasn't been legal to own people in this country for more than a century and a half."

"I just mean—"

"You just mean you think I'm the boss and can issue some order from on high that any artist under contract has to follow."

"Yes," he replied. "I think you can, and I think you should."

"You think I should?"

"You should," he replied. "Really."

Ruby shook her head and picked up the paper again. She doubted that, but she was just curious enough as to what had brought the President to her office at this unbearable hour to at least have a proper look at the thing that had his knickers in a knot.

"Well, let's see, it says here—" She stopped herself and looked up at her guest, a little horrified. "You want to use *that* song?" she asked, wide-eyed as she took another sip of her coffee.

"Yeah. It's a hit."

"That it is," Ruby allowed. "And I can't say I hate to break this to you, but it appears your advertising person is either woefully out of touch or you have a saboteur among your ranks."

"Why do you say that?" Prather asked, scooting forward to sit on the edge of his chair.

"Do you have any idea what 'Get Ready for It' is about?" she asked.

Prather shook his head as he sipped his coffee. "Just what the words say. Just that something big and powerful is coming."

"Yeah," she said, shaking her head in turn. "That's not it."

"Well, what is it then?"

Ruby pursed her lips and folded her hands on her desk. Was she really about to say these words out loud? And to a sitting United States president?

"Lyle," she said softly. "The song is about double penetration." She looked over at him and waited for those words to sink in. "That whole album is a tribute to tentacle porn. MerMeg Gilal is a scion of consensual kink and fat positivity, and it's no wonder she wants nothing to do with your re-election campaign."

Prather sat still for a moment. Then he shook his head. "She still shouldn't be able to tell me I can't use her song."

"Prather." Ruby leaned forward against her desk as she took a deep breath. "It doesn't matter a hill of beans to me that you decided to skate atop the frozen lake of fascism in order to win votes. But I'm not going to blame anyone who refuses to dive in after you when the spring thaw comes. Something, something, wind up all wet; the metaphor tracks. Now, I don't care if you want to keep in touch with me in hopes of keeping in touch with Loki, but the fact of the matter is you're a despicable human being, and you've done an abysmal job as president. And I'm certainly not going to punish any of my artists who refuse to have their work associated with you."

"But it's free speech!" Prather exclaimed. "Shouldn't I be able to use any music I like?"

"Tell me you know nothing about this business without *telling me*," she snarked in reply. "The short answer is no."

"But you could make her if you wanted to. You could tell her she had to or else."

"You're right." Ruby picked up her coffee again and eased back to recline in her chair. "I could. But I won't."

"Why not?" he asked, the whine from earlier returning to his voice. "You know there's a lot I can do for you when I get re-elected."

Ruby rolled her eyes. "Lady Vengeance told me to tell you she's voting for the other guy."

That stopped him for a moment. He sputtered audibly and then frowned back at her. "And what has that got to do with anything?"

"She told me to tell you."

"Answer my question!" he demanded.

"And which question was that?"

"Why won't you make MerMeg let me use her song? In fact, why don't you just make it a policy for all the acts you own to let me use their music if they want to keep their jobs?"

"Again, I tell you I don't own anyone."

"You know what I mean."

"I suppose I do," Ruby replied, taking another sip of her coffee. "Honest answer?"

"Yeah."

"Because I'm afraid a few of them might do the right thing. I'm afraid there are some of them who would walk—leaving the company out of all their future projects and making me look like a fascist asshole in the process. You want that song so bad?" she asked, half-rhetorically.

Prather nodded.

"Commission a cover. You'll still have to pay for it, but you'll have a version all your own that you can use whenever and wherever you damn well please. Don't want to do that? Then I suggest you find an artist who isn't repulsed by you and look through their catalog. You and your staff find someone who can stand the thought of having their music associated with your campaign, and I'll issue you unlimited license. Free of charge."

"You ... you will?"

"If it will keep you the hell out of my office at eight o'clock in the morning," she replied. "Yes. Either your own version of 'Get Ready for It' or anything by an artist who consents. Satisfied?"

Prather set down his coffee so he could cross his arms over his chest. "I guess."

"Good," Ruby said, standing from her seat and reaching across her desk for a handshake. "Then we have a deal."

"I guess we do." Prather stood as well and reached out to take her hand.

She gripped it a little too tightly. "And I'm not to hear of you or your goons harassing any of my artists to garner consent," she said, enough magic behind her words to know he not only heard but *felt* what she was telling him. "If it gets back to me that you've done anything stronger than saying 'please' to try and persuade anyone to let you have your way, you will regret it."

The feel of the magic as it passed over and settled on them was soothing to Ruby. It tingled on her tongue, spicing up the flavor of her coffee as she took another sip. She wondered if Prather could even feel it. But no matter, he was bound by it whether or not he was aware.

He wanted to dally and to chat, two things in which Ruby had absolutely no interest. What she wanted to do was head back up the elevator to her very warm bed where her very attractive lover was still tangled in her very soft sheets. But she couldn't very well tell the President that.

It had already been a long day, and it wasn't even nine o'clock yet.

CHAPTER NINE

Since borrowing the equipment from the University had been Kara's idea, all involved agreed she should take the lead on learning and using it. It didn't take her long to decide on a divide-and-conquer approach. After having their faces scanned and uploaded into the building's AI, the four women went through the documentation that had come with the machinery, divvying up the folios according to how esoteric and experimental each device appeared to be.

They'd agreed to read all they could overnight and meet back in the so-called war room after breakfast the next morning. Yumi, Lisa, and Friday were already buzzing around the room when Kara stumbled in just after ten.

"You're here early." Kara set her water bottle on an end table and moved to grab one of the chairs Ruby had gotten the staff to bring up on her departure the night before.

"The professor's way of writing is, um—" Yumi looked for the right word.

"Yeah," Kara agreed, not waiting for her to find it. "I understand."

"I only got so far into this documentation before my eyes crossed and I had to do something else," Lisa said.

"I got through all of mine okay," Friday added. "It reads like a scientist wrote it—I'm used to that. But this feels kind of like when I was learning to change the oil in the car; I need to be looking at what I'm doing while I'm reading the book, or my brain is never going to connect the things."

"Gotcha," Kara replied. "And yeah, it's a lot. Honestly, I'd rather we take our time and be sure we know what's what before trying to make all this stuff work. I'm not sure we're going to fully understand it even after we've read through all the paperwork, but I definitely think it's better we do our best to know as much as we can before we try to use it."

"So what do you think we should do now?" Yumi asked.

"I think we just start with the stacks we had last night," Kara answered her. "We'll start over, read them again, this time with the machinery right here in front of us so we can look at it and figure things out better as we go. Then, I think every time one of us gets through with one—feels like we're starting to understand it—we'll call everybody else over and see if we can explain it."

"*Everybody*, everybody?" Yumi asked. "Or just us?"

"If you're asking whether we need to wait until Miss Killingsworth is available," Kara replied.

"No," Yumi said. "I meant whether you think we should call Jaccob. He's a tech guy. This stuff is kind of his thing. He'll probably understand it all a lot better than anybody except for you."

"Yeah, he probably will," Kara replied. "But I don't care that much. We're here to work on this, and I think we keep things between the four of us. If Stardust starts asking, I don't care if anybody tells him stuff. I just don't think we're doing anybody—especially ourselves—any favors waiting for him to come get up to speed all the time. He doesn't work here. And I don't think we need to wait for him."

"Yeah, okay." Yumi looked at Lisa. "What?"

"You called him *Jaccob*," she said, scandalized. "Mr. Stevens. *Stardust.*"

Yumi shrugged.

"Works for me," Friday added. "I'm all in favor of anything that gets us through and out of here as quickly as possible. And if that means not waiting for Stardust, then I'm good with that."

"All right," Kara said. "Let's get to work then."

"I'm going to get water before we get started," Yumi said. "Anybody want anything?"

"You can bring me one," Lisa replied. "The sparkling kind."

Yumi nodded.

When she'd checked in on them the night before, Miss Killingsworth's assistant had assured them they had the run of the small refrigerator in the sitting room. She'd also told them they were welcome to the wine rack and were allowed to call down for cocktails or snacks whenever they chose. None of them had quite had the courage to open a bottle of wine or call for room service, but the variety of strange and expensive-looking bottled waters had been too much to resist. Yumi, in particular, had made liberal use of the little fridge behind the bar.

So when she came scurrying back into the room empty handed, the others couldn't help but look up.

"Yumi—?" Lisa asked. "What's going on?"

Yumi's eyes were wide. She was shaking her head and gesturing vaguely with both hands in the direction of the sitting room. "Um ... guys?"

"What is it, Yumi?" Friday asked. "You look like you've seen a ghost, and I'm pretty sure our boss has this place on the kind of magical lockdown that would make that impossible, so—"

"Yeah," Lisa added. "What's up?"

"I—" Yumi shook her head as she ran her fingers through her hair. "Um—"

"Words, Yumi," Lisa said, "you know some."

Yumi, her hair now a comical mess, turned and pointed into the sitting room.

"Yumi," Friday said sternly. "For real. Spit it out."

Yumi's eyes got even wider as she took a deep breath. She folded her hands in front of her face and squeezed her eyelids shut. "I am, like, ninety percent certain Lady Vengeance is asleep on the sofa."

"What?" Lisa looked dubious but walked toward the sitting room anyway.

"I said—" Yumi shook her head again and gestured back over her shoulder. "—Lady Vengeance is asleep on the sofa. *In there*!"

"Okay, Yumi," Lisa said, as she continued across the room and into the vestibule. "I heard the words you said. But I don't think I actually understand what you're saying."

"Come with me," Yumi said, taking Lisa by the arm and yanking her forcibly across the vestibule and into the sitting room. Yumi moved on her tiptoes, flawless and graceful, and Lisa tried to do the same, albeit not as well. The two of them crossed the polished white floor toward the small congress of sofas in front of the TV.

They only stopped once they were able to see over the back of the couch facing the television.

"See!" Yumi pointed downward, and Lisa craned her neck to look where she was indicating. Sure enough, there was a woman sound asleep—or passed out maybe—on the sofa. She had lightly tanned skin, purple-streaked black hair, and she was wearing an oversized sweatshirt, faded black leggings, and slouched socks.

Lisa only knew Lady Vengeance from the comic books, but she agreed there was a definite resemblance. Older, maybe, but possibly not so much older as to account for the actual years between the comic's creation and the present day. Eyes wide, Lisa shook her head and gestured for Yumi to follow her back into the war room.

"Okay," Lisa said, as soon as she was sure Friday and Kara would hear her without any need to raise her voice. "So there definitely is somebody asleep on the sofa. And, like, Yumi isn't being ridiculous when she says there's a real, non-zero chance that person is Lady Vengeance."

"No way," Kara said, not even bothering to look up from the console she'd been adjusting the dials on for several minutes. "Lady Vengeance lives in Seattle."

"And yet," Yumi said back.

"And yet." With one hand on Yumi's shoulder for balance, Lisa bent down and slipped her shoes off. She frowned over at the others as she pulled her phone from her pocket and scurried away from them, back across the sitting room floor. They watched as Lisa pointed her phone toward the sofa and captured a moment of silent video before shutting the phone off and sliding back across the floor toward the others.

"Why'd you take a video?" Kara asked before she even looked at the screen. "That's kind of creepy."

"Because my phone makes a sound when I snap a photo but not when I make a video," Lisa answered her. "So since I didn't want to wake her up, I took a video."

"It's still creepy," Kara said.

"Yeah, well," Lisa said, "I'll delete it. It's not like I want to keep it. But I think you should look."

Kara took the phone from Lisa's hand and looked at the image that was still on the screen. "Damn, you're right, that does look like Lady Vengeance. But I still don't think it's her."

"Why not?" Yumi took Lisa's phone from Kara. "You do know I know her, right? Like ... I slept in her bed one time."

"You what?" Lisa asked, her face suddenly screwed into a frown.

"She wasn't in it at the time," Yumi said. "It was at ... you know what? It's complicated. I'm just saying I know Lady Vengeance when I see her, and I'm pretty sure that's her asleep in there."

"Lady Vengeance lives on the other side of the country," Kara repeated, finally standing from her seat. "She has no reason to be on this coast, let alone on that sofa."

"But she—" Yumi began again.

"You know what?" Kara pulled her phone from her pocket. "I'm just going to ask."

"What?" Friday asked, finally drawn into the conversation whether she wanted to be or not.

"I just texted Miss Killingsworth," Kara replied. "I asked her."

"You what?" Yumi asked.

"You heard me," Kara said. "I asked her. I said 'hey, did you know there was someone asleep up here on the sofa, and should we send you a photo because it might be Lady Vengeance?' And I left it at that."

Friday shook her head, as did Lisa. Yumi turned back around to face the sitting room as Kara's phone chimed with a message.

Kara picked it up to read the screen and shrugged. "Huh. Well, will you look at that."

"What?" Lisa asked.

"Looks like Yumi was right," Kara replied.

"I was?"

"Yep." Kara nodded and turned the phone around so Yumi could see the reply for herself.

"I know you're working," Yumi read aloud, "but let V sleep if you can. She has trouble with time zones. I'll make sure she's up in time for her flight back to Seattle." Yumi looked away from Kara's phone and back into the sitting room. "Holy shit," she said, trying to contain her volume, but unable to contain her enthusiasm.

"Yumi?" Lisa said.

"Holy shit!" Yumi exclaimed again, louder this time—she really couldn't help it.

"What part of 'let V sleep' didn't make sense to you?" Kara asked.

"Like—" Yumi said. "Maybe you don't understand. But Lady Vengeance was probably my first girl crush—certainly the first one I was aware of and figured out. And, like, no matter how many times I've met and talked to her, I still have never managed to keep any part of my cool around her. And now I'm supposed to be working, figuring out this super complicated equipment so we can maybe catch some time-traveling bad guys, only she's asleep in the next room. It's going to be a little hard for me to concentrate."

"Asleep on your boss's couch," Friday reminded her.

"Yeah. Oh. Um." Yumi looked over at Lisa, who was watching patiently. "I mean—"

"Babe." Lisa shook her head. "You're so cute. And ridiculous."

"Listen," Friday said, also standing from her chair. "I get that she may be partially responsible for your queer awakening, or whatever. But as far as *her* awakening, I think we want to put that off as long as possible. I'm only guessing here, but I figure someone who goes by 'Lady Vengeance' might not be the best person to wake up before she's ready."

"Uh, yeah, I guess," Yumi said. "I just ... I can't even—"

"You're right, you can't," Kara said, shutting off the screen of her phone and sliding it back into her pocket. "And you won't. If she wakes up and comes in here, then it's up to you whether you hold your shit together or decide to go full fangirl. But unless or until that happens, we're here to work. We're trying to get things set up to catch whoever's been tampering with spacetime, and now that we've got the equipment to do that, we should get it all networked together and calibrated so we can actually do what we were hired to do."

Yumi frowned, but she went back to her seat.

"Going to get my own water now," Lisa said, half-smirking at Yumi. "Should I bring you one?"

Yumi spun her chair to face the console of the machine where she was sitting but nodded.

Learning the machinery proved to be interesting, and occasionally wildly frustrating. It didn't take Kara long to figure out that these contraptions were little more than glorified prototypes. Several of them might not even qualify as "glorified". It was clear from the user interfaces these machines had been designed by the professor for his own use and documented in such a way as to allow him to make a later version more usable and less unwieldy.

Hours into the process, with Lady Vengeance still sound asleep on the couch in the next room, the bunch of them decided they couldn't handle another moment in the technological quagmire without having something to eat. Yumi, in her continued exuberance for using their expense account, suggested trying to get a table at Two and Two, a hip downtown restaurant that would ordinarily have been a good bit outside their price range.

"Trust me, babe," she said to a dubious Lisa. "It's on point."

Lisa seemed hesitant. "And you want me to call?"

"Totally," Yumi said. "Do your thing."

Using her best customer service voice, Lisa made the reservation for four. The other three watched in awe as she managed to get a table with no apparent trouble. They were divided on whether or not she misrepresented just how come it was they were coming from the Ruby Tower, but none of them were particularly bothered by it.

Lunch took long enough that they were still at the table when Kara got a reply to the email she'd sent off to Dr. Kummerfeldt, explaining a few of the many eccentricities of one of the machines she'd found particularly baffling. And by the time they all made it back to the penthouse, Vivienne Cain was no longer in evidence.

Yumi, who'd made no secret of her hope of running into Lady Vengeance when they returned, was audibly disappointed by her absence. Soon enough, she was able to distract herself with the wiring of Professor Kummerfeldt's Geiger counter while Lisa synced a few of the other devices with their borrowed atomic clock.

Not all of the machines came online, but a few of them worked, at least. And as much as "some" was an improvement over "none," Kara suggested it might be worthwhile to bring in some help with the technical workload.

"Some help?" Yumi asked. "You mean your robot?"

"Babe," Lisa said. "Lumien is a sophisticated AI powered by extraterrestrial technology. Be nice."

"Yeah, I mean Lumien." Kara bit her lip, considering.

Kara had left her robotic sidekick at home for this job for a number of reasons, but the team welcomed his efforts to comb the internet for clues now that she had her employer's blessing to task him with such. Having him working remotely also meant he could be on task twenty-four-seven without disrupting Kara's need for sleep or focus. But having computing power added to the team's ability to understand the workings of their loaner gear might be worth the other inconveniences.

"Tell you what," Kara said. "Let's take the weekend, and we'll assess our progress before making a decision as to whether to call in robotic reinforcements."

"Why?" Yumi asked. "It's not like there's nothing for him to do. Plus, I've never met a robot—" She noted Lisa's stern look. "—advanced AI, uh, person."

"That's just it," Kara said.

"You mean about the contract?" Friday asked, lifting her work goggles up onto her forehead.

Kara nodded. "Miss Killingsworth knows Lumien exists as an entity, but my impression is she has little to no understanding of his actual nature or capabilities."

"And you'd rather not go into detail on that front if you don't have to," Lisa said.

"Exactly. Not to mention that anything Lumien finds gets passed along to Cassidy for deeper investigation. And I'd hate to foul that piece of the plan by bringing him into the building or onto Miss Killingsworth's network."

"Right," Yumi said. "That's tricky."

They all nodded in agreement. Having Lumien working off-site, and therefore able to pass along information to Cassidy, was a bit of a loophole in the magically enforceable NDA, but it was working so far.

Kara had been around long enough, and the others were quick enough on the uptake, to know better than to incite the wrath of an impossibly powerful sorceress, so the less they had to share about what was going on outside this building, the better. Making sure to neither stymie the work, nor out their intentionally anonymous colleague, nor anger their employer, was going to be a fine line to walk, but it would be worth it to get this project done and over with as efficiently as possible.

In the meantime, they'd just have to focus on these machines.

~

Over the course of the afternoon, the four established dominion over the setup and base function of some of the easier to understand pieces of equipment: two differently calibrated Geiger counters, an instrument that detected trace levels of specific isotopes, a small nuclear clock, and a set of power management and surge protecting devices.

Meanwhile, Kara kept the most interesting and complex piece of machinery to herself. It was a large and colorful contraption Professor Kummerfeldt had simply named "The Ometer," and it appeared to simultaneously track the displacement of certain atmospheric elements that the professor hypothesized would be momentarily affected by the sudden incursion of matter and energy from out of time.

Not only did Kara find it the most intriguing piece of machinery in the room, but of the four of them, she clearly had the best chance at understanding the apparatus and what it did. It was a sensitive and complicated beast of a thing, as large as an arcade racing game with a spool of paper and a set of needles that made it look like the overgrown bastard child of a polygraph and a seismometer. It was strange and interesting, Kara had never seen anything like it, and she was bound and determined to figure it out and get it to work.

It wasn't exactly her scientific forte, but at least she understood the mechanics—in theory.

And even the parts she didn't understand were fascinating. Fascinating enough, in fact, that she completely lost track of time fiddling with the thing. Jaccob had arrived to pitch in with the machinery in the late afternoon, just as the curtains that covered the glass wall of the room had begun to automatically open themselves.

By the time the crick in Kara's neck was bad enough she decided to take a break, it was already long past dark out.

"Was anybody going to tell me the sun went down?" Kara asked.

"I mean—" Lisa said. "The windows are open. Figured you could see."

"And we also all figured you were pretty much in charge," Yumi replied, "so, like, it wasn't really on us to tell you stuff."

"You and Stardust seemed to know what you were doing," Friday added. "We didn't think it was a good idea to interrupt what was going on to suggest that maybe it was time for us to be done, or have dinner, or whatever."

"Yeah," Lisa concurred. "We were mostly just waiting for the two of you."

"Oh. Yeah, well—" Kara shrugged. "Maybe don't do that? I have a tendency to hyperfocus, and if it's left up to me, there's every chance we'll be here 'til four in the morning sometimes."

"And to be honest," Jaccob added, "I was just tinkering. And I'd probably have kept tinkering until I got hungry, ordered a pizza from my phone, and kept tinkering until it showed up."

"Speaking of which," Yumi said. "I am kind of hungry."

"Yeah," Kara added. "Pizza sounds pretty good. You all want to come down to my condo, and we'll see who delivers?"

"You want Cicardi's," Jaccob said.

"What?" Yumi asked.

"Cicardi's," he repeated. "It's the best you're going to get in this part of town. Believe me. Mike and Chuck had us try every pizza in the zip code when we first moved in."

"Oh yeah," Friday said. "I forgot you live here. Well, not *here*, here, but ... you know."

"I do know," Jaccob replied. "And I'll tell you what. I'll spring for the pizza if you'll invite Mike."

"Oh, you don't have to do that," Yumi said. "Miss Killingsworth gave us an expense account."

"We had lunch at Two and Two," Lisa said.

"But inviting Mike is no trouble," Friday added.

"I'd really appreciate it," Jaccob said. "He's trying to be tough and all, but he's frustrated. He can't see his girlfriend, he can't go out, he can't even really work. We're only five days into this, and he's already bored to tears and lonely as hell."

"Well, we can definitely include him in pizza," Yumi said. "I can't do dairy, so we're already going to have to order more than one."

"Kara," Jaccob said, as the younger heroes headed out of the machine-filled room and back toward the elevator lobby. "Do you want me to stay here and see if I can crack this thing, or would you rather I not mess with it when you're not here?"

"Whichever is fine," Kara replied. She had to admit she kind of liked the fact he was asking. One of the reservations she'd had about taking this job was that she didn't want to be taking orders from Stardust. That he was willing to defer to her was a pretty nice turn. "But if you get it working right, you've got to promise to call me so I can come back up here and see it."

"What the *hell* are all of you doing here?"

The lot of them stopped in their tracks. Somehow, they had managed to forget their machine room was located inside Miss Killingsworth's actual residence, and that, at half past eight o'clock at night, there was every chance of her being in it.

"We're ... um ... just finishing up," Lisa answered her.

"We were about to go downstairs and order some pizzas," Yumi added.

"Oh, no," Ruby replied. "You do not want to do that. The pizza in this part of town is awful."

"Jaccob recommended a place," Yumi replied. "He says it's Mike's favorite. And their website says they have vegan cheese, so ... we're good."

"Mm-mm," Ruby sounded. "I've tried that place, and I assure you it's terrible, no matter what Jaccob says. He may be good at lots of things, but he knows nothing about pizza."

"It's still probably better than the pizza we're used to," Lisa said.

"That may very well be," Ruby said. "But the fact remains it's objectively bad. My kitchen doesn't go home until ten. I'll have dinner sent up."

"We were going to invite Mike," Yumi told her.

"Invite him," Ruby said. "What's one more?"

"Have you eaten?" Jaccob asked Ruby.

Ruby narrowed her eyes. "You know the answer to that, or else you wouldn't have asked me."

"What if I take us all out?" he asked her. "Mike could come to dinner, too, if we're all there, right?"

"What if we just call Mike to join us and have dinner brought up here for everyone?" she countered.

"That was easier than I expected," Jaccob replied, nodding his agreement.

Ruby sighed. "It's been a day. I don't seem to have it in me to resist my friendly neighborhood hero telling me to eat something."

"Well, all right then," Jaccob replied, smiling back at her.

It was a small victory, but he'd take it.

Maybe his feelings were about Ruby in particular, or maybe it was just his aversion to working with someone who didn't seem to like him very much, but he was hoping to make things a little more friendly. A casual dinner with the group would be a good start.

"And speaking of long days," Ruby said, turning to the others. "I'm not going to be an ogre about your work hours. But if you're going to be here after dark, I would appreciate a heads up. I do occasionally entertain in this space."

"Right," Yumi replied, nodding.

Friday rolled her eyes, and Lisa snickered.

"Am I missing something?" Ruby asked the group.

Yumi smiled nervously, looking back and forth between Lisa and Friday, clearly unsure what to do next.

"Just ask her," Lisa whispered.

"Ask me what?" Ruby asked.

Yumi didn't answer.

"Yumi, sweetie," Lisa cajoled, "just ask. We all know you want to."

"Um—" Yumi began, wringing her hands at her waist and shuffling her feet. "How, um ... How do you know Lady Vengeance?"

Jaccob perked up. "What's this about Vivienne?"

Yumi looked to him. "How do *you* know Lady Vengeance?"

"A while back, a demon got into my building," Ruby replied, as though Jaccob had never spoken. "Vivienne happened to be in town. I convinced her to help me get rid of it. Turns out we get along. So now we get together when we can. I take it you're a fan?"

"Oh, yes, ma'am." Yumi's cheeks were a little pink.

"That's one way of putting it," Lisa teased.

"Yeah," Friday added, "I'd say 'fan' is a bit of an understatement."

"I wish you'd said something earlier," Ruby said to Yumi, ignoring the heckling. "I'd have introduced you."

"Oh," Yumi said, "we've met. We've even teamed up a couple times. It's just—"

"Ah," Ruby replied. "I see. The next time she's in town we'll be sure to have you four over for drinks."

"Yeah?

"Oh, absolutely," Ruby said. "Vivienne gets adorably flustered in the presence of fangirls. And I can't say I don't enjoy watching her squirm."

"That—" Yumi's eyes got wide as she shook her head. "That would be really cool of you."

"Consider it done." Smiling sweetly, Ruby pulled out her phone to type a message.

Jaccob stepped in closer and put his hand on Ruby's elbow.

"Vivienne—" he said, shaking his head with narrowed eyes and a confused half-scowl. "She was here?"

Jaccob knew the two women were acquainted with each other. Sort of.

That demon hunt Ruby just referred to had gone off the rails, and she'd called him for help when she'd gotten desperate. He'd been vaguely aware the two of them had stayed in touch, owing to the fact he'd been in touch with Vivienne—he and Vivienne had even had a bit of a fling last winter after Liz first filed for divorce. Now it seemed as though Vivienne had not only been in town, but as close as the next building. That nobody had thought to tell him about it felt off, and a little upsetting.

Ruby shook her head in turn and placed her hand on his shoulder. "Full offense, Jaccob. But any right you had to ask after my overnight company expired when you took yourself off the guest list."

Jaccob's cheeks turned red. He had no idea what to say back to that. She had every right to draw that boundary. He had been the one to walk out of her life; the fact they were newly on speaking terms again didn't give him access to everything he cared to know—even if the thing he cared to know centered around her relationship to someone with whom he'd been involved. He supposed he could always just ask Vivienne, but even that felt like it might be crossing a line.

Maybe he should just let it go.

~

Ruby smiled before she turned to walk into the other room. There was something wildly satisfying about denying Jaccob information around her personal life—especially where she and Vivienne were concerned. She had gotten involved with Vivienne for reasons having nothing to do with the ability to mess with Jaccob's head, but she had to admit to herself she enjoyed that fringe benefit.

It was all she could do not to silence her work phone during dinner. She did send a rather rude message to Lyle Prather himself, to whom she'd smartly never given her personal number, that she would absolutely rescind all offers of cooperation if he didn't leave her the hell alone outside business hours. If she was going to deal with abominable politicians, it was going to be limited to weekdays between ten and four.

When she was sure she'd finally rid herself of the President for the night, she tucked the device under her arm and reached for the decanter to refill her wine glass.

Ruby had let Yumi turn on the television and had agreed to have dinner served casually on the counter in the sitting room. Mike had been happy to come up, both because he was glad to be around other people—especially people close to his own age—and because he'd been fed by Miss Killingsworth's chef before, and the food was never disappointing.

"You're mighty popular, Miss K," Mike said, as he reached to take the decanter from her hand.

"If only that were true," she replied, as she handed it over.

"I don't know," he teased, "sounds like your phone's blowing up."

"That it is," she agreed. "But would you believe it's been the same man all night?"

"Ooh," Mike sounded, grinning back at her in a way that turned his face into a perfect clone of his father's. "A persistent suitor?"

"Oh, gods no." Ruby scowled, as she shook her head. She took another sip of wine.

Over at the TV, Yumi seemed to have discovered the console access, and had challenged Jaccob to a split-screen deathmatch of some kind. She dispatched him quite messily, then was up dancing in victory while Lisa and Friday applauded. Jaccob shook his head and demanded a rematch. Ruby looked away. It wouldn't do to keep looking at him.

"I don't know, Miss K," Mike said. "Sounds like the lady doth protest too much."

"If you must know," she said, "it's Lyle Prather. He's mad at me, and he doesn't want me to forget that even for a moment."

"The President is mad at you?" Friday had wandered over for another piece of wood-fired pizza cooked by a four-star chef. "Like ... personally?"

"I suppose it's more like he's mad at me professionally."

Ruby turned from the bar and headed back to where the others were sitting around the television. Jaccob was doing better at the game this time, but only marginally. It was kind of amusing to see him get smacked down by a teenager, even if it was only in a video game.

"You've got the President mad at you?" Mike asked, spooning additional potatoes onto his plate before following Ruby. "After we came to his place and nearly got blown up, you'd think he'd say he's sorry and keep his distance."

"You'd think. But the man has never been known for his good sense." Ruby turned her attention to Lisa. "Miss Yamamoto."

"Yes?" Lisa turned in her chair. "Miss Killingsworth?"

"You mentioned an interest in coming to work for me once this assignment is over."

"Yes, ma'am."

"I have a little pop quiz for you."

"All right." Lisa set her plate on the table and turned the rest of the way around.

"Imagine you're in artist management," Ruby began. "And a no-good sonofabitch politician comes to you complaining that your artist won't grant him a license to use her song in his political ads because she loathes and despises him and everything he stands for. What do you do? What do you say to him?"

"I think that depends," Lisa answered with a shrug.

"Answered like a true Poli Sci major," Ruby said.

"Yeah, that's probably true," Lisa said. "But I really do think it depends."

"Care to elaborate?"

"Sure," Lisa replied. "Yeah. So, like ... If he's really married to that song—like, it's the only one that will do, and there's no convincing him otherwise, then I'd say he ought to hire someone else to sing it. He'd have to pay for it—probably a lot of money, but he'd wind up with a version he was allowed to use. Although I think I'd still try and get him to rethink that and to pick a song by a different artist, one that shares his politics or is at least neutral. Because even with a cover by a band that doesn't hate him, he's opening himself up to the original artist who does."

"He is?" Mike asked.

Ruby nodded. "Elaborate, Miss Yamamoto."

"I mean ... when you're using a song from someone who can't stand you, then every time you play it, you're giving that artist the chance to remind people they can't stand you. And if that artist has influence, then you may be doing yourself more harm than good."

"Oh, you really do want to work here, don't you?"

"Yes, ma'am."

"Well," Ruby said. "That was a good answer. It was the right answer. And, in fact, it's almost exactly the answer I gave first thing this morning to the hopefully out-going President of the United States."

"You want to come work here?" Mike asked Lisa, as he perched himself on the edge of the sofa across from her.

"I think so."

"That'd be cool," Mike said. "Especially since you already know the boss. Although I'll warn you, she can be a real taskmaster."

Jaccob laughed under his breath.

"I heard that," Ruby grumbled.

"I mean—" Kara said, reaching for the seltzer bottle where it sat on the end table. "She does want to be warned if we're going to be in our work room after dark."

"And she makes us leave by eleven," Yumi added, stomping Jaccob's avatar into the digitized ground.

"Before it was your work room, it was my party room," Ruby reminded them. "And pugnacious presidents of the United States notwithstanding, I do occasionally enjoy a surprise visit. And I like to know ahead of time where I can and cannot expect to privately entertain."

"Wait," Jaccob said. "He was here, too? Prather was here?"

"First thing this morning," she replied. "He and his lawyer showed up unscheduled and unannounced in my outer office at eight a.m. Bridget had to get me out of bed to come talk to him."

Jaccob's eyes got wide.

Ruby inclined her head and raised her eyebrows. She was sure there was something he wasn't saying. "Say it."

Jaccob crinkled his forehead and shook his head.

"Just—" he said, pausing to take a sip of wine, "You already hate the guy. And you're, um, not at your very most agreeable when you first wake up."

"It's true. Yet another bullet you continue to dodge," she added smugly, quirking her lip at Jaccob's recollection of what it was like to wake up beside her. "The only things that kept me from dumping a mug of scalding hot coffee right down his front were my dire need for caffeine and my concern for the condition of my office floor. As it was, he remains very lucky I didn't have him forcibly removed from the premises."

"Can you do that?" Yumi asked. "Are you allowed to just throw the President out?"

"This is private property," Ruby said. "There are whole sections of the Bill of Rights that say I can abso-damn-lutely boot the President, or any other government official without a properly executed warrant, out on their asses for any reason I please or no reason at all. I tolerated Prather this morning because listening to him whine in my general direction seemed like the least troublesome of my options. Had I known he'd be spamming my DMs all day, I might have chosen differently."

"But you didn't block his number," Friday said.

"Oh, I've done that several times," Ruby replied. "But the man appears to have infinite cell phones. There's no sense trying to block him. He's like a cockroach—he'll keep coming back. Best to just remind him to stay in his lane and tell him to shut the hell up over and over until he does."

"If you say so," Friday replied.

"If it were up to me," Ruby told her, "I'd find a way to block everyone who's ever gotten themselves involved in politics."

"You know, I could probably do that for you," Jaccob said.

"Excuse me?" Ruby asked over the rim of her wine glass.

"There has to be a way to make that happen," he said.

"Don't tease me, Jaccob," she said, "Not while I'm fragile and sleep deprived."

"You've never been fragile a day in your life," he replied. "And I'm not teasing. There's got to be a list somewhere, or a registry. There are rules around political communication. If I can get ahold of whatever registry exists, I can generate a block list and upload it to your phone."

"I swear to the gods, Jaccob," she said. "I know I give you grief about the whole 'Good Guy' thing, but if you manage to make this happen, it might be the most genuinely heroic thing you've ever done."

"I'll see what I can do. And you still need to forward me that email," he added, getting up from his seat to refill his glass.

"I'd say I'm sorry, but I honestly just haven't gotten around to it. What with the President getting me out of bed this morning and all." Ruby rolled her eyes as she pulled out her phone. "Personal email or business?"

"Just ... just my personal one is fine," he said.

Quickly, and without bothering to say another word, Ruby forwarded the damnable message, waving her phone in Jaccob's general direction before setting it on the sofa beside her.

It was a jovial evening, mostly, that wound down on its own around ten-thirty, a fact for which Ruby was silently grateful. Eight a.m. wakeup calls two days in a row had her running as close to ragged as she could ever remember feeling.

~

"Hold on a minute," Ruby said quietly to Jaccob as the others waited for the elevator, giggling over something Yumi had said. "Don't go just yet. I want to talk to you."

Jaccob stopped cold in his tracks. Nodding, he shoved his hands into his pockets in an attempt to look at least a little less awkward than he was feeling.

He watched Ruby say goodnight to Mike and the others at the elevator as the doors slid shut. Rather than approach him afterward, she crossed directly to the bar to refill her wine glass from the carafe that sat there.

"Thanks for staying behind," she said, gesturing to the barstool on the far end as she leaned against the marble counter from behind it. "I promise I won't keep you. But I find myself second guessing something, and I want to get your read on the situation."

"Yeah. All right." He settled into the seat and turned sideways, leaning against the bar and looking at her. It was unlike Ruby to second guess herself at all, and even more out of character for her to admit to such a thing.

Maybe she really *was* feeling fragile and sleep deprived.

"I think I may have over-reacted," she said bluntly, sipping her wine with a shrug. "In my rush to protect Mike, and myself, and my business, I may have locked Mike down a little tighter than is strictly necessary. I'm thinking we may want to loosen the reins a bit."

"Oh." Jaccob nodded, making mental note not to react to the way she was using the word "we". "Okay."

"I mean," she began again. "We have no evidence whoever is behind this trouble has the ability to disguise themselves, and even if they did, I know you have gadgets that could detect that. And although I do suppose there is the possibility of a 'themselves from the future' situation, I'm still not sure that keeping all visitors away is the right call."

"You're thinking you want to let him see his friends?" he asked.

"Friends?" Ruby shook her head and sipped her wine. "No."

"Oh—"

"But I've had security on Katy since she moved here. And, provided we keep good tabs on her, I think it should be safe to let them around each other."

"You have security on Mike's girlfriend?"

Ruby nodded over her wine glass. "I do."

"Why?"

"Because sometimes unhinged people think they can get close to celebrities by taking out the people they're already close to. And I won't have that sweet girl in danger because she happens to have turned the head of an up-and-coming rock star with a billionaire father. So I put a quiet, unassuming detail on her. She's aware they exist but doesn't ever interact with them. I had my security chief talk with the team leader today, and there hasn't been anything of concern. I want to let them see each other," she said. "And to that end, I'd appreciate it if you could invite Katy to stay with you."

"You would?"

"Mmm."

"With me."

"Yes."

"But I've never even met her."

"All the better then," Ruby said. "You two could get to know each other. She's a nice girl. You'll like her. In fact, she reminds me a lot of you. I think the two of you will get along famously."

"Why with me?" he asked. "Instead of over here?"

"Because if they wanted to live together, they would. That's not a decision I'm going to make for them. I don't want to do anything that could screw with their relationship or fuck with their boundaries. But I also don't want to punish Mike for something that's being done to him—or through him to me. It doesn't seem fair. But just because something feels safe at the moment doesn't mean we can presume the future. And I can't think of any place safer for Katy to be right now than down the hall from a Big Damn Hero who just happens to be her boyfriend's father. I figure you let her stay with you, and we can let them see each other. They can even have overnights if they want to—your place or his, they'll be equally secure either way."

"And you think she'll agree?" Jaccob didn't hate the idea, although he wasn't sure how he felt about inviting his son to have overnight visits with his girlfriend in his former bedroom.

"I honestly don't know," she replied, standing up straight again and pouring the last of the wine from the decanter into her glass. "But I think it's worth making the offer. And I think, if she says yes, it'll make Mike happy. Since you said the main reason you agreed to work with me on this whole thing was that you wanted things between the two of you to get better, I figure this might be a good way to help make that happen."

"You really look after him," Jaccob said, not bothering to keep the sound of his admiration out of his voice.

"I may be a sorceress, Jaccob," Ruby replied. "But, despite some people's impressions to the contrary, I am not the wicked witch. When someone is important to me, I do my best to keep them happy."

"Yeah," Jaccob agreed, casting his eyes downward as he slid off the barstool. "Yeah. I get that."

"Just think about it, all right?" she asked.

"I will," he said.

"Well, that's all a person can ask," she replied. "Good night, Jaccob. I presume you can see yourself home?"

"Yeah," he said. "Yeah. Good night."

CHAPTER TEN

Two days of being woken up too damn early had been enough to make Ruby decide to take the next day off. Not that she ever took an actual day off, but she did on occasion choose to work from someplace other than the office. That was especially true on weekends and *especially* true when there was no way to know when her next moment of possible downtime was coming.

The four young heroes in her employ were out for the day, to do some shopping they declared un-doable by an assistant before moving on to an eavesdropping session at one of The Hollows' seedier dive bars. Yumi and Lisa had both said something about makeup and skin care, Friday had been very anxious to check out a once-a-year event at the botanical garden, and Kara had mentioned her intention to pick up components from home she thought might make the machinery in the war room a little more user friendly. Wherever they were, they'd be out for the day and well into the night.

And since Ruby had the place to herself for what might be the last time in a while, she figured she might as well take advantage of that.

It was a nice enough summer day that she'd decided to see to the day's work while out on the terrace. And, owing to the fact it was Saturday, her workload for the day was light enough to allow for including a bottle of very good tequila in the program.

Ruby figured if anyone deserved a little top-shelf day drink at the moment, she did.

Having her penthouse open to four boisterous young capes, being targeted by time-traveling culprits with dubious motivation, and having her very brief visit with Vivienne interrupted at eight in the morning would have been enough to drive her to drink—and that was before considering either that interruption had come in the person of Lyle Prather or the fact she was once again in consistent communication with Jaccob Stevens.

She might just decide to drink the whole damn bottle. And, finding herself blessedly alone as she had, she'd be drinking as much as she pleased in a comfortable silk georgette shift, floppy sun hat, and oversized sunglasses with her hair pulled back in a low ponytail.

There was a time when she'd never have dared set foot on her terrace looking anything other than flawless. In the days when she was in the business of seducing Jaccob, she'd carefully curated every look that might be visible from his place across the sky from hers. There was a period of several months when one of the things that mattered most to her was what impression she might be making on her handsome neighbor if he happened to glance over.

These days, she could not care less whether she looked alluring while sipping tequila in the sun.

These days her romantic life was as satisfying and uncomplicated as it had ever been. For one thing, she had Vivienne, who understood her on a level maybe no one else ever had. From her associations with the music world, her understanding of magics, and her own unresolved feelings where Jaccob Stevens was concerned, Vivienne just ... got it. Adding the fact that the two of them were very intentionally not exclusive and perfectly happy when the other found satisfaction with another partner—provided it didn't foul up any plans they'd made together—meant this was perhaps the most stress-free relationship Ruby had ever known.

She was fully content and fulfilled in her personal life for what might have been the first time ever.

So, of course, the universe had fucked with her. *Of course* she'd had to yank Jaccob Stevens back into her orbit just as she was getting comfortable.

She knocked back the last of the tequila in her glass and immediately refilled it.

This might have been her fourth refill, or maybe her fifth. It didn't so much matter; a little tequila buzz never hurt anyone. She'd only just taken her next sip when a vexing and unmistakable sound reached her ears.

Ruby rolled her eyes and wished silently for the Stardust suit to be both *outbound* and on the other side of the building. She had a strong feeling that, now they were back on what he'd think of as speaking terms, her friendly neighborhood superhero would consider it impolite not to pop over and say hello were he to fly by when not on his way to an emergency.

She really didn't want to have to deal with him right now.

Or ever.

At all.

But she could tell within moments she wouldn't be getting that wish today. Back when she and Jaccob were involved, Ruby had learned how to triangulate the distance and direction of the Stardust suit in flight just from the sound of its repulsors. And in this moment, he was over the plaza, closing at a casual speed, and would be flying past her seat just soon enough there was no chance of scurrying inside in time for a clean getaway.

Best to sit still and hope he didn't notice her.

Not that there was any real chance of that.

He was waving at her as he came in for a landing on her patio just far enough away from where she sat to keep the suit's jet wash from blowing her dress or her hair out of place.

Infuriatingly polite, that man.

~

"Heya, happy Saturday!" Jaccob said, stepping toward her. "Whatcha doing?"

Ruby slid her sunglasses down her nose far enough to glare at him over the top of them. "You know, for a fellow wearing a million dollars' worth of visual augmentation technology, your powers of observation are alarmingly less than astute. I'm drinking tequila on my balcony. In case it wasn't obvious."

"I really do love your way with words, Ruby," he said, shaking his head as he stifled a chuckle. "You're the only person I know who can make a man enjoy being insulted. You do it so eloquently."

"Do not ever use the word 'love' in my presence, Jaccob," she snapped. "It's tacky."

"I don't think you've ever done that before," he said.

"What?"

"Called me 'Jaccob' while I'm wearing the suit."

"Well, I've also never gotten drunk enough before lunch to say the 'L' word in front of another human being, so ... first time for everything?"

"As though you ever actually eat lunch—"

"Oh, touché, Mr. Stardust, you do have your wits about you this afternoon." Ruby gestured vaguely to the bottle. "If you'd like to drink until they depart, you're welcome to join me."

Jaccob looked around and considered her offer. It had been strange getting used to being around her again. Letting her back into his life had reminded him of how badly he'd screwed things up between them and how profoundly he'd missed her before he'd forced himself to stop thinking about her.

The problem was, of course, now he could scarcely do anything but think about her.

He'd been having to constantly remind himself that being in proximity to her wasn't the same as being close to her. All in all, she hadn't been very nice. He didn't want to read too much into her invitation to join her for a glass of 1942, but neither did he want her to read anything into a refusal.

He also didn't want to refuse.

He gave a nod and took a seat, sliding the switches on the back of his helmet to release it from the rest of his suit. He pulled the helmet off and set it on the chaise beside him.

"I looked at the email you forwarded," he said, working to remove the gauntlets from his hands. The Stardust suit was good for a lot of things but holding on to delicate glassware had proven time and again not to be one of them.

Some of the tension went out of Ruby's frown. Good.

"Anything interesting?" she asked.

"Yeah," he said plainly. "Interesting. And strange."

"Do I want to hear about it?" Ruby picked up the tequila bottle and a glass and handed them both over.

"If I know you at all," he replied, setting his gauntlets aside and taking hold of the bottle and glass. "Which, I'd like to think I still do, at least a little, you'll want to hear the shape of the problem but not the details. And I'll save the lecture on why not to open an attachment from an unknown sender for another time."

"I'm not sure how I feel about your contention that you still know me at all," she said. "But, then again, you're willing to spare me a lesson on cyber security, so maybe you do. How about let's start with those broad strokes? The shape of the problem."

"Well, the quick version," he began, as he poured his glass full of the golden, aged tequila, "is that there's some stuff that looks weird, but I'm not able to get anything useful."

"I don't like the sound of 'weird'. Especially when *you* say it." Ruby held out her phone to him. "Here. If you need to see it on my phone, look at it on my phone."

That was quite a show of trust.

"Yeah." He traded her the tequila bottle for her StarPhone and then had a sip of tequila from his glass. "It's ... it's unlocked?"

"It is," she affirmed. "You're a Good Guy, remember? I think I can trust you not to rifle through my pictures, read my texts, scroll through my contacts ... You'll do what you need to do, and you'll hand it back, because you, sir, are infinitely trustworthy when you're wearing that suit."

A pit formed in Jaccob's stomach. He was pretty sure why she'd made the distinction—why he was only trustworthy in her eyes as his alter-ego. Everything he'd ever done to hurt her had been while wearing his normal clothes.

He didn't like that she held that opinion. He didn't like the fact she held his hero self apart from his day-to-day self. But he was glad for the little bit of trust she still had in him—even if that only existed when he wore his super suit.

Her email icon was in the top right corner of her home screen. He tapped it, and Ruby's email loaded immediately. There was only one message visible: from an address consisting of a jumble of numbers and letters and with no subject line, but a large attachment. That was it.

"Inbox zero," he commented, as he clicked the message. He wasn't sure why he felt so compelled to make small talk, but there it was.

"I can count the number of people with that address on one hand, Jaccob," she said. "Two of them are on this balcony right now. Suffice to say it doesn't get a lot of traffic—yet another reason this is so concerning. If we really are dealing with time travel, then I have to wonder when and how sometime in the future my personal email gets leaked."

"Right. Yes. I can see where that would be a concern."

Jaccob pressed a brushed metal panel on the left wrist of the Stardust suit and waited while a compartment popped open in a way Ruby had once likened to a high-end cassette player. He smiled a little at the memory.

"What?" she asked.

"Nothing." Jaccob reached into the compartment and pulled out a cable, which he immediately plugged into Ruby's phone.

"Far be it from me to question the particulars of a hero doing heroics." Ruby frowned as she sat up straighter to try and get a better look at what was happening with her phone. "But ... what, exactly, are you doing right now?"

Leaving the phone tethered to the arm of his suit, Jaccob set it on the chaise beside him and took another sip of tequila. It was good stuff. "What little I was able to get from the forward didn't make any sense. None of the metadata attached to the message lined up with any known technology. How much do you know about email?"

"I know how to read it," she answered snidely. "And how to send it. I know who to call when it isn't working. And I know which superhero to contact when I find it's delivered me a mystery."

"All right." Jaccob nodded. "Do you also know that every time you send an email, you're sending along a bunch of other things with it?"

"What other things?"

"Well," he replied. "That depends."

"Oh, goody," she snarled. "That sounds helpful."

"It can be," he assured her. "There are several different factors at play, but a lot of the time, an email will come with all sorts of additional information attached. Things like the sender's time zone, whether it was composed on desktop or mobile—sometimes down to the exact device's make and model. And occasionally you'll get the sender's IP address."

"And you're telling me my mysterious sender managed to get into my inbox with none of this information attached?"

"I'm telling you I'm not exactly sure."

"Way to inspire confidence," she snarked. "Some hero—"

"The truth is I don't think there's much here." His cheeks were getting hot, and he could only hope he wasn't turning visibly red—or if he was, that she might attribute it to the tequila and not to his chagrin at her comment. "But there is something. I just can't make heads or tails of it from the forwarded message. So I'm downloading it straight from your phone to the hard drive in my suit. From there, my AI and I can take it apart bit by bit and see if there's anything deep in the code that might lead us in a useful direction."

"All right." She polished off the booze in her glass and picked up the bottle for a refill. "I take it back. You're still a hell of a hero."

"Hopefully I'll have something more substantial in a day or so," he said. "But what I can tell you right now is that your hypothesis is looking more and more plausible."

"And why is that?"

"Like I said," he answered, reaching for the bottle from her to top off his glass. "What little I was able to get from the forwarded message doesn't match anything I've ever seen before—neither the info embedded in the email itself nor the attachment. So it's a reasonable theory that maybe it originated on a device that hasn't been invented yet."

"Oh," she said. "I suppose that does make sense."

"Yeah," he said, somehow unable to help himself smiling at her. "I'm going to get to the bottom of this. You called the right hero."

"It appears I did," she replied, holding out her glass in his direction.

He smiled brighter and clinked the rim of his glass against hers.

"We're making good progress on the main plan, too," Jaccob said. "The girls tell me they should have the equipment up and running as soon as Monday night or Tuesday."

"They've said the same to me," Ruby told him. "They're all out today. Hence the chance to drink on the balcony undisturbed—heroic neighbors notwithstanding. But Kara assures me it's all in service of the goal. They'll have the machines on in a day or so, and hopefully we'll find our culprit soon after that. With any luck, we'll dispatch with the meddling bastards within the week, and then you and I can once again be rid of each other."

She sounded relieved.

The pit was back in Jaccob's stomach. How was he going to tell her that his urgency to solve this puzzle had nothing to do with wanting her out of his life again? What could he say that wouldn't sound hollow or pitiful but would let her know he was increasingly glad they were back on speaking terms? How could he articulate his hope they could move forward from here and not go back to the tension of the past two years?

Even if there wasn't any sort of possible future where they could be close again, mutual avoidance and trying to pretend they'd forgotten the other existed while simultaneously living next door to each other and running in many of the same social circles was no way to live.

"I don't think you'll be rid of me so easily," he said finally, hoping it was the right thing to say.

She replied with an amused smile and a quirk of her eyebrow. "We'll just have to wait and see about that, won't we?"

"To that end, do you still have the bracelet I gave you?"

"I should remember if I'd gotten rid of that many diamonds."

"Can you bring it to me?"

Her eyes flicked to him over the rim of her sunglasses. "That's a new low."

"No, uh." Jaccob shook his head. Maybe the tequila *was* getting to him. "It's not ... I don't want it back."

"Oh?"

"I just want to make sure it works," he said. "I'd ... I'd like you to start wearing it again."

"You would, now?"

"Look," he said, his shrug almost lost in the bulk of his armor. "We really don't know what we're dealing with here. If whoever sent this message did it because they mean you harm, then there's probably a bigger attack coming. And I'd like to be there to back you up if it does."

Ruby frowned. It wasn't a small thing he was asking. When she came to him for backup when Vivienne was possessed by a demon whose influence had threatened to swallow the city, she was desperate. Was she that desperate now? Desperate enough to wear the bracelet that would call him automatically if she found herself in a certain kind of trouble?

"I'll have it sent over," she said finally. "So you can look at it, tinker with it, do whatever you're heroic little heart desires. But no promises on wearing it when you're through."

"Okay," Jaccob replied. "It's a start."

"A start?"

Uh oh. Jaccob tried to reassure her with a smile. "I mean, you said I was trustworthy in the suit, not that you wanted me around."

Oh no.

For a long time, he'd thought he and Ruby were done. He might have even been able to convince himself he was happy about that state of things. But he knew now he hadn't been. This was a chance to make things, if not right, then better, and he was going to take it.

"It's just ... last time I put a plan in place, and it went sideways, you were quick to dismiss me. I was sure I'd never hear from you again, even in an emergency. And—"

"And?

A light beeped on Jaccob's gauntlet. "Oh," he said. "Downloaded."

"Okay."

Jaccob was quick to return Ruby's phone, but he was in no hurry to get to someplace to examine the download.

"Do you need to—?" She gestured toward Starcom Tower with her drink.

"Not really." He checked with the suit's internal AI that the whole thing had been transferred successfully, but after that, he tucked the cable back into the compartment, closed it gently, and relaxed into his drink. "This is really good tequila."

Ruby relaxed somewhat. "That it is."

Only two hours and a dry bottle later did he decide it was time to go.

~

It had been an oddly pleasant afternoon in Ruby's estimation. Sunshine and good tequila certainly accounted for some of it, but she had to attribute the rest of her satisfaction to the company—a fact about which she wasn't sure how to feel.

She and Jaccob kept the conversation light but had never had to resort to actual small talk. Talking in turn about the problem at hand, favorite places to buy and to drink tequila, and the kinds of business issues only a fellow CEO would understand, with the occasional detour into the topic of Mike's general well-being and his relationship with Katy, had reminded Ruby of how easy Jaccob could be to talk to.

She wasn't sure she liked how much she liked spending this time with him.

She wasn't ready to start sharing secrets with him or anything, and she likely never would be. But it had been nice to talk to someone who understood her life so well. She'd never been in the habit of keeping up with friendships, especially not with those she used to sleep with, and she had no idea whether she'd feel the same way after she sobered up. But for the moment, she was kind of glad Jaccob had intimated he wouldn't be waltzing out of her life and closing a door between them as soon as they'd solved the mystery at hand.

She supposed time would tell.

CHAPTER ELEVEN

The Hollows had long been the part of town where the denizens of wickedness were known to congregate. Which was exactly the reason Yumi, Lisa, Friday, and Kara were headed there on a Saturday night. They'd agreed to this sleuthing errand during their meeting with Miss Killingsworth on Tuesday evening but had decided to hold off until Saturday to make an actual visit.

Denizens of wickedness tended to be known quantities. A group of unfamiliar young women showing up asking questions in a dive bar filled only with its regulars would likely draw suspicion. But The Hollows had enough of a reputation for being adjacent to supervillainy that on weekends, it also became the go-to hangout for hipsters and college kids who wanted to play at being bad for a night.

A handful of newcomers in Macky's on a Saturday was par for the course.

When the group of them arrived, Cassidy was already waiting at a table in the back. Kara spotted her immediately and signaled for the others to follow.

"I'm right behind you," Friday said. "Just give me a minute." She waved the others off and headed to the bar.

Kara led Yumi and Lisa toward the back of the room, where they all slid into the booth beside Cassidy.

"How long have you been here?" Lisa asked, gesturing to the two empty glasses on the table.

"Not that long," Cassidy answered. "And one of those was water. I may have been out of the game for a while, but I know better than to get shitfaced alone in The Hollows on a Saturday night."

"Yeah," Kara said, "good thinking. Anything interesting?"

"Not even a little," Cassidy replied.

A server with a dyed-black buzz cut and large gauge earrings approached their table. "Hey there," the server greeted them, slapping beermats down on the table in front of each of them. "High roller up at the bar says you're on her tab. So what're you having?"

Kara looked askance at Friday, who was leaning on the bar, waving a credit card in the air, obviously buying drinks for several of the people seated nearby. "I'll have whatever you've got in a can that passes for a red ale. Bring it to the table unopened. I'll be back." She scooted herself out of the booth and stood up.

"Everything okay?" Yumi asked.

"Just gonna go have a chat with our 'high roller' over there," Kara replied.

Cassidy nodded. "Good idea. I know we want people to talk, but I'm not sure waving your credit card around and acting like you're made of money is the way to go in a place like this. No offense," she added, turning to the server.

"Oh, none taken," they replied. "I know where I work. And, yeah, your friend over there is doing the thing most likely to get her info skimmed and her pocket picked."

Kara nodded in agreement before turning toward the bar. "Friday," she called out, as soon as she was sure she'd be in earshot. "What are you doing? And here I was thinking you were the one of our college contingent who actually had some sense."

"Relax," Friday replied, beckoning her closer. "It's a prepaid card. I took a couple grand out of our expense account this afternoon and transferred it onto here. That way we can leave it with the bartender, buy drinks and whatever, without handing over any personal information. It's a ... burner credit card."

"I take it back," Kara said. "That's some good thinking."

"Did you think Yumi was the only one who knows how to use an expense account?" Friday asked quietly. "I've got this. Go sit down. Have a drink. If I get anything interesting from anybody, I'll come tell you."

Kara shrugged, but did as she was told, returning to the table just as the server was walking away.

"So, what's up with that one?" Cassidy asked.

"She seems to have covered all her bases," Kara replied. "And she says she's got things handled for the time being, so I'm going to sit here and let her handle them until I see evidence she needs our intervention."

"Friday's got a good head on her shoulders," Lisa said. "And although I'm kind of surprised that she's suddenly the life of the party over there, I have no doubt she can handle herself. I think we can relax for a few minutes."

The four of them sat back, Kara and Cassidy sipping on beers while Yumi and Lisa split a soda, watching Friday play spendy social butterfly up at the bar. It was remarkably entertaining to see her acting like such a party girl.

Her beer nearly finished, Cassidy gave the others a nod. "I think I'll go to the bar to get my next one, make sure everything is copasetic."

"I'll come with you," Kara said, scooting out of the booth behind Cassidy. "I'm about ready for another beer, too, and I'm curious to see if this sudden shift in demeanor is netting Friday any information."

They were halfway to the bar when a voice sounded near the door. "The hell?!?" a woman exclaimed. Her outburst was followed by the sound of a slap.

The bellow of "Ow!" came from a man in the crowd.

"You bitch!" some other woman shouted.

"He grabbed my ass!" the first voice insisted.

"Fucking liar," the other woman said. "My boyfriend wouldn't do that!"

"Don't call her a liar," another man yelled.

"The fuck you gonna do about it?"

It was then that the whole bar erupted into chaos. The two men swung on each other at the same time, while the two women took to shrieking and scrapping right alongside them. Nearby patrons began throwing ice cubes and beermats, egging on the combatants with hoots and cheers while a tangle of hapless coeds made for the door.

In a beat, the bartender was standing on the prep sink, stomping his heavy-booted foot against the bar top in an unsuccessful attempt to get anyone's attention.

"Ah, dammit," Friday muttered, pulling herself up to sit on the bar. Having gained an adequate vantage point, she sent a tangle of vines in the direction of the brawlers.

The men were caught up first, their ankles bound up so tightly neither was able to remain upright. They fell to the floor in almost perfect unison as the vines wound their way up and over to bind the women's arms to their sides.

Unable to punch, slap, or claw, the two women resorted to body slams and headbutts, both of them still screaming obscenities as they continued trying to knock each other to the ground.

Kara moved toward the commotion, the assembled crowd so stunned by the sudden appearance of weaponized plant life she had no problem getting through. She slid a pair of tiny metal buttons from the underside of her belt buckle and pointed one at each of the two young women. With a slide of her thumb over the sensor, Kara activated both devices at once, leaving the two women stunned enough they had no choice but to disengage.

The taller one slunk down to sit on the floor while the smaller one crept backward until she could lean against the bar just ahead of where the bartender's boot was still pounding.

"Nice," Friday called to Kara over the strange silence that had fallen over the crowd.

"Comes in handy," Kara replied.

The silence was broken then by the sound of shattering glass at the back of the room. One, then another, then another, the tiny explosions rang out, drawing the attention of anyone who wasn't completely caught up in the goings-on near the front door.

Cassidy had her hands in fists as she stalked purposefully toward the far end of the bar. Two men, neither of them employees, had come around behind it while the commotion had everyone's attention on the other side of the room. One was working a crowbar in and out of the cash register while the other had his hand in the cash tips.

The two fell in tandem as Cassidy approached, covering their ears with their hands and squeezing their eyes shut as they crumpled into the fetal position on the floor amid a rain of glass shards. Another bottle shattered then, a bright green schnapps from the second shelf splashing onto the incapacitated perps, who cried out when the alcohol stung the tiny cuts left by exploding glass.

"The hell?" the bartender yelled from his perch. "Could you not destroy the inventory?"

"Yeah, okay," Cassidy agreed, as Friday vaulted over the bar to tie the two would-be thieves in vines that matched those on the brawlers.

"And put that away!" The bartender pointed at Yumi's sword, which she'd had at the ready, but hidden beneath the table, since the start of the fracas.

"Yeah, okay," Yumi agreed. "We're good."

"Okay." The bartender shook his head as he hopped down off the sink and started toward the mess at the other end of the bar. "Jesus," he said, as he got closer.

"Yeah, sorry about that," Cassidy said. "It was the fastest way to stop them. I wasn't thinking about the liquor bottles and the glassware and stuff."

"Your powers?" Kara asked.

Cassidy nodded. "Yeah. I can make sounds that humans don't so much hear as ... *experience.* It works to stop a bad guy in his tracks, but sometimes nearby glassware gets caught in the radius."

"How did you know?" Friday asked Cassidy. "To stop them, I mean ... What made you look back here while all the madness was going on up front?" She gestured to where a bouncer was bodily dragging one of the men up off the floor and toward the exit.

"It isn't the oldest trick in the book," Cassidy explained, as Kara came around the bar to join them, "but it's not exactly new. Create a huge distraction at one side of the room to get everybody facing that way so you can clean the place out while nobody's looking. Used to happen a lot in concert venues."

"Well, it was good thinking," Kara said. She clipped her two stun buttons back onto her belt as she looked down at the bound-up thieves on the floor.

"Yeah, I guess," the bartender said. "But I can't say we'd have lost any more in a robbery than all this broken glass and wasted liquor is going to cost us."

"Oh, we'll cover that," Yumi said, as she and Lisa joined the others. "Just get us an invoice."

"Yeah," Friday said. "We can pay for it. And we will pay for it. On one condition."

"Is that condition that I don't throw you out of here right now?" the bartender asked. "Because it's pretty clear you all have powers, and that one—" He pointed at Yumi and frowned. "—can apparently pull a magical sword out of thin air. And that's pretty much the kind of hero shit people come into this bar to get away from."

"Hey," Yumi said, obviously offended, "I summoned my sword, but I didn't pull it. I kept it under the table in case I needed it and then when I didn't, I put it away."

"Yeah, I guess that's true," the bartender replied.

"And I'll tell you what," Friday said, "we'll be happy to leave. And pay for all the damages. But only after you tell them what you told me."

"What I told you?"

"About that fifty." Friday pulled a bill from her pocket and stuffed it into the tip jar, then looked him in the eye.

"Oh," the bartender shrugged. "Yeah, okay. Have a seat."

"Cool," Friday said, moving out from behind the bar and indicating the others should do the same.

The group of them filed around to the outside of the bar and took up a series of seats that had emptied when the fight broke out, as the bouncer and a barback made their way behind the bar to deal with the thieves and the mess respectively.

"There's not a hell of a lot to tell," the bartender told them, pulling a pint glass from beneath the bar and filling it with ice from someplace unseen. "Coupla weeks back, some guys came up in here I'd never seen before. Now that's not that weird. Middle of summer, tourists in town, people hear about Macky's as the place the local villain set hangs out, and they come in to check out the scene ... or whatever. But these two guys were different. I thought I smelled cop on them, quite frankly, but then they opened their mouths. Too smart to be cops. But still dumb enough to come in here acting like cops. But then they started drinking and generally started chatting up the clientele. One of my regulars got to telling me they were looking to hook up with a time-traveling supervillain if we could point them to one. But then when they went to leave, they tried to pay with a counterfeit fifty."

Kara nodded at the bartender, then looked over at Friday. "Why did I need to hear that?"

Friday shook her head.

"Tell her how you knew it was a counterfeit," Friday said, nodding as the bartender sprayed juice from a dispenser gun into the glass of ice.

"Cause I ain't a fool," the bartender said back.

"Yeah," Friday said, "I get that part. Details please. Tell her what you told me."

"The bill was a mess," the bartender replied, hanging the dispenser gun back on its hook and pulling out a pill container from his pocket. "It was the wrong color, first off. Not nearly green enough. And even if it'd been dark enough back here I didn't notice that, the issue date was twenty-twenty-*five*. You believe that shit? Damn thing said it hadn't been minted yet. Dude seemed kind of embarrassed when I pointed out that little typo. I mean ... this is The Hollows, but I ain't no spring chicken. Don't try me with a damn fifty says it's from the future, you know? I get it was part of their 'time travel' schtick, but I got bills to pay *this year* so I ain't messing with that shit, ya know?"

"Yeah, I do know," Kara replied.

"See," Friday said.

"I'm beginning to," Kara answered her. "So what did they do then?" she asked the bartender. "How'd they pay their tab?"

"The guy and his buddy dug around in their pockets until they found enough real money to cover their tab. Wasn't that high. Looked to me like they were trying to break that bad fifty into real fives and tens from my till. Only I ain't falling for that bullshit. They paid and they left, and I ain't seen 'em since." He pulled two pills out and popped them into his mouth, washing them down with the juice he'd just poured himself.

"And you say that was a couple of weeks ago?" Kara asked him.

"Yeah. Two weeks. I remember 'cause it was the same day I got this." He pulled up the sleeve of his flannel shirt to reveal a tattoo of a cartoon bank robber holding an old-style money bag. "And it just stopped peeling today. So, yeah ... two weeks."

"Lines up with the day of the email," Friday said softly to Kara.

"Yeah, I hear you." Kara turned her attention back to the bartender. "Could you describe these guys?"

"Like I said," the bartender answered her, rolling his sleeve back down, "cop vibe. White guys, thirty or so, short hair, clean cut. Like ex-Marines, only a little soft in the middle, if you know what I mean. Prolly wearing vests under their brand-new tee shirts that still had the wrinkles in 'em from being folded up in the store. Notches on their belts where a holster ought to go but knew better than to wear one into a bar in The Hollows. Fuckall white guys. Prolly voted for Prather."

"All right," Kara said, "thanks."

"That help?" he asked.

Kara nodded. "It might. Appreciate it."

"Yeah, and I appreciate you ladies breaking up a fight and stopping a robbery. So I guess we're square. Insurance should get the rest, right?"

"Probably," Cassidy agreed. "But if not—"

"Yeah," Yumi said, "we'll check in. Because, seriously, we can pay for the damages. So if we owe you—"

"But right now, we're going to get out of here," Cassidy said, standing from her barstool. "In twenty minutes, it'll be like we were never here. Hopefully you can get your night back on track."

The bartender nodded as the five of them stood up and started for the door. Cassidy led the way down the block and around the corner. Once they were in a well-lit gravel parking lot with no one else in sight, she stopped and turned to Kara.

"So what are you thinking?" she asked.

"Could be nothing," Kara replied. "But also could *not* be nothing."

"I feel like I'm missing something?" Lisa, who'd been uncharacteristically quiet since the fight broke out, said to both Kara and Cassidy.

"Couple of dudes in Macky's two weeks ago trying to pass a fifty with dates on it that say it won't be minted for another five years," Kara answered her. "Bartender wrote it off as a bad counterfeit job. But anybody who's going to bother with trying to print U.S. currency isn't going to make a mistake like that. There's a lot that goes into counterfeiting—don't ask me how I know—and the bartender didn't mention anything about the security strip or the watermark or the holographic ink—"

"He did say it was the wrong color," Friday reminded her.

"Sure," Kara said, pulling her phone from her pocket and swiping around on the keyboard for a moment. "But something tells me he hadn't heard about this." She turned the screen sideways so the others could see.

"The mint's about to change the color," Lisa said, her eyes wide as she looked up at the screen.

"Yep," Kara said. "The new fifties won't be as green. So these guys had a bill with a date that hasn't happened in a color that's just rolling out."

"And they were here on the same day Miss Killingsworth got the email," Friday added.

"Yeah," Cassidy said. "That does sound like it might not be nothing."

"Exactly," Kara said back. "It very well could be something. Now we've just got to figure out what."

CHAPTER TWELVE

The tidbit about that fifty with an impossible mint date pumped up the whole team, but it lit a bit of a fire under Kara in particular. The bartenders in The Hollows could think it was a bad counterfeit all they wanted; the truth of the matter might be much more interesting. And the four young women plus their secret accomplice tasked with investigating the potential of time travelers visiting Cobalt City agreed it was very likely evidence of exactly that.

All four of them were in the war room early on Sunday morning, bound and determined to get the professor's array online as quickly as was safe. Kara said it felt decadent to call Ruby's personal chef for lunch and dinner, but she was willing to deal with it if that meant not having to look up from her work. Lisa handled the back and forth with the kitchen and the bar, and the food came and went in a way that might as well have been magic.

The four of them worked all day and late into the night on Sunday to finish getting the machines individually calibrated, and it took them nearly all of Monday to get them networked in the way Professor Kummerfeldt's documentation said would be most effective. By lunchtime on Tuesday, they were making their final inspection of the setup.

After two and a half days of exhaustive effort, and a thorough assessment done with a sandwich in one hand and a multimeter in the other, Kara declared it was time to switch the whole thing on.

Lisa messaged Ruby, who appeared in the war room within moments. The elevators in this building really were something else.

Kara was doing a final check of the cables while the others worked to thread new rolls of paper into the machines that output their data as tracings.

"We're just about ready," Kara told the others.

"Should we be waiting for Stardust?" Yumi asked the room, as she made the final check of the cables she'd run most recently.

"We should not," Ruby answered.

"I thought he said he wanted to be here." Lisa shut the access panel she'd been checking underneath and stood up from the floor, setting her multimeter on the console in front of her before wiping her hands on her pants.

"Oh, I'm sure he did," Ruby replied. "But I don't want to put this off any longer, and he's a bit busy at the moment."

"Huh?" Yumi asked.

"Train wreck," Ruby said. "Happened before dawn this morning. A freight train got into it with a commuter train. I'm surprised you hadn't heard."

"We've been a little head-down getting this stuff set up," Friday said.

"Well yes. That's fair. But Jaccob's been on the scene all day." Ruby pulled her phone from her coat pocket and opened a news app to the live feed from the helicopter. "It looks like they may be finishing up. But even if he's headed back already, it could be a while."

"Yeah, okay. That settles it. We will not be waiting for Jaccob." Kara moved to the front of the room, to a panel she'd brought in herself and installed to make the startup and shutdown go more smoothly. It made sure the machines powered up and down in the sequence they required for optimal functionality. As best as she'd been able to tell from the piles of documentation, some of these things were built as add-ons to others, and those pieces needed to be turned on in a specific order to be sure they would all connect properly on startup.

There were a few that wouldn't boot at all if their parent device wasn't up and running for them to connect to—a fact Kara had learned the hard way during the process of individual calibration. The best Kara or Jaccob could tell, this machinery had never been up and running all at once and as an interconnected system before. So the two of them had spent a little extra time building in breakers and monitors as additional insurance against things melting down or exploding.

It had taken days of reading and re-reading, wiring and re-wiring, and networking cabinets and components. But they were finally ready to start the whole system up and see if they could find what they were looking for.

And everyone was more than ready to get this mechanical show on the road.

Had it been anyone other than Jaccob "Stardust" Stevens who had expressed a desire to be there when things kicked off, Kara might have considered waiting until he could get back from attending to a train wreck. But there was something satisfying about denying him the chance to be part of this moment. She'd probably have to unpack those feelings later, but right now she was too excited to get the machinery up and running to care a whole lot about anything other than whether the array was going to work.

Kara flipped the first breaker, took a deep breath, and looked around at the others as they watched the machines begin to power on. "Well, here we go."

Ruby pulled her phone back out to snap a photo.

"You sending that to Stardust?" Kara asked, walking to the far side of the room to make sure the tape was feeding through the Ometer, now that it was under normal operation.

"I suppose I should do that, shouldn't I?" Ruby said. "I was just going to send it to Mike—figured he'd appreciate knowing things are progressing."

"Text anybody you want," Kara said. "It's your project."

"Indeed. But you're the one who knows what the hell is going on here. You—" Ruby paused. "You *do* know what's going on here?"

"I do," Kara replied, "for the most part."

"For the most part?" Ruby asked. "But you're sure you were ready to switch this all on?"

"Yeah," Kara said, "I am. I know which of the machines are actively scanning and which of the machines are passive detectors. I even know what they're all scanning for and trying to detect, although I'm not entirely sure why the professor chose the things he chose. But I know what all these machines do and, I think, what we're looking for. We've learned everything we can from the manuals. The only way to learn anything more about these things is to switch them on and experience them while they're in use."

"Well, all right then," Ruby concurred. "Let's go."

The startup sequence was simple and straightforward now that Kara had taken the time to set it up that way. She switched on the next set of breakers, then a third, then another, making sure each volley of machinery was booted and online before moving to the next.

The machines spun up with a roar and a hum that reminded Ruby of early supercomputers and reel-to-reel tape duplicators.

"So now we wait?" Ruby asked once the machines had all settled into a soft whirr.

"Now we wait," Kara said back.

The moment felt a little bit anticlimactic. The machinery hummed, buzzed, clacked, and tweetered, but nothing of import seemed to be happening. Nonetheless, Kara was satisfied. Everything appeared to be working the way it was supposed to.

"Well, good," Ruby said after a moment. "I see you have this all in order. I'll be in my office. Feel free to message if anything interesting develops."

"Yes, ma'am," Lisa replied.

"Will do," Kara said.

Ruby was barely three steps toward the door when a crack, not unlike thunder, sounded from above—unusual to the extreme on a sunny July day. Next came a clatter, like a chopper had landed on the deck of the helipad but without its attendant rotor wash or engine rumbling.

"What the hell?" Ruby headed toward the door to the patio rather than the elevator bank. Yumi and Lisa sprang from their seats and followed her, with Friday and Kara not far behind.

Ruby pulled open the patio door, looking both ways and then up the stairs. She paused as she spotted a thing on her helipad that the shift in her shoulders told the others wasn't supposed to be there. That had to be what they'd heard from inside.

The edifice was oddly shaped, a square base with straight rectangular sides that resolved into a pyramid peppered with lights and antennas at the top. Made mostly of glass, maybe, or plexiglass, with rounded corners built of brushed chrome and reflectors placed at uneven intervals all over, the contraption was the strangest piece of machinery Kara had ever seen.

And that was saying a lot.

"Stay behind me," Ruby instructed the others, starting toward the stairs to the helipad.

All four of them nodded.

"Wait, what's—?" Yumi seemed to be having trouble making out her fellows. Even Ruby, just ahead of them, was little more than a blur of gray-green linen and ginger hair.

"They'll have a hard time seeing us," Ruby said. "And it muffles our steps."

"Do you think it will keep me from summoning my sword?" Yumi asked.

"Probably. I can let it go if I need to, but let's hope it doesn't come to that."

Ruby scurried up the slatted stairs at a clip the rest of them were surprised was possible in heels that high. Yumi and Lisa were one step behind her, with Friday and Kara bringing up the rear.

Just as the group reached the top of the stairs, two men emerged from the machine, visibly surprised at how exposed they were on the open deck of the helipad. They were dressed in khakis and polo shirts with the clear outline of bullet proof vests underneath—the absolute image of a pair of plainclothes campus police.

"Like cops, but not," Friday whispered to Kara.

"Yep," Kara replied, nodding. She did her best to look past Yumi, Lisa, and Ruby, to get a good look at the contraption—that just might actually be a time machine—parked not fifty feet away from them. "Damn."

"What's—?" the taller one mumbled, gesturing vaguely to where the women were standing, his head shaking as he took his first unsteady steps across the concrete deck.

The other one reached for the gun on his hip.

"Shit," Yumi said under her breath. "I may have superpowers and all, but I can't deflect bullets with my bare hands. I need my sword."

"Fuck," Kara whispered back. "You know, I have things we could use against guns, but I don't have any of them *here*."

Ruby had her phone out, likely to summon building security, but unless they had an office hidden on this patio somewhere, there was no way anyone was going to get there in time—not if one of the intruders was about to open fire.

"Who's there?" the short one yelled. He drew his weapon and pointed it in the general direction of the group. Sweeping his pistol back and forth as though it were some sort of laser sensor, he walked slowly toward the blur that was the approaching women.

"Do you have a plan?" Lisa whispered. "You look like maybe you have a plan."

Ruby nodded, a gesture barely visible through the veil of her magic. "Just stay behind me."

The sound of her voice must have spooked the armed intruder. There was full-scale panic on his face. He was shaking all over. He had hold of his gun with both his trembling hands, scanning the space in front of him with his eyes and his weapon.

"Calm down," the other man said to him.

"Do you see that?" the armed one asked.

"I don't know what I'm seeing," his colleague replied.

"There's someone here."

"I don't see anybody."

"Yumi. Sword time?" Lisa asked in a whisper.

"I'm trying," Yumi said between clenched teeth. "This magic is no joke."

"Over there!" the armed intruder shouted, gesturing with the pistol in the women's general direction.

"We're here to work," the other one reminded him. "Don't get jumpy."

A gust of wind blew past them then. It was enough to startle the man with the weapon beyond his ability to maintain control. He opened fire without a second thought, squeezing off six shots in the space of a breath.

Lisa screamed. Yumi reached out and grabbed her by the arm, as Friday and Kara threw themselves to the ground.

Ruby, however, stood fast. She flung her hands out in front of her, sending a burst of magical energy out in all directions.

The force of it was unreal and unnatural, sucking all the air from their lungs and knocking all four of them flat. The helipad's light poles quaked, their bulbs shaking loose and shattering into pieces so fine they scattered on the wind like errant glitter. The foreign contraption teetered on its base, nearly knocked over by the force of the magic.

Yumi's powers ignited. Time slowed and she watched in awe as the six bullets impacted the magical shield one after another, breaking as they ricocheted off its visible umbra, their fragments flying back toward the shooter and his accomplice.

The gunman cursed as the shrapnel bit into him. Both intruders scrambled backward, tripping over a carpet of jumbled vines as they fled toward the machine that still wobbled between them and the elevator door.

"Shit!" Friday yelled, panting. "That didn't—"

Ruby crumbled beneath herself, her body hitting the flagstones with a disturbing thump. And in a split second, the magical corona dispersed, as did the blur they'd all been under.

The men latched themselves into their contraption without any acknowledgement of what was still going on outside.

Yumi sprang to her feet, Muramasa suddenly burning in her hand as she raced forward, determined to be the thing between her friends and the gunman should he decide to fire again.

Friday was on her feet as well, shaking her head as she threw her hands forward. The thorny ground cover sprang to life then, vines winding upward and out until they formed a nearly solid wall between the women and the intruders in their contraption.

Lisa dropped to the ground beside Ruby to check her pulse and her breathing. Kara watched through a tiny break in the vines as the strange men and their machine flickered in and out of view before disappearing, seemingly into thin air.

"What the hell?" Yumi asked no one in particular, as she moved to stand beside Lisa.

"Yeah," Kara said. "My thoughts exactly."

CHAPTER THIRTEEN

A predawn summons to a multi-train collision and derailment was the kind of thing that could make Stardust second-guess his decision to un-retire from the hero business. His back was sore, his eyes were strained, he was hungry and tired, and he needed a shower in the worst way. But he'd done good today.

Every muscle in his body ached, but every person involved in that wreck had been accounted for. And as far as Jaccob was concerned, that was more than worth all the time he was going to have to spend with heating pads and Epsom salts. It had been a long day, and it was barely midafternoon. He was flying home at a slightly faster clip than normal—ready to change out of the pajamas he'd been wearing under the Stardust suit all day, have a quick shower, and sit down with a cold drink—when an orange light flashed in the lower left-hand corner of his heads-up display.

Orange lights meant building security. It could be anything from an unruly visitor in the lobby to a bomb threat to a fire in the lab. Whatever it was, he needed to know before he landed on a possibly locked-down building.

"Show me the building alert," he instructed, "and tell me the nature of the emergency."

The suit's AI did as she was asked, bringing up a schematic of Starcom Tower. "Shots fired," the AI replied.

Stardust sped up a little. Gunshots were definitely an emergency. "Location?"

The map of Starcom Tower zoomed out in front of him, and an orange blip appeared in what looked like empty space beside it.

But it wasn't empty space.

Jaccob had designed these alerts to be sensitive up to 100 yards in any direction from Starcom Tower—a reasonable precaution for a superhero moving his family into the only inhabited building for blocks. The neighborhood had grown and improved since then, but he'd never bothered to recalibrate. He had, however, come to know what that particular block of space actually meant.

The gunshots hadn't been in his Tower. They'd been in *Ruby's*.

Jaccob's heart leapt into his throat, and he upped his speed again.

Flying at nearly full power now, he strained his eyes as he approached. The shooting must have been on the terrace, otherwise the sensors on Starcom Tower wouldn't likely have picked it up. Ruby's building was hardened as well as his own was, and an emergency any place inside would be unlikely to trip an alarm next door.

The first thing he made out clearly was a strange machine standing near the center of the helipad. Certainly not a helicopter, it looked like a bastard cross between a space capsule and a vintage concept car. The second thing, equally bizarre, was an eight-by-five-foot wall of vines and brambles standing on its far side. "What's that on Ruby's helipad?" Stardust asked his AI.

"Unidentified." He'd programmed the voice with a female-sounding British accent, thinking it would be calming. It was not.

"I know it's unidentified. I'm asking you to identify it!"

"Unidentifiable," the AI replied. "More data required for analysis."

The bizarre machine vanished as Stardust watched, flickering in and out like a glitching hologram before it disappeared altogether. Owing to the altitude and angle of his approach, the machine had taken up most of his field of vision; his heart leapt into his throat when he could see the scene it had blocked from his view.

Yumi stood just beyond where the machine had been, Muramasa drawn and flaming in her right hand. The vines, he could reasonably guess, were Friday's doing; she stood alongside Yumi, shaking her head as she held out her hands toward the wall of greenery. Kara staggered around the conjured plants toward the empty space left by the vanishing machine.

Stardust felt a sick and terrifying sense of déjà vu when he spotted Ruby. She lay on the metal deck of the helipad with Lisa kneeling beside her. And she wasn't moving.

Stardust sped up again. Even though he could barely see through the tears that had suddenly filled his eyes, the only thing he could think of was getting to her.

He almost lost control of himself as he came in for a landing, stumbling forward to burn off the last of his inertia as his repulsors shut off.

Yumi reacted to his appearance like he was a newly arrived threat, spinning to face him with eyes blazing red, but Friday shouted her name, and she lowered the sword. Her expression was hard and scared.

"What happened?" Stardust dove the last few feet to kneel beside Ruby. His stomach was churning, and he was fighting back tears, but he knew better than to let his feelings distract him from dealing with the situation at hand. Half a lifetime of hero work had taught him how to ignore his emotional state for the duration of a crisis.

And whatever was happening right now, it qualified as a crisis.

"We turned on the machines," Kara said, hands on her head in frustration. "The array was working. Everything was working." She blew out a sigh, then dropped to one knee, looking carefully down at the concrete of the helipad for ... something.

"And then we heard a noise out here," Lisa said, seemingly on the verge of tears. "And we all ran out, and there were—"

"One of them had a gun," Friday said, her summoned foliage beginning to wilt behind her.

"She saved us," Yumi said, her tears as prominent in her voice as they were on her cheeks. "He started shooting. I didn't have my sword, and—" She gazed down at Muramasa as though it had betrayed them.

Stardust nodded, his thoughts racing. He looked to Kara, who was making her way back toward them. "You turned on the array?"

"Yes," Kara said.

"Are the machines still running?"

"Yes."

"Go shut them down!" Stardust insisted.

Kara turned and ran without asking why.

There were more questions; there was more he wanted to know. But the rest of the story didn't matter right now.

What mattered was the unconscious woman on the ground in front of him. She was breathing; that was good. The last time he'd found her in this condition, she hadn't been. Her breaths came fast and shallow, though; that was less good.

Stardust pressed the two middle fingers of his left hand against the pulse point in Ruby's neck; he'd made this upgrade to the suit some time ago but had barely had occasion to test it. He was glad he remembered it was here.

"Analysis," he said.

"Working," the calm, British-sounding voice of the suit's AI said. He wanted to scream at it to work faster, but he'd learned those kinds of outbursts often earned him a response in defense of the system's pace, taking computational power away from the function he was trying to rush along.

So he didn't say anything. What he did do was use his other hand to slide the release on his visor. He needed to look at her with his own eyes.

"Come on—" he whispered, hopefully quiet enough for the suit not to hear him. Whether or not it did, the answer came only a moment later.

"Temperature," the suit's AI began, "ninety-nine point two degrees Fahrenheit. Mild tachycardia: heart rate one-hundred-twenty beats per minute. Likely cause: tachypnea. Respirations: seventy per minute."

Stardust nodded. That made sense, didn't it? She was breathing fast, so her heart rate was up, and her temperature was elevated but not enough to really worry about. He scooped her into his arms and stood up, all the pain in his back and shoulders momentarily forgotten. But before he could fire the jets in his boots, he froze.

She needed a doctor. She needed ... But he couldn't bring himself to take off. The last time he'd flown her to a hospital—leaving from almost this very spot—that had been the beginning of the end for them. Something inside of Jaccob wouldn't let him do that again.

Plus, this time was different. Right? She was knocked out, but she was breathing. She was breathing, her pulse was steady, and *this wasn't like the last time.*

"Dulcamara!" he shouted at Friday, using her superhero name instead of her civilian one—he was talking to her hero-to-hero.

"What do you need?" she asked, jogging in his direction.

He gestured with his head that she should follow him as he started toward the elevator. "See the two chevrons on my left shoulder?"

"Yeah," she replied, pointing at the two raised outlines in the light blue metal of the Stardust suit.

"Press them."

Friday did as she was asked, pushing down on the two chevrons and trying not to look too astonished when they sprung up out of the suit, revealing a hidden compartment containing a tiny cell phone.

"Call Dr. Hao! Tell her where we are. She'll know it's an emergency coming from this number. Tell her to hurry."

Friday nodded as she reached into the compartment and took hold of the diminutive device. She pressed the phone's only button, which Stardust knew would reveal the familiar user-friendly default home screen of a StarPhone.

Stardust continued toward the elevator, carrying Ruby.

Yumi dashed ahead to press the call button.

The helipad had been a last-minute addition to the Ruby Tower, and as such, the architectural plans hadn't called for the elevator shaft to extend this far. But after an unexpected visit from President Prather had required him to be walked through the penthouse sitting room to reach her office, Ruby had insisted on having the addition built.

Stardust hoped the single car that was able to reach this level wasn't currently sitting in the ground-floor lobby.

The elevator opened after a moment, and he scrambled aboard, hoping his permissions where elevators were concerned were still as intact as Ruby had intimated they were. This elevator wasn't supposed to stop on the forty-eighth floor, and he was going to need it to. Still cradling Ruby in his arms, Stardust snatched open the elevator's control panel and keyed in an access code he had to hope still worked.

The touchscreen flashed solid green before the elevator's master menu came up. Stardust input the instruction for the car to take them to the forty-eighth floor and held his breath while the command processed, and the doors slid shut.

As soon as they were underway, he took a moment to look down at Ruby again.

Bruises were forming around her eyes, and blood had begun to trickle from her left ear. That could mean a head injury. It could mean all manner of things. But there were no visible bullet wounds, so that was good.

The elevator stopped on the forty-eighth floor, and the doors slid open, revealing a solid wall on the other side.

"Dammit!" Stardust spat. How could he have forgotten getting an elevator to stop on an unscheduled floor didn't do a person any good if there wasn't a way to get off that elevator when you got there?

He quickly ran through his options. He could take this car down one more floor to the Goblin Entertainment offices and then switch elevators to Ruby's private car; that one had a door to forty-eight. The problem with that, of course, was with how many employees would see him carrying their unconscious boss from her outer office to her inner office. He still knew Ruby well enough to know she would hate that.

There was also the possibility of taking the car back up two stories to the vestibule—if he did that, he'd have the choice between getting into the elevator with a door on forty-eight or running down the two flights of stairs. He wasn't sure which of those would be faster.

But he did know the absolute fastest way to get where he was going.

"You're gonna have to forgive me," he whispered, as he stepped back from the door and charged the blaster built into his right gauntlet. Bending his body to shield Ruby from the blast, he fired a pair of Starbolts at the wall, leaving an uneven hole, about five feet wide and tangled with snarls of broken rebar and severed wiring, into the forty-eighth-floor hallway.

Trying not to think about how much damage he'd just done to her recently renovated penthouse, Stardust carried Ruby through the opening he'd made, across the debris-covered carpet, and down the hall to her bedroom. He only just managed to turn the handle, the gauntlets of his suit making his hands almost too wide to fit in the gap between the knob and the jamb.

Her room was mostly the way he remembered it. There were a few throw pillows he didn't recognize, and a chair at the foot of the bed that used to sit in the closet, but aside from those small details, Ruby's bedroom was the same as it had been the last time he'd been inside it.

He raced across the plush carpet, closing the distance between the doorway and the bed in seconds and hoping he hadn't tracked too much dust in from the hallway. He lay her down carefully, propping her head against the large, square pillows in damask shams he knew were just for decoration but couldn't be bothered to move out of the way.

Doing his best to tamp down the feeling he was intruding, Stardust unfastened the buttons on Ruby's blazer and examined the white silk of her blouse for any sign of an entry wound. Thankfully, there was nothing. Save for the blood he'd seen on the side of her face, she didn't appear to be bleeding.

That was good.

But this was bad. The bruises around her eyes had gotten darker, and her color was all wrong. Whatever was happening here was more than met the eye, and it was more than the limited diagnostic capabilities built into the Stardust suit would be able to discern.

He felt helpless. And terrified.

Dr. Hao would come, and quickly, he was sure. It was part of the deal they had. He provided the budget for everything she needed not only to keep the city's heroes taken care of but also to fund her free clinic. In exchange, she'd helped him install and calibrate the first aid upgrades to his suit and allowed him to put some Stardust tech into her vehicle, which she agreed to use to affect a quick response to anything he deemed an emergency. He was also on the hook for any traffic fines or insurance deductibles she incurred in the process.

When they'd made the deal, he'd mostly been thinking about his kids, and what he would do were either of them to ever come to harm while he was unable to disengage himself from some battle with villainy or another. And although this was not that, it was absolutely emergency enough to want to use every tool he could access.

In fact, this was so far beyond anything he had ever seen, Stardust wondered whether modern medicine would be enough. It felt more like a miracle was necessary.

A pit formed in his stomach. He knew just the god to ask to perform one.

Without stopping to consider what a bad idea this might be, Stardust tore out of the room, sprinting down the hall outside, stopping only when he reached the elevator door. He punched the button impatiently. While waiting for the car to arrive, he flipped the switches, one after the other, that would cue the Stardust suit to remove itself from his body. He didn't want to show up where he was pretty sure he was heading dressed for combat. He was going to beg a favor. And if he was right about the being he was about to invoke, the less power he projected, the better.

When the suit was off and folded but the elevator car still not in evidence, Jaccob decided he wasn't going to wait any longer. Most people wouldn't know there was another way to get where he was headed, but Jaccob knew this building almost as well as he knew his own. There was a way, and he was going to use it.

Leaving the Stardust suit folded beside the elevator, Jaccob ran to the giant painting that concealed the door to the emergency stairs. The magnetic lock disengaged with a click as the canvas popped away from the wall and swung open an inch on its hidden hinges.

Jaccob hurled it aside, figuring he could replace the damn thing if he broke it—hell, he'd already be paying to rebuild the whole adjacent wall, what was a framed canvas in the grand scheme of things? It especially didn't matter, as he knew this piece of artwork was a reproduction and not at all dear to its owner. He shot through the open door and darted down the stairs, past the marker for the forty-seventh-floor offices of Goblin Media, and down another flight to the unmarked door to the forty-sixth.

He'd only guessed what he might find here, but under the circumstances, it was worth a try. There were tears in his eyes as he burst through the door, and he couldn't decide whether or not he was surprised at what he saw on the other side.

But at least it confirmed he'd come to the right place.

"Loki!" he screamed. He knew he sounded unhinged, but he couldn't be fussed to care. "Loki! Where are you? Please!"

Jaccob had long suspected there was something untoward with the forty-sixth floor of this building. Ruby claimed it to be empty, but there was no sense in keeping a full floor of a tower this size unfinished and unused. Loki had been on the roof with Ruby the last time Jaccob had found her unconscious. He'd needled Ruby about her association with the god of mischief a few times but had never come out and asked her for details. And other than the few mentions she'd made in the process of assuring Jaccob and the others their time-traveling quarry wasn't magical in nature, she'd kept mostly mum about it.

It was something Jaccob had often wondered about.

And for Ruby's sake, Jaccob was glad he'd guessed right when he'd thought perhaps Loki had a base on this floor of her building. But seeing it with his own eyes still felt like he'd uncovered a betrayal; yet another feeling he didn't have time for at the moment. He'd cope with his feelings around Ruby keeping this secret some other time. Right now, he needed to save her life.

He tore through the room—the large, open floor punctuated with gold and marble statuary, red velvet curtains, and intricately patterned carpets. On one end of the space sat a golden throne, and on the other an enormous four-poster bed piled high with pillows, with a red satin canopy impossibly suspended above it.

"Loki!" he shouted again, choking back a sob. "Loki, it's Ruby! Please! We need your help!"

"I do not care for being summoned!" Loki's voice replied from nowhere at all and yet everywhere at once.

Jaccob turned around and around, searching frantically for the source of the sound. A moment later, it revealed itself; the god, clad in blues and blacks, complete with a cape and diadem, sat draped across the golden throne Jaccob was sure had been empty just a moment before.

"Please," Jaccob yelled again.

"What are you on about?" Loki asked, turning to sit almost properly in the seat.

Jaccob found himself fully tongue-tied. He didn't know a damn thing about what had happened upstairs, other than the fact of his absence and what little he'd let Kara and the others tell him. He wasn't sure he even had the vocabulary to recount what was going on.

"I don't—" Jaccob took a deep, shaky breath and tried again. "Ruby. Magic ... and gunshots. Upstairs."

Jaccob wasn't sure he was communicating, but he could tell he'd gotten something across. Loki sprang from his seat, dashing past Jaccob toward the still-open doorway to the stairs, his cape nearly hitting Jaccob as he passed.

Jaccob turned and followed, racing to keep pace as Loki bounded up the two flights of stairs.

It stung a little when Jaccob realized Loki knew where to go. He tried to put it out of his mind, the wonder about how often the god had taken these stairs up the two flights. There was enough to worry about in the here and now for him to start borrowing that kind of trouble.

Bursting through the still-open door to the forty-eighth floor, Loki was down the hall and at Ruby's bedside so fast Jaccob was barely able to keep up. Yumi and Lisa were already in the room by the time Jaccob followed Loki through the door.

"Holy crap!" Yumi said, as the god of mischief swept in.

"It's fine." Jaccob didn't have time to explain.

If Loki even noticed them, he gave no sign.

Cape billowing behind him, Loki rounded the foot of the bed, not even bothering to stop before sliding onto the satin duvet. He reclined on the bed beside Ruby, leaning his face down until his forehead was resting on hers. Loki brought his hands to Ruby's face, stroking his knuckles against her temples as he closed his eyes and took several deep breaths.

Moments later, just as the silence in the room was beginning to grow awkward, Loki snapped his head sideways and his eyes flew open. His face was red, and a sound not unlike a growl filled the room from all directions.

Loki glowered at Jaccob, then turned to give the same admonishing glare to Yumi and Lisa where they stood by the foot of the bed. He then turned his face back toward Ruby and cupped her cheeks with his hands.

"The good news is," he said softly, "if this was going to kill her, it would have happened in the moment."

"You're sure?" Jaccob managed to ask.

Loki looked up at him and scowled. "How dare you question a god?" he spat, taking hold of Ruby's hand. "Your puny mortal meatsacks aren't built to channel arcane energy, and she's got power beyond what any human should be able to wield. She threw everything she had at stopping that bullet."

"Six," Yumi blurted out.

"What?"

"Six," she repeated. "There were six bullets. She ... she stopped six bullets."

"Mjolnir!" Loki cursed. He leaned down and pressed his forehead against Ruby's again, squeezing her fingers with his right hand as his left combed through a tangle in her hair.

Jaccob's face was getting hot. He'd spent the last few days trying to convince himself that his feelings for Ruby were at most remnants of something long past. But seeing Loki being so tender with her—taking her hand and stroking her hair like that—had his guts in a knot over emotions he was not at all ready to entertain.

"Please." Jaccob hated swallowing his pride like this, but his heart wouldn't let him do anything else. "Please, if there's anything you can do—?"

"I just told you," Loki replied, looking up at him. "An overload of magic did this damage. And yet you somehow think applying more magic could make things right?"

"I don't—"

"You're damn right you don't." Loki turned back to look at Ruby for a moment before standing up to scowl more pointedly at Jaccob. He took a step closer, until the two men were standing nose-to-nose, and snarled, "You never deserved her."

Loki turned his head to glare at the young women with narrowed eyes. Then, with a flourish of his cape, he stormed out of the room and disappeared back down the hall.

For a moment, all was silent. Jaccob had no idea what to say or to do. He'd just been called out by the god of mischief and, what's more, he'd probably deserved it.

"I'm ... um ... I'm going to go down and wait for the doctor with Friday," Lisa said after a minute.

"Yeah, okay." Jaccob understood. This day had already been far too terrifying and far too intense and now it was suddenly far too awkward.

"I'll go with you," Yumi said, taking Lisa's arm as the two of them headed out of the room a little faster than might have been polite.

Jaccob wasn't sure what to do next. He shoved his hands into the damp, sweaty pockets of the plaid flannel pants he only now realized he was still wearing. He'd been in the Stardust suit since an hour before dawn when the first report of the train accident had rung his alarm. He should probably feel embarrassed that he'd just barged into the sanctum of an immortal god in pajama pants and a free tee shirt from a radio promotion at Icons, but he was too full of worry and upset to give a damn.

He needed a shower, and he wanted a change of clothes, but he wasn't about to leave. Not until after Dr. Hao got here. There was a time he'd have jumped into Ruby's shower and asked Mike to run across the street for a set of clean clothes, but today that felt like overstepping. He wouldn't make that presumption. What did he care what Dr. Hao and the girls thought of his appearance, anyway?

And if Ruby woke up and told him he looked slovenly, well ... that was the best-case scenario. It would be worth it just to hear her voice and to know she knew he was here.

Jaccob walked slowly to the side of the bed and sat down beside Ruby in the spot Loki had just vacated. He reached over and picked up her blazer where he'd tossed it onto the bed, folding it neatly before draping it over the chair that now stood beside the footboard. He slipped her shoes off her feet, carefully, as he remembered there was something special about the ones with the red soles.

He wasn't sure whether he was imagining things or if she looked even worse now than when he'd first brought her in here. Jaccob let his eyes close as he reached for Ruby's hand.

He had a lot to do. There was paperwork waiting for him back at his office regarding the train wreck he'd spent all day attending. Someone would need to call Arsho or the head custodian to come up and assess the mess so they could start clearing the dust and debris from the hallway. And he should probably get started on finding a contractor who could patch that wall as soon as possible—he shouldn't make his mess into anyone else's problem. But all Jaccob wanted to do was sit and hold Ruby's hand.

The mess would keep. So would the paperwork.

CHAPTER FOURTEEN

"You said there was shooting?"

Dr. Hao was a diminutive woman, petite in every dimension, with graying black hair she wore in a short bob and an unassuming demeanor that made her imminently approachable. And yet, when she spoke, everyone sat up and paid attention.

She had gotten to the Tower in under ten minutes. Even with the Stardust tech in her car, Jaccob had to figure she couldn't have been all the way at her house in Morriston when Friday called her. Friday, Yumi, and Lisa had met her in the lobby and shown her to Ruby's room, briefing her as best they could on the situation during the elevator ride.

She immediately ran Jaccob out of the room, closing the door behind her while she looked over Ruby. He'd spent the intervening minutes mostly pacing the hallway, trying not to imagine the worst.

Mike had arrived just after the doctor, and Katy wasn't far behind him, carrying with her Jaccob's phone and a change of clothes Mike must have directed her to from his closet.

Kara and Yumi took turns recounting the events of the afternoon to Jaccob while Friday and Lisa followed Katy back up to the sitting room to bring down water for everyone. Mike excused himself to make a few calls, and a pair of valets with snack trays showed up in the hallway suspiciously close to the moment of his return.

Jaccob knew he should eat. He'd been going nonstop since before dawn, and it was well past lunchtime, but he didn't have an appetite. It was all he could do to gag down a bottle of water in an attempt to stay hydrated enough to remain functional.

A change of clothes and a drink of water weren't enough to make him okay, but Jaccob was grateful for feeling a little more like himself by the time Dr. Hao emerged.

"Yeah," Lisa answered the doctor's question. "That guy fired six times."

"Well," Dr. Hao said, "there's no evidence of any gunshot wounds."

"She stopped it with magic," Yumi said. "I saw it. It was—"

"That makes sense," Dr. Hao said, as though magic was just as ordinary a tool as a bulletproof vest. She turned her attention to Jaccob, who was fidgeting.

"How is she?" he asked.

"Her pulse was a little thready when I got here. But it's improved now. Her breathing's normal and her blood pressure's back up. She's not responding to stimuli, though, so I ran an EEG." Dr. Hao gestured to the leather case she carried that Jaccob knew contained some of the most advanced portable medical equipment in the world. "And even though she's unresponsive, her brain activity looks more like deep sleep than coma. Your reports of magic use, especially using magic to stop bullets, lead me to believe the magic just overwhelmed her body. Everything from the systemic dysregulation to the capillary damage points to extreme thaumaturgic shock."

"That's what—" Jaccob began. But then he caught himself. He didn't need to bring up Loki in front of people who weren't already in the know. "That was our best guess."

"In my experience," Dr. Hao said, "the best thing to do is to let her sleep. She might wake up tomorrow morning good as new, like nothing ever happened. But I have to admit this is the worst case I've ever seen. We're just going to have to watch and wait."

"How long 'til we worry?" Katy asked.

Jaccob shook his head. He'd almost forgotten Katy was here. He wasn't sure how he felt about getting his son's unsuspecting girlfriend mixed up in all this. And he wasn't sure how to express the degree to which he was already worried.

"Give it a day," Dr. Hao replied. "If she's not awake by this time tomorrow, call me. I'll come back, run a repeat EEG and maybe give her some fluids."

"Okay," Jaccob said.

"Have someone look in on her every few hours," the doctor instructed them.

"We can do that," Lisa replied.

"I can help, too," Katy said. "I know y'all are in the middle of something."

"We can figure it out," Jaccob said to all of them.

"Let me know if anything changes," Dr. Hao said.

"What—?" Jaccob started, stumbling over his words as he shook his head. "What might change? What should we be looking for?"

"Fever," Dr. Hao responded, "cold sweats, anything that looks like a seizure. I'm leaving you with a scan thermometer and a pulse oximeter. Her temperature should stay between ninety-seven and ninety-nine and her O2 sat above ninety. Anything out of that range, call me immediately. Otherwise, just let her rest. Keep her comfortable. And I'll be back tomorrow."

"Yeah," Jaccob said back. "Okay."

~

"Fuck." Cassidy knocked back her second shot of whiskey, eyes wide at the revelations Kara and the others were sharing.

"I know, right?" Friday said, sipping her fruity cocktail through its straw. Normally she didn't like to drink on the job, but tonight she figured it was okay to make an exception. "That's pretty much what I said."

"It was wild," Yumi added. "This wacky-ass machine landed on the helipad, and we ran outside, and one of the dudes who got out of it got spooked and started shooting, and then she threw up some sort of magical forcefield thing that stopped the bullets and freaked out the shooters and so they got back into whatever that machine was that brought them there and just ... fucking vanished."

"Yeah," Lisa said.

"Had to be a time machine, right?" Cassidy asked. "Any other tech you can think of that can vanish like that?"

"Not that I can think of," Kara said.

"And it couldn't be magic," Cassidy said.

"It couldn't?" Yumi asked.

"No way," Cassidy replied. "The wicked witch is liable to have that place warded tighter than a nun's asshole. Anybody trying to use magic in that building without her literal blessing would be in for a whole world of hurt. Since you say they were conscious, and upright, and not writhing in pain or bleeding out of their eye sockets, I'd say they weren't using magic."

"Well, okay then," Friday said.

"I was able to summon my sword, though?" Yumi looked to Friday. "And your vines—?"

"Your sword didn't show up until after she was unconscious," Lisa reminded her.

"And what I do isn't really magic," Friday said. "At least it's not my magic. It's Freya's. I just channel it, and the rules for gods are different. Even so, the vines didn't take their full form until she was out cold, either."

"Shit," Lisa interrupted them, holding her hands out in front of all of them to stop the conversation.

"What is it?" Friday asked her.

"Are we violating our NDA?" she asked. "Speaking of ... bleeding out of the eyeballs and stuff—"

"I don't think so," Kara replied, sipping casually at her beer as she shook her head. "As long as we're just talking about what we went through, about what happened to *us*, then we should be okay. *We* saw the strange men and their machine. *We* got shot at. *We* got protected. That's our story, not her secret."

"And if you were worried about accidentally revealing she's a magic user," Cassidy added, "don't. In case you couldn't tell from my earlier comment, I knew that already. I've known it for half my life."

"Really?" Kara asked her.

Cassidy nodded. "The first time I worked with her she was ... what ... seventeen maybe? Way too young to be put in charge the way she was."

"Story time?" Yumi asked.

"Sure, yeah," Cassidy said. "I was touring. It was ... I want to say '97, '98 maybe. I had a string of shows in shopping malls. And Ruby wound up working for the tour. Then, suddenly one day, everyone—the stage manager, *the tour manager*—the whole damn crew just started deferring to her. Like, out of nowhere. One day she was a really broody intern with a completely ambiguous job description who seemed thoroughly allergic to work, and the next day she was running the show: changing the choreography, adjusting the sound mix, and bossing around the roadies. And nobody questioned it. It had to be magic. There's no other explanation."

"Did you question it?" Lisa asked.

"Nah," Cassidy admitted, shaking her head. "The fact is, as annoying as she could be, she made the show better. A better show has better attendance, sells more tickets, makes more money. So, since she didn't seem to want to use her powers on me, I decided not to say anything. I just did my job, did my best to avoid her, and took a bigger paycheck home at the end of the tour than I probably would have otherwise."

"Then she went on the be the boss?" Friday asked.

"Not right away," Cassidy replied. "But I'd say she charmed her way up the corporate ladder pretty quickly."

"She is really good at her job, though," Lisa said.

"Yeah, I'll admit to that," Cassidy said. "The company's done great with her in charge—gone from Goblin Records to Goblin Media to Goblin Entertainment Worldwide. That doesn't change the fact she used magic to get where she is. And who knows how much magic she uses to run the place. She's evil. She's a self-centered, wicked, narcissistic capitalist. The fact she's also made other people money while she's built her empire doesn't mean she isn't evil."

"Yeah." Friday sipped her cocktail and nodded. "I feel you."

"She used magic to save our lives," Yumi said. "And put herself in a coma doing it. I don't know how you can still think she's evil after that."

"She saved her own life," Friday said. "We just happened to be standing behind her."

"I guess that's true," Lisa said.

"And we haven't even told you the wildest part yet!" Yumi exclaimed.

"Excuse me?" Cassidy asked. "A time machine lands on the roof, the dragon lady uses magic to stop six bullets, knocks herself into a coma, and runs off the bad guys, and that's not the wildest part?"

"It actually does get weirder," Kara agreed. She waved at their server, gesturing her request for another round of drinks.

"So," Yumi began, "Stardust showed up, like, right after this. And he freaked all the way the fuck out. And he told Friday to call Dr. Hao, and then he picked up Miss Killingsworth like he was in some kind of old movie and got into the elevator. But then I guess he forgot that elevator didn't open on the floor he wanted, so he blew a hole in the wall to get out of the elevator. Then he took her down the hallway to her room and I guess he was still freaked the fuck out so then he ran off and changed out of his super suit somehow and then a few minutes later he came back just wearing his pajamas and he had Loki with him."

"Wait ... what?" Cassidy asked. She finished the whiskey in her glass and looked dubiously at Yumi.

"She's telling the truth," Lisa said. "I was there."

"I'm just—" Cassidy said. "I'm just having to picture Jaccob Stevens in his pajamas trying to talk to the god of mischief."

"It was a lot," Kara said. "When I asked you if you wanted to meet for drinks, it was only half because we needed to meet. The other half was that we needed to drink."

"Yeah," Cassidy agreed, "I can imagine."

"And it felt weird to order drinks from Miss K's bartender when she's ... ya know ... in a coma downstairs," Yumi said.

"I also just wanted the hell out of that building for a little while," Friday added.

"That, too." Kara reached into her pocket and withdrew a small plastic envelope. She slid it across the table toward Cassidy. "Here. These are the printouts I talked to you about. They're not great. The cameras up on the helipad aren't the best. But at least they're in color. Starcom probably has the tech to enhance the images, but Jaccob is an absolute mess right now, and quite frankly, I'd rather not interact with him if I can help it."

"Nah," Cassidy said, "that's cool. If the pictures were too good, that'd probably draw suspicion anyway."

"I hadn't even thought of that," Kara said, "but you have a point. Anyway, those two men on the roof today, they fit the description of the so-called counterfeiters we heard about at Macky's. I think it's worth asking around. Because if this is them—"

"Yeah." Cassidy slipped the envelope into her bag as the server returned with a tray of fresh drinks for the five of them. "I get it. That would be one hell of a data point. I'll do a little digging. See what I can turn up."

"Cool," Kara said. "When those fuckers landed, our machines went batshit. The war room looks like an earthquake hit it right now."

"Oof," Cassidy said. "And you'd only just gotten that stuff working, right?"

"Literally moments before," Kara replied. "Needless to say, we're going to have our hands full repairing a room full of priceless, *borrowed* equipment. So we appreciate the help with the field work."

"No worries," Cassidy said. "I can handle that."

CHAPTER FIFTEEN

The door was ajar, but Jaccob felt the need to knock anyway. There was something about barging into Ruby's bedroom uninvited that just didn't feel right. He rapped his knuckle gently against the frame three times before pushing the door open just far enough to see inside. The lights were out, save a tiny lamp on the near side of the bed that shone just enough for him to make out the contours of Ruby's face.

Dr. Hao had come and gone in the mid-afternoon as promised, checked Ruby's vitals, and given her a fluid bolus. She declared Ruby's condition unchanged and promised to come again tomorrow. She assured Jaccob her patient was, as best she could tell, stable, but had once again stated plainly that she'd never seen thaumaturgic shock this severe, and she wasn't sure what its course would look like. She had agreed, though, there was little more a hospital could offer by way of care than what they could accomplish in the penthouse, and there would be no harm done by letting Ruby sleep this off in her own bed.

So at least Jaccob could let go of his guilt over not having flown her straight to an emergency room.

Somehow, in the past thirty hours or so, flowers had managed to appear on practically every available surface of Ruby's bedroom. Apparently everyone who might want a favor from Miss Killingsworth had decided to send her flowers upon hearing she was under the weather. As Jaccob understood it, Arsho, the building's manager, had seen the whole shooting through their security cameras and had alerted the appropriate company people to their boss's coming absence. He wasn't sure what details they had and had not shared, but he could tell from the proliferation of vases the news of Ruby's illness-slash-injury had gotten out.

He tried not to think too hard about the fact this wasn't the first time Arsho, or the company, had had to deal with this kind of thing. He'd already resolved this wasn't going to be like last time. This time she would wake up at home, and this time she wasn't going to wake up alone.

Yumi, Lisa, and Katy were checking on her regularly throughout the day, and Jaccob had been by last night to sit with her for probably longer than was appropriate considering the current status of their relationship. And now he was back again, for a second night in a row ...

Ruby lay on her back with her head resting on a little cushion in a damask pillowcase. The oversized pillows in their fancy shams were nowhere in evidence. He wasn't sure whether it had been Dr. Hao or one of Ruby's household staff who had tucked her in, but she looked cozy and comfortable. It would have been easy for someone to pretend she was just sleeping normally.

Not for Jaccob, though. He knew better.

For one thing, she was on the "wrong" side of the bed—in the same place he'd laid her when he brought her down from the helipad. Probably nobody else knew she normally slept on the far side, or that she never, ever slept on her back or with a lamp turned on. She wasn't sleeping. This wasn't normal.

Still, he couldn't help himself but to tiptoe as he approached her bedside, as though he was afraid to wake her. That was silly, and he knew it. He'd be happy as a clam if she were to wake up, although perhaps a little awkward if she asked for an explanation of what he was doing in her bedroom in the middle of the night.

Or maybe not. If she really were to wake up and find him here, he'd have a pretty easy time explaining himself. This trip.

Jaccob slipped the little box out of his pocket and set it on the nightstand, taking care not to bump the rather substantial bouquet sitting beside the lamp. He stood back for a moment, looking at Ruby and then again at the box, and changed his mind. He picked it back up and shook his head as he opened the box at its hinge and looked down at the diamond bangle inside.

He'd wanted to have this back to her sooner. And he'd spent the hours since the shooting—when he wasn't at her bedside—

doing almost nothing but getting it back into working order. Was it the right thing to do, giving it back at the earliest possible moment, even though she was unconscious and wouldn't know until she woke up? Or was this a coward's way of handling things: leaving the bracelet where she would find it without his having to be present for the exchange?

Jaccob shook his head and frowned. When did things get so complicated?

Jaccob knew the answer to that question. He just didn't know what to do with it. In the months and years since he'd walked away from Ruby in St. Joan Hospital, he'd done his best to keep his feelings toward her locked down tight. He'd never dealt with them, never processed them, and, as it turned out, never let them go.

There would have to be a reckoning around that sooner or later, but here at her bedside while she was unconscious from thaumaturgic shock didn't feel like the time.

Maybe it was the familiarity of it all that was getting to him. He'd seen her like this before—like this, only to the extreme. That night when he'd found her near death on her balcony had stuck with him, as had the memories of the first few days afterward when all he'd been able to think about was how close she'd come to being gone from his life forever.

And how quickly he'd run away from her once he knew she would recover. And how many of the days between had he been awash with regret over that?

But this time was different. This time there were no secrets between them, no betrayals. And this time, when she woke up, he was going to do things differently.

It felt like a second chance. And he was determined to take it.

And the first thing he would be doing differently this time was to make sure she knew, from the moment she woke up, that he wasn't going anywhere.

He set the open box back on the nightstand.

She'd see it when she woke up and know he'd been here. Jaccob turned his head to sniff at one of the roses in the vase beside it, glimpsing as he did a card that read: "Feel better, Ginger. <3-V. P.S. If you don't like the arrangement, yell at me, not the florist."

Jaccob shook his head. The idea of Vivienne sending flowers to Ruby was bizarre—honestly, the idea of Vivienne sending flowers to anyone was hard to wrap his mind around. But there they sat: flowers on his ex-lover's nightstand sent by his one-time flame.

The two women's friendship was one of those things he'd probably never understand. Of course, he didn't exactly understand Ruby's friendship with Loki, either, but the god's reaction to seeing her in this state was enough to tell Jaccob their connection ran deep. He was starting to realize how little he'd bothered to get to know her when they were together, and how satisfied he'd been with that at the time.

Jaccob had no idea what the way forward was going to look like. But he knew he had to try and make things right, or at least as close to right as she'd let him.

Starting with this.

"I'm so sorry," he whispered to her, dodging blossoms as he bent down to gently kiss her forehead. "I'll do better. I promise."

~

Getting the war room back up and running was proving to be more of a chore than first predicted. When Kara had headed back in to shut things down at Stardust's insistence, she'd found most of the array offline already. The Ometer had thrown three of its seven needles and one of its ink reservoirs had burst and was leaking bright blue out the bottom seam of its cabinet. Three machines had cracked LCD screens, one of the pressure gauge housings had fallen over onto its side, and nearly all had at least one blown fuse or fried wire. And the guts of the Isotopeter still weren't quite cool enough to thoroughly inspect, almost forty-eight hours later.

Only the Geiger counters and the atomic clock seemed to have come through unscathed.

It had been frustration after frustration trying to triage, diagnose, and repair the array. Kara had been in a particularly bad mood, and the others weren't handling things much better.

Having Miss Killingsworth in a coma was not exactly good for morale. And not knowing whether it was safe for them to turn the machines back on once they finished the repairs was bad for their ability to get this mystery solved. Kara wasn't sure whether activating the equipment in the war room had been the impetus for the attack on the penthouse, but all involved agreed it was too much of a coincidence not to be wary.

They were probably only a day or so out from being ready to turn the array back on again, but Kara wasn't sure how she felt about doing that without checking in with Miss Killingsworth first. And she certainly wasn't about to ask for Jaccob's thoughts on the matter.

As best Kara could tell, he'd been spending most of his time obsessing over the security footage and what defenses the building did and did not have against a possible repeat attack. But it was obvious to Kara he'd lost his usual focus; he'd been kind of a mess since the shooting. Katy was doing her best to help, but even the doting attentions of a young woman who seemed to care only for others' comfort had not been enough to keep Jaccob on an even keel. As far as Kara was concerned, he could stay in his fancy Stardust cave until he got his head screwed back on straight. They had a big, dangerous mystery to solve, and a bunch of borrowed equipment to repair; nobody had time to coddle an off-kilter hero.

Even if another tech genius probably would be a big help putting the busted machinery back together.

This equipment needed all the help it could get.

The closer they looked at each individual machine, the more Kara became convinced that the armed men who had landed on the helipad had indeed gotten there by traveling through time. The machines looked, almost to a circuit, as though they'd been overwhelmed and overloaded. And if time travel was the thing they'd been built to detect, then the best explanation for those machines' current state was they'd detected a hell of a lot of it.

Most of the array was already approaching functional again when Kara finally ruled the Isotopeter cooled enough to start on.

"Goddammit," Kara mumbled, shaking her head as she scooted away from the open panel on the back of the still-warm apparatus. She ran her hands through her hair, took a deep breath, and considered what to do next.

"What's up?" Yumi asked.

"There's a crack in a metal drum," Kara said. "Part of the motor ... a thing that spins around and drives the whole thing. Giant fucking crack. I'm going to pull it out, but—"

"Well, shit," Friday said.

"Exactly," Kara replied. She turned her head toward the pile of bankers' boxes in the corner. "Any chance anyone saw a five-inch-wide solid metal drum in with all the spare parts and paperwork?"

"Not that I remember," Lisa said. "But I don't think I went through everything. I stopped looking after I found the spools of wire you asked me for."

"Yeah. Okay." Kara ran her fingers through her hair again and headed toward the pile of boxes. She doubted she'd find a spare metal drum, but she was pretty sure she remembered seeing the specs for the motor the drum was part of, and that would be a good place to start in sourcing a replacement.

A quick and cursory glance into all the boxes was enough to tell Kara she'd been right about not having any large components hiding in there. She considered for a moment calling the professor, but she thought better of doing so before having the documentation in her hands. She knew from experience they'd be talking in circles around each other if she wasn't using the exact terminology he expected.

And whether or not the professor was going to be able to assist with repairing or replacing the part, having the documentation readily available would likely be helpful in the long run. There was also the concern of just how powerfully she didn't want to tell the professor about literally all his equipment getting fragged.

Professor Kummerfeldt's filing system seemed to exist in a liminal space between "quirky" and indecipherable, and Kara was three boxes in before she even began to understand that there was any system at all. But it was at the bottom of the fourth box that she found something interesting.

It wasn't the manual or any of the documentation for the Isotopeter—nothing that looked useful on the surface. Instead of research and development information, the bottom half of that box was filled with rolls of paper Kara was quick to recognize as tracing tapes from several of the apparatus in their array. Whether it was due to frustration with the Professor's so-called system or just the way her brain worked, she began unrolling and examining the papers.

Kara wasn't sure how long she'd been head-down, but she knew she was seeing a pattern when Friday approached her.

"Did you find it?" Friday asked.

"Not yet. But I want you to look at something." Kara got up from the floor where she'd been sitting and crossed to the table at the end of one of the rows of machinery. She'd pulled all the tracings from the day of the shooting, but she hadn't bothered to put them away yet. Kara gathered the three tapes from the corner of the table then spread them out in overlapping rows.

"What is this?" Friday asked. "What am I looking at?"

"See this?" Kara asked, pointing to a tall and oddly shaped multi-line spike on all three strips.

"Yeah."

"These were recorded during the shooting," Kara explained. "Or, at least between the time we turned the machines on Tuesday and when they went haywire and stopped working. This big spike, this weird skyscraper-looking thing, as best I can tell from synching the Ometer and the atomic clock over there to all the cameras in this building and the ones next door, this spike corresponds to the moment the attackers landed."

"Holy—" Yumi said, moving to look over Friday's shoulder at the tracing.

"Yeah," Kara said. "And—"

"So wait," Lisa said. "Are you saying—?"

"I don't know what I'm saying," Kara replied. "But what I do know is that, although correlation does not mean causation, we have a tracing here that correlates perfectly to the moment the attackers arrived. And we also have those." She pointed at the tapes on the floor where she'd just been sitting.

"What are those?" Yumi asked.

"Those are some old tapes I found when I was looking for paperwork on the Isotopeter or a spare drum to replace the one that cracked. All of those came here with the machines when they were delivered," Kara said. "Each of you pick one. Doesn't matter which. Open all the tapes, lay them out like this, and have a look."

Lisa was first to the pile in the corner; she picked up three of the rolls of paper, handing one each to Yumi and to Friday before beginning to unroll the one she'd kept for herself.

"What are we looking for?" Friday asked, as she began unrolling the tape in her hands.

"I don't want to say," Kara replied. "Not yet. I want to know if you see what I saw when I looked at those."

"You mean this?" Yumi asked, holding up her unrolled tape with one hand while pointing at the tracing with the other.

Kara nodded.

"Damn," Friday said, looking back and forth between Yumi's unrolled tape and her own.

"You see it, too?" Kara asked.

"How could I not see it?" Friday shook her head as she looked back at the tape in her hand. The tracing was unmistakable. The spike was smaller, but identical—the self-same shape as the giant one corresponding to the appearance of the attackers on the helipad.

Lisa turned hers around, too, revealing another skyscraper-shaped tracing.

"And there's this one," Kara told them, joining the others in the corner and picking up a partially unrolled tape from the box.

"Do these all match?" Yumi asked, gesturing to the half dozen rolls of paper still rubber-banded together.

"All the ones I looked at do," Kara replied.

"What makes that one special?" Friday asked, gesturing to the one in Kara's hand.

"It's the second largest," Kara said. "Not as big as the one from the day of the attack, but bigger than all the others by a good degree. Only that's not the most interesting part."

"It isn't?" Lisa asked.

"No, it's not," Kara replied. "See, when I started looking through these, I realized what the pattern might mean. The shapes are all the same, but the sizes differ, and my guess is maybe the relative size could be an intensity thing. And in cases like this, intensity is as likely to equal proximity as anything else."

"Yeah, okay," Friday said. "That makes sense."

"This one in my hand," Kara said, "the second largest ... It's from the day Miss Killingsworth got the email."

"It's what?" Lisa asked.

"Yeah," Kara said. "The day she got the email. The same day two guys tried to pass a fifty that hadn't been minted yet at Macky's. When Cassidy gets back to us after talking to the bartender, I'd bet our whole proposed bonus it's going to turn out the guys on the roof and the guys with the fifty were the same two guys."

"Which means—?" Lisa started a sentence but didn't manage to finish it.

"Which means that this array," Kara picked up her train of thought and continued, "threw the same tracings on the day of the email and the day of the attack."

"So whatever it is those two events have in common," Friday said, "is the thing that gets measured by this array of machines."

"This array of machines that are designed and set up specifically to detect the atmospheric indicators of time travel," Lisa said.

Kara nodded.

"Holy fuck!" Yumi exclaimed.

"Couldn't have said it better myself," Kara said.

"We've got to call Jaccob," Lisa said.

"I don't know about that," Yumi countered.

"Why not?" Lisa asked.

"You know as well as the rest of us he went kind of batshit after the attack," Yumi reminded her. "He's almost never on our gaming server, and when he is, he's actually playing worse than he did the first time I kicked his ass. It isn't even fun to beat him anymore. And I don't think he's been back over here since Tuesday, either, even though he said he'd be coming to take a look at the machines with us and see if he could help figure out what the hell went on."

"Oh, he's been here," Kara said.

"He has?" Lisa asked.

"How do you know that?" Yumi asked.

"Starcom got me access to the cameras, remember?" Kara shrugged. "To see if I could sync the tapes to anything interesting? I have automation set up to tell me any time anyone sets foot on this roof—seemed like the safe thing to do while Miss Killingsworth is in a coma and all. During the day, there's been some work crew or another, and sometimes somebody cleans the balcony, but then at night sometimes Stardust shows up. Only, not *Stardust* Stardust. Just Jaccob in his regular clothes, but he gets over here by flying, so—"

"I can't decide whether I think that's really sweet or really creepy," Friday said.

"Well, I think it's sweet," Lisa said. "And I say again that I think we should call him."

"Yeah. You're probably right," Kara agreed. "I'm pretty sure he'll be interested to know about the correlation. I'm going to spend a little more time with these tapes. And there's another one of these machines that, I think, is going to tell us where the disruptions happened. It stores data on magnetic tape instead of outputting paper tracings, but I shouldn't have a hard time finding the days and times we're looking for. If it confirms the two we think were here in Cobalt City really were, then we can look more closely at where it says other disruptions have happened, and then chase local news around those places to see if there's anything we find suspicious."

"Yeah," Lisa said. "That makes sense."

"Plus," Yumi added, "If there's anybody in town with a machine shop that could fix that drum—"

"You've got a point there, too," Kara said. "And perhaps giving him an assignment will get Jaccob out of his funk."

"What should we be doing?" asked Friday, as she began to re-roll her tape.

"If you want," Kara replied, "you can go through the rest of the paper tapes in the box and pull out the ones that match our pattern while I start on the magnetic tapes."

"Yeah," Friday said, "I can do that."

"Want me to call Jaccob?" Lisa asked Kara. "Tell him to come get the drum and see if he can either get it fixed or get started on a new one?"

"Yeah, that ... the hell?" Kara looked over her shoulder and frowned. There was a ringing, banging noise coming from the next room. "Someone's at the door. Probably one of the maids locked themself out."

Miss Killingsworth hadn't made a habit of keeping that door locked, but with Jaccob coming and going in the middle of the night, she had no doubt he'd have locked it behind him when he left.

"I'll go get it." Friday offered. She headed across the vestibule and into the sitting room. As she rounded the corner toward the door to the veranda, she was able to see who'd been knocking on the glass and she paused.

"Well, damn," Friday said, as she quickened her pace toward the door. "Yumi! You'll never believe who just showed up!"

Angel DeSantes—also known as A-Girl, petite, blonde, internationally internet famous, and supposed to be in Seattle—swept into the room like the sunshine after a storm.

"¡Hola chicas!" she said with a big smile.

She'd obviously flown here under her own power, as evidenced by the fact there were no aircraft in sight and yet she'd knocked on a fiftieth-story door instead of a ground floor one. She wore cargo pants, a tank top, and a denim jacket and had a backpack slung over one shoulder with the helmet to her super suit clipped around one of the straps. She was definitely not who anyone had been expecting.

"Angel?" Friday greeted the newcomer with a mix of confusion and elation in her voice.

"¡Mi corazón!" The perky blonde lunged forward, grabbing Friday around her waist in a hug so intense it could easily have been mistaken for a restraining maneuver. She kissed her on both cheeks.

"Um—" Yumi said, walking into the room as Angel let go of Friday. "Not that it's not really great to see you and all, but ... what are you doing here ... exactly?"

"Well." Angel shrugged as she turned to hug Yumi as well. "Aunt V said you all could use somebody bulletproof."

"She wasn't wrong," Friday said. "That is, we did get shot at. And the only reason we didn't get *shot* shot was that Miss Killingsworth stopped six bullets with her magic and that put her in a coma. So if someone else were to come and shoot at us, or those guys were to show up again, there's every chance having somebody bulletproof hanging around could actually come in very handy."

"But," Yumi added, "were working on a kind of top-secret thing. And we all had to sign a magically enforceable NDA. So I don't know if we can tell you what we're doing or let you see the stuff in the other room or help us out at all without getting into kind of serious trouble with our boss."

"Oh, no worries," Angel said. "I know all about what you all are doing here."

"You do?" Friday asked.

"Yeah. Aunt V explained everything when she asked me to come help. Someone with an unknowable IP address emailed Miss Killingsworth a file of someone singing a song that Mike Stevens had barely finished writing and she thinks it's some future bad guy with a time machine, so she called Stardust—because he's a tech guy and also Mike's dad, which outweighs the fact he's also her ex—and he called all of you. And then a professor at your school who studies the possibility of time travel in his spare time lent you a whole banquet room's full of equipment to hopefully help you track down if that's really what was happening and when you finally got it all hooked up and calibrated and working, then ... BAM! Bad guys on your roof, huge gunfight. Miss Killingsworth saved the day, but it left her unconscious, Stardust is feeling hella guilty, Loki is big mad, you guys still don't know if it was the machines that caused the bad guys to show up, and having somebody bulletproof could prove super useful either way." Angel shrugged again. "That about it?"

"Um ... yeah," Yumi said. "That's pretty much everything."

"I even saw pictures," Angel said, "of all the machines and stuff. So I'm pretty sure you guys won't be in trouble if you let me hang around."

"Wait, how does V even know all that?" Yumi made a face. "Ruby's, um—"

"You know, I didn't ask," Angel replied.

"Well," Friday said, "however you came to be in possession of this information, I think you're right. I'm pretty sure letting you in here won't get us in any trouble. Welcome to the team, A-Girl. You can stay with me while you're in town. That is ... provided you don't mind sharing a room with a bunch of plants."

"I like plants," Angel said.

"Come meet the rest of the team," Yumi invited her.

Angel smiled back and nodded her agreement.

When Yumi and Friday returned with the newcomer, Lisa was re-rolling all the paper tracings.

Kara, meanwhile, lay on her side with her head inside a medium-sized magnetic gauge, in the final phase of attaching a replacement for its blown LCD screen. A hammer and a ratchet sounded in turn, occasionally punctuated by soft curses at the machine's design, as well as its recent damage.

"You won't believe who just showed up," Friday called out to the others.

"Yeah?" Lisa jogged over and froze in the doorway. She bit her bottom lip as she slowly backed up—and into the machine Kara was working on.

"Hey," Kara said, scooting out from inside the cabinet, "what's up?"

Lisa could only point.

Kara stood up and took Lisa by her shoulders, turning her around so they were facing each other. "Is everything okay?"

Lisa still couldn't answer. She just looked up at Kara, eyes wide, and tried her best neither to scream nor fall down.

"Shit." Kara let go of Lisa and slid the concussion taser from where she'd had it clipped to her belt. If those damned intruders had come back, she wasn't about to let them get shots off again. Kara dashed past Lisa, through the vestibule toward the sitting room, her weapon in front of her but not yet ready to fire until she got a better read on the situation.

"Hey!" Friday said, as she spotted Kara. "No need for that. It's just Angel."

"Angel?" Kara asked.

"Hi." Angel stepped forward and smiled. "I'm Angel. A-Girl."

"Famous recording artist, movie star, and influencer, A-Girl?" Yumi asked. "Seattle-based superhero, daughter of Athena?"

Kara shrugged.

"Hey, sweetie, you okay?" Yumi asked Lisa, who had tiptoed back into the vestibule and was halfway hiding behind Kara.

Lisa, her eyes still wide, just shook her head. She pointed sneakily at Angel and continued to barely manage to remain upright.

"Oh, that's right. Angel?" Yumi took Angel by her arm and led her past Kara toward where Lisa was standing. "I want you to meet my girlfriend, Lisa. She's a big fan. "

"Uh-huh," Lisa managed to say.

"Hi, Yumi's girlfriend, Lisa!" Angel lunged forward to hug Lisa with almost as much aplomb as she'd hugged Friday. "It's really nice to meet you."

"Uh-huh," Lisa said again.

"I think she's a little starstruck," Friday said to Kara.

"Starstruck?" Kara asked, as she clipped the concussion taser back onto her belt.

"A-Girl is really famous," Yumi informed her. "Lisa's, like, her biggest fan."

"Uh-huh." Lisa seemed on the verge of collapse.

"What are you famous for again?" Kara asked Angel, crossing her arms over her chest. She knew there were probably oodles of twenty-year-old blondes who were plenty famous in their own circles who she'd never heard of, but she was curious as to what exactly this one was capable of. And if they were going to be working together, then she figured it was best to know.

"Hero stuff mostly." Angel shrugged. "And I've done some movies and music and stuff. But really I'm just popular online."

"She's being modest," Friday said. "Yeah, she's popular because she's blonde and pretty, sure. But she also does a lot of good and saves a lot of people. She's completely impervious. Like bulletproof, which could come in real handy here if our rooftop visitors decide to show up again. Plus, she can fly, she has super strength, and super speed—"

"Super strength?" Kara interrupted.

"Yeah," Angel said.

"Come with me." Kara headed back into the war room. "I have a few pieces of heavy machinery that will be a whole lot easier to fix if we can move them."

"Oh, yeah," Angel said. "Sure. I can do that."

"And I don't know if you overheard," Yumi said, taking hold of Lisa's hand again as they moved to follow Kara and Angel. "But she already knows everything we're doing. She even already saw pictures of the array. So we can talk to her about stuff and we're not in any trouble."

"Oh, that's good to know. I was going to let her walk in alone and see for herself and then not tell her anything. Everything she finds out on her own isn't on me. But it'll be nice not to have to mind what I'm saying." Kara paused, turning to look back at Angel. "How, exactly, do know about all this already? Is that part of your power set?"

"Oh, no," Angel said. "My aunt just told me."

"Your aunt?" Kara asked.

"Lady Vengeance," Yumi answered.

"Yeah." Angel nodded, as she gave Kara a thumbs-up.

"Well, okay then. It's that one." Kara pointed to the Isotopeter. "There on the end. If you could just pull it out into open space, that would make it a lot easier to get into the guts of it and get the drum out that needs replacing."

"No problem." Angel casually dropped her backpack as she walked between the rows of machines to the one Kara had indicated.

"Carefully," Friday said, as Angel reached out to take hold of the machine. "It's busted already, but it's priceless, and it's borrowed, and the plan is to be able to put it back together."

"Right. Got it." Angel took gentle hold of the machine, placing her fingertips on either side of the cabinet and pulling it slowly across the floor until it stood squarely in the middle of the walkway between the row of machines and the wall. "Like this?"

"Just like that," Kara replied. "Thank you. And welcome."

"Sure," Angel said. "Happy to help."

"Yeah, you're going to be good. Always nice to have somebody with super strength and super speed on the team. Also nice that you came pre-informed, so we don't have to—" Kara's voice trailed off at the sound of an unfamiliar beeping sound.

"What the—?" Yumi asked.

"Oh, shit." Kara dug her phone out of her pocket. "That's Cassidy's ring. You swear to me she's trustworthy?" she asked Friday, gesturing vaguely toward Angel.

"For sure," Friday said. "Yeah, she's cool."

"Okay, good." Kara poked the screen to answer and set it to speaker. "Hey, Cass. What's up?"

"I take it we're safe to talk?" Cassidy asked.

"Oh yeah," Kara said. "We're all here, Jaccob's not, and the employer is still out cold. We've got a new person here, but she got filled in already by someone who didn't have to sign an NDA, and since you didn't sign one either, I think we're all good."

"Cool," Cassidy said. "So my next question is: 'are you sitting down?' Because you are not going to believe what I'm about to tell you."

"Is this about the pictures from the security footage?" Kara asked.

"Yes and no," Cassidy replied.

"Yes *and* no?" Friday asked.

"I don't think any of you will be surprised that the bartender at Macky's said the men in the pictures could have been the men with the bad fifty," Cassidy replied.

"Not even a little bit," Kara said.

"Yeah," Cassidy said. "That's not the thing you need to be sitting down for. The big news is something Lumien found."

"Oh?" Kara asked.

"It seems there's a piano player working a Texas showroom who all sources say is supposed to be dead."

"Come again?" Friday piped up.

"As best Lumien or I can tell, this guy died in 1931. Lumien's done everything in his seemingly considerable power to out him as an impostor—trying to find any trace of who he was before he popped up on a marquee in Lapis, Texas—but there's nothing. This man showed up a couple of weeks ago, seemingly out of nowhere, and was apparently the star of the show the next day. And Lumien can't find any record of him before then."

"Except that he's supposed to be dead?" Lisa asked.

"Yeah, so, we've seen his face," Cassidy told them, "and he looks like the guy who died in 1931. And I don't mean I think that, I mean Lumien ran some software he has that says so. Look. Maybe it's nothing. Maybe he's just an impersonator. But Lumien did everything he could to trace this guy and prove he was an impersonator, and all clues lead to his not having existed until this show. Except for the ones that say he was born in 1894 and murdered in 1931. Lumien says there's no making sense of it, which to me says this warrants further investigating. If I was a time traveler looking to fuck with a music executive, snatching up a long-dead musician just before he was scheduled to be murdered is exactly the kind of thing I would do."

"Uh-huh," Kara said, "me too. That's definitely a lead worth chasing."

"I thought you'd think that."

"Thanks, Cassidy," Kara said. "Tell Lumien to pop everything he has into our cloud workspace, and I'll take a look."

"Okay, cool," Cassidy replied. "And if there are any developments, I'll keep you posted."

"All right. Talk to you later?"

"I'll call if there's anything."

"Cool. All right. Bye."

"Welp," Kara exhorted with a shrug, hanging up her phone and sliding it back into the pocket of her shorts. "Looks like we really do have to call Jaccob now."

"How come?" Yumi asked.

"Because as much as I will allow this guy in Texas could possibly be there as a result of time travel, he could just as easily be the kind of everyday impersonator known for playing hotel showrooms. Lumien did what he can do, and that's a good start, but before we jump the rest of the way to the conclusion Cassidy has already drawn, we should put his face through Starcom-level facial recognition software. And hologram detection. And I'm not talking about the off-the-shelf stuff. We're going to need to get the top tier, not for sale version, and the only legal place to get that is straight from the source."

"Wait, do you mean Jaccob Stevens?" Angel asked, brightening.

"Yes?" Kara quirked an eyebrow.

"Sorry, I'm kind of a fan." She looked a little like Lisa had upon seeing her a few minutes ago. "He's dreamy. For an old guy."

"You'll have to excuse her," Yumi said. "She's terminally heterosexual."

Lisa heaved a sigh—both relieved and a little disappointed.

"Can one of you send him a text?" Kara looked back at the Isotopeter and shook her head. "I'm sure I'm going to need his help getting this damned drum repaired, too. I'm gonna get started taking this side panel off so we can see what else is busted."

CHAPTER SIXTEEN

The headache should have been a bigger clue. It was the first thing Ruby was aware of when she awoke, and it was perhaps the most powerful headache she'd had in recent memory. Not long after that, she began to feel all the other aches, the tightness in her muscles, and the fact her mouth was maybe the driest it had ever been. But it was the heaviness in her limbs and eyelids that jogged her memory.

There had been a gunman. And she'd tried to stop him. As best she knew, she *had* stopped him. But she didn't really remember much.

This, though—this feeling—*this* she remembered. This was drain, and it was bad. The last time she'd felt this lousy at the hands of her own magic had been on the heels of her battle with the demon Azazel in hopes of rending Vivienne, and her building, from his clutches.

At least that time she'd remained conscious. Not so today, it appeared. She sat up slowly, on the wrong side of her bed, noticing as she did the number of flower arrangements displayed all around the room. Probably whoever had put her into bed had mentioned illness or injury to someone in the office. Bouquets had been known to appear at lightspeed on such occasions.

Ruby turned slowly, moving the covers aside as she slid her feet off the bed and onto the floor. Whoever had tucked her in had also changed her clothes, leaving her in only the slip she'd been wearing under her gray linen dress suit. She wondered if they'd taken it to the cleaners; if she'd passed out on the terrace, which she must have done, she could only hope her suit had survived its unexpected meeting with the flagstones.

The lights in her bedroom were off, and Ruby knew better than to try and use magic to turn them back on. When the drain hit this hard, she needed to go easy for at least a day or two. She reached over and switched on the lamp atop the near nightstand.

There were flowers there, too: a big bouquet of roses and peonies with a card that read "Feel better, Ginger, <3-V. P.S. If you don't like the arrangement, yell at me, not the florist." The smile that spawned made Ruby's head hurt worse, but she couldn't help herself. She'd have to find out how Vivienne got word and got flowers onto her nightstand so quickly.

There was another item on the nightstand, too. And this one didn't need a card. A familiar platinum bangle inlaid with diamonds sat in a hinged velvet box just beside the vase containing Vivienne's flowers. So Jaccob had been by; that was interesting. Not as interesting as, say, where her phone had wound up, but interesting nonetheless.

She lifted the bracelet from its box and looked at it closely. It was pristine, polished to a high shine, and its diamonds sparkled brilliantly in their settings. She hadn't remembered it well. Somehow her memory had dulled it with the satin of patina and turned the diamonds dim, small, and unimpressive. But that wasn't how she found it now. The bracelet was a thing of beauty, and a technological marvel, and the man who'd once cracked the hard shell of her heart had once again asked her to wear it for his peace of mind.

She had half a mind to put it on right now.

But she thought better of it. The bracelet's defining feature was the fragile hinge that would summon Stardust on the double were it to be damaged. And with the way she was feeling at the moment, she'd be as likely as not to break it just getting dressed.

Which she figured she really ought to do.

The small clock on her vanity, visible from where she sat, told Ruby it was ten 'til six, so she'd been out for a while. Suddenly, the only thing that mattered was finding out what had happened while she was down. She needed to know that Lisa, Yumi, Kara, and Friday had come through all right.

She got to her feet slowly, knowing well enough from experience that standing up too fast would mean either a powerful bout of nausea or passing out again, and she had no interest in inviting either of those outcomes.

As quickly as she could without aggravating her headache, Ruby made her way into her bathroom, where she brushed her teeth and wiped the mascara smudges from underneath her eyes before tossing back a pair of pain killers.

She found her phone on its cradle in her closet and tucked it under the belt of the simple black dress she pulled on over the slip she couldn't be bothered to change out of. She stepped into the first pair of black shoes she saw—low-heeled slingbacks—and combed her fingers through her hair. The glamour she tried to throw to combat the dark circles under her eyes made her head throb at the temples, and what was worse, it didn't land.

She'd have to do without any magic at all, probably at least until tomorrow. So she stopped by her vanity to dab on a bit of concealer before heading upstairs.

Stepping out of her bedroom, Ruby saw the first evidence that maybe things in the rest of the building might be worse than she feared. The wall of her hallway just beside the elevator was a gaping, jagged hole, exposing the open shaft and cables of the penthouse guest elevator. The damage to the sheetrock was easily large enough for a person to step through. Whatever had happened here couldn't have been good.

If this was any indication of the condition of the rest of her building, there was every chance the proverbial headache was about to be just as powerful as the literal one. Ruby did her best not to let her imagination run away with her as she waited for the elevator. She'd check in on the condition of her top floor, and hopefully grab a bottle of water from the fridge in the sitting room if all was well. Depending on what she found there, she'd start calling and texting accordingly.

Best not to jump to any conclusions. She could wait the three minutes to see the top floor with her own eyes.

If the place was a crime scene, Ruby wasn't sure what she was going to do about that. It felt like only yesterday the repairs had been completed in the wake of the demon occupation, and she absolutely did not relish the idea of going through another major reconstruction project so soon afterward—or *ever* if she was being honest with herself. But the damage outside her bedroom was enough to tell her she ought to brace for the worst.

She'd woken up in her own room, at least; that was good. Had the Tower taken too much damage from the intruders, she'd likely have been taken someplace else. The fact she was safe and sound and tucked into bed just three floors down from the scene of the attack allowed for the possibility her building remained sound.

But there was also a giant hole in the hallway outside her bedroom, so the inverse was equally likely to be the case.

More important, even, than the building were the four young women who'd been on the terrace with her. Ruby knew they were all in the hero business; that's how they'd wound up on this job to begin with. But she also knew Kara's great power was in technology, and Yumi had been concerned with her ability to summon her sword with Ruby's magical shielding in effect. As best she knew, Lisa had no real powers at all beyond smarts and organizational skills—more of a "woman in the chair" sort of cape, but she kept them all on task. And she had no real idea how Friday's powers worked outside her relationship to the goddess Freya.

Something she knew for sure about all of them was that none had been armed with a pistol. Or wearing a bulletproof vest.

Relief was awash over Ruby when she stepped from the elevator on the fiftieth floor and heard all four of their voices coming from the next room. She rounded the corner and was surprised to see the group of them in the war room, sorting through papers on both sides of a little table Ruby didn't remember having been there earlier. A fifth young woman she didn't recognize was there, too, casually lifting a metallic contraption that must have been ten times her own weight.

Jaccob was also with them. He sat on a rolling stool with his back to the door, dressed in gray chinos and a button-down shirt with its sleeves rolled up almost to his elbows. Ruby wasn't exactly surprised to see him; he'd been around a lot during this project. But seeing him sitting there working—the muscles in his forearms flexing as he fiddled with whatever was in front of him—stirred something in her she had no interest in paying attention to.

"Everything all right in here?" she called into the room.

Yumi sprang from her chair, Lisa whipped around to face Ruby, and Friday dropped the notepad she was holding. Jaccob nearly fell off his stool in his haste to turn in his seat.

"Oh!" the newcomer said. "Hi!" Which was immediately followed by her dropping the piece of equipment she'd been holding.

"Jesus!" Yumi exclaimed.

"You startled us," Lisa added.

"Apparently," Ruby replied.

The lot of them were clearly surprised to see her. Had they thought she'd be down for the night? And who the hell was the new arrival? Super strength, bit of a klutz, early 2000s Latin pop vibe with a hint of a modern edge. She seemed familiar, but Ruby's head was still foggy.

"It's good to see you," Kara said, rising from her seat as well, but with far less haste or apprehension. "But yeah, we're a little surprised you're here."

"How are you feeling?" Jaccob asked Ruby, standing slowly from his seat and beginning to walk toward her. The look on his face was something between terror and amazement, and he was approaching so slowly Ruby wondered whether she'd made a mistake by not spending more time fixing her face and her hair. She was sure she looked like hell, but that hadn't mattered much when she'd been worried about her people and her building.

Now that she could see everyone was all right, it was beginning to matter quite a lot.

"I suppose I've been better," she answered, hoping to mitigate the unease on Jaccob's face, and the obvious disquiet of the others as well.

"You should probably sit down," Lisa said.

"It's just a headache," Ruby replied. "And a little magic fatigue. It'll be fine."

"Do you know how long you've been unconscious?" Yumi asked her.

"Well, let's see," Ruby said. "It was just about two when we switched those machines on, and now it's nearly six. So ... four hours, give or take?"

"Yeah, no," Yumi said.

"I really think you should sit down." Lisa indicated the nearest chair. "Please?"

"What's going on here?" Ruby asked. "Why are you all looking at me like I've suddenly grown a second nose or something? And while we're at it, would someone like to introduce me to the new girl?"

"Hi." The blonde Latina stepped forward and put out her hand. "I'm Angel ... er ... A-Girl. I'm ... um ... Vivienne's niece?"

"Well, would you look at that." Ruby took the proffered hand and shook it briefly. Quite a grip this Angel had. "And here I was impressed she'd managed to get flowers here so quickly. Now I come to find out she sent me a whole blonde."

Angel smiled. "Well yeah, an impervious one, too. She said some assholes were shooting at you. And that you tended to get shot when that happens? Something about not taking cover like a normal person?"

"That sounds like Vivienne," Ruby said. "She's told me about you, a little. But apparently not about how fast you can fly. It seems you made record time getting here from Seattle."

"Ruby," Jaccob said, placing his hand on her elbow, "Angel didn't get here all that quickly, and you weren't just out for a few hours. The attack happened at two o'clock on Tuesday. It's almost six on Friday. You've been in a coma for three days."

"Three days?" That certainly explained everyone's surprise at her having turned up in the war room. Things were making sense now. "No wonder I'm thirsty."

"Let me get you some water," Jaccob said, squeezing her elbow before dashing away toward the mini fridge in the sitting room.

"That would be lovely." Ruby turned to the others and asked, "How much coffee has he had today?" as quietly as possible once she figured Jaccob was out of earshot.

"Probably too much," Friday said.

"He's just been really worried about you," Lisa told her. "I mean ... we all have. Please will you sit down?"

"Why don't we all go sit down?" Kara suggested. "There have been some developments in the past few days. I feel like we ought to get you updated, if you're up to it."

"Sitting down and hearing an update?" Ruby gestured for the others to follow her as she turned and headed into the sitting room, "I think I can handle that. Can we start with what happened to my wall downstairs?"

Jaccob intercepted Ruby on the way to the sofa, placing an already-opened bottle of her preferred variety of sparkling water into her hand and making the rest of the walk just behind her. She took a seat on the near sofa, and Jaccob sidled up next to her.

"That was my fault," he confessed. "You were unconscious, I wasn't thinking, and I got into the elevator on the helipad completely forgetting it wasn't supposed to open on the forty-eighth floor. I was able to override the car and get it to stop, but there wasn't a door, and it seemed like the fastest thing to just blast through the wall. I've already made some calls about getting it repaired."

"And here I thought having a specific insurance rider for Stardust-related structural damage felt excessive."

Jaccob's face turned red, and Ruby tried her best not to laugh.

"I told Arsho to send me the bill," he said. "So at least your premium won't go up."

"Well, thank heaven for small blessings," Ruby said, sipping at her water bottle as she shook her head.

"Anybody else want a water?" Yumi ducked behind the bar.

"Nah," Kara said, just as Friday said, "I'm good."

"I'll take one." Lisa turned to Ruby. "Is there anything else you want? Food? Juice? Coffee? I can call down, so you don't have to." She took the seat on Ruby's other side and pulled her phone from her pocket.

"No, thank you," Ruby said. "But I appreciate the offer. And I'm impressed at how well you're adapting to life in the Tower. We may make a junior executive of you yet."

Lisa beamed at the comment, and Ruby smiled back at her. Yumi was there with the water just a moment later. She handed a bottle to Lisa then settled in on the other sofa where Kara, Friday, and Angel were already sitting.

"So you say there've been developments," Ruby said, raising her eyebrows as she brought the bottle to her lips.

The rest of them nodded.

"There's a lot," Kara said. "Jaccob, you've heard most of this. Unless you really want to stick around for a second recap, it's probably a better use of your time to keep working on the drum."

"Oh." Jaccob snapped his head around to look at Kara. "Yeah. I think I'm going to take it over to my machine shop. I'll have an easier time figuring out if it's fixable over there, and if it's not, I'll get started right away on fabricating the replacement."

"Drum?" Ruby asked.

"When the attackers landed on the helipad," Lisa said, "all the machines were registering off the charts."

"Evidence those things are connected?" Ruby surmised.

"That's the hypothesis," Kara said. "But it's just a single data point. Not enough to know for sure."

"And when everything went all bonkers," Lisa added, "a bunch of stuff wound up broken. We've spent the last three days trying to put it all back together."

"Angel's super strength has come in really handy when we've needed to move stuff," Friday said, "but some of the parts need to be replaced."

"Enter your neighborhood tech billionaire, his mechanical prowess, and that fancy damn machine shop he has next door," Kara said, once again looking at Jaccob pointedly.

"And you think you can fix it?" Ruby asked Jaccob as he stood.

"I think so, yeah. And, like I said, if I can't manage to fix it, I've got the means to make a new one. One way or another, we'll have a new cylinder this weekend." Jaccob set his hand gently on Ruby's shoulder. "It's good to see you," he said softly. To the others, he added, "I'll bring the drum over as soon as it's done," before heading back into the war room to retrieve the item on his way out.

"Is he all right?" Ruby asked.

"Hell if I know," Kara said.

"I think the shooting freaked him out," Yumi said. "He's been kind of all over the place: keeping odd hours, sucking extra bad at video games, barely talking to us even when he's over here. But he seemed to perk up when you came in; I think he'll be okay now."

Friday nodded. "You're alive and kicking, there's extra security on the roof, we've got Angel with us for extra personal security, and he's got a gizmo to tinker with. I say give him a day or two, and he'll probably be back to normal."

"For that very specific, Jaccob Stevens value of 'normal'," Ruby retorted.

The other five laughed.

"Now." Ruby looked pointedly at Kara. "Developments."

"Right," Kara replied. "I have to preface this by saying I'm not sure we're ready to draw conclusions yet, but all signs point to those men on the roof having an energy disruption signature in common with whoever sent you that mysterious email."

"Energy disruption signature?"

"There's a shape," Kara explained, "a pattern created by the combination of tracings the Ometer generates. It's a way the convergence of the different measurements expresses itself. And a series of correlating readings from several of the other instruments."

"I think I'm following," Ruby said.

"Well," Kara continued, "it turns out the machines were running in Professor Kummerfeldt's lab the day you got that email. And the tracing from when the shooters landed is too similar to be coincidental."

"But you're not ready to draw conclusions?"

"I think it's safe to say the two things are related," Kara replied. "And also related to a story we heard in The Hollows about a couple of men trying to pass a fifty-dollar bill with a date on it that said it hadn't been minted yet. Everyone mostly wrote it off as bad counterfeiting, but there's a tracing that lines up with right around that time—the same day you got the email that kicked this whole thing off."

"Sounds like you may be onto something."

"We may be," Kara replied, "because there's more."

"There is?"

"Yeah," Kara said. "There's one more ingredient, but we haven't verified it yet, and I don't want to jump to any conclusions."

"How soon will you know?" Ruby asked.

"Maybe tonight," Kara replied. "At least we hope so. In the meantime, we're working on getting the array repaired."

"How bad is the damage?" Ruby crossed her arms over her chest.

"Not *bad* bad," Kara answered her. "At least not as bad as we first thought. It mostly looks like the whole system just overloaded. That is, several of the machines look to have gotten a higher load of whatever it is they measure than they were designed to cope with. A lot of fried wiring and a couple of cracked screens—all stuff we've been able to put back together pretty easily. One of them busted an ink reservoir and lost a few of its tracing needles, and then there's that cracked drum Jaccob's working on."

"So," Ruby said, taking another sip from her bottle of water, "we can, at least, draw the conclusion that whatever that was that landed on my roof is possibly connected to the email?"

"Yes, ma'am," Lisa said. "That part we're pretty sure about. It's whether we have a lead to chase to find out more that we're not ready to commit to yet. It has to do with something Lumien uncovered. But we don't know yet whether it's a real thing that's worth chasing. And we're also not sure if switching on the array somehow sent out a signal, and that's why the shooters showed up when and where they did. We're working to get it fixed so we can switch it back on and see whether they show up again."

"Security came up and put in additional cameras," Friday told her. "And Jaccob says he's been working on field emitters and a targeted EMP, so if they do show up again, we should have an easier time dealing with them."

"And you also have me," Angel said. "Super speed and super strength. And as I mentioned, I'm bulletproof, so—"

"Yes, I can see where that might help," Ruby said. "But first you've got to get the machines fixed?"

"We're working on it," Kara assured her.

"We thought we were almost done," Lisa added. "But then Kara looked inside the Isotopeter and found the cracked drum."

"So we're just waiting on Jaccob?" Ruby asked.

"Not entirely," Lisa said.

"Not yet," Kara corrected her. "The rest of the machines are mostly ready. We'll need to fill the replacement inkwell and do some calibration on the Ometer. And there are still a few wires that need running inside the Isotopeter before we'll be able to slot the drum back into place and finish rebuilding the motor. But most of that should be done tonight. And then we'll just be waiting on Jaccob."

"All right," Ruby said, "Good. And this other thing? The Lumien thing?"

"We're working on that, too," Kara said. "I may have word as soon as tomorrow. I just don't want to move on something if there's any chance it could be a false alarm."

"I suppose that makes sense," Ruby said. "We have quite enough to deal with already—with a blown array and a giant hole in my wall—not to waste our time chasing wild geese."

"My thoughts exactly," Kara said. "We're going to hang out here for a few more hours, get the rest of the machinery put back together. Then I'm going to head downstairs and spend some time on this other problem. We first got wind of it yesterday, and I had Jaccob bring over some software that should be done installing by now. Provided that's all working when I get downstairs, I'll spend the rest of the night verifying our suspicion and hopefully have something for you by morning."

"Good," Ruby said, finishing her water and setting the empty bottle on the table in front of her. "But don't work too late. I'm not paying you enough for you to pull an all-nighter."

"With all due respect, ma'am, yes you are," Kara said. "And even if you weren't, I want to get to the bottom of this. Because if it turns out this thing is what we think it is, then we'll have a real, serious lead to chase that just might get us closer to the answers we're looking for."

"Well, I do like the sound of that." Ruby smiled at Kara as she stood, prompting the others to stand as well. "I'll let you get back to work. I apparently have three days' worth of emails to catch up on, in addition to a seemingly unshakeable headache and sudden but overwhelming urge to bathe. Let me know in the morning if you get anywhere."

"Will do," Kara assured her.

Ruby nodded as she walked away. Three days in a coma was a lot to process, as was the revelation the attack was likely related to their ongoing investigation. That Jaccob had been noticeably worried was also interesting.

But first things first. She'd take another dose of pain killers, get in the bathtub, and call Vivienne. She'd been worried enough to not only send flowers but also her super-powered niece. It would be unkind not to let her know she was back up and about. She didn't like the idea of Angel getting that news to Vivienne before she could.

Then a glance at work, a bit of a nightcap, and early to bed. The only remedy for drain this bad was rest, and she intended to get plenty.

But first, a bath.

CHAPTER SEVENTEEN

Ruby awoke to a text from Kara saying there was more to discuss around the Lumien situation. She'd said she hoped to have something by morning, and apparently she did. Excellent. Ruby messaged back inviting Kara and the others to brunch, then alerted the kitchen to the plan once her invitation had been accepted.

The staff set things up in the formal dining room. Platters of meats, cheeses, pastries, and soft-boiled eggs, along with carafes of juices, bottles of prosecco, and pots of tea and coffee, were waiting for Ruby when she arrived. The cook's assistant offered her a bellini off a silver tray, and she took it gladly before dismissing the young woman back to the kitchen.

This was a work meeting, not a formal party, and Ruby had seen how uncomfortable some of her employees got in the presence of household staff. Best to let them serve themselves and avoid the topic coming up.

All five young women arrived at the same time, dressed in very individual interpretations of appropriate attire for a business brunch.

"Come in. Have a seat. Everything's on platters," Ruby told the five of them as they claimed chairs. "Just help yourselves."

"Wow," Yumi said, taking stock of the spread on the table. "This looks amazing."

"My chef likes breakfast," Ruby replied, "and I never eat it. So I'm sure she had a good time putting this together. We've also got bellinis, orange, apple, grapefruit, and tomato juice, plus coffee and sparkling water. If you want anything else to drink—cider, vodka, what have you, I can call down."

"I think this will be fine," Lisa replied. "More than adequate."

"Glad you approve. Once you're all settled, I'm anxious to hear what Miss Sparx has to tell me. But first—" Ruby turned and looked at Angel where she sat on the opposite side of the table. "Miss DeSantes."

"Me!" Angel perked up. She had only just taken hold of the pitcher of orange juice. The sound of her name must have pulled her focus, as the glass vessel slipped from her hand, canting sideways as it began to fall.

The whiff of magic Ruby sent to right the carafe as it landed made her eyes ache, but it was worth it not to have the whole meeting derailed by soggy pastries and a ruined tablecloth. She took a deep breath and nodded before looking back at Angel.

The young hero's eyes were wide, and her hands were folded contritely in her lap.

"I have spoken to your aunt," Ruby said to her, choosing to address neither her clumsiness nor the magic that spared the group its consequences. "While she did admit to having sent you here, she wasn't exactly forthcoming as to why. Vivienne being Vivienne, I'm not terribly surprised at her inability to tell the whole truth, but the fact remains I feel like I'm missing some vital information. So I'm going to need you to fill me in."

"Well, Angel's impervious to pretty much everything," Friday said. "She's been on bodyguard duty for us ever since she got here."

"She mentioned as much yesterday," Ruby said, "as did Vivienne on the telephone. And I have no doubts as to her possible utility. I'm merely trying to gauge motivation."

"Miss Killingsworth," Angel said, pushing her chair back and standing from her seat to address Ruby. "Honestly? Aunt V sent me because she heard what happened and it kind of freaked her out. And when she told me about what was going on, what she said was that you'd used your magic to stop a bunch of bullets and that you'd knocked yourself out in the process. She said your magic is powerful enough to stop bullets, but also it's sophisticated enough that blunt force casting like that is kind of a waste—especially when you've got someone like me who can just take the bullets for you and leave you and your magic available for nuance and finesse."

"Vivienne said that?" Ruby asked her dubiously. "She used the words 'nuance', 'finesse', and 'sophisticated' in the same sentence?"

"She did."

"And she sent you here to take bullets for me?"

"Yes, ma'am."

"And do you always listen when Vivienne tells you to put yourself in the line of fire to protect someone of her acquaintance?"

Angel shook her head. "No, ma'am."

"Then how about you tell me why you did so this time, and we can start this conversation over from an honest place?"

Angel frowned. She hung her head for a moment and sighed before shrugging and looking back up at Ruby. "Truth be told, Miss Killingsworth, I've kind of been trying to get an introduction ever since I found out you and Aunt V knew each other. I don't know if you know this—that is, I don't know if it's risen to the level of your notice—but I'm an entertainer."

"You're A-Girl. Correct?"

"Yeah," Angel said. "Um, yes. I am."

"I've heard 'Glow'. It's not bad."

"Oh," Angel said. "Thanks?"

"I love that song," Lisa said, looking nervous again. "It is literally my favorite song." At least she was talking.

"It is," Yumi said. "She plays it, like, ten times every day."

Angel flushed a little, which was adorable. "I mean, in addition to all the hero stuff ... I did a movie where I played my mom. And I do some music stuff."

"Selling out the Showbox isn't 'some music stuff'," Yumi contended.

"I watched that whole live stream!" Lisa's eyes had gone wide. "Twice! It was *amazing*."

Ruby smiled faintly. A fan. That made sense.

"Anyway," Angel said. "I thought that, if I got to meet you, we could talk about it. You make people into stars, and if that's what I want to be, then you're the best person to get to know to help make that happen. So when Aunt V said you could use somebody bulletproof on your team, I thought this might be my chance."

"And?"

"And I want to help," Angel said. "Once I got here and I saw it was Yumi and Friday working on this—they're my friends—I got kind of excited at the possibility of a team-up with people I actually like. So ... yeah. I came here partly for selfish reasons. But I really do think I can help. And I want to help. So, please, can I help?"

Lisa made a little "eep" sound and covered her mouth with both hands.

"I appreciate your honesty," Ruby said. "And the fact of the matter is I hadn't thought ahead to the possibility of needing as much muscle as you bring, but indeed it has presented itself. It'll be Monday morning before we can get the contracts in place, and I can't promise you anything entertainment-related will come of this. But if you'd like to stay and work with us for the duration of this crisis, then I'm happy to have you."

Angel's whole bearing bounced upward, enough so that she hovered for a moment, a cushion of pink energy appearing beneath the soles of her sneakers. "Thank you! I won't let you down."

The others seemed almost as pleased as Angel was—Yumi springing from her chair to clink her champagne glass against Angel's, and Lisa doing a little fist pump. Friday and Kara raised their glasses as well.

"You're welcome," Ruby replied stoically, taking the opportunity to sip at her champagne with the others.

"Now," she said at length. "For the original reason we're gathered. Miss Sparx, what is it you have for me?"

"There's a lot." Kara took two eggs and a silver egg cup from the serving dish. "To recap super quickly," she began as she started in on cracking the egg in the cup, "we had a really distinctive reading on the Ometer when the attackers landed on the roof—it was the last reading we got before needles started flying off and everything basically started breaking. Then, when we went back through old tracing tapes from the machine, we found several smaller instances of similar readings. Best guess was same thing but lower amplitude."

"Yes," Ruby said, "I remember you telling me that."

"Now," Kara continued, taking a bite of her egg, then pausing to add salt and pepper to it, "from the best we're able to tell, amplitude is distance."

"That makes sense," Ruby replied. "So it looks like there's a pattern? Like whatever happened here on Tuesday is just an extreme example of something that's happened several times before?"

"That's just it," Lisa said, unfolding a linen napkin into her lap. "Maybe not an extreme example. Maybe it was an identical example at extreme proximity. Because the one from the day of the shooting is the biggest tracing of the shape in question, but the *second biggest* is from the day you got the email, which also possibly lines up with the fifty-dollar bill thing."

"I see," Ruby replied. "You're saying these incursions may be regular things, recorded at varying amplitudes based on the event's proximity to the array."

"Yes, ma'am!" Yumi snagged a pastry off a silver tray.

"While that makes sense, it's little more than you told me yesterday. What is it you learned last night?" she asked pointedly in Kara's direction. "What's the new thing I needed to hear this morning?"

"It pertains to what Lumien found," Kara said.

"I'm presuming you're about to tell me he's uncovered something useful? Because, although I don't mind feeding you all, if it was a dead end, this meeting could have been an email."

"I don't think we can declare anything useful just yet," Kara replied, popping a croquette into her mouth. "But what we've got is definitely interesting."

"I'm not sure my constitution can take much more *interesting*," Ruby said.

"That's understandable," Angel asserted.

"Care to elaborate, Miss Sparx?" Ruby asked then, reaching for the carafe of bellini.

"Yeah." Kara leaned back in her chair and crossed her arms over her chest. "This all goes back to the clues we found in the Professor's paperwork."

"In the tracings?"

"Exactly. My methodology on this is, if we take the readings from the day of the attack as our base ... our zero, and the readings from the day of the email to represent a radius as wide as the farthest point in the city from where the instruments were at the University, then we can postulate the distance from the Professor's lab to any of the incidents the tapes recorded. When we triangulate from that data, we have distances to add to the dates and times the machines recorded. When we plug in those distances, more than half of them would put the incursions in the middle of the ocean, which helped narrow down the search. We were just about to get started checking local news and blogs for every place on dry land one of these tracings might have led us to when Lumien found something he thought was worth passing along. And, as it just so happens, what he found lines up exactly with one of the tracings."

"And?" Ruby asked expectantly.

"And there's a musician headlining a residency down in Texas who's supposed to be dead," Friday blurted out before Kara had the chance to say anything more. "Sorry, it's just ... wild. I didn't mean to step on your explanation, Kara."

"It's fine," Kara said. She turned back to Ruby and shrugged. "I didn't want to tell you until you had context."

"All right, I'm listening." Ruby folded her hands around the stem of her glass and leaned back in her chair, sipping at her bellini with her eyebrows raised.

Throughout Kara's long explanation, the group slowed down in terms of eating—all except Angel, who seemed to take that as an indication she should start finishing off each and every platter.

"His name's Simon Floyd," Kara said. "He's a piano player, and everything I can find says he died in 1931."

"And that's not, like, a rumor," Angel said, piling the last of the bacon onto her plate from the gilded platter. "It's not like a 'Paul was the Walrus', 'bare feet on the album cover' kind of thing. He has an obituary. We read it."

"And he's playing a residency in Texas?" Ruby leaned forward and set down her half-empty bellini, snatching up the Prosecco and topping off the glass without bothering to add any more peach. The idea of yet another time-traveling musical act was more than she wanted to think about sober.

"That's what it looks like," Lisa said. "Five shows a week, starring a dead guy."

"And," Kara continued, "his show opened not long after one of these events we've been looking at, one that happens to be right on the bullseye of where one of these data sets is pointing."

"So, it stands to reason," Yumi said, "that whoever is behind this went back in time, snatched this guy up right before somebody murdered him, then brought him to Texas and put him on stage."

"Starcom has some really excellent, and I mean accurate-to-the-point-of-terrifying, facial recognition technology," Kara told Ruby. "That's the stuff I had installing on my machine when we talked yesterday. And based on what we've gotten from that, either this guy in Texas is really who he claims to be, or he's had some truly excellent plastic surgery. The match is that close. And I don't know if you know this about me, but I'm kind of an expert in holograms, and I can tell you our man isn't using any."

"And I take it I'm not the only one presuming this fellow was nowhere near famous enough to warrant an impersonator with this level of dedication?" Ruby asked.

"Yeah," Kara replied. "Pretty much."

"Is there any unexplored chance he's doing this with tech?" Ruby asked. "I know those things exist. Jaccob once used a gizmo like that to make Vivienne look exactly like his ex-wife."

"He did *what*?" Angel asked, the look on her face making it very clear to the rest of the group what she thought about that.

Ruby chuckled. "Nothing so interesting as what I presume you're thinking. They were trying to foil an assassin. Which they did."

"Tech like that can fool most people, even me ... sometimes," Kara said. "But it leaves traces on camera. Most humans wouldn't be able to spot those, either. But the software Jaccob lent me absolutely can. And there's nothing."

"So if this was the kind of thing Jaccob could make, it would also be the kind of thing Jaccob's stuff could spot?"

"Yes. And Lumien is an extra layer of surety," Kara added. "If this was tech, we'd know. Which means we know it isn't."

"I'm going to trust you on the tech front," Ruby said, "and move on to my next question. Magic can do this, you know? A proper glamour from a sophisticated enough sorcerer can make anyone look like anyone else. Could that be what you're seeing?"

"I guess it could be," Kara replied.

"But why?" Lisa chimed in.

Ruby looked to her. "I beg your pardon?"

"Why?" Lisa seemed to overcome her star-struck hesitation when there was a mystery on the table. "Why this musician? Why now? If he's an imposter, then what's his motivation? That's the part I don't get. We just watched you knock yourself out with magic, and I can't imagine a person making themself into a whole other person would be easy. So if it is magic, then what on earth is this guy's reasoning for turning himself into this particular, not-terribly-famous-when-he-was-really-alive piano player? Because he's not just doing it for the hour he's on stage every night—he's walking around like that all the time."

"He could just be crazy," Yumi said.

"What?" Lisa asked.

"Like an obsessed fan," Yumi replied. "Like a total weirdo. Like the biggest fan this guy ever had who just happens to have been born years after he died. Some kind of misunderstood swing dance jazz geek who decided he wanted to be Simon Floyd when he grew up and then found a way to make it happen."

"While I will acknowledge madness is always a possibility in cases such as this," Ruby allowed, "it still sounds like this is something worth investigating. You said he was headlining five shows a week." Ruby turned in her seat to look at Kara. "Where is that? What's the venue?"

"Hold on," Kara replied, taking out her phone, "I have it. Here it is. He's playing the showroom at someplace called the Golden Century in Lapis, Texas."

"Lapis, Texas?" Angel said. "I don't think I've ever heard of that place."

"Consider yourself lucky," Ruby replied. "Lapis, Texas, is where good taste goes to die. Imagine everything obnoxious about country and western music, turn the volume up to eleven, then spray paint it gold, and you'll have an idea of the town's aesthetic. It's where geriatric has-beens spend their twilight years and ambitious up-and-comers try to one-up each other without having to resort to auto-tune."

"Sounds awful," Friday said.

"It is awful." Ruby once again poured her glass full of prosecco. "The whole town is awful. But I find it interesting he's playing the Golden Century, of all possible places."

"Why is that?" Lisa asked.

"Because that's where the company puts people up in Lapis. I've been twice myself. Arranging travel and accommodation should be no problem."

"So you think we should go?" Yumi asked.

"I do."

"If you'd like," Lisa said, pulling her phone from her pocket, "I can book all our tickets. I presume you'd rather fly first class ... if you tell me when you're hoping to leave, I can look—"

"I don't fly commercial unless Vivienne makes me," Ruby interrupted her. "I happen to own several aircraft; transportation won't be a problem. My scheduler can handle our travel. A usual trip to Lapis is a Monday mid-day flight and a Wednesday return; plan for that unless I tell you otherwise."

"Oh my. It's really hot in Texas." Lisa turned her phone around so the others could see the "92" on her screen.

"That it is. I am presuming the five of you may not have appropriate clothing for the climate. And on top of that, I'm also presuming none of you has ever been a VIP at a dinner show in an inexcusably pretentious five-star resort and are thusly lacking the wardrobe for that as well. So I'm going to send you to see my girl at J. Dene. Her name is Catherine, her assistant is Elle, and between the two of them, they'll get the five of you all fixed up. And I see the look on your face, Miss Yamamoto," she added, shaking her head at Lisa as she continued typing on her phone. "This will all be on my account. No need to worry about the expense."

"Oh," Lisa said. "Yes, ma'am. Thank you."

"You can head down whenever you're ready," Ruby told them. "I'll have a driver meet you."

"Wait," Friday said. "You mean you want us to go right *now*?"

"Finish breakfast first," Ruby replied. "But yes. Nothing fits anyone directly off the rack, and even on a rush job, tailors need time to work. So the sooner the better."

"Yeah," Lisa said. "Okay."

"I mean it, though," Ruby said, standing from her seat. "Eat your fill. You can take your drinks with you. I'll send instructions to the boutique; they'll be waiting whenever you arrive. I'll have Jillian get your itinerary to you as soon as it's final. In the meantime, handle your shopping and get your things packed. I'll see you on Monday. And Angel, you'll want to be prepared for an early morning. Brunch is one thing, but I'd rather not have you getting on the plane without a properly executed contract. Your reputation precedes you, dear, and my insurance policies are very particular about such things." Ruby turned on her heel then and was out of the room before Angel had a chance to reply.

~

There were enough nerves between the bunch of them that brunch was over rather quickly, and with very little additional chatter. The food was good enough to hold their attention and keep their mouths busy until all five of their phones sounded simultaneously, announcing the car waiting for them outside.

"I didn't know she had my number," Angel said quietly.

"Yeah," Friday said back, topping off her glass with juice, "she's creepy as fuck. You get used to it."

Angel finished off the last of the pastries, then the five of them left the formal dining room and turned toward the stairs they'd taken down from the fiftieth floor to get there. The dining room was on the penthouse's middle level, the forty-ninth floor, and the elevator they normally took only had access to fifty. This morning had been the first non-emergency trip the group had made into the lower floors of their employer's penthouse, and both those times, they'd taken their usual route to the top and the stairs down from there.

"Think we could just take this elevator?" Angel asked, pointing to the subtle call button built into the wall on their way to the stairs.

"I don't know," Yumi answered. "Ya think?"

Angel shrugged. She went over and pushed the button, pointing at it when it lit up.

"If I understood Jaccob when he set us up with access," Kara said, "if this elevator shows up, we're allowed to take it."

"Yeah," Lisa said, gesturing to the light on the call button as it went out. "I don't think Miss Killingsworth would expect us to take the stairs back up a floor just to take a different elevator to the street level."

"You sure about that?" Friday asked, as the doors to the lift slid open.

"I'm sure it's here," Kara said, shrugging as she stepped aboard. "And I'm sure as hell not going to stand there and let it leave without me."

The others followed her into the car. This elevator was something else. A funhouse of reflective surfaces, the interior of the elevator was nothing but polished chrome on all sides, hung with a set of actual mirrors on both the doors and back. And it was tiny. It was a tight squeeze for five people; clearly Miss Killingsworth never intended this elevator to accommodate multiple passengers.

It was a short ride to the ground floor, but the car was still so cramped the five of them were plenty happy to clamber out of it when the doors opened. They dashed through the little marble-clad lobby and out onto the sidewalk beneath the green velvet awning to see their ride waiting for them.

What Miss Killingsworth had described as "a car" was, in fact, a stretched Mercedes S-class painted dark gray with mirror-tinted windows and a driver standing by to open the door for them. With varying degrees of surprise and excitement, the five of them climbed in and made themselves comfortable.

The ride to the shop, an all-but unmarked boutique in Regency Heights, was smooth and short. The group was met at the door by a gentleman who introduced himself as the shop's manager and a younger man who kept silent but handed each of them a bottle of sparkling water as they passed. They followed the manager up a set of stairs and into a cozy nook on the upper floor, where they were invited to sit on a too-large, disturbingly modern, black buttoned-leather sofa that easily fit all five of them with room to spare.

Reactions to all this were mixed. For two out of the five—Friday and especially Lisa—they only knew from television that stores like this existed, but being inside one was so far out of their experience, neither of them was sure how to react. Yumi and Angel were both more used to situations like this, and they had an easy time enjoying themselves. Kara, by contrast, seemed totally neutral toward all of it.

It was only a moment before Catherine made her appearance. A Rubenesque lightbulb of a woman, she was golden-haired and rosy-cheeked and dressed from head to toe in colorful layers of silk and chiffon. She wore large gold earrings, necklaces of varying lengths, and bangles on both her wrists. If a person could exist as the aesthetic opposite of Ruby Killingsworth, this woman was it.

"Hello, ladies!" she greeted the five of them. "This is your first time shopping with us, is it not?"

"Um." Between the presence of Angel and the whole vibe of the shop, Lisa could barely form words.

"Yes," Yumi said. She put her hand on Lisa's knee. "This is her first time doing anything like this at all."

Lisa mouthed a quiet "thank you."

"Well, all right then," Catherine said. "Welcome in. Can we offer anyone a drink?"

All five of them looked down at the unopened bottles of water they'd been handed upon arrival and frowned.

"The guy downstairs already did that," Kara told her then.

"All right," Catherine replied. "Miss Killingsworth is partial to crémant while she's shopping, but she's also never here before noon, so I wasn't sure. If anyone changes their mind, just let a staff member know, and we'll get that right to you. Now, I understand we're headed to a Texas showroom full of pretentious nincompoops, is that right?"

"I guess?" Friday replied. Ruby hadn't mentioned anything about pretentious nincompoops, but it sounded plausible.

"Well," Catherine said, "We'll get the five of you all set. Elle will be up in just a moment with a tape, and while she gets your measurements, we'll have a chat about your personal style and what kinds of things you like to wear. Then we'll start pulling pieces and get to work. The fitting rooms are just behind me." She gestured to a narrow hallway with a curtain swagged to its side. "If you'd like to go and get changed, Elle will be right with you."

Before anyone could respond, Catherine was gone again, through a door they hadn't seen just beside the giant mirror the sofa was facing.

"Get changed into what?" Lisa asked, clearly confused.

"I've been to this kind of place before," Angel said offhandedly. "There's probably a robe in the fitting room."

With an "eep," Lisa clammed up and took shelter behind Yumi.

Angel, who was admiring herself in the mirror, didn't seem to notice. She brushed her hair back with one hand and bit her lip.

"Huh," Kara said, standing up and shrugging as she moved toward the hallway Catherine had indicated.

The five of them found their way into the fitting rooms, where, in fact, knee-length robes of taupe satin waited for them. As promised, Catherine's assistant, Elle, a tall, visibly muscular, raven-haired beauty, joined them presently and began taking down measurements.

The whole process felt a bit invasive, but none of them actually complained, at least not to the boutique's employees. The conversations were mostly limited to what kinds of things each of them liked to wear normally and how they saw themselves going into this show in Texas.

Most of them didn't have the heart to say they had absolutely no idea, although Kara was bold enough to mention her dislike of dresses. Only Angel had a list of preferences and tastes, which Elle noted dutifully. It was only after the sales staff had left them to pull try-on items that it occurred to anyone just how fast things were moving.

"Um ... guys?" Yumi addressed the others loudly enough she hoped she could be heard in her fellows' respective dressing rooms.

"What is it, Yumi?" Angel asked.

"Well," Yumi said, "apparently we're all going to Texas on Monday, and we're going to a fancy show to see if the guy who's starring in it is actually supposed to be dead and maybe traveled through time. But do we have any idea what we're supposed to ... ya know ... *do* with him when we get there?"

"What do you mean?" Kara asked.

"I mean—" Yumi pulled open the curtain at the front of her fitting room and leaned against the wall. "How are we going to know for sure whether or not this is our guy and what are we supposed to do if we figure out it's him?"

"That's a good question," Angel said, also stepping into the doorway of her fitting room. "I mean, I guess I could rough him up a little? Grab hold of him and fly really, really high and threaten to drop him if he doesn't tell me the truth. But if that's the plan, then I'll need to wear my A-Girl costume under my dress, which means the measurements that lady just took don't work anymore."

"You know, I hadn't thought that far. Give me a second." Kara pulled her phone from the pocket of her borrowed robe and shot off a text. "This whole thing is the boss's idea, and if she has more ideas, we better—"

A reply came almost immediately.

"Client says she's got it handled," Kara said.

"What?" Lisa asked, finally poking her head through the fitting room curtain.

"I just sent her a text," Kara explained, also drawing back the curtain on her fitting room. "She said, and I quote: 'We can talk details tomorrow. He'll tell me who he is, what happened, and where he came from. Because I won't give him any other choice.' Sounds like the short answer is 'magic'."

"Y'all don't find her just a little bit terrifying?" Friday asked, coming out of her fitting room to sit on a nearby ottoman.

"Oh, absolutely," Kara agreed. "I'm real glad we're on the same side."

"For the moment," Friday said.

"Do you all think it's a good idea to just let that be the plan?" Lisa asked, moving to join Friday on the ottoman.

"It's her gig," Kara reminded her. "It's her plan, it's her magic."

"Yeah, but," Lisa countered, "her magic is what knocked her into a coma she just woke up from. Don't you think we should maybe come up with some ways to try and keep that from happening again?"

"I think she's the client." Kara cracked open the water bottle she'd left on the end table. "I think she's in charge. And I also think she's an adult. She doesn't need us to take care of her."

"I'm just saying—"

"Lisa does have a point," Yumi said. "I don't think it would be good for any of us if our boss was to wind up having a magic-related medical crisis in a hotel in Texas."

"Yeah, that's fair," Kara said. "Let me see what I can do about loading the facial recognition program onto something portable. And maybe I can even get my hands on some magic detection software—I know there's a guy in Colorado who's been doing some heavy work in that area. I'll set us up as best we can to answer every possible question with tech. She'll only need the magic if, after all that, all signs still point to this guy being who we think he is."

"Sounds good," Angel said. "I'll plan on packing my costume but not wearing it under my dress. If I have to, I can get changed pretty quickly. Super speed and all that."

"Yeah," Lisa said. "That works. It's a good plan. Kara makes sure it's worthwhile to use magic in the first place, and we have Angel standing by in case Miss Killingsworth needs backup or rescue."

"That's probably the best we're gonna do," Kara said with a nod. "Now, let's enjoy the rest of this day. Somebody look up what crémant is so we can decide if we want some."

CHAPTER EIGHTEEN

Ruby couldn't quite believe it when she realized she'd be blessedly alone all afternoon. It had only been a few short weeks, but she'd already forgotten what it was like to have the apartment all to herself with no chance of intrusion. It was, in fact, her preferred way to pass the time, and she was pleased to have found herself in such a state. She had a cloud full of tracks to listen to while she made a packing list for her housekeeper and a dolcetto in an ice bucket waiting for her to pop the cork.

It would make for a lovely way to spend a Saturday, result in a decent amount of catch-up following her brief incapacitation, and offer her enough peace and rest to hopefully shake the last of the malaise still clinging to her from the recent unpleasantness. The day was even just overcast enough she wouldn't have to squint to see her screen. The clouds had also kept the morning cool, a welcome change from last week's high temperatures and a stark contrast to what she knew was coming in Texas.

Best to enjoy it while she had the chance.

Ruby stepped off her elevator into the wide-open fiftieth floor in a blue shantung off-the-shoulder jumpsuit and favorite Chanel sunglasses with her hair in a low ponytail and her earbuds in her hand, heading directly for the terrace where her wine, and an afternoon of peace and focus, awaited her.

And was taken quite by surprise when she rounded the corner just in time to see Jaccob Stevens walking into the sitting room through the patio door.

"Jaccob," she greeted, sure he hadn't yet noticed her there.

"Oh," he sounded, clearly startled. "I was ... um ... looking for Kara."

Ruby pulled off her sunglasses. "She's not here."

"Oh," Jaccob said again. "Do you know if she's downstairs? I'll just text her to come up."

"No," Ruby replied. "She's not here at all. Neither are the others. They've all left on an errand. It's just me."

"I'm sorry. I didn't mean to bother you. I really thought the girls would be here."

"Do I look bothered?"

"No, I guess you don't. But still, I didn't mean to barge in. It's just that I got this thing fixed and I figured Kara would want it back as soon as possible."

"First off, it isn't barging. I flat-out told you to stop knocking and just let yourself in."

"The door was locked, so I wasn't sure. But you said, so—"

"I did say. And while it is true that the revelation of the possibility for armed aggressors to land on my helipad seemingly out of thin air has prompted me to finally make use of the lock you so generously installed on that door, I have, as I suppose you are now aware, left the coded entry as it was. Had I meant to keep you from coming and going as you pleased, I'd have had the code changed."

"Right. And I'm glad you locked the door. That was really scary."

"I know you've put in additional security measures. And I have temporary custody of a bulletproof blonde bodyguard. But the lock still felt prudent."

"It was. I mean it, I'm glad. I'm also glad you don't mind me letting myself in. This thing got pretty fragged, and the Isotopeter can't run without it. I thought I was going to have to machine up a new one, but I managed to—" His voice trailed off. He was sounding like an awkward schoolboy. "Anyway, I fixed it. It's fine now. I'm just gonna—" Jaccob gestured vaguely toward the war room.

"Be my guest." Ruby gestured and stepped aside, allowing him to pass. She followed him out of the sitting room and across the vestibule and watched as he tiptoed over the tangle of cables and piles of paper to the open side panel of the machine he'd come to repair. There were tools scattered on the floor near the opening and Jaccob picked up two of them, sliding them into his pockets before crouching down onto all fours.

"You, um ... gonna watch me do this?" he asked, looking up at her from his spot on the floor.

"Why not? It isn't like I've got anything better to do." She could drink wine and listen to music any time. Having him in the apartment already canceled out the peace of solitude; she might as well keep him company. Additionally, there was something about being alone with Jaccob that appealed to her in ways she didn't want to think too hard about. Especially in light of how flustered he'd gotten of late when in close proximity to her. Given the right impetus, she might even bring up the bracelet. "Watching a gentleman work with his hands seems as good a use of my time as any."

"Yeah, okay." He turned his attention back to the machine, picking back up the drum before ducking his head into the cavity in the Isotopeter.

Ruby propped herself on the edge of a small table and tapped at her phone to check on the status of Monday's travel plans. Satisfied things were adequately in motion, she set her phone and earbuds beside her and looked back at Jaccob. He'd crawled into the open side of the machine far enough his entire torso was hidden from view. She watched as he reached into the pocket of his blue jeans and withdrew the ratchet he'd only just picked up.

Jaccob lay on his side facing away from her, and Ruby tried not to let herself admire his backside, finding that practically impossible given their relative positions. She had half a mind to snap a picture and send it to Vivienne, sure she would enjoy the view as well. But before she could, Jaccob began to audibly grumble and started to back his way out from inside the machine.

~

"Everything all right?" Ruby asked, as Jaccob climbed out.

Jaccob nodded, flopping down to sit inelegantly on the floor. "Yeah. It's just dark in there."

Not that Ruby Killingsworth ever let herself look less than divinely sculpted, but Jaccob could see she was feeling better.

Whatever thaumaturgical trauma or whatever entailed, she seemed to be recovering. She looked good. Way too good.

He pulled his phone from his pocket. "I'm just going to message Kara and get her to bring me a flashlight."

"I told you already. Kara's not here. She and Lisa and Yumi and Friday and Angel are all off on an errand."

"Oh." Jaccob frowned. "Right. Well, damn."

"Seriously, Jaccob?"

"What?"

Ruby rolled her eyes and stood from her perch on the table. "I may be no tech genius, but I can follow instructions. And I believe myself perfectly capable of holding a flashlight."

"You—?" He sat up straighter and looked back at her, confused. "Really?"

Ruby picked her phone up then and activated the flashlight feature. "Really," she assured him, waving the device in his direction.

"Yeah, okay. I just didn't think you'd want to get down here on the floor. You're not exactly dressed for crawling into machinery."

"The floor's been mopped, and I have a good dry cleaner." Ruby lowered herself to sit beside him on the floor and shone the light from her phone into the mechanical cavity. "Really, I'm happy to help."

"Well, all right," he said, turning to smile at her.

The movement brought their faces extremely close together—far too close together. He recognized the impulse to lean in and kiss her just in time to turn away and try to get ahold of himself. This wasn't the time, no matter how opportune it seemed.

They weren't there yet, maybe they never would be. He might have spent the past several days thinking about wanting to get close to her again, but she'd been asleep through all of that.

He swallowed hard and turned back to his task. Crawling back inside the machine, Jaccob picked up the drum and slid it into its intended spot. It was much easier with a little light.

"Is this okay?" Ruby asked, scooting closer and angling the phone in such a way as to get as much light onto the metal drum as possible.

"I think so." He picked up his tool and got to work on the installation. He managed to get the first few connections made without difficulty, but when he moved in closer to reach for the connections on the far side, his shoulder wound up blocking the light entirely. "Oof. Not anymore."

"Here." She moved her body even closer as she extended her arm to its farthest reach. "Does that do it?"

"Almost." Jaccob scooted himself sideways then, ducking his head to try and let the light past him to where he needed to see. He managed to find a position that was functional, if not comfortable, only to find his arm once again in the way of the light when he reached up to continue the repair. "Hmm ... can you—?"

Ruby scooted closer still, until her torso was pressed against his back inside the tight quarters of the machine's maintenance cavity. Propped up on her right arm, she was able to reach the light above Jaccob's shoulder, directing its beam onto the drum from an angle his arm wouldn't block.

"How about this?"

Jaccob's breath caught in his throat. There was very little space inside the Isotopeter; as a result, Ruby was fully spooned up behind him, her phone hand resting on his shoulder, and her face so close he could feel her breath on his neck and his ear. It would be too easy to close his eyes and lean into her ...

But he couldn't do that.

"Are we good?" she asked then.

Jaccob knew better than to say his first answer out loud. "Yeah, um, that's ... good," he managed to say after a moment.

Too good, he thought.

He tried his best to concentrate on getting the drum replaced and not on how good her body felt pressed against his.

"I ... I should tell you I just talked to Arsho this morning," he said, in hopes a change of subject might help. "You can expect a crew here some time on Monday to start work on your hallway."

"That's convenient," Ruby said, moving to rest her chin against his shoulder beside where her hand was propped.

"It is?"

"Indeed, as I prefer not to live within a construction zone, and it just so happens I'm leaving town on Monday."

"You are?" Jaccob stopped what he was doing and turned his head just enough to catch her gaze. "Are you sure you're up to that?"

"Up to what?"

"Are you sure you're well enough to travel?"

"Jaccob, consider that I am currently crammed inside a piece of experimental machinery, into which I have voluntarily crawled with a flashlight in my hand, in order to help you repair said machine. And here you're asking whether I feel like I'm well enough to board a luxury aircraft."

"Yes?"

She sighed. "Yes, Jaccob. I'm fine."

He nodded then, deciding to drop the subject for the time being and concentrate on getting the drum reattached. He made quick work of the last two bolts and slipped his ratchet back into the pocket of his jeans.

"All done?" she asked.

"For now. You want me to try and get out of here first?"

"Not worth it," she said back, already having doused the light from her phone as she started the process of wriggling out of the machine cavity.

~

Ruby backed the rest of the way out before giving him the all clear.

She was already on her feet by the time he scooted his way back out from inside the machine. He wasn't looking at her as he removed tools from his pockets and replaced them, along with the other implements scattered on the floor, back into a canvas satchel that was sitting open just on the far side of the Isotopeter. He seemed a little forlorn.

Ruby was beginning to think Jaccob really was about to leave well enough alone and mind his own damn business when he looked back at her.

"So ... um ... Where are you headed to on Monday?"

Ruby smirked as she raised her eyebrow. "You're far too transparent, Mr. Good Guy. This isn't small talk. If you're going to grill me about my travel plans, can we at least do this over drinks?"

"I don't mean to grill you. I'm just worried that—"

"Drinks," Ruby repeated.

It was half invitation, half demand. If he was going to insist they talk, she was going to insist they drink, especially seeing as he'd been keeping her from the lovely bottle of wine already on her patio. She turned away then, heading back across the vestibule and into the sitting room. By the time she made it to the end table where the decanted Scotch was kept, Jaccob was right beside her.

"It's just—" he began again as he moved to sit on the sofa.

"It's just nothing, Jaccob," Ruby interrupted, picking up the decanter and pulling out its stopper. "Kara's automaton found evidence of something that appears pertinent to our situation. There's data to corroborate her theory from a couple of those machines in there, and the thing I'm absolutely not going to do is fail to follow this lead."

"You could let the girls go without you," Jaccob suggested. "They're supposed to be handling the investigation; that is what you're paying them for."

"While I appreciate the point you're making," she said, as she poured liquor into a pair of Glencairns. "I'm not sure how I feel about your calling them 'the girls' when they are, in fact, grown women. And what I am sure of is the fact they wouldn't possibly have the access I do."

"Access?"

"The lead is a musician," she explained, handing a glass to him as she came around to sit on his other side. "One presumed dead since 1931 but who appears to be alive and well and playing a showroom in Lapis, Texas, in a hotel that's doing its best to turn kissing my ass into an art form."

"Lapis, Texas?"

"I'm going to take your lack of familiarity with the place as evidence of your good character. It's an inexcusably gaudy hellscape of late-stage capitalism—a whole town themed around old-style country music. It may well be the absolute worst city on the face of the planet."

"Sounds like you hate the place."

"Oh, I absolutely hate the place."

"But you still think it's a good idea to go?"

"A good idea? No. But I don't have a better one. So here we are." She took a sip of her Scotch and shrugged. "The good news is that travel to Lapis is a semi-regular thing, so there'll be no trouble managing logistics. And I can play it like any other work trip. Of all the places this fool could be playing, he happens to be somewhere easy to justify visiting."

"And you're sure you're up to making the trip?"

"It's a trip, Jaccob. A few hours on a private jet, a few minutes in a limousine, a couple of nights in a truly obsequious hotel, an hour watching a dinner show, and a brief-yet-hopefully-informative conversation with a musician who may or may not have traveled through time to get there. There's nothing to be 'up to'."

"I mean, sure, if you were healthy."

"I'm fine!" she insisted, throwing her head back in frustration before looking him squarely in the eye. "I knocked myself out with drain. Not for the first time, might I add."

"You were out cold for three days with what the doctor said was the most severe case of thaumaturgic shock she's ever seen."

"And now I'm up and about and crawling into machinery," she said, "and drinking Scotch and squabbling with a superhero."

"Three days, Ruby. You were out longer than you've been back. Are you sure this can't wait? Are you sure you're well enough to do this now?"

"Physically? Yes. I'm quite well." She couldn't decide whether his concern was more endearing or annoying. A lot of things with Jaccob were like that. "I am all recovered, and perfectly capable of a little business trip—even if it is to the Opry's armpit."

"Physically?"

"What?"

"You said you're quite well, physically. Which makes it sound like maybe there are ways you're not well yet." Jaccob took a generous sip of Scotch. "I'm worried about you."

"Not to worry, Jaccob. This isn't some sort of mental health crisis. It's not a case of my delicate female nerves being still frazzled by my recent run-in with a lead-based memento mori."

"I didn't mean—"

"If you must know, it's only *magically* where I'm still not a hundred percent. And that's not really a thing you care about, now is it?"

"Ruby, that's not fair."

"Oh?"

Jaccob seemed to shrink. "I only mean I'm trying to be better about that," he said softly. "And I think I have been. The part I don't think is fair is you acting like you're talking to me from two years ago. I'd like to think I've grown since then."

Ruby shook her head and reached across him, snatching the decanter off the end table to refill her glass.

"Maybe you have," she allowed.

She poured another ounce of Scotch into her glass, then reached past Jaccob again, resetting the bottle where it belonged and ending up seated a good bit closer to him than she had been before.

"I know I was closed-minded," he said. "And I know I didn't handle myself very well."

"That's very self-aware of you."

"I have a very good therapist."

"So it seems."

"I wish I'd done better. But it's just not something I understand. And I've always been leery of things I don't understand." Jaccob met her gaze. "But the thing I *do* understand, is that you used magic to save your own life, and the lives of those four girls—young women. You used magic the same way I would have used tech. A man opened fire in your direction, and everyone got out alive. If I couldn't respect that, what kind of hero would I be? Hell, what kind of *man*, for that matter? Your magic—that thing I was so scared of—saved the day. And that makes me want to stop being so scared. It makes me want to understand."

Ruby considered. "You know you can talk to me."

"Can I?"

"My door's been open, Jaccob. I think I've made that clear."

Jaccob nodded, casting his gaze to the floor as he took a sip of Scotch before looking back at Ruby. "So—" He frowned a little as he worked to formulate his question. "What do you use it for?"

"Use?" She shook her head. "What do you mean?"

"I mean the magic. What do you use it for ... when you're not being shot at?"

He had really asked. She hadn't expected him to. Strange.

"All sorts of things." She could tell from the look on his face he'd been hoping for more of an answer than that. "Mostly little stuff. I can open a door with my hands full, switch on a light without leaving my desk. I can turn a lock. I can steady an object or knock it down without ever having to touch it. I can break a thing, possibly even mend it."

She idly wondered how that Stardust statue at the University was faring right about now.

"I can change the way something looks," she said. "Counter a bad hair day or cover a bruise, hide the logo on a coffee cup so the paparazzi doesn't know where my assistant gets my espresso when we're out, or make a famous face just unrecognizable enough for an artist to come and go from someplace without being clocked by photographers."

"That sounds like it could be useful."

"It is." Ruby swirled the amber liquid in her glass as she studied his face. He didn't look afraid—nervous, maybe—but not afraid. There were things she was absolutely not going to tell him, but it seemed pretty clear that he wanted to know more. "And that's most of it. Little things that make life easier."

"Are there ... bigger things?"

"Indeed." She chuckled under her breath a little. "You know some of it. That whole demon fighting business, you were here for that. Portals to other dimensions, other places along the Coil, exorcisms ... all sorts of rites and rituals can honestly be performed by anyone with the time and the know-how. But power helps. A lot. And then there's the really wild stuff."

"How wild?"

"Well, I did help slay a dragon once. Technically, I suppose I did that twice. But I really only count the second time, because the first time, Loki did all the heavy lifting, and the dragon didn't seem to know to fight back. The second time I wound up with ichor in my hair and ruined a very nice ball gown."

"You ... slayed a dragon?"

"I didn't do it alone. But I was definitely a party to the slaying. I held it still while my counterpart put a sword through its innards."

"I'd say that counts."

"I think any time a mortal being is in the same room as an unkillable fire-breathing lizard with teeth the size of your average traffic cone and the mortal gets out alive, it counts as something."

"I'm—" Jaccob shook his head and chuckled. "I'm just trying to picture you fighting a dragon in a ball gown."

"Believe me." She knocked back the last of the Scotch in her glass. "If I could have avoided it, I would have. But when an actual god shows up in your office panicking over a dragon they're convinced is about to come gunning for the both of you, there's hardly a choice not to get involved."

"I can only imagine."

"Hope it stays that way."

"Was that ... right after we—? When weird dragon stuff was happening all over town?"

"It was. Let me guess, you did a bit of slaying yourself?"

"Sure did. Helped put down a big attack on the city. Saved a triple-seven full of unsuspecting passengers, among other things. Screwed my back up pretty bad in the process."

"Ah yes." She snickered. "The ever-tumbling sands of time. Even a hero can't stay young forever."

"So I've learned." Jaccob took another sip of his Scotch as he began to laugh softly.

"What? What's funny."

"I was just thinking. That's a strange thing for us to have in common. Dragonslaying."

"We live in Cobalt City, Jaccob. Strange things are what all of us have in common. But I will say, you being the hero and all, if I am ever faced with such an adversary again, I am far more likely to call you than I am to try and handle things myself. What I learned from that experience is that combat magic is not my strong suit. I'd rather not have to do that again."

"Don't sell yourself short. You've proven yourself plenty capable. You stopped six bullets."

"And knocked myself into a three-day sleep. No thank you. And again, I'm still not all the way back to full potency. It's a severe pain in my ass, and I'd rather not buy tickets for a repeat performance."

"I can understand that. And I wish I'd gotten here in time."

"If only people would be more considerate when timing their railroad accidents."

"Yeah," he said with a sad smile and a shrug. "I mean, I know that part wasn't my fault, but—"

"No buts, Jaccob." She interrupted him, daring to set her hand on his knee. "You were dealing with a train wreck. A multi-train

train wreck at that. You pulled ... how many people out of upturned and fiery passenger cars and got them to safety?"

"I don't know. I wasn't counting."

"Well, I bet someone was. I'm sure if we went looking, we could find it online. You did good, like you always do. And we all survived."

"You did. I'm just ... I'm nervous for a next time."

"A next time?"

"Whatever it was the shooters wanted, whatever it is they thought they were doing by coming here, you know they didn't do it. I've seen the tape. They landed, got out of their contraption, saw you, opened fire, freaked out, turned tail, and ran. So depending on what it was they were after, there's every chance they'll come back. And if they do come back, they're likely to come back better armed."

"I suppose you have a point. And I'm guessing you may have some ideas as to what we should be doing, aside from Vivienne's niece serving as bodyguard and all the security upgrades that are already underway?"

"What you're doing already *is* my idea. And having A-Girl around helps. But you're about to leave town. Which means you'll be out from under the protections we've built into the Tower. If whoever is behind this is after you particularly—" He shrugged before looking her in the eye. "Would you let me ... maybe ... put some tech on you for this trip to Texas? I've been working on a new generation of Starbands, and—"

"And here I was just thinking I'd ask you along."

He blinked in surprise. "You were?"

"I was. As you mentioned, we don't know what our attackers want nor when or how they're likely to strike again. And, as I recall, the last time someone could have blown me to a million pieces, the fact I was standing next to you is the thing that prevented that from happening. Especially in my current, not-fully-operational state, I feel safer with you nearby. And also—" Ruby sighed as her voice trailed off.

"Also?"

"Something, something ... adult conversation," she said after a sip of her drink. "As fractious as this can be sometimes, I can't say I haven't enjoyed having you around."

"I'm enjoying having you around, too." Gently, ever so gently, he laid his hand atop hers where it still rested on his knee. "And I'll be happy to come with you to Texas."

"You're sure? You'll come with us to hillbilly Vegas? Just like that?"

"Just like that. I don't have anything pressing going on elsewhere next week. And I'd rather be close by in case another gunman shows up—"

"Agreed. Angel is a dear, and I'm sure she means well, but she isn't exactly the most coordinated bodyguard I've had in my employ. I'd very much appreciate it being your turn to stop the bullets."

Ruby was smiling, and Jaccob smiled back.

"Something like that," he said, squeezing her hand.

"It's a plan, then," she declared, turning her hand in his until she could squeeze his fingers in return. "Monday morning." She stood up then, patting his knee as she did. "I should work on packing. As should you. The showroom's summer formal, so be prepared."

"I can handle that," he replied, before finishing his drink and standing as well.

"Jaccob. Do not take this the wrong way, but I'm talking about the sartorial standards of a bunch of gatekeeping pretenders to the nouveau riche. And you are a divorced man over forty who works in tech. Forgive me for not believing you."

Jaccob couldn't help himself but to laugh. "You've seen me dressed up before."

"And you've always looked irresistibly handsome. In Cobalt City. I'm telling you these Texas assholes are on a whole other level."

"So noted." Jaccob set his hand on her arm as he dared to lean in and kiss her cheek. "What is it they say in Texas: not my first rodeo? I promise you'll approve of my dinner attire."

"I'm going to take your word for that," she said. "Because you're a Good Guy, and my understanding is you Good Guy types don't lie to women's faces."

"I do my best. And I'll let Kara know I got the cylinder reattached." He set down his Scotch glass as he turned to go. "If she needs anything else, she knows to call me. And if you need anything—" He cast his gaze to the floor. "—you can call me, too."

"So noted. Either way, I'll see you on Monday."

CHAPTER NINETEEN

Unaccustomed as she was to group travel without her scheduler aggressively handling her retinue, Ruby had prepared herself for Monday morning's departure to be a pain in her neck. She'd been greatly and pleasantly surprised when she'd gone to meet the car to the airport and found the others already inside.

Even Jaccob had arrived uncharacteristically early. He and Yumi were chatting about a particularly eventful late-night gaming session during which, he continued to assert, he had come very close to winning. Ruby couldn't help herself but chuckle at Yumi's patient disagreement with that contention.

The ride to the airfield, timed to just miss the after-lunch rush of city traffic, was smooth enough and got them where they were going just in time to get aboard and get seated for their scheduled takeoff.

Ruby liked it when things went to plan. She also liked the expression on Jaccob's face when he got a look at the G-700 on the tarmac.

"Told you," she said quietly in his ear when she noticed him ogling her plane. She'd teased him over text when she'd sent him the travel itinerary about how her newest plane was bigger and faster than anything in his collection, including the Stardust suit. The resulting banter might even have qualified as flirting, had Ruby cared to think of it as such. She enjoyed seeing how right she'd been in predicting his airplane envy.

"Yes, you did," he replied, as he headed up the boarding stairs. "This is a seriously nice aircraft."

"That's why I bought it."

Jaccob chuckled as he followed her up the stairs and onto the plane, where the cabin steward was waiting with a tray of glasses filled with champagne. The five young heroes traveling along with them had already claimed their glasses and were settling into seats.

Ruby gave a nod to the steward and took her usual chair across the aisle from where Yumi and Lisa were sitting. Jaccob took the seat across from her, slipping a tablet from the leather satchel he'd brought onboard and setting it down on the table in front of him.

"Trashy romance?" Ruby asked him.

Jaccob laughed as he shook his head. "P and L."

"In August?"

"Amended from June."

"Oh, geez," Ruby said, cringing a little. "Better you than me."

"Hopefully I can get through this on the flight," he said, as the plane's engines spun up for departure. "I'd like to be able to enjoy Texas."

"Nobody enjoys Texas, Jaccob," Ruby said. "Especially not where we're going. But if there's one thing I can think of that's absolutely less fun than an evening in Lapis, it's a past due P and L."

The plane was moving within moments of everyone getting seated, and airborne shortly after that. Ruby sipped her champagne and tried not to laugh too hard at Jaccob's expressions of annoyance at the document he was reading until the pilot announced they had reached their cruising altitude, at which point she pulled out her phone and turned her chair around to better address the others.

"You all might find this interesting." She set her phone down on the small table between herself and Jaccob as music began to play from its tiny speaker.

"I can amplify that if you want me to," Jaccob said, his voice low enough not to fully drown out the sound of the song. It was an old tune—jazzy with a lot of woodwinds and a strong back beat. There were snaps and pops in the recording, as though it was playing from a turntable instead of a next-generation smartphone.

"No need for that," Ruby said. "I just thought everyone might like to hear our undead headliner."

"Wait," Kara said. "That's him?"

"He's the pianist," Ruby said.

"Neat!" Lisa said. "Did you find this online?"

"Quite the opposite," Ruby replied. "I did a little poking around in the corporate databank, just to see if we had any record of the guy. As it turns out, we did. He played on two of the Cobalt Blues and Jazz Company's 78s in 1930 and '31. Cobalt Blues and Jazz is one of the three early labels that merged to form the original Goblin Records. So I ducked into the archives Sunday morning and dug up the records. I didn't think it was a good idea to bring a couple of archival 78s and a player on the plane with us, but I thought you might like to hear the music anyway."

"That's a pretty low-quality recording," Jaccob said, shaking his head as he frowned at Ruby's phone. He toggled a switch on the tablet he'd been reading and looked expectantly at Ruby.

"It's a cellphone recording of a ninety-year-old record playing on a seventy-year-old turntable," she said. "It's a wonder it sounds like music at all."

"I get that," he replied. The sound from Ruby's phone stopped then.

"What did you—?"

"Wait for it."

The music continued after a pause, coming now from Jaccob's tablet. Most of the snaps and pops were gone, as was the base-level hiss inherent to external turntable recordings.

"Did you just hijack my device?" Ruby asked.

"Could you maybe not say 'hijack' while we're on a plane?" Friday asked. "I don't love flying, even with two flying superheroes here who could theoretically rescue us were something to go wrong."

Ruby nodded once, but never looked away from Jaccob. "My question stands."

"I just intercepted your audio," he said, "cleaned up the sound."

"Filtered out the character is more like it," Ruby replied.

"I just thought," Jaccob said, shrugging as he pushed his tablet across the table toward her, "I know you're a piano player. If you're going to use his playing style as part of the means to verify this guy is really who he says he is, you might like to hear him without any unnecessary noise."

"Partial credit for good intentions," she replied softly.

"I'll take it."

They listened to the end of the song, and the next, until the cabin steward emerged from the forward galley with platters of cheese, fruit, nuts, and charcuterie, all of which he left on the console across from the sofa where Friday, Kara, and Angel were sitting.

"Ooh," Yumi said, springing from her seat. "Snacks."

Lisa followed her out from around the table, and the two of them headed toward the trays of food.

"Is this a television?" Lisa asked, pointing at the sliver of LCD screen protruding from the console behind the snack plates.

"It is," Ruby answered her, turning in her chair just enough to look Lisa in the eye. "There's a remote back there, beside the sofa. Feel free to turn it on. It has all the streaming services, and the in-flight Wi-Fi is more than adequate to the task." She turned back around and slid her phone off the table. "If you want," she said to Jaccob, "you can use the aft cabin to get the rest of your work done. The TV shouldn't bother you back there."

"It's all right," he said, putting his tablet back in its leather case. "I'm going to take a break for a little while, have a snack. Can I get you anything while I'm up?"

"No thanks," she said. "All I need from you right now is a bit of the truth. You had a remarkably easy time just ... taking over my phone. Should I be worried about that?"

"Nah," he said. "StarPhone security's best in the business."

"Says the man who runs the company."

"To one of my biggest clients."

Ruby smiled at him and shook her head.

"What?" he asked.

"One of your biggest clients," she said, softly enough she could be sure the others wouldn't overhear.

"I mean—" he said. "You are."

"I just find it interesting," she said, "with our history, that's how you think of me: very valuable ... *client*."

"That's not—" he stammered. "I mean I only ... We were talking about data security is all."

"It's all right, Jaccob," she said, interrupting his rambling before he could reach anything approaching a point. "You can stop. We *are* a major client, and I appreciate the fact that never changed. After what transpired between us personally, you could easily have chosen to cancel our contracts; in fact, I was braced for you to do that. And I'm sure if Elizabeth still had a seat on the board, she'd have insisted on it. But you didn't."

"I would never do that." He shook his head. "Even if Liz had said to, I wouldn't have done that."

"You're a good businessman, Jaccob. Better than most people give you credit for. You know I respect that."

"I appreciate your saying so."

"Good. But," she said, a little louder, "the next time you take over my phone without asking, I may start canceling accounts anyway."

"That's fair," he said, eyeing the array of snack trays by the television. "I really was just trying to help, though. I'm actually surprised you had to record it like that. I figured you'd have a record player aboard this thing already. I mean ... in your line of work and all—"

"Oh, I do," Ruby said. "But it's a modern machine; it doesn't play at 78 RPMs."

"You have a record player?" Angel asked. "On your airplane?" She was sitting between Friday and Kara on the sofa, holding a tiny plate piled high with cheese and fruit.

"You ask that like there's not also a TV," Friday said, gesturing to Angel's other side, where Kara was using the television remote to page through the menus of the various streaming services available on the flight.

"Okay," Angel said. "But a record player's a lot less common than a TV. Like, there are TVs on regular planes."

"Like Jaccob said," Ruby told them, "in my line of work, it makes sense. I have all sorts of musical equipment installed in this aircraft: turntables, cassette decks, compact disc players, computers, amplifiers, equalizers ... I could probably produce a record right here in this cabin if it came down to it."

"Somehow I'm impressed but not surprised," Kara said.

"Yeah," Friday added, popping a cube of cheddar into her mouth, "I stopped trying to wrap my head around any of this stuff a while ago."

"I just—" Lisa was shaking her head and holding out her nearly empty glass of champagne from takeoff. "How am I ever going to get back on a regular airplane after this?"

"I rode in a private plane once before," Angel said. "And I have to say, the struggle is real. That's part of why I usually just fly myself places now. Unlimited leg room! Plus—" She winked at Lisa, who blushed. "I'm faster."

"Angel, stop teasing my girlfriend, or she's going to explode."

"No I won't." Lisa shrank down. "Probably."

"Commercial planes are fine for what they're good for," Ruby said. "But this is better. We come and go as we please, there's never a queue for the washroom, the liquor quality is whatever I say it is, and I can pack my full-size sunscreen if I damn well please."

"Oh," Yumi said. "I hadn't even thought of that."

"I did," Lisa said.

Ruby chuckled. "Well done."

"Not having to worry about clear plastic and tiny shampoo is definitely a benefit."

"I see you also hit up the boutique for appropriate travel wear," Ruby said.

"You did?" Friday asked.

Lisa shrugged. "Catherine said Tencel pants were the way to go for a long plane ride. And that a well-made white tee shirt would be worth whatever I, or in this case, you, paid for it. And you said you didn't mind if we abused the expense account a little, so—"

"You keep proving you belong here, Miss Yamamoto," Ruby said.

"Thank you." Lisa smiled so widely it made her nose wrinkle. "Although I don't think I'll ever get used to this."

"Oh," Ruby said. "You will. You'd be surprised how quickly you acclimate to the way we do things. And you have to know, you're coming on board with an advantage most new hires don't have. That is, I know I can stand being around you. Which means you're likely to be invited on these kinds of trips from the word 'go'. I specifically bought the big airplane so I can travel with staff whether or not I'm traveling with artists."

"How do you even buy an airplane, anyway?" Yumi asked.

Ruby knew for a fact this wasn't her first experience with private aircraft either. Her father, Akira Kujikawa, CEO of 2K Industries, owned at least one business jet, and though Ruby and Akira had never met personally, she knew the type: conservative, stoic, politically connected. That Yumi had taken a job at a burger delivery service in the city suggested she wasn't exactly on the best of terms with her wealthy aerospace family. This probably wasn't just idle curiosity.

"How do you buy anything?" Ruby asked, shrugging as the steward refilled her champagne. "You see an ad, you make an appointment, you put down a deposit, you choose your cabin configuration and your finishes, you hire a pilot, you pay the balance, and you take delivery. Then you figure out where to park it."

"And I thought it was hard to park my car in the city," Friday said.

"So you picked all this out?" Yumi asked. "Like, you got to pick the furniture and stuff?"

"To some degree," Ruby said. "More where it goes than what it is. Gulfstream has pretty exacting requirements for, you know, safety. But the furniture's nice. It's cushy, the chairs recline. And the leather is stain resistant. As a matter of fact, Miss Kujikawa, not too long ago, Lady Vengeance lost a battle with a full tureen of tomato soup in the chair you just vacated, and as you can see, no evidence remains."

"Lady Vengeance ate soup in that chair?" Yumi asked, sitting up straighter to look back at the seat she'd been in for takeoff. "In the chair I was sitting in?"

"More like she failed to eat soup in that chair," Ruby answered.

"Sounds like Aunt V." Angel giggled at the mental picture.

Ruby frowned as her phone began to vibrate against the table in front of her.

"Everything okay?" Jaccob asked.

"Probably not. It's the work phone; my office is usually pretty good about not sending emails while I'm in the air. Which means this might be an emergency." She swiped her screen on as she lifted her device from the table and snarled comically when she saw what was there. "Oh. It's nothing important. It's only the President."

Yumi shook her head. "Your life, Miss K. I swear. The idea that an email from the President of the United States is nothing important—"

Ruby shrugged. "Were it any other President, maybe I'd feel differently."

"Cheers to that," Jaccob said, raising his half-full glass of champagne as he settled back into his seat with a plate full of black olives and pickled peppers.

"Oh," Ruby said, still looking down at the screen of her StarPhone. "Gold star to you, Miss Yamamoto."

"What?" Lisa asked. "Why?"

"This message here from Prather," Ruby said. "It seems he's found a bluegrass duo from Muscogee, Oklahoma, to record 'Get Ready for It' for him. You have good instincts. The idea of you working for me after this is all over with is sounding better and better."

"So you're going to give them permission to record it?" Yumi asked.

"We don't have to," Ruby said. "It's called Compulsory Mechanical License. They can record it, and we can't stop them. All they have to do is pay us."

"I didn't know that," Yumi said.

"Yeah, me neither," Jaccob added.

"Most people don't," Ruby said. "But it's true. Anyone can cover any song at any time provided they're willing to pay. I'm not surprised Prather decided to go this route. And I can't wait to call Meg and tell her."

"You think she'll be mad?" Yumi asked.

"On the contrary," Ruby replied. "She'll be thrilled."

"Because she'll get to yell about how lousy it is?" Angel asked. "I mean ... I'm guessing a bluegrass duo from Muscogee isn't going to do justice to 'Get Ready for It'. That song *slaps*."

"You're halfway there. Again, I say, good instincts. You're all too young to remember this, but you're not," she added, as an aside to Jaccob. "I don't know if any of you were paying attention at the time, but there were a few years in the late nineties and early aughts when country sensation Mac McMantus and R&B/soul supergroup Up and Under got into a bitter rivalry and kept recording each other's songs."

"Oh, I do remember that," Jaccob said. "Liz and I danced to 'You're My World' at our wedding."

"Country or R&B?" Ruby asked.

"Um—" Jaccob thought for a second. "R&B."

"I vaguely remember when that was going on," Kara said. "I wasn't into any of that music, but most of the people I went to school with liked one or the other. There was a lot of taking sides."

"Would it surprise you to hear we did that on purpose?" Ruby asked.

"Wait, what?" Lisa said.

"Both of those acts were signed to Goblin subsidiaries," Ruby said.

"You did that on purpose?" Jaccob asked, looking a little shellshocked at the revelation.

"In fact," Ruby said, "The whole damn production was my idea. It started when both acts wanted to record 'Absolutely'. The demo wasn't very exciting. It had a sort of Swedish pop feel to it, but anyone with any chops could tell it was a good song. I was a newly promoted mid-tier executive at the time, and I'm honestly not sure why I wound up in the meeting where the two managers were dithering over who would get to record the song, but I piped up and said they both ought to do it. Country and R&B didn't play on the same stations, the audiences barely had any crossover in those days, so why the hell not? Double the airplay, double the record sales, double the money. I couldn't see a downside. And everybody went for it. The two songs hit the airwaves, and their respective charts, within weeks of each other. We were all thrilled. It was the media that suggested a rivalry, and we just ran with it."

"Whoa." Angel made a "mind blown" gesture.

"So that whole thing was completely fake?" Kara asked.

"Entirely manufactured," Ruby said. "Every other quarter, we'd have the managers in for a strategy meeting, and I'd make a point to leak it to the press they were coming, ostensibly for the label to force them to shake hands and call off the rivalry. In reality, we were sitting in a conference room listening to demos to figure out what song to have both of them record next. We made sure to alternate who got to release the track first, so each new duplicate would feel to the audience like retribution for the last time. Much like Miss Sparx's schoolmates, most of the English-speaking world picked a side. Meanwhile, both acts, and both labels, were raking in money hand over fist. It was one of the greatest stunts in the history of our business. I'm all but certain the orchestration of that scheme is what put me on track to eventually earn the office which I now occupy."

"Boss bitch, confirmed," Yumi said.

"And you think you're going to do something similar with MerMeg and Prather's Okies?" Angel asked.

"I think I'll call them 'Prather's Okies'," Ruby said. "That's good. Catchy and dismissive at the same time. And no, not exactly. That rivalry was fake. This one will be very real. But we can use the lessons we learned then to make the most of what's about to happen now. I already warned Meg this might happen, so she's had time to start gathering her thoughts. We'll wait for the news to hit something a little more public than my inbox to issue the official statement we already have prepped and ready. Next, we'll book Meg or a surrogate in every market where Prather schedules an appearance from now until the election."

"So," Yumi said, "instead of coming out in support of his opponent, you're just going to put on a better party across town? Draw the crowd away?"

"I don't know how the crowd situation will work out," Ruby answered, sipping again at her champagne. "But I do know what the local media coverage will probably look like. President former TV man isn't going to be top story in any city he visits between now and November."

"Hell yeah," Yumi said. "Get 'im, Miss K."

"Damn," Lisa said. "That's harsh. And, like ... amazing."

"Yeah," Jaccob said. "Remind me to stay on your good side."

"Who says you're on it now?" Ruby asked him, smirking over her champagne glass. "But yes, Meg is either going to have those Okies on their knees groveling for her blessing of their underwhelming cover, in which case she'll be able to get them to also denounce Prather, even if he gets to keep using their song. Or we'll set out to squash them like the pissants they are. Either way, we win. Prather loses."

"That's—" Lisa said. "Wow."

"Miss Yamamoto," Ruby said, "I think I'd like you to handle some of this."

"You would?"

"I would. Keep track of your time," Ruby said, "and I'll see to it you're fairly compensated. But I feel like we ought to take advantage of the fact that you're not officially on our payroll yet."

"Ma'am?"

"I just think that you doing the research, getting a list of what cities the floundering fascist road show is planning on playing, and shooting a few emails to venues to check their availability on those days won't raise the kinds of red flags that might pop up were someone under our corporate umbrella to be doing those things. Especially when the emails come from a Texas IP address. See, Jaccob," she said, sipping her champagne as she glanced sideways at him, "I listen when you talk." Ruby turned back to Lisa. "Do you think you can handle this?"

"Um ... yes, ma'am," Lisa replied.

"Good," Ruby said. "And I really don't mean to monopolize your downtime. If you want to send these inquiries from the pool or the bar, that's fine by me. I rarely care where the work gets done as long as it's getting done. Let me know when we can start booking venues. I'll get you the means to do that, and then I'll get you on the phone with Meg and her manager so you all can start making very quiet travel plans."

"On—" Lisa blinked rapidly and took a sip of her drink. "On the phone with Meg?"

"Is that going to be a problem?" Ruby asked, setting her champagne glass down as she turned her chair to better face Lisa. "Because if you're going to work for me, you're going to be working with celebrities. It's literally the job description."

"Oh ... um ... no, ma'am," Lisa said. "It's not a problem, it's just ... it's a lot. But if I can sit across from A-Girl and keep calm, I can talk to MerMeg on the phone."

"It is a lot," Ruby said. "I appreciate you taking it seriously. And speaking of A-Girl, I think you should loop Angel in on this. The only thing I can think of to make a MerMeg appearance more exciting would be to add a pretty blonde superhero songstress to the bill."

"You mean that?" Angel asked, leaning forward on the sofa and turning to look Ruby in the eye.

"Of course I do."

"I think that would be amazing. I'm happy to help."

"And I think it will be fun to remind Prather that his side doesn't have the market cornered on hot young blondes," Ruby said.

"Oh, hey," Angel said, taking the remote from Kara's hand and pointing it at the television. "Look! Kara found a travel special on Lapis. We should watch this."

The others nodded their agreement as Angel punched the button to start the program.

Ruby turned her chair again, startling Jaccob, who had been gazing at her in wonder this whole time. She smiled wryly as she picked back up her champagne.

"Congratulations," she said softly.

"Huh?" Jaccob frowned.

"Your P and L is no longer the most annoying thing on this flight."

CHAPTER TWENTY

Part hotel, part "experience," the Golden Century was the kind of destination that could only exist in Texas. A mere ten minutes away from the tiny Lapis airport, the resort's main tower reached sixteen stories into the sky, the whole thing a sheet of gold-tinted windows that reflected the afternoon sun with enough intensity a person had to squint behind their sunglasses to look directly at it in daylight. Its lower floors, however, were fashioned to look less like a modern hotel and more like an oversized copy of the sort of mid-century bungalow most often found on a Palm Springs postcard.

It was, in a word, tacky.

But that was by design. And what's more, it was entirely fitting with the aesthetic of Lapis, Texas. The whole town was a made-up destination in the middle of what had very recently been absolute nothingness. Lapis was a false oasis in the tumbleweeds dreamt up by developers and tax assessors to draw exactly the clientele it did: a mix of somewhat-locals and cross-country travelers all in search of a wholly manufactured "wholesome" travel experience.

The Golden Century was the pinnacle of a certain style of tribute to bygone luxury. Not one inch of the place was truly high-end, but no one who chose to vacation in this city would likely be able to tell. It was the nicest place in Lapis by a long shot, but that didn't make it a quality accommodation.

"Anybody else feel too ethnic to be here?" Friday asked the others.

"Nah," Yumi said. "We work for the rich white lady, so we're gonna be okay."

"I heard that," Ruby said, not bothering to turn around and face them.

"Hey, it's a genuine concern," Friday said. "I'd really rather not spend the next couple of days being mistaken for one of their maids."

Ruby stopped cold in her tracks and turned around, catching Friday's gaze immediately. "While we are here investigating the possibility of someone going back in time, *we* have done no such thing. This, Miss Jones, is nothing more than a run-of-the-mill theme hotel. All the aesthetic, none of the bullshit. A taste of the mid-century, but missing the racism, sexism, misogyny, homophobia, antisemitism, and other nonsense that plagued this country in that era. Or," she added with a tiny frown, "at least not any more of that stuff than exists anywhere else in this day and age; we are in Texas, after all. However, even with that consideration, you are here with me, and this hotel knows better than to dare treat any member of my complement with anything less than the utmost care and respect. You're perfectly welcome, and you're perfectly safe. Now, can we please check in? I've got work to do."

Friday was frowning, but she nodded.

They'd walked no more than half a dozen steps into the lobby when they were accosted by a tall woman in a modern suit wearing a name tag that identified her as the hotel's manager. She was flanked on all sides by a cadre of uniformed bellmen who could have stepped directly out of an Audrey Hepburn movie.

"Miss Killingsworth," the woman addressed Ruby, "We have your rooms ready."

Ruby nodded, but neither did she slow her walk nor do anything else to acknowledge the approaching assembly.

"Mr. Stevens," one of the bellmen addressed Jaccob. "If you'll come with me, I'll show you to Get Smart."

"And Miss Sparx?" another one called.

"Yes," Kara replied, moving through the crowd toward the sound of her name.

"I have you in the Buck Rogers suite. If you'll come with me."

"Okay," Kara replied. "Sure."

"Miss Yamamoto, Miss Kujikawa," one of the young men read from a card, managing to almost pronounce both Yumi's and Lisa's surnames correctly. "You're going to Gunsmoke."

"Miss Jones and Miss DeSantes," the last one read from a pair of cards.

"That's us," Angel said, raising one hand and grabbing hold of Friday's free hand with the other.

"You will be in Bewitched and Superman respectively," the bellman told them.

"Bewitched?" Friday asked.

"Superman?" Angel asked.

Those might have been rhetorical questions, but the manager had an answer anyhow. "All our suites are entertainment themed."

"Ah." Friday shook her head, but she broke off with the others to follow the bellman.

"Ladies," Ruby called out before any of them could get too far. "I'll see you tomorrow night, ten to seven, dressed for evening, in front of the main showroom doors. Your time is your own until then. Enjoy the hotel, go out on the town ... I don't give a damn. But don't be late, don't be sunburned, and don't be hungover. Do you understand?"

A chorus of nods and sounds of affirmation followed, along with one disappointed sigh.

Ruby clucked her tongue. "Miss Kujikawa, I heard that."

All that agreed, the hotel staff started to move again, leading the others toward the main bank of elevators at the center of the lobby. Ruby made brief eye contact with the manager, who fell into step beside her as they began walking as well.

"I have you in the Presley suite, as always, Miss Killingsworth," the manager said. "I've had the Scotch decanted and the piano tuned. Is there anything else you require before this evening?"

"No, thank you," Ruby replied. "I have a car coming in an hour, and I'll want to leave out the back."

"Would you prefer to use the loading dock?"

"Oh, no," Ruby said. "The side door will be fine."

"We'll have fruit and cheese for you when you return," the manager said.

"Good," Ruby answered. "Yes. Have a bottle of Burgundy up there as well."

She followed the manager down a hall and around to a bank of elevators that were hidden from the main thoroughfare. The manager pulled a badge from her belt and placed it against a palm frond carved into the brass façade of the wall, causing the elevator doors to slide open immediately.

It was a short ride up the sixteen floors, and Ruby followed the manager down the familiar hallway and through the double doors of the Elvis Presley suite. The luggage had come in a separate vehicle from the airport, and the butler was finishing her unpacking as she arrived.

By the time the staff was done in the room, Ruby had a little more than forty minutes to freshen up and get changed for her outing.

The Elvis Presley suite was every bit what a person would expect when they heard the words "Texas Opulence." The whole thing was done in shades of gold, with walls and shelves paneled in imitation burled maple, and a gleaming white grand piano beside the heavy-draped windows in the corner of the main room. The salon also featured a marble bust of The King himself on a pillar between a pair of white Naugahyde chairs, all across from a too-long green velvet sofa. The matching sofa table and coffee table, done in gold-tone and glass, were piled with welcome gifts: an arrangement of yellow roses peppered with purple camellias and peonies sat beside a card hand-signed by the hotel owner, and Ruby's preferred Scotch had been decanted into cut glass with a matching ice bucket and tumblers.

The bedroom walls were covered in what only the most discerning guests would be able to tell was polyester—not silk—taffeta, and the furniture, all ivory with gold dry-brushed shading, was the style of 1970s-era Rococo revival construction that wouldn't have been out of place in Graceland itself.

If there was ever a place more phony, Ruby Killingsworth had never seen it. She could only hope Simon Floyd would prove to be more genuine than the goose down in the bedroom comforters.

But that was tomorrow's problem. Tonight's problems were something else altogether.

Ruby had never enjoyed Texas fashion sense. The aesthetic of wearing soft and flowy dresses with denim and boots was a perfect storm of stacking her least favorite fashions into a single look.

But then again ... when in Rome ...

For tonight to go the way she needed it to go, she'd have to blend in. So it was, albeit begrudgingly, dressed in a navy-on-black brocade print silk jersey midi dress and blazer-cut denim jacket that she stepped out of her suite for the evening's excursion. There were some aspects of summer fashion that, thankfully, were universal enough not to be subject to regionality, so a nude pump was perfectly reasonable, which Ruby found comforting, as she refused to become so Texas as to wear either cowboy boots or a hat.

She'd be seated most of the night anyhow, and it was going to be dark. Nobody would be able to tell she hadn't gone wholly native.

She was halfway to the elevator when she heard footsteps behind her. Ruby frowned. Unless the hotel had done something they shouldn't have, her party had this whole floor to themselves—meaning whoever was behind her was someone she knew, and therefore someone she would likely have to speak to.

But whoever it was would have to speak first.

Ruby slowed her walk a little. If she had to make pleasantries with one of her employees, she didn't mind, provided they were headed to the same elevator she was. Then again, there was every chance it was a member of the hotel staff who would let her go on her way.

But no, she was sure within moments that wasn't the case. Because the moment her pace slowed, the footsteps behind her quickened. Whoever was coming was trying to catch up. And that meant she was going to have to be pleasant.

"Hi," she heard just as the other person caught up to less than a pace behind her.

It was Jaccob's voice.

What the hell?

"Jaccob." She slowed her walk further, so he'd have a slightly easier time catching up but didn't fully come to a stop. She had a car waiting and a place to be.

"I was ... um—"

Ruby did stop then, turning on her heel to face him. When Jaccob got tongue-tied, there was only one way to snap him out of it, and that involved looking him square in the eye. He stopped abruptly as soon as she turned, wringing his hands at his waist and fidgeting a little.

"Yes?" she asked.

"I don't—" he began again. "I don't know what the others are doing, but I was going to, that is, I was about to come and ask if you'd like to, go get some dinner maybe?"

"While that is very dear of you, I think you can probably guess I have plans and am on my way out."

"Oh. Okay. Yeah. I'll ... uh ... see you tomorrow then."

Ruby looked back at Jaccob. Had he meant that like a date? Or was he really just so lonely and out of sorts he hadn't thought about what asking her to dinner might sound like? Either way, he looked a little pitiful. She couldn't help herself. "Although I suppose you could join me. How do you feel about country music?"

"What?"

"You know what? Never mind. Are you coming or not?" She was in a hurry, and whether or not he tagged along for her outing, Ruby was going to be in the elevator within the next fifteen seconds.

~

Jaccob wasn't sure of the last time he'd been so confused, although there was every chance Ruby Killingsworth had been involved in that, too. "Um ... sure," he said finally. "Yes. *Yes.*"

Ruby nodded and kept walking, pulling her StarPhone from her jacket pocket as they headed toward the elevator. She pressed a button and spoke into the device. "Slight change of plans. Tell them I'll have a plus one. He drinks whiskey, same as me."

Jaccob followed her the rest of the way down the hall and into the elevator, half afraid to ask her what was going on and half just relieved she'd invited him out with her instead of shooing him down the hall.

Ruby typed on her phone for most of the elevator ride, and when the doors opened on the ground floor, she slid the device into her pocket then took off through the lobby at a clip that made Jaccob have to scramble to catch up to her.

"Everything okay?" he asked, as he followed her down a nondescript hallway.

Ruby only nodded. She neither spoke nor looked back at him. That was her game face, and he went along with it.

The dark-tinted glass door at the end of the hall came open as they approached, and Ruby charged through it, then straight into the open door of a town car parked beside the adjacent curb.

Jaccob followed her into the car, getting himself seated just as the driver shut the door behind him.

"Sorry about that," Ruby said, as the driver took his seat and put the car in gear. "I needed to get out of there without being spotted. I don't have time to 'celebrity' right now. I'm sure you understand."

Jaccob nodded. He did understand. He remembered a time in the early Stardust days when he couldn't reliably go into any public place without being asked for an autograph. These days, he was just as apt to get obscenities flung his way. Damn Prather. Nonetheless, he understood not having time to deal with the public.

It was a short car ride, probably less than a mile, and Ruby spent the majority of it looking down at her phone just as she had in the elevator. When they stopped, it was outside what looked to be an old-fashioned saloon. Jaccob knew just enough about this town to know it was probably a reproduction. The driver let the two of them out of the car and dashed past them to hold open the door to the building.

Ruby led the way down a narrow hallway, past a doorman and a coat check, and up a shallow ramp beside a bar that spanned the width of the building. At the far end of the large room was a stage, with tiny round tables filling the floor in the middle distance.

"Good evening, ma'am," a woman greeted Ruby as she slid from the end barstool to meet the newcomers at the top of the ramp. "We've got your table ready, with a second chair and a second glass. Is there anything else we can do for either of you?"

"Not at the moment, Patricia," Ruby said. "Thanks. But he's liable to get hungry."

"Kitchen's closed on Monday," Patricia replied. "But I can have Max bring up a basket of popcorn just as soon as it's popped. Or I can—"

"I'm sure that will be satisfactory, thank you." Ruby cut her off before she was able to make any further offers.

Patricia was visibly relieved. She smiled back at Ruby and nodded. "If you're ready, you should head on up. The show's going to start any minute."

Ruby inclined her head toward Patricia, then blew past Jaccob toward the opposite wall. Patricia followed, reaching past Ruby to pull back a black velvet curtain that Jaccob had mistaken for a decorative wall hanging.

Ruby ducked through the opening it exposed and passed from Jaccob's sight almost immediately. He darted through the curtain behind her, hoping he'd be able to see where she'd gone once he was on the other side.

"What is this place?" he asked, as he followed her up the narrow flight of stairs he found behind the curtain. It was dark in here, cramped and rough—very much the opposite of the kind of place he'd imagined Ruby frequenting.

"It's Monday," Ruby said, still climbing the stairs, "which I'm sure means nothing to you. But in show business, it means the night off. So all these kids who make their living singing backup for whatever washed-up wannabe rhinestone cowboy passes for a headliner in this town get to use Monday night to express themselves *as artists.* The ones who want to dance on Broadway are doing karaoke across town at Mae's. I promise, you do not want to see that. But the ones who dream of country and western stardom come here—to the Tin Horn—for the open mic."

Ruby passed through a second set of curtains as she finished, onto a small balcony overlooking the tables downstairs. There was only one table up here, a smaller and slightly nicer iteration of the ones on the floor below. At the table were two carved wooden chairs, upholstered in orange velvet that looked long overdue for a proper cleaning, and on its top was a decanter of whiskey and a pair of matching glasses.

"And you're here to listen?" he asked, following Ruby's lead and taking a seat at the table.

"That I am." She picked up the decanter and tugged on the stopper. "Now, granted, it's mostly small-pond big-fish from podunk who are somehow unaware their careers are peaking at this very moment, but every now and again, there'll be someone with actual talent."

"So this is a scouting mission?"

"You might call it that. Think of it as the industry equivalent of kissing frogs in hopes there may be a prince in the bunch."

"So why the cloak and dagger?" he asked. "Why don't you let them know you're here? Won't they give a better performance knowing there's somebody important in the audience?"

"The answer to that question is no. Jaccob. They're children. Imagine you're Chuck's age. It's your first summer away from home, or at least your first time making a living as a performer. Eight shows a week, you're appearing in the ASCAP Jamboree or the Canned Music Revue playing to drunk tourists and evangelical bachelorette shindigs. Once a week, you get a night off from whatever overproduced hootenanny pays your bills and you come down here to play music you believe in—your own music—to be onstage as yourself, instead of Cowboy Wahoo or Calamity Dame or third dancer from the left in the back. Imagine how much that relaxes you. Imagine how free and creative you feel in that room full of other Cowboy Wahoos and Calamity Dames all here to take a night for being authentic, vulnerable, heartfelt." Ruby took a breath. "Now imagine you find out the single most powerful person in the entire world of entertainment is in the audience. How does that make you feel?"

"Nervous?"

"You're damned right it does. When word leaks that I'm in town, everybody sucks. Like clockwork. Their nerves take over, their fingers don't work, they can't remember their own damn lyrics. It's a shit show. That's why I like to land in the late afternoon, check into the hotel in the early evening, and come straight here. The fewer people aware I'm around, the better. And I promise you, once there's been a shift change at the hotel, everyone in town will know."

"It's nice of you to want them not to be nervous."

"Please do not ascribe benevolence. It's an act of pure self-interest. I'm telling you, they're all terrible when they know I'm here. Hell, sometimes they're terrible anyway."

"Hence the whiskey?"

"Precisely." She poured his glass full, then repeated the action with her own. "What we're most likely to witness tonight are a bunch of self-indulgent ballads, a few novelty songs that aren't really all that novel, and a steady stream of closet cases in snakeskin boots who've convinced themselves the ability to play C, A minor, F, and G qualifies them to be the next Conway Twitty."

"If it's that bad, why do you come?"

"Because, like I said, every once in a while, there's some talent in the bunch."

"And what do you do if you like someone?"

"I alert the appropriate label rep. They'll fly down here, give the lucky bastard a proper audition, and if all goes well, we pluck them from obscurity and make all their wildest dreams come true."

"That's kind of your thing, isn't it?"

"Making dreams come true? Oh no. My thing is making money. If someone's dreams come true in the process, then bully for them, I suppose." Ruby turned her attention back to her phone.

It wasn't long before a young man appeared on the balcony with a basket of popcorn and a small bucket of ice with tongs. The house lights went down just as he departed, and Ruby refilled both whiskey glasses as the first of the night's performers took the stage.

The show was amusing, if not what anyone might call high quality. Every now and then, Ruby would whisper a voice memo into her phone, but mostly she sat back in her seat, sipping her whiskey and frowning. Jaccob did his best to enjoy the performances, and the popcorn, and to applaud appropriately at the end of each songwriter's presentation—even for those acts not particularly worthy of much applause. He could celebrate their courage, at least.

Occasionally, he caught Ruby side-eyeing him applauding some particularly out-of-tune crooner. He would smile, and she'd roll her eyes, and they sipped their drinks. It was nice.

Every once in a while, he'd offer her some opinion or commentary. Sometimes she'd answer him with a snarky comment of her own, and once she even laughed out loud. But mostly she'd just smile and nod or pat his arm. Jaccob tried not to get his feelings hurt over her lack of engagement. It wasn't like this was a date, or any sort of plan they'd made together. This was her letting him tag along while she was working.

So he mostly let her work.

He munched on the popcorn until it ran out and drank whiskey until the decanter was low. He figured Ruby would want the last, and he wasn't wrong. She was knocking back the tailings as the lights came back on at the end of the show.

She looked at him expectantly, then stood up, and headed quietly for the curtained-off door to the staircase. Jaccob followed her down the stairs and out into the little vestibule where they'd been greeted.

"Sorry for the hurry," she said quietly, as they approached the door to the outside. "But if I'm not out of here by the time they're all done congratulating each other, then I'm stuck dodging sob stories and demo recordings for at least an hour, no matter how hard I try to get out the door. I'll have the car here in a minute."

"Why don't we walk?" Jaccob suggested. As soon as the words were out of his mouth, he couldn't believe he'd said that. There was no way she was going to agree. But for whatever reason, he decided to press the subject. "It's a nice night. It can't be more than a mile. And we've been sitting for most of the day today—"

Ruby crossed her arms over her chest and scowled at him. "Do I look like a person who walks places voluntarily?"

"No," Jaccob answered sheepishly.

"Well." She sighed in resignation. "You *did* just put up with two hours of less-than-stellar country music. And I suppose there's a first time for everything. And it is a nice night."

"Isn't it?" Jaccob asked. "And it wasn't that bad."

"Don't make me regret this."

"Wouldn't dream of it."

He put out his arm, she rolled her eyes, and she stepped out alone into the warm Texas evening.

~

The sun had long since set, but a person could barely tell from the lights in Lapis. The Tin Horn was half a block off the main drag, and the world only got brighter as Ruby and Jaccob turned the corner onto Lonestar Street to head back to the Golden Century.

Lapis at night was quite something, and Ruby could tell Jaccob had never witnessed anything like it before. Part Sunset Strip, part theme park, and part country music video come to life, the street was lined on both sides in flashing neon and twinkling lightbulbs. Fake gas lamps were swagged over the street itself, and boot-shaped installations sat on every corner, concealing stairways to underground crosswalks.

A stage in front of one of the venues featured a dozen old-timey can-can dancers, and a pair of Rodeo Clowns chased each other around a mechanical bull in a pen outside another. Hot dog carts and cotton candy wagons dotted the sidewalk, along with the occasional vendor of frozen lemonade, roasted peanuts, and caramel corn.

"This place is wild," Jaccob said.

"It certainly is something," Ruby said. "It's not exactly my cup of tea, but people seem to like it. I only come here for the music, and even that isn't always worth the trip. But it's a convenient cover for why we're really in town, so I'm not complaining."

"Can I ask you a question about that?" Jaccob said.

"About what?" Ruby asked, sublimating a little bit of unease. "Our time-traveling pianist?"

"No. No. About the music."

"What about it?"

"Was it just me, or ... I mean, I know I don't know anything about the music business, but—"

"Spit it out, Jaccob."

"Did we just hear a bunch of the same song?"

"Three chords, and the truth," Ruby replied with a shrug.

"Huh?"

"They say that's all you need to make a country song. And a lot of these kids seem not to have figured out maybe they ought to include a little more than the minimum."

"Was there anybody you thought was any good tonight?"

"Maybe. That little blonde ... Dree Gordin ... I keep thinking about her."

"The one you said sounded like she'd been dismissed from the Chipmunks Union?"

"You overheard that?" Ruby asked. She hadn't realized he could hear the things she'd been quietly saying into her phone.

"I wasn't eavesdropping. I swear. I just—"

"Jaccob." Ruby stopped him before he spent any more time trying to explain himself. "You heard correctly. She's got no future as a vocalist, but her couplets were catchy, and her hook was good—sophisticated. Of course, it could be a fluke, that happens all the time. Lots of people have one good song in them and that's all they'll ever do. But if that little ditty she played tonight is indicative of her larger body of work, there may be a lucrative future for her writing songs for other people to sing."

"Are you ever not working?"

"Oh, please. As though you're not assessing the communication and security needs of every building you ever set foot in. I saw you checking out the cameras behind the bar at the Tin Horn."

"Yeah, okay—"

"It's the job, Jaccob. You know that. If I wanted a day off, I'd quit, and let someone take over who doesn't want a day off. It's not like I need the money or like I have anything left to prove. It's just who I am. It's how I think. You of all people should understand that."

Jaccob nodded. Ruby was sure he did understand. Hell, he'd tried to retire several times, but he'd always come back to Starcom. The company had grown to what it was because he couldn't help but tinker and innovate. It was one of the many ways the two of them were alike—one of the reasons they'd had such an easy time understanding each other.

They walked slowly back toward the Golden Century, Jaccob stopping every so often to patronize one street food vendor or another. At one point, Jaccob even offered Ruby his arm again, and this time she took it, much to his obvious surprise and delight. They walked arm-in-arm until he needed to dash away again, this time in pursuit of a box of caramel chestnuts. He was like a kid set loose at a circus, seemingly compelled to examine every sideshow, sample every available delicacy, and dally along every inch of sidewalk, prolonging their time out under the lights.

Ruby decided she didn't mind. Monday was the slow night in Lapis; it was unlikely for her to be accosted on the street by aspiring musicians. And she knew Jaccob wouldn't mind a hasty exit if that happened, because he knew what it was like to be recognized. He knew the discomfort of being eyed by every stranger passing by.

That was probably why he was having such a good time. No one in Lapis knew Stardust was in town. And he wasn't as much of a celebrity here as back home in Cobalt City. He wasn't this town's hero. Jaccob had made it clear plenty of times that he didn't regret being open about his super identity, but Ruby also knew how he occasionally envied those who kept their identities secret.

For one thing, it made for more carefree nights on the town.

He was having fun, and she figured it was worth it to let him. Between his day job as a billionaire tech mogul and philanthropist plus his night job as Cobalt City's preeminent superhero, she couldn't imagine the last time he'd been allowed to galivant along a city street with impunity. In fact, she wasn't sure the last time he'd been able to do anything anonymously. There were places in the world where she could go with little chance of being recognized, and she had magic to assure her privacy everyplace else.

Jaccob had neither of those things. He was as world-famous as any of her headliners, and he had no way to keep from being recognized, save from a slow night on the main drag during an unplanned and unannounced trip to a strange Texas town.

She almost felt sad for him when they reached the door of the hotel. Almost. What easily could have been a twenty-minute walk had taken them well over an hour, and it had been after ten when the show at the Tin Horn let out. It was late even without considering the fact her body was very much still two time zones ahead, and she'd been on her feet for almost long enough to rethink her eternal aversion to cowboy boots.

Tomorrow was a big day: she was sure she'd have work to do in the morning, and she wanted to be fresh and well-rested for the evening show and the task she had set out for afterward. Ever since the shooting, her magic hadn't felt quite right, like it didn't sit well in her body, and she needed everything to be working perfectly to get what she was after from this Simon Floyd.

Jaccob finished the last of his snacks as the two of them walked through the doors to their hotel. He tossed the empty box into a receptacle by the lobby entrance then absently wiped his hands on his pants.

There were whispers in the lobby as the two of them made their way to the elevators; Ruby noticed, but she decided not to point it out. In Lapis, it was just as likely folks were recognizing her as him, and she didn't want to spoil his fun by alerting him to the fact they had an audience.

Fortunately for both of them, when the elevator doors closed, they were the only ones aboard.

"This was a lot of fun," Jaccob said, as Ruby scanned the key card that let the elevator access their floor. "Thanks for letting me tag along."

"It was fun. I'm not used to having someone to talk to when I need to tune out the performers for sanity reasons. I'd say we should do it again, but this feels like a little far to travel just to hear bad music and eat snack foods."

"Yeah." Jaccob shoved his hands awkwardly into his pockets.

Ruby resisted the urge to invite Jaccob back to her room for cheese and wine. He'd been acting strangely these past few days, and she feared having him alone with her in a hotel room could end poorly.

As could the kiss on the cheek she had to stop herself from giving him as he paused at her door. She didn't need that kind of distraction going into tomorrow.

If things were going to get tense between her and Jaccob, they could wait until after she was finished with the man she'd come here to question. For now, she needed rest and focus—two things that Jaccob Stevens had a reliable record of disrupting.

CHAPTER TWENTY-ONE

There were few places on the planet as aesthetically unappealing to Ruby Killingsworth as the lobby of this hotel. Gold-tone fixtures and palm frond wallpaper had never been to her taste, and the two of those together made for a visual assault the likes of which she preferred to avoid whenever possible.

Tonight, of course, it wasn't possible. When she arrived at the pre-arranged meeting point at ten minutes to seven as planned, the five young women in her employ were there and waiting. Her gentleman comrade, however, was not; Ruby grumbled under her breath at his tardiness.

Her displeasure, though, was tempered by the job the sales associates at J. Dene had done dressing the five young women who'd be joining her for dinner tonight.

Angel was a vision in a dusty pink strapless Matoshi. This young lady wanted to be a star; clearly, she already knew how to dress like one. Lisa's frock was a rainbow of Siriano chiffon that would absolutely have been too much anyplace on earth that wasn't Texas (save perhaps on a float in a Pride parade) but was perfectly appropriate to the locale and the occasion. By contrast, Kara had chosen to wear a black silk tuxedo with navy metallic pinstriping and a navy sequin shell that would have been far too understated for the venue had the stylists not paired it with a pair of intricately beaded velvet loafers. Yumi looked sleek and modern in an indigo fit-and-flare gown, and between the draping of Friday's peridot-colored evening dress and the gladiator sandals she wore it with, Ruby had to stifle a laugh at how out-of-pantheon the avatar of Freya had chosen to appear.

All five of them looked lovely, and Ruby couldn't help but to be pleased with that. Proud, even.

Ruby herself had on a sleeveless, floor-length, boatneck couture gown in a shade of silver that made it appear from a distance as though it could have been spun from liquid metal. It clung just so to her chest and her hips; it was sexy without trying too hard. She wore with it a pair of silver opera-length gloves and diamond earrings large enough to impress, but not so large as to make people wonder as to their authenticity.

And as Jaccob Stevens dashed toward them in the very nick of time, the expression on his face told Ruby the look was having precisely the desired effect.

He was dressed for a summer formal just as promised: tuxedo pants, a white dinner jacket, black tie, and patent shoes. On just about anyone else, the ensemble could easily have looked like a weak attempt at James Bond cosplay. On Jaccob Stevens, it looked exquisite. And here she'd been worried about his fashion sense. Apparently, her doubts as to his ability to meet the "summer formal" brief had been misplaced. The man had definitely understood the assignment.

His eyes were wide as he came to a stop near to where the others were standing.

"Nice of you to join us," Ruby said coolly. The very last thing she was about to do tonight was let on that she still found Jaccob attractive. Those were thoughts for another day.

Or for ignoring wholesale until they went the hell away.

~

"I'm not late," Jaccob contended.

"Cutting it kind of close, though," Kara replied, showing him the time on her smartwatch. They'd agreed to meet at ten 'til and it was six fifty on the nose.

"I'm right on time."

"But Miss Killingsworth says on time is late," Lisa reminded him.

"I like that one," Ruby said. "She's my favorite."

"I'm sorry if I made you wait," he said. "You ... that dress—" Jaccob suddenly found himself tongue-tied. Shaking his head, he finally settled on, "Wow. You ... you look stunning."

Ruby pursed her lips and smirked. "Say you like my dress all you want, Jaccob, but consider removing the air of disbelief." She folded her hands at her waist as her face relaxed. "Telling a woman she looks nice in a tone of voice that says you hadn't thought it possible may not be the compliment you think it is."

Jaccob was suddenly even more flustered than he'd been a moment before. He still hadn't gotten his mind all the way around his feelings for Ruby, but he hated to think she was really under the impression he'd been surprised to find her so attractive.

The fact was, she'd taken his breath away.

If he were bolder, he'd say so, even in front of the whole team, several of whom were watching this exchange very closely. As it was, he did his best to smile and nod.

"This way," a uniformed maître d' called to the group of them from just inside a door he'd pushed open.

"That's our cue." Ruby gestured with her clutch for the young heroes to go in ahead of her.

If Ruby noticed Jaccob offering her his arm, she didn't acknowledge it. He decided it was better to just presume she hadn't seen. He waited while she passed through the door just ahead of him, silently keeping to the agreement they'd made on the plane for him to watch the backs of the rest of the team.

The maître d' led them across a brief terrace and along a wrought iron rail toward the center of the cavernous hall.

The showroom was a large, open auditorium, with rows of high-backed booth seating extending down a steep slope toward a modest dance floor, beyond which was the purple velvet stage curtain. A well-stocked bar stretched across the back wall, and several small tables peppered the top level.

The room was empty save for a handful of white-coated service personnel who seemed to be doing a final check on the setup. The maître d' signaled for the group to follow as he started down the center ramp toward the front of the room.

Jaccob was aware of two opposing paradigms in situations such as this. Either the VIPs (of which he understood Ruby was perhaps paramount in this town) would be seated early so they could be settled and served whilst the hoi polloi were being tended to, or the VIPs would be given someplace private and comfortable to wait while the auditorium filled and then seated at the last possible moment. This was clearly going to be the former.

They were led to one of the largest tables situated only one step above the dance floor. From here, they'd have an unimpeded view of the stage, and the quilted velvet seatback attached to the semi-circular booth meant they'd remain unseen by the patrons seated behind and beside them.

Angel climbed into the booth first, with Lisa and Friday seating themselves on either side of her. Somewhere along the way, Lisa seemed to have got over her fangirl awe of Angel, and now they were chattering like old friends. On either side of them came Yumi and Kara, leaving Jaccob and Ruby to sit on the ends. Seated across from her, Jaccob couldn't help but to look at Ruby; she really did look incredible. He was a little thankful when a waiter approached with champagne cocktails, as it gave him something else to look at. With the way she looked tonight, he was going to be hard pressed to keep himself from staring.

And he was feeling awkward enough without her catching him at it.

~

The service staff kept their drinks topped off as the showroom filled, swapping the champagne bucket for a fresh one as the first bottle waned, and taking orders for proper pre-show cocktails as the second bottle ran dry. When no one bothered to ask them for ID, the young heroes had agreed to a little champagne before curtain, but it was only Kara, Ruby, and Jaccob who asked for spirits when the time came. The others made themselves happy with soda water and mocktails; they were at work, as Friday was quick to remind everyone, and they needed to keep their wits about them.

Even so, Ruby put in a request for another bottle of champagne just as the din of the crowd began to reach a level that might indicate the show would be starting soon.

"You okay?" Jaccob asked her. "You look nervous."

"I don't get nervous," Ruby snapped in reply, sharper than she had meant to. "I just haven't had to do this in a while."

"Right."

"You feeling up to it?" Lisa asked her. "I mean ... you look incredible—like, completely flawless and all—but also you were in a coma four days ago that both a god and a doctor told us was because you used more power than a human body really ought to handle, so ... maybe it's a little soon to be leaning on magic so hard. You know? No one's going to be mad if we need to make a Plan B."

"I'll get to your question in a moment," Ruby replied. "But first I'm going to need you to back up a little. Did you say you consulted with 'a god and a doctor'?"

"Oh, yeah," Yumi said. "Jaccob didn't tell you?"

"I'm afraid he didn't." Ruby looked across the table at Jaccob, who returned a sheepish shrug as he sipped his cocktail.

"Wow," Yumi said. "Yeah. So. Um ... Stardust showed up, like, right after you went down. Then he kind of freaked out and took you downstairs while Kara turned off all the machines, in case that's what made the shooter show up. And Friday called Dr. Hao, and then Jaccob ran off right as Lisa and I got downstairs, and then he came back with Loki."

"Oh, really?" Ruby asked, making eye contact with Jaccob over her glass as she slowly sipped her champagne.

"I was worried," he said. "I panicked."

"And at what point did you put a hole in my wall?"

"That happened between the 'freaked out' and the 'ran off' portions of this retelling," Jaccob answered her.

"I see." Ruby nodded, unable to help the smile that erupted. That explained a lot, most specifically how Vivienne had known about her injuries in time to send flowers; Loki would surely have called her at the first opportunity. It also told her a lot about where things stood between herself and Jaccob. Her relationship with Loki had been among the topics of their parting conversation, and Jaccob had made no secret of his distaste for the idea. That he'd been willing to find Loki and ask for help spoke volumes about how far he'd come in the past two years.

"You're a Good Guy, Jaccob," she said quietly. To Lisa, she added, "And yes. I am feeling up to it. In fact, this will probably feel good. I've been taking it very easy, and I think it's high time I get back on the horse, so to speak."

"Good," Lisa said, raising her glass in Ruby's direction.

The lights went out just as waiters approached with the first course of the night. Dinner was a pre-fixe seven courses consisting mostly of various meats and seafoods. Yumi grumbled under her breath a little about being a vegan in Texas, but the baked potato on its own was more than enough to fill her up and the flambeed apple dessert was absolutely delectable. Everyone at the table agreed the food was rather tasty—even if Miss Killingsworth didn't eat nearly enough of it.

Dancers performed on the parquet floor during the dinner service, a variety of salsa, samba, and Argentine tango featuring pairs sporting increasingly lavish costumes.

It was only as the desserts were being cleared that the dancers left the floor and a light hit the purple velvet drape beneath the showroom's proscenium arch.

"Ladies and gentlemen," an unseen announcer's voice boomed through the auditorium. Ruby frowned into her champagne; unsurprisingly, it seemed Lapis, Texas, had yet to grow beyond binary forms of address. "The Golden Century proudly presents: Simon Floyd and his orchestra!"

The lights changed again, getting darker in the house as bright floodlights and a pair of follow spots landed on the stage where the curtain was slowly opening at the center.

"Kara?" Ruby asked.

"I'm working on it. It's darker in here than I was expecting. I'll need to adjust for it."

"Adjust for what?" Angel asked.

"The camera on this thing needs to be calibrated for scanning a bright stage in a dark room," Kara replied, pointing to a tablet computer in her lap, just barely visible over the lip of the table. "We all figured it's worth it to get this Floyd guy into the facial recognition/comparison software live and in person to double check our theory before we send Miss Killingsworth in to grill him with magic. It'd be an awful waste of energy if it turns out he's just a lookalike."

"Right. Good." Jaccob sounded to be in agreement, but a frown creased his brow. "Floyd—"

"I've also got to dim the screen so we don't look like we've got our own personal spotlight at this table," Kara added, still not looking up.

"Shit. Simon. Floyd—"

Ruby frowned up at Jaccob. It was very unlike him to swear at the table, and whatever had prompted the outburst appeared to have him in a particular tizzy. He was gaping at the stage, his eyes wide as he shook his head slowly.

"Jaccob," she said, "are you all right? You look like you've seen a ghost."

"Yeah ... The name sounded familiar, but ... I didn't ... I mean ... that's—" He looked at Ruby and took a deep breath.

"What is it, Jaccob?"

"I know that guy. And he's dead."

"Didn't we know that?" Yumi asked. "He died in 1931. Or ... he was supposed to. That's why we're here?"

"No," Jaccob said. "No. Kara, can I see that for a second?"

"Yeah, sure." Kara handed over the tablet, making a point to keep the screen facing downward.

"Jaccob," Ruby said, "considering your retrograde taste in music, the fact you recognize a Depression-era pianist comes as very little surprise to me. What I'm not understanding here is the panic. Care to explain? Please?"

"Simon Floyd. I knew I knew that name from somewhere, but—" He typed furiously at the tablet's onscreen keyboard alternately with poking and swiping at his smartwatch.

"Jaccob, that's not—"

He cut her off. "I'm telling you, I've seen this guy before, and he was dead."

"I'm afraid you've lost me," Ruby said.

"Yeah," Angel added, "I think you've lost all of us."

Jaccob shook his head, still typing. "Simon Floyd. He was a piano player, witnessed a mob hit, murdered. In 1931. Cremated. Reanimated by his voodoo girlfriend. He worked with Wild Kat and the Mysterious Five. He was part of the Protectorate!"

"The Protectorate?" Kara asked, frowning.

"He went by Mister Grey," Jaccob said, "but he vanished, and—"

"Shit," Kara said. "You're right. I don't know how I missed it, but ... yeah. Simon Floyd is Mister Grey. Oh my God."

"Except Mister Grey was a pile of ash, and Simon Floyd is a very much alive human being playing piano on that stage right now," Jaccob said, passing the tablet back to Kara.

"So it appears what we have here," Ruby said, taking a rather pronounced sip of her drink, "is a man who performed on two records now in my corporate archive, who was murdered in 1931, turned to ash, and then was later re-animated only to become a member of a team of heroes of which our very own Stardust was also a member, who at some point vanished and is generally presumed to be gone for good?"

"That's what it looks like," Kara replied, still looking at the pictures on the tablet.

"And now he's shown up, alive and well, once again fully corporeal and not at all made of ash, playing the showroom in a hotel that prides itself on sucking up to me."

"Yeah," Kara said. "Just in time for you and Stardust to be back to pal-ing around thanks to an email that got you all freaked out about someone messing with Mike."

"Anyone think there's any chance at all this isn't deliberate?" Ruby asked the group.

"You mean, like a trap?" Friday asked.

"I mean *exactly* like a trap."

"Ooh." Yumi perked up. "This just got exciting."

"It's been entirely too long since I punched something," Angel said.

"You thinking you want to call this off?" Jaccob asked Ruby.

"Absolutely not," Ruby replied. "But I think we can all agree things just got a little more interesting. There appears to be a plan afoot. Whether or not Mr. Floyd here knows he's part of it remains to be seen."

"So you're still going to question him?" Lisa asked.

"You're damn right I am."

"You sure?" Jaccob asked.

"Do I appear at all hesitant?" Ruby snapped. "I did not come all the way to low-rent Republican wanna-Vegas to walk away without answers. It's just that now I'm going in armed with better questions."

"What do you need from us?" Angel asked.

"Sword time?" Yumi suggested.

"Just—" Ruby replied, taking a deep breath and fixing her concentration on the stage. "Just keep quiet and watch the show. Let me work."

"Yeah," Angel said, sounding a little disappointed. "Okay."

~

They team waited, sitting back with their drinks to watch the show while Ruby started to work. Jaccob, however, couldn't help but watch Ruby instead of the orchestra. He'd always hated magic, feared it, felt repulsed by it. But he was learning.

And the idea of watching Ruby work, especially in that dress, was a whole lot more appealing than looking at the fully human incarnation of Mister Grey up there on the stage.

He was also a little bit fascinated by the idea Ruby was working magic right there across from him. She looked focused, thoughtful, and a little stern, but not in any way he might have imagined a sorceress looking while working a spell.

It would have been mesmerizing even if she hadn't shown up tonight looking like an absolute goddess. Jaccob wasn't sure he could ever be fully comfortable with magic but watching her here tonight made him want to try.

When Ruby very suddenly snapped her head sideways and caught him looking, Jaccob felt his mouth go dry. He was ready to get called out for staring and already mentally forming his apology when she reached out her hand and said, "Jaccob, dance with me."

At least one of the team gasped. Lisa was staring at them with wide eyes. Angel looked back and forth between the two rapidly.

"What?" Jaccob asked.

"I need to get closer," Ruby said.

"What?" he asked again.

"Godsdammit, Jaccob." Ruby pulled her napkin from her lap and folded it aggressively on the table beside her plate. "Must I really describe the intricacies of magical influence at the dinner table?"

"Maybe?"

She shook her head and sighed. "Closer, Jaccob. For reasons I do not fully understand, I don't think this is working. I'm not sure I can do it from here. We need to talk to him, meaning I need to get close enough to get the magic to work."

She was mad. Jaccob wasn't sure he'd ever seen her this agitated, and that included when she'd just survived a bombing and had to throw the sniveling, cowardly President of the United States off her aircraft. He honestly had no idea why she was suddenly in such a foul humor, nor what getting closer to the stage would do for her ability to work the magic she intended.

But asking too many questions right now was unlikely to do anyone any good. Best just to do as she wanted and find ways to fill in the information later. He quickly folded his napkin on the table and stood from his seat, reaching out his hand to Ruby as she also stood.

He kept hold of her hand on the short walk down the single step and across the patterned carpet to the parquet dance floor.

"So you just want to ... dance?" Jaccob asked, sliding his arm around her waist.

"I want a pretense to get as close to the stage as a person can get in this place without arousing suspicion," she replied. "And since what lies between our seats and that stage is a dance floor full of reveling patrons, dancing seems the most practicable solution."

"Oh. Right—" Jaccob chewed at his lower lip as they began moving to the rhythm of the music coming from Simon and his band. He tried his best not to pull her too close or hold her too tight as they turned across the floor. But it was hard. Ever since she'd helped him replace the drum in the Isotopeter, he couldn't help himself but think about the way he'd felt with her body pressed up against him.

Having her in his arms again felt good. But he couldn't let that pull his focus. This wasn't a social dance.

The dance floor was crowded, and Jaccob wasn't sure of the etiquette. He'd never had to dance with an agenda before. He was a little surprised Ruby was letting him lead. The music was smooth, and quite easy to dance to, but his nerves were making him graceless, and he knew it.

"You're ... um ... you're wearing your bracelet." He gestured with his head to the bangle on her right wrist. He was used to chatting with his dance partners, and the silence between them felt particularly awkward.

"Not because you told me to," she said bluntly. "It's just that diamonds go with everything."

"I believe I said similar when I gave it to you the first time."

"I may remember something like that."

"Do you really remember?" He turned them around the dance floor to move closer to the stage.

"Of course I remember," she said. "It was in the car on the way to the Pops."

"I'm surprised."

"You know, Jaccob, contrary to my very carefully curated public image, I do not actually have men presenting me with diamonds every time I climb into the back of a limo."

Jaccob felt his cheeks turning red. He hoped the dim light was enough to keep her from seeing.

"Isn't it romantic," he said then, after a beat.

"What?"

"It's ... it's the song," he stammered, acutely aware in that moment just how awkward he was being. "Isn't it romantic."

"Yes, Jaccob," she snapped. "That's nice. I appreciate your skill at 'Name That Tune.' But I am trying to concentrate."

"Oh."

He tried his best not to look as forlorn as he felt. After a moment, it was clear he shouldn't have worried about his expression or what color his face might have turned. Ruby wasn't looking at him.

Her gaze was fixed over his shoulder, her attention solely on the stage behind him. Her lower lip was quivering, and there was a furrow in her brow Jaccob was pretty sure he'd never seen before. This had to be the magic. No more talking for the time being. He watched her face and continued to lead her gently in enough of a dance to not tip anyone off to her ulterior motive.

Her eyes narrowed, but never blinked. Her teeth clenched, and tension grew in her fingers where they rested on his arm. Her hand trembled in his grip, and the color seemed to be slowly draining from her face. Jaccob wanted to ask if she was okay, but the little bit he understood about magic told him it was probably better not to break her concentration. He just did his best to keep them dancing and moved around as naturally as possible while making sure she could keep her line of sight.

As the song finished, the other couples stepped apart to applaud along with the patrons still in their seats. Jaccob looked back at Ruby, unsure as to whether he ought to let her go. But it was barely a moment before her whole body relaxed. Her eyes blinked shut, and she smiled before stepping away and clapping her gloved hands softly as though nothing unusual was happening at all.

She inclined her head toward Jaccob before stepping away and turning to walk back to the table.

"Everything all right?" he asked, as he caught up and put his hand on her back.

She replied only with a curt nod, never breaking her stride. When she reached the table, she snatched up her glass and knocked back the last of her champagne.

"The band will be taking a break in a moment." She shook her hair from her shoulders and flashed a smile to the others at the table.

As the applause faded, the band began to set down their instruments. The band leader, a tall Latinx man with a streak of white in his ink-black hair, announced they would be back shortly, and invited the audience to give another hand for Simon Floyd.

"That's my cue," Ruby said. "I'll see you all in the morning."

As the audience continued to applaud, Ruby strode away from the table and across the dance floor toward an unassuming door beside the stage. It opened as she approached and then closed itself behind her.

"What—?" Jaccob half-asked, as he slid himself back into his seat.

"She did it," Lisa said frankly.

"She did?" Jaccob asked.

"Yeah," Yumi said. "This was the plan."

"There was a plan?"

"Yeah," Friday said. "There was ... I mean, there is. Apparently she didn't tell you about it."

"That whole thing," Lisa said, "just now, with the dancing. She was doing magic. This isn't a scheduled break. She got them to take a break. And now she's gonna talk to Floyd—get him to tell her everything about how he got here."

"And she's recording it," Kara added. "Everything goes the way it's supposed to, we'll have a lot of good information in the morning."

Jaccob resisted the impulse to ask the others what they knew about the plans for the rest of the night. There were a lot of hours between this moment and morning, and he didn't like where his brain went every time he wondered about that apparent gap in the plan.

There was something uncomfortable and undeniable about the way he felt. He'd been well aware for some time that he had unresolved feelings where Ruby Killingsworth was concerned. But watching her walk away, ostensibly to spend the night with another man—in what way he wasn't altogether sure—had his whole gut in a knot. He slid back into his seat and reached for his own glass of champagne.

"How long," he asked the others, "are we expected to stay here?"

CHAPTER TWENTY-TWO

It didn't take the group long to come to the consensus that being the first ones to leave after the band took their unexpected break wasn't the best idea. And Angel made the point that it wouldn't be polite for them to leave a half-drunk bottle of champagne in the bucket. So the six heroes spent the better part of the next hour still in the showroom sipping champagne and listening to the house band, minus Simon Floyd, play their next set.

It was late by the time the group left the showroom, and Kara decided to knock on their boss's door on the way to their rooms. Yumi and Lisa, both equally curious as to what Miss Killingsworth's conversation with a potential time traveler might have been like, joined her at the door. Jaccob took his time walking past, probably hoping for a glimpse of Ruby.

When there was no answer at the door of the Presley suite, everyone headed off to their respective rooms to change out of their evening clothes and wind down for the night. Except Angel, who decided it was her job to be as close to their boss as possible in case she found herself in need of impervious assistance. Yumi declared her intention to order another baked potato from room service and then log on to the gaming server and give Jaccob another virtual smackdown just as soon as she got changed. Lisa also thought room service was a good idea, while Friday wanted nothing more than to look in on the automation Kara had helped set up in her condo to make sure her plants were faring well in her absence.

It was nearly two hours later when a message appeared in the group text. "Do you want the recording now, or would you rather wait until morning?"

"Be right there," Kara texted back before throwing a sweatshirt on over her pajamas and heading out of the Buck Rodgers suite.

Yumi and Lisa were already in the hallway when the door closed behind her. Both of them were dressed similarly to Kara, in hoodies and pajama pants, Yumi wearing a pair of rubber flip-flops while Lisa was in her stocking feet. Angel, dressed for bed in a one-piece pajama in the A-Girl colors, complete with matching furry boots, came ambling out of her room moments later.

"Wow," Kara said, as they fell into step toward the far end of the hall. "You all as excited as I am to get our hands on this recording?"

"Yeah," Yumi said back. "I mean ... kind of."

"Kind of?"

"Mostly I want to see what a billionaire's hotel room looks like," Lisa said with a shrug.

"And I mostly want to make sure Miss K is all right," Angel added. "You know ... the whole 'magic, coma, magic' thing. I'm supposed to be protecting her, and she just got done with a big magic thing. So I just ... I wanna make sure she's okay."

"Yeah, sure," Kara said. "That makes sense. Friday didn't want to come?"

"She didn't feel like waiting up," Angel answered. "She went to bed as soon as she was done looking in on her plants. I figured if her phone didn't wake her, I wasn't going to."

The bunch of them hurried down the hall, and Kara knocked quietly on the unassuming double doors of the Presley suite. Realizing the door was already propped open with the swing bar, the group of them crept inside.

"Shit," Lisa whispered, as the four of them rounded the corner into the suite's main area. "I think this room is bigger than my parents' house."

"It's certainly bigger than anyplace I've ever lived," Angel replied. "And I've lived a lot of places."

"It's too much," Kara agreed. "But we're here to work."

They headed across the marble entryway and onto the gold-tone carpet toward the sofa and chairs.

Ruby stood to greet them when they came in. She looked ... different. Her hair was loose, not just down and unpinned, but also free and flowing, as though she'd brushed all the style and product out of it. Her face, although not bare exactly, was unmade enough to make her look altogether different from the way she'd looked just a few hours ago. And she was wearing a long sleeve emerald-green silk wrap dress with a low plunge and a flowing skirt that billowed apart with every step enough to expose what some people would call a scandalous amount of leg.

She looked relaxed, not *tired* exactly, but not as sharp and buttoned-up as she usually appeared. Maybe this was just how she always looked after midnight. But it wasn't how she always looked to the group of them.

"Your device is on the coffee table," Ruby said to Kara. "You're welcome to grab and go, we can debrief in the morning. But if you'd like to stay for a drink, you're welcome. We check out tomorrow, and there's a decanter full of Scotch. We might as well drink it. And while you're here, I'm happy to answer any questions about my chat with our Mr. Floyd."

"I could drink. I mean—" Angel shrugged. "I'm impervious, so the whole 'don't drink on the job' thing doesn't really apply to me anyway."

"It's past midnight," Ruby reminded them. "It's officially after hours."

"I'd like to hear your impressions." Kara crossed to the coffee table to pick up the device Ruby had left there for her. "And I'm not opposed to Scotch."

"The good news is the man had no problems sharing." Ruby moved to the table behind the sofa where the half-full decanter of Scotch was waiting. "He definitely tried to talk my ear off. And the best I can tell, he absolutely was snatched up from the 1930s and brought here in a contraption not unlike the one we got a glimpse of on my roof."

"That *is* good news," Lisa said, picking up glasses as Ruby filled them and passing them out to the others.

"But calling that 'the good news' kind of implies there's bad news," Yumi added, taking both glasses from Lisa's hands and passing one to Kara.

"That there is." Ruby handed two more drinks to Lisa and then poured a last one for herself. "It seems our friend Mr. Floyd was on several of the more popular recreational substances known to the prewar jazz scene when it happened—not the hard stuff, though; he went on a little rant against heroin, come to think of it. But still his memory is a little fuzzy. I got the distinct impression he's not entirely sure this whole experience isn't just a synergistic effect of absinthe and mescaline."

Kara chuckled as she sipped her Scotch. "Sounds like you had an interesting conversation." She pulled a set of earbuds out of her pocket and plugged them into a jack on the side of the recorder in her lap.

"I look forward to your listening to it," Ruby replied.

Kara put a single earbud in her ear as she flipped a small switch on the back of the device. "Damn," she said after a moment.

"That doesn't sound good," Ruby said, moving to sit on the arm of the side chair farthest from the door.

"I think it's the battery," Kara said, flipping the switch again and pulling the earbud from her ear. "I made it as small as I could while making sure we'd get the resolution I want. Small device means small battery, and with the time I had, it didn't seem worth it to try and make it energy efficient. So I'm not surprised the battery is almost dead. I'm going to go plug it in and start the data transfer." She stood up then, knocking back the rest of the Scotch in her glass before pocketing both the recorder and her earbuds. "See you guys later."

She left the room quickly, and Lisa moved to take her seat on the sofa. "So how come you think he's really from the thirties? If he said things were all weird and like an absinthe trip, what is it that makes you think he could really be from back in time?"

"Aside from the fact that this particular man has too many connections to our little adventuring party to be sheer coincidence," Ruby replied, sipping her drink, "it was his manner of speaking. One of my first jobs with the company was with the old guys. They were fifty years past their prime, but get enough of them in a room together, and you might as well have had a time machine. The slang is different, the cadence ... it's just different. Most modern depictions are caricature, and most films from the period have a particular stilt to the dialog. And he didn't sound like either. He sounded like those old men used to sound."

"Wow," Lisa said.

"That's really interesting," Angel added.

"Hello?"

There had been only the briefest knock on the door before the voice called out.

All four of the women sitting in the parlor of the Presley suite turned their heads just in time to see Jaccob coming around the corner from the entrance. He was still in his tuxedo pants and shirt, with the sleeves rolled up over his elbows, his cummerbund and tie missing from the outfit entirely. His shirt had come halfway untucked, and he'd traded his patent leather formal shoes for driving loafers. He looked a mess, but, then again, he was skulking around a hotel hallway in the middle of the night, so at least he was dressed appropriately to the activity.

"Mr. Stevens," Ruby greeted him. "To what do we owe the honor of your presence?"

"I was out getting ice and I saw your door propped open," he said. "Everything okay?"

"Oh, yeah," Angel replied. "Kara must have left it propped. She went down to her room to copy the recording. Miss Killingsworth had it propped open for us, and I guess she didn't think to shut it behind her."

"Drink?" Ruby offered, holding up her glass of Scotch.

~

"Um—" Jaccob frowned.

He didn't exactly know what he'd expected when he'd come down the hall to knock on Ruby's door, but he was self-aware enough to know had he not found it propped open on its swing bar, he very likely would have chickened out. And he was absolutely sure he hadn't been prepared to find her holding court with two of the young capes he'd brought into her employ and Vivienne Cain's super-powered niece.

Could he sit and have a drink with them without making an ass of himself? His track record thus far hadn't been stellar. Maybe he should just decline and head back to his room ...

"You know what?" Lisa said, patting Yumi on her leg and making a face. "It's kind of late. We should get going. Early flight tomorrow." She turned her head and made the same face at Angel, who narrowed her eyes before responding with a nod.

"Um, yeah." Angel gulped down the whisky in her glass before taking hold of both Yumi's and Lisa's glasses and polishing those off as well. "Yeah, it's late. We should ... we should definitely go."

She'd barely finished her sentence when Lisa started for the door, tugging Yumi behind her. Angel caught up quickly and in the space of a breath the three of them were gone.

"Asking again, would you like a drink?" Ruby said to Jaccob, as she watched the three young women leave the room.

"Um ... sure. Yeah." Jaccob sank down onto the couch as Ruby crossed behind it to where the decanter and ice were standing.

Jaccob recognized her green silk lounge dress as having been in her wardrobe when they'd been a couple. He'd found it alluring then, and tonight he couldn't help himself but to watch as the skirt moved along with her, giving him all-but-inappropriate glances at her bare legs as she walked.

"So do you want to tell me what you're really doing here?" she asked, as she pulled the lid from the ice bucket.

"What?"

"You weren't out getting ice."

"What?"

"You don't go get ice. You call for ice. Same as I would. So I ask again. What are you doing here?"

"I—" Jaccob took a deep breath. "I wanted to ask how things went with Floyd."

"No, you didn't."

"Ruby—"

"Just be honest with me. If you really wanted to know about Floyd, you'd be talking to Kara, because I know you know she's the one with the recording. She's the one who has the accurate info. But you didn't knock on Kara's door, you knocked on mine."

"I just ... I wanted to see you." Jaccob fidgeted, for a moment moving to put his hands in his pockets, but then thinking better of it when his position on the seat made it difficult. He was sure he'd managed to look awkward in the attempt.

"You know that's probably just magic," she said.

"You promised you'd never use magic on me," he reminded her.

It was the promise she made the last time they'd spoken before they might never have spoken again—when she'd first admitted the fact of her magic to him. He hadn't taken it well, but he remembered that promise, at least. A little shadow crossed her face at the reminder.

"I did do that, didn't I?" Ruby rolled her eyes a little as she plinked two cubes of ice into a glass. "No, I can assure you I have not directed any sort of enchantment your way. But you were right there while I was working on Floyd, and I think I've been pretty open about the fact that things haven't been quite right for me since ... the incident. So although I haven't thrown any magic at you intentionally, spillover is certainly a possibility."

She filled both glasses with Scotch and then handed one to Jaccob over the back of the sofa before replacing the stopper and taking a sip from her glass.

"I ... I don't think that's it."

"No?"

"I don't think that's it, because it's not just tonight."

Jaccob's mouth went suddenly dry. There it was, what he'd been trying to say to Ruby since they'd been back on speaking terms—or at least the first few words of it.

"Oh." Ruby took another sip of her drink and eased herself down to sit on the arm of the sofa. She seemed intrigued. "And here I thought having an hours-long conversation with a man thought long dead who'd almost certainly experienced time travel would be the highlight of the trip." She gestured. "Go on. I'm listening."

"Yeah, it's just ... I—" Jaccob took a deep breath. "I really hate the way things ended between us."

"And you weren't even the one who got dumped while in a hospital."

"Yeah," Jaccob replied. He took another deep breath and did his best to summon some courage. He'd come here to say these things, and by golly he was going to say them. "I screwed that up. I know I did. I was angry and upset and I felt lied to and—" He closed his eyes for a moment and fidgeted absently with his beard. "By the time I realized how bad I'd fouled things up, Liz was back and ... and I thought I could just go on with my life—try to forget."

"And how's that working for you?"

"Yeah. Not ... not great. And then when Liz left again, and ... I don't know. What I do know is that when I was awake in the middle of the night, feeling sorry for myself, feeling lonely, you were the person I wanted to call."

"So why didn't you?"

"What?"

"Call, Jaccob," Ruby said, leaning against the back of the sofa as she swirled the Scotch in her glass. "Why didn't you call? I haven't changed my numbers—any of them. Hell, you could have just shown up. My door is twenty yards from yours. And even if it had been locked, which you now know it never was, you're the one who installed the lock. You have the code; you've had it all along. You could've just let yourself in. You didn't even have to knock."

"I don't know why." Jaccob looked down into his glass of Scotch, as though the answer to her question might suddenly appear inside it. "I think I was scared," he said after a moment. "I think I didn't know how to begin—how to say I'm sorry. And I felt like I didn't have any right, like I had no place stepping into your life again after the way I'd walked out of it. But then one day there you were, standing in my office, and—" He trailed off, shaking his head and staring into his drink.

"No, no," Ruby said. "You have to finish that sentence. You don't get off the hook that easily."

"Well," Jaccob nodded and then took a sip of Scotch. "Oh, this is good."

"No changing the subject, either."

"Right. Yeah. So you were just ... you were back in my life, and I figured things would, I don't know, naturally progress, maybe? And maybe they have, in a way. But I've been thinking about it a lot, and I know things aren't going to just happen all on their own, and I couldn't figure out what I could do that might move things forward."

"Big damn hero short on grand romantic gestures. Who would have thought?"

"Turns out I'm kind of a coward," he said.

"Must be," Ruby replied, leaning forward to place her glass on the table in front of her. She folded her hands in her lap and shrugged. "You had two years, Jaccob. You could have found a way to say *something*."

"I'm um—" He tensed his jaw and knocked back another belt of Scotch. "I'm saying something now?"

Ruby shook her head and stood up again. She crossed her arms over her chest as she looked down at him. "You know I'm seeing someone."

The realization hit Jaccob like a brick upside the head. "V ... i ...vi ... vi ... Vivienne?" he stammered.

It was a question, but it wasn't. It had been as plain as day, had it only ever occurred to him to consider it. He knew the two of them had been in touch, and that Vivienne had spent the night in Ruby's place just a couple of weeks ago. When he thought about it, everything about the two of them together made sense. He was sweating all of the sudden, his head swimming with the realization and with a series of mental pictures he couldn't help his brain conjuring up.

"Mm-hmm."

"I'm sorry," he said. "I'll go. I didn't mean—"

But before Jaccob could finish his sentence, Ruby was gesturing for him to stay seated. She had her phone in her hand, perched atop her upturned fingers. It was barely a moment before the brief sound of a ring gave way to a familiar voice.

~

"Hey, you," Vivienne said, "How's Texas?"

"It's hot," Ruby replied.

"And it's after midnight," Vivienne said back, "you should be sleeping. You know you're not well yet, and—"

Ruby interrupted her before she could get any farther into her expression of care and concern. "You're on speaker, V."

"Oh?" Vivienne asked, sounding intrigued. "And why is that, pray tell?" It was clear to Ruby by her lover's tone that Vivienne was expecting the answer to be something salacious. This was going to be a fun surprise.

"Because Jaccob is in my hotel room," she answered.

"He is?"

"Mmm—"

"And how did that happen?"

"Would you believe he knocked?"

"Really?" Vivienne's voice had a fake incredulity that told Ruby everything she needed to know about Vivienne's opinion on her guest. Yes. This was a very fun surprise. "He didn't break down your door insisting you were in need of rescue?"

"Alas, no," Ruby replied, "that particular fantasy will have to wait for another day."

"Sad." Vivienne paused, and there was the sound of her drinking something. Probably bourbon. "So. What's he wearing?"

"Half a tux."

"Ooh, your favorite. You gonna take it off him?"

"I'm considering," Ruby answered. "Thought I'd get your opinion on the matter first."

"Are you planning on inviting Loki?"

"Oh, no. Even if I wanted to, Loki won't set foot in Texas—something about an angry mob and a Bible college. They've been a little light on the details."

"So it's just the two of you, then?"

"That's the idea."

"Pics or it didn't happen," Vivienne teased.

"I ought to just snap one now," Ruby said. "Jaccob has turned the most delightful shade of scarlet."

"Oh, I bet. Hello, Jaccob!"

"Um ... hi ... um, Vivienne," he said. His cheeks were bright red, and it seemed he couldn't figure out what the hell to do with his hands.

"You two enjoy yourselves," Vivienne said. "And you'll call me when you get home tomorrow?"

"You know I will."

"All right then," Vivienne said. "Have a good night. I'll talk to you tomorrow."

Vivienne hung up, and Ruby slipped her phone back into the pocket of her dress. She snatched her glass from the table then turned away from Jaccob, taking several steps toward the hallway before turning back.

"Well," she said to Jaccob, frowning. "Are you coming?"

Jaccob leapt from the sofa and followed after a beat.

~

When Jaccob rounded the corner into the bedroom, Ruby was already by the nightstand on the near side, sliding her phone onto a charging cradle. She narrowed her eyes as she turned back to look at him.

"Everything all right?" she asked.

"This is—" He shoved his hands into his pockets as he took a deep breath. He was completely overwhelmed, and it was obvious.

"You're not trying to tell me you showed up in my hotel room at half past midnight with your heart on your sleeve and this wasn't what you hoped would happen?"

"You know," he answered her, shaking his head and allowing a tiny laugh at himself, "I don't think I thought it through. I just wanted to see you. I just wanted you to know I wanted to see you."

"And now you see me," she said, starting back across the room toward him. "And I see you." She didn't stop moving until she was close enough to reach out and place her hands on his chest. Her touch was gentle, but deliberate, and she tilted her chin upward to look him in the eye. "And if that's all you wanted, then here we are."

"I don't know what I want." He moved his hands from out of his pockets to either side of her waist.

Ruby saw her chance and she took it, raising up onto her toes to gently press her lips against his. In an instant, what he wanted became abundantly clear. Jaccob leaned into the kiss, moving his hands from her waist to her back, and pulling her gently toward him until their bodies were pressed against each other. She threaded her arms around his neck, kissing him in precisely the way she remembered he liked.

They went on like that for a minute or more, Jaccob taking the lead after a moment, and Ruby letting herself be held, kissing him deep and hard, but without an urgency or needfulness. When the time felt right, she leaned away from him, just enough to catch her breath. He was breathing hard, his body was hot, and his face was flushed. He was smiling at her through half-lidded eyes when she looked back up at him.

"Do you know what you want now?" she whispered.

He kissed her again.

CHAPTER TWENTY-THREE

Jaccob could tell something was wrong with Ruby from the moment he woke up. She was sitting on the edge of the bed with her legs over the side, wearing an ivory satin nightgown she'd apparently put on some time in the night and with one arm in a matching dressing gown she hadn't yet managed to get over her shoulders.

"Hey," he said softly. "You all right?"

When she didn't respond, he slid out from under the covers and snagged a hotel robe from the back of a nearby chair, throwing it on as he made his way to the far side of the bed.

"What's wrong?" he asked, reaching out to place a hand on her shoulder.

"I ... I don't know." Ruby closed her eyes and shrugged. "I don't think it's a hangover, but ... maybe I had too much champagne? Maybe chasing it with Scotch was a bad idea?"

"I've seen you drink your weight in champagne. Hell, I've seen you drink *my* weight in champagne, and you never woke up like this. I don't think it's a hangover."

"Yeah, I don't know."

Jaccob turned and sat down on the bed beside her. "I think I should call Dr. Hao. If this has anything to do with what you've been through—"

"No. No, it's not ... Don't do that."

"What can I do, then?" he asked, placing his hand gently on her knee.

"Hand me my phone," she replied quickly, gesturing to the device in its charging cradle.

"Sure, okay," he said, reaching past her to grab her phone from the nightstand and place it carefully into her hand. Jaccob couldn't help but notice she didn't take proper hold of it. Her eyes were half shut and her breathing seemed slow and labored. "What else?"

"You're not going to let up until you feel like you've helped, are you?"

"You know me so well."

"All right. Yeah. Um ... Grapefruit juice. Call down to room service and get them to bring up a carafe of grapefruit juice. And make sure it's the real stuff—bitter, straight from the fruit. None of that sweetened juice cocktail bullshit they serve to tourists."

"I can do that. Anything to eat?"

"No. And then go find Kara and the others. Tell them the flight's delayed. Tell them we'll leave here at three. And that we'll be using the loading dock, not the front door."

"Okay."

Ruby shifted her gaze enough to get a look at him. "You might want to get dressed first."

Jaccob's face flushed as he pulled his robe closed. "Yeah. I probably should do that." Jaccob stood up then, leaning over to kiss the top of Ruby's head before fastening the robe properly around his waist. "I'll call down for your juice first. Then I'll go get dressed before talking to the others. I'll come back and check on you later."

"You don't have to do that."

"I know I don't have to, but I think *you* know I'm going to anyway."

Ruby chuckled a little under her breath as she nodded gently. "Right."

"I'll be back."

Jaccob slipped out of the bedroom and used the phone in the salon to call down for grapefruit juice—a thing which the hotel's butler was prepared for Miss Killingsworth to request. Jaccob managed to get to his own room without encountering anyone in the hallway. He showered and dressed quickly before knocking on Kara's and then Friday's, Yumi and Lisa's, and finally Angel's doors to let them know their departure would be delayed.

He was thankful none of them had questions. If one of them had asked after Ruby, or how he knew the plans had changed, or why he was the one spreading the word, he wasn't sure how he'd have explained himself.

By the time Jaccob made it back to the Presley suite, the juice had already been delivered. The carafe of murky, off-white liquid stood in a silver ice bucket alongside a tiny crystal goblet. An insulated bowl of nugget ice with attached tongs accompanied the juice and glass, as did an embroidered napkin and a fresh yellow rose. All of it was positioned atop a lace and linen tablecloth—it was by far the fussiest room service delivery he had ever seen.

When Ruby had said this place was trying to turn sucking up to her into an art form, she hadn't been exaggerating.

Jaccob quickly popped a few bits of ice into the goblet and poured it full of juice before heading back to the bedroom to check on Ruby.

He found her curled on her side with her head on the pillow. She was wearing her dressing gown properly, her hair looked recently brushed, and she had her phone in her hand. It was an improvement, but not much of one.

"I brought your juice," he said, when he saw her eyes open.

"Thank you," she said softly. "Just set it on the nightstand."

"Are you feeling any better?"

"I brushed my teeth, so, yes. But not in the way you're probably asking."

"Anything else I can do for you?"

"No. Just be ready to go at three. I've already moved the flight back. And the car will meet us in the loading dock. In case I'm not feeling better, I'd rather not be seen in the lobby."

"All right. Sure. Only I'm not leaving you alone like this."

"Jaccob—"

"No," he cut her off before she could start. "Five days ago, you were in a coma. And right now, you've barely got the energy to hold on to your phone. You don't want me to call a doctor yet, fine. But someone ought to be with you in case you get worse. So either I call Angel, your self-appointed bulletproof bodyguard, to come in here and sit with you, or you're stuck with me."

"Suit yourself," she said after a beat, finally rising to sit on the edge of the bed as she reached for the glass of juice he'd left on the nightstand. "I suppose this is what I get for going to bed with a Good Guy."

Jaccob felt his face flush. They hadn't talked much last night. In fact, they hadn't talked hardly at all—their energies had been decidedly focused on *other things.* He had no real idea of the status of their relationship, other than the fact they'd spent last night together. He knew what spending the night with someone meant to him, but he had a very strong feeling it might not mean exactly the same thing to her.

"Looks like it," was all he managed to say.

Ruby drank half the juice from the goblet before setting it back on the nightstand and lying back down on her side on the bed. Jaccob reached over and pulled a blanket over her feet.

"I'll leave you be," he said. "Get some rest. I'll be just in the next room if you need anything."

He bent down and kissed her cheek again before heading back out into the suite's main salon.

~

Jaccob spent the rest of the morning and early afternoon surfing the hotel's television channels and playing games on his phone. Every once in a while, he'd hear Ruby stirring, so he'd send her a text offering her more juice and asking if she needed anything additional.

Ruby was well in to her second carafe of juice and halfway through a bottle of sparkling water when she invited him to come and sit on the balcony with her while the butlers came in to pack her bags. By that point she was dressed and ready with her hair done and her face done. Most people would never have been able to tell there was anything wrong with her at all.

But Jaccob was not most people.

And he'd done what most people wouldn't. Despite Ruby's insistence to the contrary, he had called Dr. Hao. After he'd seen how much a trip to the bathroom mirror and back had taken out of her, he couldn't help himself. The doctor shared Jaccob's suspicion that Ruby's malaise was magic-related and told him to do whatever he could to keep her from using further magic, at least until the doctor had a chance to look into things more thoroughly.

Jaccob didn't mention how impossible it was to keep Ruby Killingsworth from doing anything she had a mind to do, but he felt lucky that she seemed disinclined toward magic for the moment. By the time they were ready to leave for the car, she'd pulled herself together enough to make the trip on her feet, but he couldn't imagine she'd be up to any tricks on the way.

There was nobody else in the penthouse-level hallway when Jaccob and Ruby headed to the elevator, the luggage having gone down earlier, and the others apparently out ahead of them as well. In the absence of other people, Ruby didn't seem to mind Jaccob's arm around her. She even leaned against him a little for support. But when the elevator doors slid open on the basement level of the hotel, Ruby Killingsworth strode across the rug and down the hall to the tunnel where their car was waiting as though nothing could possibly be wrong.

It was only once they were settled and on their way that Jaccob was able to figure out she'd just been in a hurry to sit back down. And when the car pulled up beside the plane on the tarmac, Jaccob could tell she wasn't really up to standing again. He got out of the limo ahead of her, holding his hand out in a gesture he was sure would be mistaken for run-of-the-mill chivalry.

The look she gave him was all the thanks he was liable to get, but she took his hand nonetheless. He led her to the aircraft's stairs and let her up ahead of him, keeping his hand on the small of her back as they went. The others, who had been busy teasing Friday about an apparent flirtation with the drummer of the hotel's poolside reggae band, followed behind them, still giggling.

If Jaccob's experience with his own young adult daughter was any indication, they likely hadn't noticed anything was off with their boss. It was a good four hours back to Cobalt City, and he could only hope Ruby would either feel better by the time they got back or agree to let him summon the doctor to have a look at her.

Either way, she had the next several hours to be still and rest, which was something she'd never have done if there wasn't a long flight on the agenda. So at least that was a blessing.

~

Something was wrong with Ruby; Lisa was sure of it.

But Miss Killingsworth didn't seem like the kind of person who'd appreciate being asked if she was all right. The quickness with which she'd pivoted from comatose to pretending nothing had ever gone wrong was enough to tell anyone who was paying attention that asking her how she was doing wasn't the best idea. Rather than take it as a genuine expression of concern, there was every chance Ruby would accuse the asker of drawing attention to her possible infirmity. So Lisa didn't ask.

Instead, she waited until Jaccob followed Ruby to the aft cabin of the aircraft to bring it up with her fellows.

"Did you notice—" she began.

"That Jaccob hasn't been able to keep his hands off Ruby all day?" Angel said. "Yeah, I noticed."

Lisa, who had not noticed that, looked back at Angel and frowned. "That was not what I was about to say."

"Then what was it?" Yumi asked. "Because I spent the whole ride over here trying not to notice Angel's thing, so maybe I noticed your thing and maybe I didn't."

"That Ruby's not okay," Lisa replied.

"She looked fine to me," Friday said.

"No," Kara said. "No, Lisa's right. Something's off."

"Maybe she just didn't get a whole lot of sleep last night," Angel suggested. "If you know what I'm saying."

"Eww," Friday sounded.

"Huh?" Kara asked.

"Yeah, you two weren't there," Angel said, pointing at Kara and Friday. "Jaccob showed up in her room last night, right after you left, Kara. Then the rest of us left, and the next thing we know, it's morning, and he's the one telling us the flight is delayed, when that seems like the kind of news that should have come in a text from her scheduler."

"Yeah," Lisa said. "The flight was delayed because she's sick. And Jaccob came to tell us about it because he knows she's sick and wants to take care of things for her. And you're talking about him having his hands all over her? He did no such thing. He walked her up the stairs with one hand holding her elbow and the other on the small of her back. Not like he was trying to cop a feel but like he was afraid she might fall."

"Honestly," Kara said, "I think you're both probably right."

"Huh?" Yumi asked.

"I think they probably slept together," Kara replied. "And also, there's something wrong. I think two weeks ago, Jaccob wouldn't have been so tender with the way he helped her up the stairs, and I also think two weeks ago, Ruby would sooner have taken a tumble down those stairs than let him help her at all. And there is definitely a difference between the way they're acting toward each other now versus how they were the last time we were on this airplane, meaning whatever happened to change that happened in Texas. Add to that his popping into her room in the middle of the night, and yeah, I think Angel is probably right. They probably spent the night together. But even if they did, I don't think that explains Ruby suddenly being willing to let someone help her up the stairs. So I think even if Angel is right, Lisa's also right. Something's wrong with Ruby. The thing is, I don't think that's actually any of our business."

"You don't?" Lisa asked, shaking her head and rattling the ice in her glass. "The person we work for—who, might I remind you, was in a coma last week—is visibly unwell again, and you don't think that's any of our business?"

"I mean," Kara replied with a shrug, "I guess that part's a little more our business than whether or not she and Jaccob slept together, but no. Not really."

"I guess. Maybe." Lisa took a sip of her soda and shook her head again.

"But you're worried?" Yumi asked her.

"Yeah," Lisa replied.

"You think it's going to screw things up for us?" Friday asked. "Because I feel like we've got the recording of Floyd, and we've got all that equipment back at the penthouse that's just about ready to be turned back on, and we got a look at the contraption when it was on the helipad. Plus, we've got Angel for protection now, in addition to all the security upgrades Jaccob put on the building. I mean ... I think we're good without her help for the time being."

"Okay, no," Lisa said. "I'm not worried because I think our work's gonna suffer or we're going to have a big setback that might affect our bonus, or whatever. I'm worried because she's a person—a person who's been unbelievably generous to us, by the way—and she almost died, like ... a week ago, and now she's not doing well again, and I have actual, like, human concern."

"Well," Yumi said, sipping on the botanical mocktail the steward had brought her after takeoff, "I don't think we have to worry about her. Jaccob seems to be paying close enough attention. And we're headed back to Cobalt City, where Dr. Hao will be, and to her building where, apparently, there's a god available for consultation."

CHAPTER TWENTY-FOUR

It was raining when they landed in Cobalt City. Ruby's driver met her at the top of the aircraft stairs to walk her down with an umbrella over her head. She was a little grateful for the lousy conditions, as her unusually slow and deliberate trip down the boarding stairs was easily attributable to the weather and slick shoes.

Ruby managed to fake her way off the plane and into the car. Jaccob could likely tell she still felt rotten, but her head was high, and her gait was steady, so there was little chance the others noticed anything was off. She had the bright idea to order the driver to stop at the Tower's residential entrance first, to let her employees out of the car with the quickest trip back to their accommodations.

It also meant they wouldn't see her possibly struggle to get out of the car, which was a thing she was growing increasingly concerned about. The longer she was forced to sit upright and hold a stiff upper lip, the less energy she would have to make the trip upstairs. When the car finally stopped outside her private entrance, only Ruby and Jaccob were left inside. He'd seen her at her worst first thing this morning, so she didn't much care what he saw at this point.

"I can have the driver pull around to your door," she told him. "That way you won't have to cross the street in the rain."

"I'd rather walk you inside?"

Ruby shrugged. She'd seen that one coming and didn't have the energy to push back.

He got out of the car ahead of her, holding out his hand to help her out much as he had when they'd arrived at the airfield in Lapis.

It was just the kind of casual gallantry he was prone to, and she wouldn't have thought twice about taking his hand had she been feeling herself. So she fought the stubborn urge to wave him off as some sort of proof she was okay.

Once she was on her feet, Jaccob offered his arm as he took the umbrella from the driver and held it over both their heads. Ruby took his arm then, giving a nod of dismissal to her driver as she did. Jaccob's presence beside her as she made the short walk beneath the awning to her private entrance was warm and reassuring. She didn't like how much she appreciated having someone to lean on, and she was doubly annoyed with herself at how deeply she enjoyed the fact that person was *him*.

She did her best to push those feelings to the back of her mind as the doorman pulled open the glass and brass door to let them inside. Jaccob handed the umbrella to the doorman and followed Ruby into the small receiving lobby. Ruby realized, as they approached the waiting elevator car, that Jaccob had no intention of letting her go.

"So, by walk me inside," she said softly, "you meant—?"

"Just let me get you upstairs," he implored.

Ruby shook her head but gestured for him to board the elevator alongside her. She'd managed to mostly ignore the man for the better part of the past two years; surely she could ignore him for the next five minutes.

Ignoring Jaccob proved to be, somewhat predictably, easier said than done. It was clear when the elevator doors opened again on the forty-eighth floor, he meant to see her all the way to her bedroom. It wasn't that she minded Jaccob in her bedroom—in some circumstances she'd have positively reveled in the idea—but she didn't need to be tucked in like a child. He'd been adorably sweet and attentive on the flight, bringing her mineral water while she lay in bed in the aft cabin, and staying to chat or leaving her in peace afterward according to her stated preference.

She had things to tend to, and a mind to get to sleep as soon as possible. And she didn't need company. But Jaccob seemed disinclined toward leaving, and this thing burgeoning between them was too new and too fragile for telling him outright to leave to be a good idea. If he meant to spend the night, for whatever reason, she didn't actually mind. But she would absolutely not stand for being doted upon.

He could stay if he wanted to, but she wasn't going to change her evening plans to accommodate him.

"I'm making a call," she said, less to get rid of him—because she was pretty well convinced that wasn't going to happen—and more to prepare him for the fact she was about to start talking and it wouldn't be to him. She pulled out her phone and punched the button to dial Vivienne.

"Hello, darling," Ruby said into the phone, as soon as Vivienne picked up. "I said I'd call, so I did. I'm home but I'm tired, so I'm going to bed. We'll talk tomorrow. In the meantime, could you please tell Jaccob he has his own shiny skyscraper to go home to, and if he can't at least pretend to relax, I'm going to insist he do so? Because he's hovering, and it's getting to be a little much."

Ruby continued into the bedroom, placing the phone into Jaccob's hand as she passed through the door. She gave him a look over her shoulder as she turned to head toward her closet.

Ruby strode across the room with more purpose and pep than Jaccob would have thought her capable of after the way she'd been all day. He put her phone to his ear as soon as she'd closed the closet door behind herself.

"Um—" Jaccob had no real idea what to say. "Um ... Vivienne?"

Her response was curt and to the point. "Don't you dare leave her alone."

"Wasn't planning on it."

"Is she sitting right there, or can you talk?"

"She went to get changed. She's in her closet with the door closed."

"Good. So you can tell me what the hell is going on. I got a text this morning saying the flight was delayed but not for how long, which is completely out of character for her. And now when she finally calls me, she sounds like death warmed over. What's going on?"

"She used magic before she should have, and—"

"This can't just be magic," Vivienne insisted. "I've seen her kick her own ass with magic, and this is ... this is more than that."

"It is, but it's—" Jaccob sighed and shook his head. He already knew more about magic than he'd ever intended to, but trying to digest everything he'd learned and form it all into an explanation another person could understand was a horse of a different color. "I talked to Dr. Hao. She says it's akin to someone falling on a broken bone just as it's starting to knit."

"So, she's re-breaking herself every time she uses magic."

"Pretty much. Yeah. You know when your phone's battery dies then you finally get it just charged enough to turn it on, but then the very act of turning it on is enough to kill the battery again?"

"Yeah."

"It's like that, only with her magic abilities."

"That was a surprisingly good analogy," Vivienne said. "And you're not freaking out. Kudos."

"You think I'm not freaking out?"

"Not about the magic stuff."

Jaccob paused. It was true. Somehow, it didn't seem as threatening as before. "Huh."

"Should I be getting on a plane?" Vivienne asked.

"No. No, that's a bad idea. She's doing her damnedest to keep people from realizing there's anything wrong. I feel like she'd try so hard to convince you she's fine, she'd wind up putting herself back in a coma."

"Yeah, okay; that tracks. But you're going to take care of her."

"As best she'll let me."

"You've got to do better than that," Vivienne snapped. "Listen, I know you two have a past and I know about last night. What I don't know—what you're going to have to tell me honestly—is where your head is right now. If magic still gives you the willies, if you're still holding some kind of brokenhearted grudge against Ruby ... You've got to level with me. If you're not up for keeping her alive whether she likes it or not, then you need to tell me that right now."

"No, I can. I promise."

"Okay, good."

"You're still here, and you're still on my phone," Ruby called out, as she strode back into the bedroom. Dressed now in a dark gray silk nightgown and matching lace robe, she looked even paler than she had in her navy-blue travel dress. She seated herself on the edge of the bed and looked up at Jaccob expectantly.

"I think she wants her phone back," Jaccob said.

"Sounds like it," Vivienne replied.

Ruby held out her hand and waited for Jaccob to set her device on her palm. He did so presently, and she put it back to her ear.

"He didn't leave," Ruby said.

"Don't think he's going to," Vivienne replied. "I'm not so sure he's going to chill out, either. If you need me to come smite him, let me know."

"Oh, I doubt it will come to that. But it's nice to know you care."

"Get some sleep, Ginger. And call me tomorrow."

"All right, darling. And I'll keep your offer in mind."

"You better," Vivienne replied before hanging up the phone.

Ruby ended the call on her end as well and then reached over to set the phone in its charging cradle on her nightstand. She looked up at Jaccob and frowned.

"In case you're wondering, V's offer was to fly out here and smite you if I deem it necessary."

"That's because she doesn't want you smiting me yourself."

"Is that so?"

"Yeah. No smiting. No magic at all."

"Excuse me?"

"I think you know."

"You think I know what?"

"That it's your magic. That the magic you used on Simon Floyd last night is the reason you've felt so badly today."

"Any academic sources for this theory?" Ruby stood up to pull back the covers. "Or did you come up with this one all on your own?"

"Dr. Hao," Jaccob said.

"Did you call her or did Vivienne?"

"I did."

"Jaccob—"

"What? I was worried about you."

"Were you now? Or was it just that you figured I might need saving, and since that's the thing you do best—?"

"You didn't seem interested in knowing why you felt so poorly this morning."

"What does it matter why?" She sat back down and pulled the blankets up around her waist. "It is what it is, and I have to deal with it either way."

"I just—" Jaccob was flustered. "Maybe it is my need to save people. But I wanted to know what I could do to take care of you."

"And you told Vivienne?"

"She wants to take care of you, too."

"I would think the both of you know me well enough by now to understand that I can take care of myself."

"Really? Without magic?"

Ruby was struck by how non-confrontational his tone was. He wasn't sassing her, poking her, or daring her. He sounded genuinely concerned she might not be prepared to do what she said she could do.

"Jaccob—"

"And how long until you figured that out?" he pressed. "How much more damage would you have done before you realized it was your magic that was hurting you?"

Ruby shook her head and sighed. She hated it, but he had a point. "You know, I can't say. I've gotten used to this power. Half the time I use it without thinking. Do you have any idea how long it's been since I've had to walk across a room to close a door or turn on a light?"

"I'll tell you what." He sat down on the bed opposite her. "Tomorrow, I'll take a few minutes and put all your lights on voice control. That way you can keep your seat, the lights will obey, and you don't have to use magic to make that happen."

"And the doors?"

"You can voice control that already." He reached over to pat her hand. "'Jaccob, would you please shut the door?' I doubt you were raised in a barn, so how about you stop acting like it?"

He stood up then and walked the short distance to the bedroom door. As soon as he could reach it, he turned the handle, opened it slightly, then closed it again before crossing back to the bedside.

"You're enjoying this!" Ruby exclaimed, all her feelings of warmth toward his apparent concern gone in an instant. "Poor, pitiful Ruby, all helpless and broken and needing to be cared for. Well, I'll tell you—"

"No." Jaccob interrupted her. "No, it's not that."

"It's not?"

"It's just—" Jaccob shook his head and took a step back toward her. "When we were together, you were going through something I can't even begin to imagine. I mean ... I didn't know it at the time, but you'd basically lost the principal way you interact with the world. And you didn't seem to miss a beat. Not only that, you were there for me in every way I needed someone. Meanwhile, you couldn't even tell me what was going on with you."

"Oh, right," Ruby snarked. "'By the way Jaccob, it hasn't come up yet, but I think you should know I'm the living embodiment of the thing you hate most in the world.' I'm sure that would have ended well. And quickly."

"Yeah, I know." He hung his head and clasped his hands at his waist. "I know you couldn't confide in me, and I don't blame you. I didn't make myself a safe person to talk to. And I'm sorry for that. I'm trying—" He sat on the far side of the bed and looked into her eyes. "I couldn't be there for you then, but I can be here for you now. I can tell you don't want people to see you this way, but with me ... at least I hope it's different. I've seen you with no magic. I fell in love with you with no magic."

"Don't say that."

"Why not?"

"Because it's bullshit."

"Ruby—"

"No," she stopped him before he could go any further. "It's bullshit. Love does not exist. It's a made-up aspirational state perpetuated by capitalist oligarchs in order to increase sales of greeting cards, chocolate boxes, lingerie, and acoustic albums."

"Are you really that cynical?"

"I'm not a cynic, Jaccob, I'm a realist. I've heard an awful lot of love songs in my day, and every one of them is a work of fiction."

Jaccob shook his head, looking down at the bedspread and trying to pretend there was something interesting in the damask. He hadn't really meant to admit his feelings like that, and he surely hadn't been prepared for her response.

"I'll ... um ... I'll go. I'll stay at my own place tonight," he offered. "If you'd rather—"

"Jaccob," Ruby said, "I honestly don't care where you stay tonight. I do care that you stop treating me like I'm everybody else. I do not need saving. You're right that you've seen me without magic before—and, as you just said yourself—I didn't miss a beat. I was fine. I was fine then, and I'll be fine now."

"Yeah. You will be fine. But you're not fine right this minute. And there's a difference. Back then you couldn't use magic, but the current problem is that you *shouldn't.* Your magic might work, but it could also kill you. Meanwhile, I wonder sometimes if you'd rather die than go without it."

"Oh, so this is a suicide watch? Jaccob, really?" Ruby rolled her eyes as she crossed her arms over her chest. "I can assure you I do not need a babysitter any more than I need a superhero."

"Ruby—"

"Or a nursemaid."

"You know." He leaned in to rest his chin on her shoulder. "Even the Stardust suit can't take six bullets without needing some down time."

"But you see, those bullets never hit me. So—"

"But they did. They may have hit your magic and not your body, but you still took the force of all six shots."

"Hrmph."

"Now, I can't imagine the amount of energy you had to generate to make that happen." He sat up straight again, then he held his hands up, jiggling his wrists just enough to make his Starbands bangle on his arms. "Except I kind of can. After the thing at the White House—"

"Thing?" Ruby interrupted. "Jaccob, it was a bombing. You make it sound like a bad cocktail party."

"After the bombing, I had to swap the batteries out. They'd discharged so completely that they needed an external component to recharge. Now—" He reached out to put a hand on her knee. "—I can't pull your batteries and swap them for fresh. And I can't just plug you into the wall and wait."

"Indeed. It turns out that people are more complex than even Stardust tech. Who knew?"

"But this is a lot alike. Dr. Hao says you depleted your batteries. And you fried your wiring in the process. There's no reason to believe your body won't repair itself over time, but you've got to take it easy and let it happen. Every time you use a near-dead battery to send current through a bunch of damaged wires, you risk affecting your battery's ability to ever recharge again, and you're risking permanent damage to all your wiring. If I'd have been where I was supposed to be, none of this would have happened. So if you—"

"Wait," Ruby stopped him, scooting away so his hand was no longer on her leg, "so this is a guilt thing? Jaccob—"

Jaccob shrugged.

Ruby shook her head again. "Newsflash, heartthrob, even you can't be everywhere and all the time. So you are just going to have to learn to live with yourself if every once in a while a person of your acquaintance has to save themselves. Some of us are actually quite capable."

"I know," he said softly. "I do. I know that. It's just—"

"It's just nothing. Get over yourself, hotshot. Not everybody needs a hero."

"I'm learning."

"Good."

"But I'd still rather not leave tonight."

"I never said you had to."

"That's good. Because I promised Vivienne."

"And we wouldn't want to incite the wrath of Lady Vengeance, now, would we?"

"Wouldn't recommend it," Jaccob said. "No."

"Stay as long as it suits you. Or as long as Vivienne thinks it's necessary. But you're not allowed to blame yourself for the shooting, and you're not allowed to treat me like an invalid."

"But you'll let me put all your lights on voice control?"

"Upgrade the building all you want. Lights, doors, windows, I literally don't give a damn—as long as you don't put passwords on things without telling me what they are."

"I can make all of it recognize you the same as the elevator."

"That's all fine then. But for the moment, if you would please get the lights. I'm going to bed. Join me if you care to, but either way I'd like it to be dark in here."

Ruby stood up again, shedding her dressing gown and draping it over the plush chair by her window as Jaccob crossed to the light switch by the door. When he turned back around the room was dim, but only just. The city lights bled in through the window sheers, keeping the room from falling dark enough for sleep. Jaccob crossed quickly from the door to the windows, pulling the heavy shades shut with unmasked urgency as Ruby chuckled softly under her breath.

"What?" he asked, turning around once the shades were shut and the room was all but completely blacked out.

"Those are on a remote control already. I could have done that with my phone."

"Oh ... I knew that didn't I?"

"Mm-hmm."

"I'll try to remember."

"Okay."

"Is there anything else? Anything I can do? Anything I can get for you?"

"Well," Ruby said, pulling back the covers and sliding into her side of the bed. "There is one thing I can think of, might help me sleep a little better."

"What do you need? I can call down, or I can go get it—" His hand was already on the doorknob when she interrupted him.

"Jaccob, I swear," she sighed, shaking her head as she pulled the covers up around her waist. "You wouldn't catch an innuendo if I taped it to a brick and flung it at your head."

"Oh." He swallowed hard. "You mean—?"

"I do mean." Ruby smiled back at him and patted the bed beside her.

"Oh."

"Well?" If he'd meant what happened in Texas to be a one-time thing, she could be fine with that. But Jaccob had never seemed the type to be into one-night stands. And he'd been the one to insist on staying over. She figured it was worth the effort to try and enjoy his company as best she could.

"Yeah. Yeah, I can do that. In fact, I'd be happy to." He slipped his jacket off his shoulders and draped it across the chair at the foot of the bed.

"Good," Ruby said. "Then come over here and do it."

CHAPTER TWENTY-FIVE

Talking her way out of bed and into the office had been more of a chore than Ruby was prepared for. She'd honestly forgotten how cuddly Jaccob could be, and how clingy. And she had grossly underestimated how hard he was going to try to get her to forgo her workday altogether. It had taken a good measure of amorous attention, along with a reminder it was a longer walk to and from the far end of her closet than it would be to and from her desk to get him to relent.

The line between sweet and overbearing was one he was doing only a fair job straddling.

But he had things to do, and eventually agreed that her spending her day head-down in her office was preferable to many other possibilities. Not the least of which being pacing back and forth while the team of heroes worked to reconcile what they learned from her time with Simon Floyd with the data they had from their machinery and its attendant records.

The way he'd kissed her goodbye had been almost disturbingly domestic, and he'd promised to be back over as soon as he could, hopefully with the first set of components necessary to start work on her doors, windows, and light switches.

Which meant Ruby's first order of business for the day was obvious. She dialed Vivienne's number as soon as she was out of the elevator car. Vivienne picked up on the second ring, just as Ruby was getting settled in her office chair.

"Hey there, Ginger. How're you feeling?"

"Much better, thank you."

"How'd you sleep?"

"Funny you should ask. Because the reason I called this early is that I think I should tell you Jaccob stayed over last night."

"I think I should tell you I told him to," Vivienne replied. "Although I'm kind of surprised he didn't mention that himself."

"He did ... in a way. But I wasn't sure how much he was improving the truth. And I want to be honest with you, so I thought I should let you know what happened—er—is happening."

"Good."

"You're sure? This doesn't bother you? Ethical non-monogamy is one thing, but I know Jaccob can be a ... sticky subject. For both of us."

"Is he taking care of you?"

"Indeed he is. Possibly too well by some metrics."

"Are you going to call things off between us and run away with him for some kind of heteronormative hero-ever-after?"

"Absolutely not."

"Then have your fun, Ginger."

"If you're sure."

"I am. You know, this was practically inevitable, right? I made peace with the possibility weeks ago."

"It was?" Ruby asked. "You did?"

"Ginger, I swear. You are possibly the smartest person I know, but you can be real dense sometimes."

"Oh really?"

"Yes. Really." Vivienne laughed for a second before going on. "Jaccob's always carried a torch for you. That much was obvious from the first time I talked to him after the two of you broke up, back before you and I ever met. He never let go of his feelings for you. He never even got real good at *pretending* he'd let go of his feelings for you. And he's less averse to magic now than he used to be—I think we both get a little credit for that one. So when you told me the two of you would be working together on this thing for Mike pretty much right after he told me his divorce was final ... yeah. Hate to break it to you, babe, but I saw this one coming."

"And you're really okay with it?"

"I really am. The man is a walking box of donuts."

"Come again?"

"You know, like when you see a box of donuts and you decide not to have one, and then all you can think of for the rest of the day is how much you want a donut."

"I'm afraid I don't follow."

"Fine." Vivienne sighed audibly. "He's like a song you can't get out of your head. The kind you can't shake until you've listened to it on loop for half an hour. The sort of thing you have to indulge. You'll just drive yourself crazy trying to resist otherwise."

"Ah, yes. A music analogy. That one I understand. And I completely agree."

"Of course you do. Because I'm right. And I mean it. Have your fun. It's no skin off my teeth. And it's not like I'm out here playing celibate or anything."

"Hmmm. I thought I heard snoring in the background. Anybody I know?"

"Can I plead the fifth on that one?"

"Only for as long as he's behaving himself."

"Well, you don't hear me asking you to undo any curses."

"Good," Ruby said. "Because I won't be doing that. Tony earned that curse fair and square, and if it's ever rescinded, it will be because he earned that, too. And as satisfying as you may find the experience, the bedroom won't be the place where that gets done. Not that I'm saying it's possible at all—"

"I mean ... that's fair."

"I know it is. And as long as he refrains from plotting homicide, he's perfectly safe. And I'm glad you're enjoying yourself out there."

"Yeah, me too. And I'm glad we're talking about it. We may both suck at relationships, but this relationship doesn't suck."

"Call it that one more time and I'll hang up on you."

"Yeah, well," Vivienne said, laughing even harder. "We should hang up anyway. I've got things to do today, and lying in bed talking to you won't help get any of them done."

"I believe we just covered that topic."

"No, I mean it. Work stuff. Restock after a busy weekend stuff. And, you know ... vigilante shit. Tony's not just here on a social call."

"All right. I have things to do, too. Apparently being in a coma for three days can really back up your inbox."

"Just ... just try to take it easy, all right? I know you've only got one speed, but I really don't want my next trip over there to be to sit beside your hospital bed."

"There's no danger of that, V," Ruby said. "I assure you. The worst has passed, and Jaccob has me on magic restriction."

"How's he gonna manage that?"

"He's decided to add voice controls to all my windows, doors, lights, and anything else he can think of that I might otherwise use magic to interact with."

"And that's going to keep you from using magic? Sounds unlikely."

"Well, it will at least keep me from using it casually. Give my batteries time to recharge, as he says."

"You know what? If it works ... good for him. I happen to like you upright and conscious."

"Liar. You like me flat on my back just fine as I recall."

"Okay, that's fair," Vivienne said. "But I stand by preferring you awake and quipping."

"Well, that's fine."

"How's Angel doing? I haven't heard from her since you all left for Texas."

"Oh, she's fine. A little intense, but—"

"Yeah, she gets that from her father."

"Did you know him well?" Ruby wasn't sure Vivienne had ever mentioned any of Angel's other relations before. It seemed strange for her to suddenly bring her father up so casually.

"Wait, you don't know—?"

"Don't know what?"

"Shit—" Vivienne took a deep breath and blew it out loudly. "Ruby, Angel is Tony's daughter."

Ruby felt all the blood drain out of her face. That was information she was absolutely not prepared to hear. She'd never thought to interrogate how come Vivienne's niece and former lover shared a surname, and as much as this explanation made sense, it made some other things very confusing.

"And I take it from the tone of your voice," Ruby said slowly, trying to wrap her mind around what she'd just learned, "that this wasn't some sort of million-dollar miracle/everything happened in a lab situation?"

"Yeah, no."

"Jesus fuck, Vivienne. He never deserved you."

"That's very nice of you to say."

"I am not nice! And I mean it. He never deserved you, and he certainly doesn't now. You ought to throw him out in the street right this second."

"How about, instead, I just leave him here and go to work?"

"If you must. But I promise you can do better."

"Yeah," Vivienne kidded, "but he's here already and you're all the way on the other side of the country. So—"

"I guess."

"Call you tomorrow?"

"Tomorrow's a mess. Saturday."

"I'll call Saturday, then. Tell Jaccob hello from me."

"I will. And do not tell Tony hello from me. I'll talk to you Saturday."

"Bye."

Even under penalty of torture, Ruby wouldn't have readily admitted to just how much weight having Vivienne's blessing for this dalliance with Jaccob had lifted off her shoulders. But it was definitely real, and she was only mildly annoyed at the self-awareness. She didn't like feelings in the slightest. And she intensely disliked the way feelings could complicate otherwise pleasant circumstances.

She'd made the mistake of not considering Vivienne's feelings about a spontaneous hookup once, and it had almost ended things between them. She had later decided once and for all that would be an unacceptable turn of events and had done her best to make amends—maybe even succeeded. Things had been delightfully smooth between them in the few months since, Vivienne's association with her homicidal former sweetheart notwithstanding.

She absolutely did not want to fuck things up between them. But she also didn't want to cut things off with Jaccob. So having Vivienne's blessing was the absolute best possible outcome.

For the time being, anyway.

Ruby couldn't help but fantasize about the fun the three of them might have together in the coming weeks or months if she played her cards right. That was certainly an adventure worth pursuing. She was sure Vivienne would be game, and she figured the two of them wouldn't have too rough a time talking Jaccob into bed with them if they put their minds to it.

It was difficult not to let those thoughts consume her thinking, but Ruby Killingsworth was nothing if not disciplined. She had work to do, and she couldn't let herself get distracted.

Fortunately, a lot of what had landed on her desk in her absence was cursory. A signature here, a quick question there, and the tacit approval of half a dozen FYI memos, and she was more than halfway through the game of catch-up when there was a knock at her door.

That was weird.

No one should be knocking at her office door. At least not without Bridget having called ahead over the intercom.

Which meant one of two things was happening. Option one: Bridget had left the desk without coverage and some employee on a benign errand was knocking as a matter of course, not expecting her to be at her desk but generally unwilling to walk into the boss's office *without* knocking.

Or option two: whoever was there had done some harm to Bridget and had a mind to harm Ruby next. It wasn't exactly a far-fetched idea, especially considering gunmen had appeared out of nowhere on her roof just last week.

Then again, would an attacker bother to knock?

They would if the double doors from her outer office to the hallway were propped open and they didn't want to raise alarm in anyone who might walk past and consider intervening.

For a moment, Ruby let herself wonder how much of Jaccob's resistance to her coming into the office today was borne out of fear of a repeat attack. Not that it mattered at all right now. But with the possibility of her magic either failing her or leaving her incapacitated, she was genuinely frightened of whatever might be on the other side of that door. She'd thought when she had the building repaired and upgraded after the demon occupation that she'd never have to feel fear in this office again. So much for good intentions.

She fingered the panic button under the lip of her desk as she called out. "Come in?"

Ruby took a deep breath as she watched the door swing open.

And blew it out in exasperation when she saw it was Jaccob on the other side.

"Hey," he said, clearly oblivious to the tension of the last few seconds.

"You're above speaking to my receptionist now?"

"Nah, nothing like that. I asked her if you were still in, she said she wasn't sure, and so I told her I'd just knock."

"Well." Ruby shook her head and worked to get ahold of the adrenaline she no longer had any use for. "While that is all fine and good, might I remind you that the week following a violent attack on a person might not be the best time to break with her office protocol."

"Oh," he said, his face suddenly grave. "Shit. I hadn't thought about that. I'm sorry."

"We live and learn. Might I ask what brings you here this afternoon? I don't recall it being Take Your Hero to Work Day."

Jaccob chuckled. "I'm here to look at this door. Turns out I have a lot of automation components next door in the lab, so I think I can start on the voice control stuff today. But I wasn't here for the rebuild like I was for the initial construction." His voice sounded suddenly sad. "And I figured all the stuff I did in here before was probably ripped out during the repairs. So I wanted to have a look at what the team put in before I showed up with a tool box and a bunch of computer parts."

"You know, I hadn't thought of that. Everything looks so similar to the way it was before, I hadn't taken a moment to consider that none of your work was likely to have survived. I'm glad you're doing this, then. It's just one more thing we're putting right."

"I'd like to think we're setting a lot of things right."

Ruby was a little bit disgusted with herself at how happy seeing that smile again made her. "Me too," she said, before she was able to stop herself.

"I'll just be a minute here. I'll do the work over the weekend so I'm not down here interrupting your workday, but I didn't think you'd mind me dropping by to make sure I had all the components at the ready."

"And your decision to come down this afternoon had nothing at all to do with wanting to check and make sure I'm sitting still like a good convalescent?"

Jaccob looked back at her and shrugged. "I'm not good at being sneaky. And I really do have to check what's up with this door."

"But—"

"But I also wanted to see you."

"I swear I'm behaving."

"I'm not going to apologize for looking out for you."

"Your co-conspirator says hello, by the way," Ruby said then.

"My—?"

"Vivienne. I talked to her about an hour ago. I know the two of you are in cahoots. Not that either of you was making any effort to hide it. But I know now she genuinely does want you here, and she has no objection to what you and I are doing. Which is good, because I like what's happening here, but I wouldn't want us moving forward at her expense."

"Yeah. No, that wouldn't be good."

"It would not. But neither is the two of you ganging up on me. I am an adult. I run a multi-billion-dollar megacorporation. I think I can be trusted to decide for myself when to come to the office, when to stay in bed, and even, now that you've shared with me what Dr. Hao said to you about my casting capacity and needing time to heal, when and how to use certain skills and when to approach problems differently."

"I'm sorry you feel like we were going behind your back," Jaccob said, turning away from the door, which had held at least a bit of his attention until now. "But I know how you are. And V does, too. You're strong and you're capable, but you're also stubborn. You'll just keep going until you can't anymore, damn anything that tries to get in your way, including the people who care about you. The problem is, this thing could kill you if you just keep going. And we'd rather have you alive and well and angry than dead or comatose from doing what you want."

"What I want is for you to figure out this door situation as quickly as possible and then go upstairs and check on the progress of the array. Because what I want most of all is to catch the bastards who've been terrorizing us."

"Yeah," Jaccob said, "that sounds like a plan."

~

"You're sure we want to do this?" Kara asked.

Jaccob wasn't sure. To be honest, he wasn't sure about much at the moment, but he *was* sure the idea of turning the machines back on was not his favorite. However, it remained the next logical step.

With the information they'd gotten from Simon Floyd, cross-referenced with the security cameras from both Jaccob's and Ruby's skyscrapers, the best they were able to ascertain was that the conveyance that landed on the helipad with the shooters inside was very likely the same one Floyd took to get to the here and now in Texas.

Of course, the man had admitted freely he'd been under the influence of hallucinogens and had no clear memory of the person who'd put him aboard the thing.

His memory was suspect, but it was all they had to go on. And the consensus was that the smart money would be in turning the machines back on. Ruby's assertion that the attackers had come once, so they already knew how to find the place and wouldn't need any sort of beacon to find it again, along with Angel's repeated reminders of her imperviousness and her commitment to Ruby's safety, had been enough to convince Jaccob that it wasn't too great a risk considering the possible reward.

There was no guarantee the shooters would come back, but there was no guarantee they wouldn't, either, and there was no way to know whether switching back on the array would have any effect on whether that happened.

Jaccob had done all he could to prepare for the eventuality that restarting the machines meant once again summoning armed hooligans. He'd spent all day Friday installing added precautions even beyond those he'd had put in immediately after the shooting. He'd armed the Ruby Tower's helipad with shield generators, stun bolt launchers, and a series of pinpoint EMP emitters, as well as more cameras than a person might have thought would fit at first glance.

A-Girl had agreed to fly cover and to be ready to take on any uninvited arrivals the moment they became visible, giving the building's defenses time to spin up and Stardust the chance to get into his suit before possible intruders could get out of their contraption.

Jaccob had also talked the other capes, as well as Mike and Katy, who were across the street in his condo, into wearing his new generation of Starbands for the duration of this crisis. These newest models were the smallest yet, with a band width of just over two inches and enough power in the rechargeable battery to activate a shield several times or even fire a single stun bolt in an emergency. He'd been working on these prototypes on and off for over a year, and he was as confident as he could be in their functionality.

The genesis of the idea had been to build a personal protection device that Chuck would be willing to wear full-time. Although he still hadn't quite talked his daughter into that, Jaccob thought the current version must be getting close. In the time Katy had been staying with him, he'd taken advantage of having a stylish young woman around to ask her opinion on the design. Katy had come through with some easy to implement suggestions, and Jaccob had taken them all to heart.

Even Ruby had agreed to let him put a pair of these improved Starbands on her for the time being, keeping to her word that she preferred to let him stop the bullets if at all possible. She'd slept in the morning after they'd returned from Texas and had gone to bed early again the next night. Now, on their third day back in Cobalt City, there was no indication left of how poorly she'd been just a few days prior.

Save, of course, for the fact she was still using magic sparingly, a condition that maybe only Jaccob could tell was affecting her mood. He was doing all he could, from tech upgrades to shoulder massages to fancy cocktails and extra attention in the bedroom to try and improve her disposition. Vivienne was a little help, texting him suggestions of things to try and warnings about things to avoid.

It hadn't been an entirely quixotic undertaking, but neither had he managed to fully remedy her foul humor.

At least she was willing to get behind him or A-Girl if the shooting started again. He wanted to believe it was something he'd said—that he'd talked her out of relying on magic when there were other options available, or that he'd talked her into letting him protect her the way he wanted to. But he was pretty sure she was just hating this temporary spate of magic restriction and was hoping to avoid a repeat.

Either way, he was happy she was at least amenable to accepting help if she were to find herself at gunpoint again. And that was something. Between A-Girl, Stardust, and personal protection tech, they were as prepared as they could be.

Kara was still waiting for an answer.

"Me?" he finally said. "No. I'm not sure. But Ruby is, and since we're all here because of her, I think we've got to go ahead."

Friday checked the Starbands on both her wrists and looked back at Jaccob where he stood between the atomic clock and the Geiger counter. "You're sure these things will work? Looks more like a pretty bracelet than a self-defense mechanism."

"That's the point," Jaccob replied. "We're hoping to take these to the consumer electronics market. The idea is to make a piece of personal protection tech that women will actually want to wear."

"They are really pretty," Yumi said. "Looked real nice on my arm while I smashed you to pieces in our game last night."

"I'm getting better," Jaccob said back. "One of these days I'm going to win one, just you wait. But also thank you; I'm pretty proud of what we've done with the bracelets."

"Yeah, they look nice," Friday said, "but do they work?"

"Come here." He gestured for her to come closer.

Friday stepped away from the Ometer and started toward Jaccob. "Okay."

"Go stand right there." He pointed to the open area between the entryway table and the sitting room.

Friday frowned, but she did as she was told. As soon as she reached an open space, Jaccob pulled a stylus from his pocket and hurled it at her.

"What the hell?" Friday cried, putting her hand up to bat the thing away so it wouldn't hit her in the face. But before she was able to, the Starband on her wrist activated and sent the stylus flying back toward Jaccob.

"What the hell, indeed." Ruby spoke just in time to distract Jaccob from his intention to catch the flying object. The stylus bounced off his chest and fell to the floor.

"Sorry about that," he said, as he bent down to pick the stray stylus off the floor. "Friday was concerned about how the Starbands were going to work. I wanted her to be sure."

"And so you're flinging things around my vestibule," Ruby replied, tucking her hair behind her ear. She looked good. Dressed down in a white tee shirt, black trousers, a denim jacket, and patent flats, and wearing her hair down loose, she'd promised Jaccob she would only "pop in" to her office for a few minutes this morning. He was a little bit surprised he hadn't had to text her to get her to come back up.

He was still in awe of the fact they were back together, and as much as he didn't enjoy seeing her distress over having to limit her magic, he really did enjoy how unguarded she was acting and the way she was letting him take care of her.

"To be fair," Jaccob said, as he walked in her direction, "you weren't supposed to see that." He slung his arm around her waist and leaned in to kiss her temple.

"You're lucky I like you," she said.

"Yes, I am." He rested his forehead against hers and smiled for a moment before leaning down to kiss her again, this time on the lips.

"More of that later," she said softly, squeezing him at his waist before stepping away. "But first we've got to get this show on the road."

"Kara?" Jaccob asked.

"Just about ready," Kara replied.

Jaccob took Ruby's hand as the two of them moved into the work room from the vestibule. Ruby didn't put up with the public display of affection for long; she smirked at him and squeezed his hand quickly before walking across the room to stand beside Yumi, who was ready to switch on the first set of machines.

"I will admit I wasn't paying particularly close attention when we did this the last time," Ruby said. "So what's the program?"

"There's a startup order," Kara told her. "I have the machines connected to breaker boxes. That way we can turn on the first wave, then the second, et cetera, et cetera. This is the same way we got it all working last time. We turn it all on, then we watch and wait."

"And, you know," Friday said, "gird our loins."

"Hey," Yumi said back, sounding as cheerful as Friday did glum. "This time we're prepared. We've all got our fancy Stardust bracelets plus two whole-ass superheroes here to fire back if anybody shows up to mess with us."

"Miss Killingsworth," Lisa said. "Do you need to put yours on?"

"Ruby?" Jaccob looked over at her with a positively stricken look on his face.

"Not to worry, whole-ass hero." Ruby reached beneath the cuffed sleeves of her jacket, one and then the other, and slid the Starbands she wore on both wrists out from under the folds of fabric. "Every time I think I'm sneaking down to the office on a Saturday morning, and there's just no way anyone's going to see me, inevitably half a dozen members of my staff have something they need to put on my desk or some other reason to come into my ostensibly empty office—outside of which there is likely no assistant, as I allow all of my support staff to spend their weekends elsewhere. And as embarrassed as these hapless intruders always are, I know for a fact the unexpected run-in with the CEO becomes the hot employee gossip of the day, and there's a non-zero chance I'll have interns daring each other to come in and also set something on my desk, knowing there's a chance they'll run into me. I didn't think I needed to show these things off to whoever happened to walk into my office unannounced. It could raise questions I don't want to answer."

"But you wore them?" he asked.

"I did," she assured him, raising both her wrists and shaking them until her Starbands clattered against her tennis bracelet and the platinum bangle Jaccob had given her. She'd been wearing it nonstop since Texas, he'd noticed. Maybe it was to assuage him, but he liked to think of it as a totem of their renewed affections.

Jaccob smiled at her. In all the time he'd known her, she'd never been good about accepting help. He was more than glad she'd been willing to make this exception.

"I'll get a set inlaid with diamonds if that'll get you to wear them full time," he said, only half joking.

She had armored vehicles, a staff of bodyguards, and, he now knew, plenty of magic to keep her safe from harm, but none of that was enough to shake his desire to protect her. As it was, he'd added a panic button to each of the two Starbands he'd given her for the duration. She could use the fields the bands generated to ward off danger, she could fire a stun bolt from each wrist, or she could call him to come save the day. He wasn't sure she'd ever actually do that, but she'd been willing enough to at least say she'd rather him be the one to take the bullets that he figured it worth giving her the option.

"I *do* like diamonds," she said.

"Jaccob?" Kara asked.

"What is it, Kara?"

"I wasn't sure before," Kara said. "But I'm starting to think we can do this your way. And the closer we get to startup, the more I think maybe we *should* do this your way."

"Your way?" Ruby asked, inclining her head toward Jaccob as she crossed her arms over her chest.

"Remotely," Jaccob replied. "I asked Kara if she thought there was a way to switch this all on without our being here."

"And is there?" Ruby asked Kara.

"I wasn't sure at first," Kara said. "A bunch of this stuff is as mechanical as it is electronic, and not all of the switches are easily triggered from afar. But I think I can do it. And if Jaccob says he has the tech to make it happen, I'm inclined to believe him."

"And you think that might be safer?" Yumi asked.

"If turning these machines on was what brought the attackers here in the first place," Jaccob replied, "then it stands to reason it could happen again. And the best way to survive an attack is to be someplace else when the enemy shows up."

"So ... what?" Ruby asked. "We switch the machines on remotely and ... let whoever shows up wreak havoc on my empty penthouse? Ransack the war room? Destroy the professor's equipment? Need I remind you that I just had this building redone, and I'd rather not have to go through that again—?"

"No." Jaccob moved across the room to stand in front of Ruby but stopped short of taking her hands. "We lock down the penthouse. Sew it up tight. Anybody asks, it's a drill I talked you into running to test all the newly installed upgrades. We'll keep a live feed running from every camera in the place, so we can see everything that happens. And I can set up extra force and taser fields to keep anyone who lands on the roof stuck where they are and knock them out so we can come back and deal with them."

"Kara," Ruby said, "pretend like Jaccob isn't here and tell me the truth. How do you feel about this plan? Would you rather be here where you can keep a closer eye on the machinery and what's going on, or would you feel better monitoring this whole operation from a safe distance?"

"I think I'd rather not be shot at again," Kara answered frankly. "I know whole-ass superhero here says it's safer this time because he's here and Angel's here and he did a bunch of stuff to the building and we've all got forcefields in our bracelets. But honestly, if he's willing to help me set this all up to be remotely operable, then my vote is to be someplace outside the potential line of fire."

"I know I'm not driving this ship," Friday said, "but I would also like to not be where there might be bullets flying. Just ... just personal preference. Walls of vegetative matter aren't all that effective against, ya know, speeding hot lead."

"So where are we going?" Ruby asked. "Jaccob, are you planning to host us all at your place?"

"I was thinking we should go to your place," he replied.

"All right," Ruby said, "now you've got me confused."

"Yeah." Jaccob shook his head and laughed softly at himself. "That sounded silly. I think we should go out to the house. I'd like to look at your overall security over there anyway. And if I'm remembering correctly, there's plenty of room for everyone. Kara and I can set up whatever equipment she thinks she'll need, including a monitor for every camera if that's her preference, in either one of the parlors or the media room."

"I hate how much sense that makes," Ruby said. "But it does. We should bring Mike and Katy along, too."

"You think?" Jaccob asked.

"I'm not saying they need chaperones," she said. "But there's an argument to be made that leaving one of the parties at whom the initial attack was directed alone in a building that may or may not be about to attract a second armed incursion, and also leaving his unsuspecting girlfriend alone in the building across the street, might not be the safest thing for either one of them. And, as you mentioned, I've got plenty of room. If we're going to the house, we're all going to the house."

CHAPTER TWENTY-SIX

"What, and I mean this with all possible offense," Ruby asked, "is that?"

Making the plan to move everyone out of the penthouse and into Ruby's crosstown mansion had gone better than anyone had anticipated. The younger capes had just enough time to pack overnight bags, while Jaccob had gone next door to the labs in Starcom Tower to gather the requisite components to set up the remote operation of Professor Kummerfeldt's equipment.

By the time Jaccob was back with all the gear, the staff was up to take the luggage. And under Kara's direction, the team was able to get things rigged up in under an hour while Jaccob made equally quick work of setting up the defenses. Apparently, the man had a glut of excess forcefield generators lying around.

Ruby had a mild suspicion Jaccob had some of these defensive measures already in place on her building, but she wasn't about to question him on that in front of the others. She'd told him he could do whatever he wanted to her building; it would be hypocritical of her to criticize his choices, even if they did seem excessive.

Kara had a gear case she hadn't sent with the staff, and Ruby decided not to ask about that, either. Mike and Katy were waiting in the garage when the others arrived, but it was the vehicle parked behind them that caused Ruby's outburst.

"I mean it," she said. "What in the escaped carnival ride version of Autobahn hell is that?"

"It's my truck," Jaccob replied, with a pride in his voice that made Ruby cringe.

It was a G-class, painted in high-gloss light blue, accented in pearl ivory, with gold shimmer peeking out in tiny bits of trim around the headlights, windshield, and mirrors. The windows were tinted at least as dark as any limousine, including the too-large sunroof. The tires, although not completely out of place on a vehicle this size, were oversized and mounted on gold-tone spoke rims polished to a high shine.

Ruby hadn't seen a vehicle this tacky since her teen years in Detroit.

"What's it doing in my garage?" she asked.

"It's equipped with everything we'll need," he replied. "Both for the remote operation of the equipment upstairs and to set up the monitors for all the pertinent cameras. Plus, I've loaded up everything I'm going to need to get started on the on-site stuff once we're at the house."

"How long will it take to transfer the equipment?" she asked. "I'd rather not be waiting in the garage while you handle all this, but I suppose the rest of us can get in the car and open a bottle while you finish up and get this out of here."

"Oh no," Jaccob said. "We're just going to take it. I'm gonna drive."

"No," Ruby said.

"Ruby—"

"No. Jaccob. I am not riding in that thing, and you can't make me."

But she could tell this was about to be an uphill battle. Yumi, Lisa, and Friday had already settled into the blue monstrosity's rearmost seat, and Mike was holding the door open for Kara and Katy to get into the middle bench. It appeared the rest of the party had already agreed to this and decided not to tell her.

Jaccob took a step toward her and shook his head. "You're right." He took hold of both her hands. "I can't make you. But I can *ask* you to please let me do this. There's so much we don't know about these people, Ruby. The idea that turning these machines back on may trigger their return is a guess. It's the best guess we have, but it's still only a guess. And if we've guessed wrong ... if these people really are traveling through time and they really do mean you harm, then there's a chance they know what we're doing, and this whole idea of not being here when the machines are turned back on could turn around and bite us. If we're potentially going to be under attack, the safest thing is for us all to be together. And all of us together in an armored vehicle equipped with next level defensive capabilities and a full suite of Stardust tech, and with A-Girl flying air cover, is the safest way I can think of to manage moving everyone across town. You don't have to ride with us. You can call your driver and get to the house in your own car. But I'm going to be terrified the whole time you're out of my sight. So I know I can't make you do anything—nobody can make you do anything, that's just who you are. But I can ask you. Please. Please just get in the car. Let me drive you with everybody else so that if something happens, I'm there, and I can do something about it. Please."

Ruby frowned at Jaccob and shook her head. "Some Good Guy you are. This is emotional blackmail." She pulled the passenger door open. The two-tone gray and ivory interior was pristine; Ruby wondered if this was the first time Jaccob had driven passengers in this thing. It smelled like new speakers and ozone, and Ruby cussed under her breath as she boosted herself up to get into the passenger seat.

Jaccob was smiling as he watched her get in. He leaned in and kissed her cheek once she was seated, whispering, "thank you," as he closed her door on his way around the front of the vehicle to get into the driver's seat.

They were barely ten minutes out of the garage when something began to rattle Ruby in a way she found positively nauseating. "Jaccob, what is—?" she paused after a moment and frowned to herself, realizing in that moment the upsetting noise was her phone vibrating in her lap. She pulled it out and chuckled. Of course it was Vivienne; who else would it have been? She said she'd call on Saturday, and it was Saturday. Also, her other two phones were down in her bag. The only other person with this phone's number was sitting beside her in the driver's seat.

"Oh, Vivienne," she said, clicking the button to answer the call as she brought the device to her ear. "What excellent timing. It seems you've caught me in the middle of a kidnapping."

"Wha—"

"Don't listen to her, V," Jaccob called out, loud enough for Vivienne to hear.

"Jaccob?" Vivienne asked.

Ruby shook her head and put her phone on speaker, holding it out so Jaccob and Vivienne would be able to hear each other better. She had the strong impression they'd been talking almost daily; at least this way she could know what they were saying to each other.

"She just doesn't like my driving," Jaccob said.

"Why are you driving?" Vivienne asked. "Miss 'Fleet of Bentleys'—"

"I do not apologize for preferring the services of a professional in this capacity," Ruby said.

"It's because none of those Bentleys can transform itself into a super suit," Jaccob answered Vivienne.

"You're still driving that awful thing?" Vivienne asked.

"Thank you," Ruby said.

"Oh, I've upgraded since the one you saw," he replied. "Same idea, though. But this one's bigger."

"Of course it is," Vivienne snarked. "And where is it you're going that you don't want to be without your super suit?"

"Anywhere with her," he said. "At least until we know more about the shooter."

"Oh, yikes," Vivienne said. "Sorry, Ginger. I didn't mean to sic the labradork on you full force."

"It's all right," Ruby said. "You'll both make it up to me in other ways."

"That I believe."

"But to answer your question, we're going to the house for a few days. Jaccob wants to inspect my security ... or something. And he insisted on driving us all in this ... Sherman tank because it's apparently got some sort of super-computer inside it. And, apparently, a hidden Stardust suit, which I suppose explains the color, but—"

"And three rows of seats!" Jaccob added. "We can all ride together!"

"Except for Angel," Ruby said. "Who probably wouldn't have fit anyway, but who has chosen to fly across town in order to spare herself the indignity of possibly being seen riding in this crime against automotive engineering."

"Attagirl."

"She offered air cover, and I thought it was a good idea," Jaccob said. "She'd have fit just fine."

"Oh," Ruby said, reminded of the others in the car with them. "I've got one of your biggest fans in the back. Yumi, say hello to Lady Vengeance."

"Um ... uh—" Yumi stammered. "Um ... hi?!?"

Friday and Lisa couldn't help but giggle beside her.

"Oh, hello, Yumi," Vivienne said.

"Hi, Miss Cain!" Mike said, likely to give Yumi some cover, as she didn't seem to be able to gather her thoughts enough to say anything back to Vivienne.

"Yes, hello," Katy said.

"How many people are in this car?" Vivienne asked.

"Eight!" Jaccob replied. He was grinning.

"Sounds cramped," Vivienne said.

"Nah," Jaccob said. "Plenty of room in the Stars Truck."

"You named it the Stars Truck?"

"It was its construction codename, and it stuck."

"But it seats eight comfortably?"

"Not as comfortably as a stretch," Ruby asserted.

Vivienne laughed. "I take it you're riding shotgun?"

"Indeed."

"You know," Vivienne said, "I don't think I've ever seen you in the front seat of a car you're not driving."

"And you won't."

"Actually—" Jaccob said, a hint of mischief seeping into his voice. He thumbed a panel on the steering wheel with his right hand then reached over to interact with the smartwatch he wore on his left—which was still steering the car.

"What did you do?" Ruby asked him.

"Check your DMs, V," he said.

"Did you just take our picture?" Kara asked.

Ruby pointed to where Kara sat behind her. She wanted that question answered.

"Yeah." Jaccob grinned even wider. "If I wanted, I could add IR, thermography, x-ray, night vision, or backscatter."

"I am never getting in this car again," Ruby grumbled.

"Ginger, you look pale. Jaccob, she looks pale. Does she look pale in person or is that just your camera?"

"She's a little pale," Jaccob said.

"Have you forgotten I'm a redhead? Fair skin is part of the package."

"I know what you look like." Vivienne sounded legitimately concerned. "But right now, I'm looking at the picture Sparkle Motion just sent me. And either you decided to forego both rouge and bronzer this morning, or you're not as well as you've been trying to convince me you are. Jaccob, is she sleeping enough?"

"I think so," he replied.

"Is she eating?" Vivienne asked. "Actual food?"

"I'm right here!"

"Not enough," Jaccob said to Vivienne, ignoring Ruby's outburst. "But I'm working on it. Do you think the staff at the house will get mad if I decide to use the grill?"

"Yes," Ruby snapped.

"Probably not," Vivienne replied. "Just don't leave it a mess. And, whatever mess you *do* make, let them clean up; you don't know where anything goes, and getting in the way of the people who do is not helping."

"So now you want to be the cook *and* the chauffer?" Ruby asked him, not at all bothering to mitigate the annoyance in her voice. "I suppose after this you'll tell me you want to sleep in the staff room."

"Don't be too hard on him, Miss K," Mike said. "Dad's just being Dad. If he wants to show off his meat-searing skills for an audience, I really think you ought to let him. He's actually kind of good at it."

"And you can promise he won't burn my house down?"

"Oh, come on, Ginger," Vivienne said. "The grill is all the way out by the pool. The worst he's liable to do is singe the pergola, and you've been talking about having that painted anyway. Let the hero have his fun."

"I am not used to being ganged up on like this," Ruby said.

"When's the last time you were in a conversation with this many people who didn't work for you?" Vivienne asked her.

"I will remind you the majority of the people in this souped-up glittermobile *do* work for me."

"Ah," Vivienne said, "But Jaccob and Katy don't. That makes two people who don't answer to you in the same car as you at the same time, plus me on the phone for a total of three, and as far as I'm aware, that's still a record."

"You are a menace, Vivienne."

"That's why we get along so well."

"I'm hanging up now."

"That's all right," Vivienne said. "I'll call you Monday."

"That's presuming I survive the weekend."

"Hey," Jaccob interjected, his face suddenly fallen into an intense frown. "That's not funny."

Ruby shook her head and sighed. "Monday, then," she said into the phone.

"Okay," Vivienne replied. "Bye." The phone chirped to signal the call had ended as Ruby turned in her seat to face Jaccob.

"I was merely intimating that I might be driven mad by having this many people in my house at once," she told him. "Not that I thought you might allow any real harm to come to me."

Jaccob's frown relaxed, but not completely. He nodded a little, then reached across the center console to squeeze her fingers briefly. He was quiet for the rest of the drive, a fact that wasn't lost on Ruby but one the others in the car likely failed to notice. Mike, who had been to the house twice before for industry parties, spent the rest of the trip answering questions about the house and informing the others he'd be spending every possible moment in or near the swimming pool.

By the time they were pulling up to the gatehouse at the foot of the driveway, he'd talked the others into joining him there just as soon as their necessary duties were taken care of.

It was only after Jaccob parked his ridiculous vehicle in Ruby's driveway that she fully understood what he'd meant by "equipped with everything." A good half of the rear cargo space robotically cleared itself out on its own, revealing both a large suite of electronic equipment and a console-lined mobile headquarters complete with screens and seating.

Jaccob pointed out the slide-out capability that could extend the vehicle's length by six additional feet, thereby making room for all the self-extricating equipment to be put to use right inside. But in today's case, he and Kara had decided to instead take over Ruby's second-floor media room. Jaccob had apparently spent some time in there the first time he'd slept over and declared the space to have adequate outlets for their power needs. He also postulated they'd have a better time tapping into the house's native security using the already built-in wiring. Ruby decided not to ask what he meant to do to access that wiring. Some things were better not to know.

Members of the household staff met the group in the driveway, and Ruby was glad she'd texted ahead to warn them as to what would be arriving. Butlers and housekeepers reported having already squared away everyone's overnight bags in their respective lodgings and that they were happy to help ferry the equipment out of the driveway and into the media room.

Yumi, Lisa, and Friday helped carry things as well, but they were barely one trip in when Angel blew past them, carrying more gear than the three of them could all together, and at impossible speed. She narrowly avoided crashing into the wall beside the door, ducking inside at the last second. It didn't take the others long to realize they were more likely to be in the way than to be of help just then. Agreeing amongst themselves that getting run over by Angel with her hands full of sensitive electronics was just not something they were interested in, the three of them left to join Mike and Katy out by the pool with a promise to come help just as soon as Kara or Jaccob gave the all clear.

Ruby had opted to spend her afternoon poolside as well; a bit of sunshine would likely do her some good, and she wanted to be as far away from the goings-on in her media room as possible. Sitting under a pool umbrella with never-ending cold drinks and the company of people she could genuinely stand being around wasn't a bad way to spend a Saturday.

It wasn't long after Angel had joined the group that Kara kicked Jaccob out, too, preferring to set her things up her way and save herself his neuroses until he could at least see what she had in mind. He arrived poolside dressed for an afternoon swim but carrying with him a case of electrical equipment and two cartons labeled "smart lightbulbs." One of Ruby's maintenance men met him at the edge of the patio with an A-frame ladder, which he positioned beneath one of the lights on the patio trellis.

Apparently, he was getting started on the outdoor lighting whether Ruby wanted him to or not, although the ladder led her to believe he'd at least run his intentions past her security personnel.

Honestly, whatever he was doing was between him and them. Ruby didn't have the bandwidth to care. If her people were fine with whatever the hero had in mind to keep her safer, then she wasn't about to argue.

Her only real concern was with the aesthetics of the project, so once she'd seen the first of Jaccob's lightbulbs installed seamlessly into one of the existing fixtures, she decided the project warranted no further attention. That was, until Jaccob took his shirt off after the third bulb was in place.

The man was an *ideal* physical specimen. Keeping up with hero work obviously required some level of physical conditioning, but his chiseled abs and muscular back truly were next level. Ruby was thankful for dark sunglasses; they allowed her to ogle his bare torso while he worked with little fear of getting caught. The view got even better when he moved to work on the lights on the far side of the pool from where she and the others were seated. Looking ostensibly straight ahead and getting an unimpeded view of his bare back and his rear end in a very well-fitted pair of McQueen swim trunks was a treat she hadn't expected this afternoon.

He left swapping the lightbulbs behind where the group was sitting for last, and by the time he got to them, Ruby was once again impressed by his stamina. It was hot as blazes out—the kind of hot that climate scientists liked to point to as proof of their theories—and he'd been up and down from that ladder for the better part of two hours—not to mention having hauled it and all the attendant equipment around from pole to pole all on his own.

And all because he wanted to feel like she was as safe as possible. He didn't need to do any of it; her security was adequate just as it was. And even if it had been found wanting in some way, he could have staffed the installation out to any of a number of her employees.

But he didn't.

Vivienne had known what she was talking about when she'd said he still had feelings. Ruby, who mostly hated feelings, wasn't altogether sure what to do with that information. But for the time being, she decided just to let herself enjoy it. It wasn't everyday she had a very attractive, half-naked hero climbing ladders in ninety-degree heat for her benefit.

The last of the lights he was changing being situated behind her meant Ruby only became aware Jaccob had finished his task when he came to sit at the foot of her chaise and cracked open one of the water bottles from the ice bucket just beyond.

"If you want a real drink," she said, "someone will be out in a minute. That is, provided you're done climbing ladders."

"For the time being. And, yeah, I'll probably do that in a minute. But first—" He took another long drink of water before reaching past Ruby to set the bottle on the nearest end table. He stood up then, slipping his shoes off and taking three short steps before lowering himself into the swimming pool carefully, so as not to create any splash. He ducked his head under the water for a moment, then leaned his forearms on the ledge and smiled up at Ruby.

"It's hot out," he said.

"No arguments there," she replied.

"I think it's perfect," Katy said from the floating lounge she'd been enjoying most of the afternoon.

"That's because you're from Mississippi," Mike said. "This is Gulf Coast heat, not Massachusetts heat. But at least the boss is letting us use her pool."

"I happen to like Gulf Coast heat," Ruby told him. "It's nostalgic."

"Where're you from, Miss K?" Katy asked.

"South Louisiana," Ruby replied.

"Well, that sure explains why you like to drink outside on a hot day," Mike said.

"Perhaps it does," Ruby replied.

"Somebody really ought to get Kara," Katy said. "I hate that she's inside while we're out here having such a nice time."

"She's working," Friday reminded her.

"So am I," Lisa said, chomping on the pineapple spear from her frozen drink, which she held with one hand as she continued typing with the other. She stood up to her shoulders in the pool, with her laptop open just on the ledge, a posture she'd adopted almost immediately upon her arrival outside.

"Does booking concert venues from the swimming pool really count as work?" Mike teased.

"I don't know, Mike," Yumi said. "Does playing guitar count as work?"

"Absolutely does," he replied. "But I can't do that from the pool."

"Sure you can," Ruby said. "You just haven't tried hard enough. I'd tell you to go get your guitar right now, but you're still on restriction."

"You're gonna like this, Miss K," Lisa said, taking another bite of pineapple. "Angel, you'll want to listen to this, too."

"Oh yeah?" Angel floated over, and—in contrast to just a few days ago—Lisa seemed totally at ease with her.

"I don't like things," Ruby teased in reply. "But tell me anyway."

"Well," Lisa said, "you'll like this. Meg said to tell you, because she's sure it'll make you smile."

"All right," Ruby said. "If MerMeg says I'm likely to smile, then there's got to be something to it. What is it you're so excited by, Lisa? Other than the fact that you've had an international pop star in your DMs all day—?"

"Well," Lisa replied, turning around to face Ruby where she sat under the shade of a giant umbrella, "I've been able to book Prather's venues out from under him in Houston, Austin, San Antonio, and Fort Worth. Apparently, the campaign is having a hard time paying its bills. Meanwhile, they've sold tickets in every one of those towns that they'll have to refund if there's no rally and no photo ops. So now we're the better show in the better venue, and if he decides to cancel because of that, his whole campaign's going to go broke—like to the level they'll have a hard time running any sort of a campaign at all broke."

"Oh, you're right," Ruby said. "I do like that. Anything that fouls a fascist's plans is cause for smiling. Doubly so when it fouls both his bank account and his authoritarian ambitions."

"Madam," one of Ruby's staff interrupted as he stepped behind her to replace her near-empty drink with a fresh one. "The kitchen would like to know if you have a preference for dinner."

"Mr. Stevens has asked to use the grill," she replied, loud enough to be sure Jaccob would hear. "I'll leave it up to the chef's discretion as to whether or not he's allowed. Tell the kitchen we'll be fine with a casual steak dinner either way. And let's do that on the patio."

"Yes, ma'am," the butler replied, looking around the group for any other drinks that might need attention before he left.

"You're really going to let me cook?" Jaccob asked, looking up at her from his spot in the pool just at the foot of her chaise.

"Not exactly," she replied. "I'm delegating that decision to my chef. If she doesn't mind, then I don't. I figure it's supposed to be a nice enough night we can eat on the patio either way. There are too many of us for the small dining room and the large one tends to intimidate first time guests."

"Oh, wow," Katy said. "For what it's worth, I love a big fancy dining room."

"Of course you do," Ruby said to her. "You were a Kappa at Baylor. I'll be sure to have the two of you out for a formal dinner soon enough. But this little weekend retreat was a bit spur-of-the-moment. I hardly prepared this bunch to have to dress for dinner."

"Have you always been this fancy, Miss K?" Angel asked her.

"Oh, heavens no," Ruby replied. "I had a miserably blue-collar upbringing and entered adulthood with nary a clue as to how the upper classes did things. Why, when I was your age, I wouldn't have known what to do with a black-tie dinner invitation if I'd been folded up and stuffed inside one."

"Says the woman who slayed a dragon in a ballgown," Jaccob said.

"Well, yes," Ruby said, "these days I can be almost as dandy as you, when the occasion warrants. Although, I will guess your ability to look dandy was probably born of success and wealth rather than a need to make up for being bullied in your teens."

"Um—" Jaccob said. "You would be wrong about that."

"Oh, please ... Are you trying to tell me you weren't the star quarterback? Voted most likely to succeed?"

"Okay," he said, stifling a chuckle. "I was voted most likely to succeed. But I, um, I didn't play ball until college."

"Really?" Ruby asked.

"Yeah, no," he replied. "I ran track, but I'm not a natural athlete. That's why the suit. I was always into building gadgets and tinkering with tech. One day, I realized that I could build myself a way to be everything I hadn't ever been."

"So you were already into the tech stuff in high school?" Katy asked him.

"Oh yeah. Big time."

"All those years as a tech bro, and you still suck at video games," Yumi joked.

"Did they even have video games when you were in high school, Dad?" Mike asked.

Jaccob wrinkled his nose. "Yes." He chuckled. "But I wasn't any good at them back then, either. I've always been more of a robotics guy. If it hadn't been for the computer lab and the metal shop, I'd have had a pretty miserable time in high school."

"Stands to reason," Ruby said. "I swear I only showed up to high school for the free music lessons."

"Wait," Mike said, "Miss K, were you in band?"

"Jazz band," she replied quickly. "Not Marching. And I was the pianist for the school orchestra."

"I was on the math team," Jaccob confessed. "But, like I said, my big thing was robotics. I was mostly into circuits and microchips."

"While I am sure the math team is not a proven path to popularity, if you were already into building things like this—" Ruby gestured with her left hand enough to make her diamond bracelet bangle against her wrist. "—surely you must have been getting noticed for it."

Jaccob inclined his head and smiled at her. "Noticed, yes. But that's not exactly the kind of thing that gets you a date for the prom."

Ruby nodded. "So who'd you go with?"

"Yeah, Dad," Mike asked, "who'd you take to prom?"

"I didn't go," he replied. "I was out of town at a robotics competition that weekend."

"I didn't go to mine either," Ruby shared.

"Yeah?"

"I was playing bass in a community production of *Jesus Christ Superstar*."

"You play bass?" Mike asked, sounding impressed.

"Not as well as I play piano," she replied. "But yes."

"Cool," Mike said.

"You know," Jaccob added. "I did theatre in high school, too."

"Really, Dad?" Mike asked. "I never knew that."

"Yeah," Jaccob replied. "I did the lights. The school let me build them a whole new lighting system that had a control board with a computer monitor and everything."

"You're trying to tell me you were a straight man hanging around the theatre department, and you didn't have girls throwing themselves at you from every direction?" Ruby asked, sitting up straighter and looking down at him over the top of her sunglasses.

"I don't think you properly appreciate just how big of a nerd I was," he replied.

"You really want me to believe you weren't cute?"

"Nah, Miss K," Mike said, "I've seen pictures of Dad in high school. He, um ... peaked late."

Jaccob let his jaw drop as he shook his head at his son's remark.

"That's all right, darling," Ruby said. "So did I. We're doing fine now, though, aren't we."

"I'd say so," Jaccob said.

"Excuse me, Mr. Stevens," an unfamiliar voice joined the conversation. The group of them turned their heads to see a member of the household staff standing behind Ruby's chaise. "If I may—?"

"Um—" Jaccob pulled himself up out of the pool and looked dubiously over at the uniformed young woman. "What is it?"

"Chef says you're welcome to use the grill," the young woman said. "But she'd like you to come into the kitchen to discuss details."

"You'll need to dry off a little first," Ruby told him. "The kitchen floor gets very slippery when wet, and the last thing we need this weekend is a concussion."

"Oh." Jaccob shrugged as he looked around at the others. "Excuse me." He crossed quickly to a stack of flawlessly rolled pool towels on a low table just behind Ruby's chaise. He patted himself dry with one as best he could before draping it over the back of the nearest empty chair and then grabbed a second one to wrap around his waist. He walked past Ruby again, careful to keep from dripping on her, to slip his shoes back onto his feet. "I'll be right back," he said, smiling down at her.

"Take your time," she said back. "We'll be here."

"I'm telling you, Miss K," Mike said, as Jaccob headed toward the kitchen. "Dad is good with a grill. Heck, you should have seen when we were in Bermuda—" His voice trailed off as a good bit of color drained from his face. His eyes were wide, and he bit his lip while screwing his face into a proper frown. "Damn. I'm sorry. I shouldn't have brought that up, huh?"

"Not to worry, Mike," Ruby said. "You can't hurt my feelings; I don't have any."

"Yes, ma'am," Mike said.

"What—?" Katy was clearly confused. "Mike, why—?"

"The trip he's referring to," Ruby said to Katy, "was two years ago—right after the White House bombing. Jaccob and I were together when they left on that trip and ... by the time they returned, that was no longer the case. It was all very messy and complicated, and I believe Mike was concerned he'd brought up a possibly painful memory. But what's past is past, and I'm quite over the whole episode. Plus, I think I'm about to hear an amusing story, and possibly have a laugh at Jaccob's expense. So please, Mike, do go on."

"Well," Mike said. "Chuck wanted the trip to be just us, and Dad's got his 500 Ton license, so we left the crew in town. And before the chef got off board, she locked up everything. The entire galley, except for one refrigerator, was padlocked closed. She even took the knobs off the stoves and the oven."

"Oh my," Katy said.

Ruby laughed softly.

"Yeah. Have you been in my dad's office?" he asked Katy.

"No," she replied. "Not yet."

"So, he has a bunch of clippings on the wall in there," he said. "Framed pictures cut out of newspapers from times he wound up wrecking things while in the suit. As it turns out, our yacht chef has her own collection. All over the galley, she has pictures taped on the walls of Stardust-related fires and explosions. And, I guess, she didn't want her galley added to the list of casualties."

"I can only imagine," Ruby said.

"But he has this grill that clamps on to the transom rail," Mike said. "And that's how he cooked everything for us the whole trip. Didn't so much as scorch the teak on the swim platform."

"Well, that's good to know," Ruby said.

"He won't singe your pergola, Miss K," Mike assured her.

"And if he does," she replied, "I happen to know we're both well insured."

Mike laughed at that, shaking his head as he jiggled the ice in his mostly empty glass. As if on cue, a pair of butlers appeared poolside, one with a tray of fresh drinks and the other with a case of tools and implements she set onto a stone and zinc counter adjacent to the poolside grill.

It was only a few minutes later when Jaccob returned, dressed now in khaki pants and a polo shirt, and followed by Ruby's head chef. "Turns out you have a whole chateaubriand in there," Jaccob reported, coming to sit on the foot of Ruby's chaise. "Chef is going to slice it up into filets, and then I'm going to do them on the grill while she handles sides and dessert. And that includes the risotto she's already started on for our vegan hero."

"That sounds like a delightful plan," Ruby said.

"Glad you approve," he replied, reaching over to squeeze her ankle. "Chef's going to show me around the grill for a minute, then we'll get it lit and starting to preheat. She said someone will bring the steaks out when it's time to put them on. I told her I could come inside and get them, but—"

"You have the staff's blessing to use the grill," Ruby said, "but I've heard no negotiation as to the kitchen. If I were you, I'd be thankful everything else is being handled by professionals."

"You may have a point."

"I've been told I'm very smart."

"You're a lot of things." He leaned in to take her hand and kissed her knuckles gently before standing up to head to the grill where the chef was waiting.

"I know we just talked about how we're not expected to really dress for dinner," Katy said, as she swapped out her empty drink for a fresh one from the steward's tray, "but I think I'll go change in a minute anyway. I just don't feel right at the table in a wet swimsuit."

"I think I'll come up with you," Lisa said, closing the lid on her laptop and boosting herself up to sit on the side of the pool. "I want to get changed, too. And I need to plug in my laptop. Plus, I want to check in with Kara and tell her there's about to be food."

"I'll go with you, too," Yumi said. "Katy's got a point about not wanting to eat in a wet swimsuit."

"Yeah, me too," Friday said.

"Good idea, I'll come too," Angel agreed, even though she appeared completely dry already.

"I suppose," Ruby said, swinging her legs over the side of the chaise, "if everyone else is getting changed, I ought to as well. I'd hate to feel underdressed at my own table."

"Don't worry, Dad," Mike called to Jaccob, as the others began to gather their things and move toward the house, "I'll stay and hang out with you while the ladies go in and get primped for dinner."

"Oh yeah?" Jaccob smiled. "Cool. Wanna ... learn how to grill a filet to impress a lady?"

CHAPTER TWENTY-SEVEN

Getting "primped" for dinner, as Mike had put it, turned out to be more of a production than Ruby had anticipated. Deciding what to wear had been easy enough, but the heat and humidity were doing unbecoming things to her hair, and it took just about every ounce of willpower she had to keep from using magic to cope with it.

She decided to wear it up in a loose bun with a scarf threaded through it to tamp down the worst of the flyaways.

On her way back downstairs, Ruby took a small detour in hopes of checking on Kara and the progress setting up the control and surveillance hub. One look at the state of the room was enough to make her regret that choice. What had started the day as a casual media lounge had been transformed into a chaotic hybrid of a cartoon superhero lair and a poorly managed live TV control room. Tangles of wire and cable ran across the floor between the dozen or more screens arranged in three separate banks around the room. Open crates and loose ties cluttered the floor, and every table, chair, and ottoman in the room had been pressed into service to house either packing crates or as-yet connected bits of technology.

Kara herself was nowhere in evidence.

Ruby decided it best to presume the others had interrupted the setup with news of dinner, and the chaos was to be remedied with haste. She could withhold judgment until she was invited in for a proper inspection. But she still took her time looking around. This was a room in her house, set up by her employees, in order to watch over her building in hopes of solving her problem. She wasn't about to let this project run roughshod over this house the way it had her party room back at the Tower; that equipment hadn't given her much say, but she was hoping to avoid a second full-scale war room.

She didn't begrudge Kara a break for dinner, but she would perhaps be sending the others in here to help her get the place in order afterward whether they liked it or not.

By the time Ruby made it back out to her patio, the preparations for dinner were well underway.

A small faction of the household staff was in attendance, setting platters and pouring drinks at the large table on the patio they'd managed to set for nine without the assembled guests seeming to have noticed.

A butler made his way through the group offering a negroni spagliato to anyone who cared for one, while the young woman who'd summoned Jaccob to the kitchen earlier went around the table pouring goblets full of water and wine.

"Ma'am," the woman with the wine bottle said to Ruby, gesturing to the fully set table as the chef approached from the kitchen with baskets of bread. Ruby nodded and headed to her seat at the head of the table.

The others caught on to their hostess's cue quickly, joining her at the table with Mike to her right and leaving the seat to her left open for Jaccob, who was still focused on grilling. The butler who'd been passing around the cocktails returned to the house, emerging a minute later with a platter he took out to the pergola to wait for the steak.

"You're letting Dad cook the steaks, just not carry them?" Mike asked Ruby, as he picked up the nearest breadbasket and offered a fresh roll to Katy.

"I said I'd trust him with my grill, not my dishes," Ruby joked.

"Okay, that's fair," Mike said.

Having handed off the steaks to the staff, Jaccob joined the others at the table, bending down to kiss Ruby's temple before taking his seat. It was scarcely another minute before the chef, along with her assistant and the two butlers who'd been looking after the group all afternoon, emerged from the kitchen, each carrying a pair of plates to the table.

"For tax purposes," Ruby said, as the staff began setting plates onto their chargers, "this is a business dinner. So I'd like to hear an update as to the state of things in the media room. Miss Sparx?"

"You, um ... looked in there, huh?"

Ruby just nodded, sipping her wine.

"It's a mess," Kara said, "but I'm actually almost done with the setup. Once I'm sure I've run all the cables correctly and the screens are all showing what they're supposed to, I'll get everyone else to come help, and we'll get those cables bundled and put away. I promise the floor won't look like that much longer."

"That's all I needed to hear."

"The plan is to get that handled tonight."

"I appreciate that. And the array," Ruby asked, "is it switched back on?"

"Not yet," Kara replied. "The setup's done. It's all wired and ready. Jaccob did most of that work before we ever left to come here. But if the point is to be able to see and control everything back at the Tower in case the bad guys come back, then I don't want to risk switching on anything that might trigger a repeat performance until we're sure we've got all our bases covered here."

"Tomorrow then?" Ruby asked.

"Hopefully later tonight," Kara replied. "Taking a break for dinner is one thing, but we're close—and that includes a remote alarm Jaccob set up to ping me if Tower security is breached. I'm inclined to get it all up and running tonight."

"Excellent." Ruby picked up her wine glass and turned to Jaccob then. "And am I to presume from the sparkly blue rolling monstrosity in my driveway that you have your super suit all prepped and ready to fly back across town and give those bastards a world of hurt if they do show up?"

"Absolutely," Jaccob replied. "And A-Girl has agreed to come with me. Security here at the house is more than adequate, plus you've got Yumi and Friday on the hero side, and Kara to handle things on the tech front. And if all that fails, you've got your bracelets. So, yeah. Bad guys show up, we've got this."

Ruby smiled and inclined her head toward him. "I'll drink to that." She lifted her glass slightly in Jaccob's direction. "And also to the fact my pergola remains intact."

"Told you, Miss K," Mike said, "Dad knows how to use a grill."

"It's a very good steak," Katy said.

"Mine's a little done," Ruby said, "but all in all an admirable job."

"Not everyone wants their steak to flinch when they go to cut it," Jaccob teased. "But I did pull yours early."

"It's a fine steak, Jaccob," Ruby assured him, taking another bite. "I'm impressed."

It was an altogether delectable dinner. The chef had made a smooth-as-silk green peppercorn sauce for the steak, as well as a truffle risotto and wilted Yamashita spinach. Even Yumi proclaimed herself more than satisfied with the food. It was as good a meal as they'd have had if the chef had done all the work herself, and Jaccob was happy to have gotten to contribute, so all was well.

Assorted desserts came with generous pours of a tawny port and espresso for anyone who wanted any. The sun was setting, and the staff lit the tea lights and pillars in the tablescape.

The atmosphere was lovely and relaxed as the last glimmer of sunlight dipped beneath the tree line. Then sounded an odd, loud click, then a diffuse buzzing. It was enough to make all of them sit up a little straighter. Everyone at the table was looking around for the source of the strange noise when, seemingly out of nowhere, the entire back lawn suddenly lit up brighter than daylight.

There was a chorus of shrieks and moans as Ruby and her guests winced, and averted their eyes from the intense, inescapable brightness.

"What the hell?" Ruby exclaimed.

"They're working!" Jaccob said. "Wow, that's bright!"

"This was intentional?"

"Oh, yeah," he replied, grinning as he refilled his water from the carafe on the table. "These are the lights I installed today. They're on an infrared heat sensor, they turn on any time the ambient light is below a certain level and there's anything alive in the yard or on the patio."

"Well, it's too damn bright," Ruby said. "Now, I understand why you did that, and I'm not going to make you fix it tonight. But tomorrow we're going to have a conversation about how we tell the system when I'd like to have a nice, relaxing evening on my patio and keep it to a pleasant glimmer out here until I'm quite done for the night. Because this, darling, is ridiculous."

"Yeah," Jaccob said, "okay."

"And in the meantime," Ruby announced to the others, "I'm going the hell inside. And I'm going to ask that the rest of you also go the hell inside. Because if these damn things are on a heat sensor and will stay on as long as there are people on the patio, then the only way to get them to turn off is for there to no longer be any people on the patio. Please."

"Yeah," Lisa said.

"Good idea," Yumi agreed.

"We've got work to do anyway," Friday said, as she pushed her chair back from the table.

"Shall we?" Ruby asked the group. She stood from her chair and, taking her glass of port with her, headed toward the French doors into her dining room.

Jaccob stood up quickly, knocking back the last of the port in his glass before following Ruby toward the house.

The others weren't far behind, some of them with dishes and glasses in hand, with clear plans to finish dessert once they were out of the glare.

"It's been a day," Ruby said to the others, as the last of them clambered into the main dining room and shut the door behind them. "I am going to sit in my room, have a cocktail, and go to bed early. You all have the run of the lower floors. Try not to be too noisy, and please don't play the harpsichord, it's due for tuning and my fellow is in Vienna." She cast a glance over her shoulder at Jaccob, who was mostly paying attention to the lights outside.

After a moment, he turned his head and looked back at her. Ruby raised her eyebrows just enough to communicate to Jaccob he was invited to join her in the bedroom. It was understood he'd be staying the night with her, but if he had other things to do, she wasn't going to bully him upstairs.

Especially if the things he wanted to do involved cleaning up the cable situation in the media room or adjusting the light level on her back patio.

He smiled back at her and nodded, turning to follow as she left the room.

Jaccob was unusually tacit on the way up the stairs, and Ruby couldn't help but wonder why. If he was having second thoughts about what had been going on between them, if something about retiring with her in front of the others was bothering him, she needed him to own up to it, and soon. But she knew him well enough to know that probably wasn't going to happen.

It had taken him years to so much as admit he had unresolved issues around the way things had ended between them the first time. Whatever he was dealing with now, he was unlikely to be particularly forthcoming with it.

"I'm going to get changed," she said, as Jaccob pulled her bedroom door shut behind them. "I'll be right back." She squeezed his hand and kissed his cheek before heading into her dressing room and closing the door part way behind her. If he got it in his head to try and make a clean getaway, she would give him the cover. She'd much rather let him slip out now and make excuses later than try and force a conversation she'd rather not have.

When Ruby returned to the bedroom, Jaccob was standing by the windows, leaning on one forearm against the glass while his other hand was in his pocket. He seemed preoccupied by something, and it probably wasn't whatever cleanup was still happening in the back yard. Ruby crossed behind him, taking a seat on the divan across from the head of her bed and pouring herself a dram of Scotch from the decanter she kept on the side table.

After a moment, Jaccob turned around to face her.

He looked pensive. Troubled. If he was having second thoughts, Ruby needed to know that now. If he was about to walk out of this room, she'd much rather he'd done so while she was getting changed. But better now than twenty minutes from now.

This was a dalliance, but (as much as she hated it) Ruby was self-aware enough to know it wouldn't be long before her heart got involved. And she was not about to set herself up for a second heartache courtesy of Jaccob Stevens.

"Everything all right?" she asked. It was as open-ended a question as she could hope to get an answer to.

"Yeah," he said, shoving his other hand into a pocket as he smiled. "I was just thinking."

"I'd offer a penny for your thoughts, but the damn things are worthless in this economy."

His smile got brighter as he left his spot at the window to sit on the divan beside her. She poured him a glass of Scotch and handed it over without bothering to ask whether he'd like one.

Jaccob shook his head and took a sip. "You—You let me cook dinner tonight even though you didn't really want to. You weren't thrilled with the idea, but you let me do it anyway. Because I wanted to. And that reminded me of something you said to me while we were talking about Mike and this situation. You said when someone matters to you, you do the best you can to make them happy."

"I am eternally in awe of the degree to which you pay attention when I talk."

"Yeah, well—"

"But I feel like you were going somewhere with that," she said, doing her best not to let his blush derail what he was trying to say. "Pray continue."

"Yeah." He took a deep breath and stood up. "It just ... I was thinking ... What you said about why you didn't tell me about your magic ... before. It was just ... it was that."

"In part, I suppose it was."

"In part?"

"All right." She untied the scarf from her bun and shook her head until her hair fell around her shoulders. "I guess we're doing this."

"We're doing—?"

"We've been dancing around this conversation for weeks. I didn't want to have it. I thought we could get away with never having it. But now that we've been sleeping together, if we want to continue sleeping together, then I think it's best we just get it over with—put everything out in the open. Because what you and I don't need is extra tension and complication."

"Um ... okay?"

"Jaccob, I didn't tell you about my relationship to magic two years ago because for all I knew, it was in the past—no more relevant to what you and I were doing than any other past relationships we never discussed."

"But you were trying to get it back. So it wasn't in the past."

"That's true, I was. I was trying everything I could think of to get my magic back, but with what I knew to be impossible odds against anything working. Meaning: I was left straddling this torturous line between trying to get back this part of myself I'd lost—that was missing—and finding a way to move on with my life without it. And you, Jaccob, fell very squarely into column B."

"I—"

"Being with you was proof I could still have good things in my life even without magic. You would never have wanted to be with me in my original and un-damaged state, and the way you looked at me ... well, it made up for a lot of what I was missing."

"I was—" Jaccob shifted. "I was your good thing?"

"You were just about the only good thing." She leaned forward to refill her glass from the decanter.

"And before you even knew whether your power was coming back, I freaked out and walked away."

"It wasn't your finest moment." Ruby took a sip of her Scotch and shrugged.

"If I hadn't—" He refilled his own glass before coming to sit back down beside her. "Would you have told me?"

"Told you what?"

"When you got your powers back, would you have told me about that? About the magic? About what you'd been going through all that time?"

"That was the idea. Yes." Ruby sipped her Scotch for a moment before continuing. "Probably not right away, but eventually. Once I understood the power and its mechanics and its limitations, yes. Once I was sure I could do so adequately, I would have explained everything. That is ... I wanted to."

"Well," he said, also taking a sip of Scotch. "If you want to explain things to me now—"

"I no longer owe you an explanation!"

"No, I guess you don't."

"Listen, if there's something you want to know, I don't mind your asking. But I see no need to fully explain myself, or what went on with me two years ago, in the interest of trying to keep you from walking out of my life. Because I've already lived that worst-case scenario, Jaccob. You walked. And I survived."

"And two years later, I still owe you an apology for that."

"Do you, now?"

"I'm not sure I've ever said I'm sorry."

"Are you sorry?" she asked him frankly. "Because I'd rather not hear it than be lied to. If you stand by what you did and how you reacted, I can respect that. But—"

"No, I *am* sorry. I appreciate what you're saying, and that you want me to be honest. And maybe I could just say 'I wish it had been different,' and you'd let that be enough. But it's not enough. I panicked. I got hurt, and I got scared. I freaked out, and I ran. I was a coward, and you deserved better."

"I appreciate your saying that."

"Look." He leaned in to pick up the Scotch bottle again. He topped off her glass and then his own as he continued. "I was a mess. I thought my marriage had ended, and I didn't understand why. But then I found this new thing with you, and it was ... it was so good. And then out of nowhere, I found out there was this whole side of you that I didn't know about, and I got scared. I thought I'd jumped into something headfirst, and I should have looked before I leapt and ... and I was just scared. And like a real goddamn coward, I turned tail and ran. You were *in a hospital* and I ... I just fucking ran. And I'm sorry."

"I accept your apology," she replied, looking him squarely in the eye as she sipped at her Scotch.

"I don't expect you to forgive me, but—"

"Jaccob, I forgave you a long time ago."

"You did? Really?"

"Really." She reached out and took his hand in hers. "My life is too damn big to hold on to small grudges. You didn't kick me while I was down, you didn't out me to the tabloids, you didn't use what you know about me to fuck with my company. You just turned your back, walked away quietly, and stayed quiet. That's just about the best a person can hope for after a breakup."

"I never meant to hurt you. And I'd never do anything to hurt you on purpose."

"I know. It's part of the whole 'Good Guy' thing." Ruby chuckled.

Jaccob wasn't laughing. He cast his gaze downward and shook his head. "I try to be that guy. Even when I'm not wearing the suit, I try to be that guy. But I don't always succeed at it. And I count the way things ended with you as one of my greater failures."

"You clearly failed so profoundly at ending things it turned out not to be the end at all."

"Or maybe it was, and we've started again."

"Perhaps, and maybe that's better."

"You think?"

"I think we're being more sensible this time."

"Sensible? Really?"

"Two years ago, to borrow your turn of phrase, we both leapt in headfirst. In your case, I think the word 'rebound' wouldn't be out of place."

"Ruby, I didn't—"

"I don't mean to minimize." She turned on the divan to face him better and set her hand on his knee. "Merely to acknowledge the fact that two years ago, you were very recently separated and probably hadn't done a lot to process that before we started spending time together."

"Okay, yeah. I guess you're right about that."

"I know I'm right. Whereas now, you're comfortably divorced. You know where your head is. And for that matter, so do I. Now you know all about the magic, that it's powerful and stable, moments of overuse notwithstanding. And you know about Vivienne. There's no chance of me having to play at monogamy. Meanwhile, I know your habits, your expectations. I know your children. That is, I know Mike adores me and while Chuck doesn't strictly need me to die in a fire, that's certainly on her approved list of ways to be rid of me."

"Chuck doesn't hate you."

"Yes, she does. Even Katy knows that, and I wouldn't have believed Katy understood the concept of hatred. But it's fine. It's not like I'm trying to get into the stepmother business. Chuck thinks hating me is somehow equivalent to defending her mother, and who am I to give a damn? I don't think we'll have a problem steering clear of each other. Two years ago, I might have felt like I had something to prove. Now—" Ruby shrugged as she squeezed Jaccob's knee. "It doesn't matter. It only matters that you and I want to continue spending time together. Or not."

"Or ... not?"

Ruby shook her head. She took another sip of Scotch before leaning forward to set her glass down on the table. She turned back to Jaccob then, adjusting her position to face him fully and placing her hands on either side of his waist.

"I like what we've got going on right now," she said. "It's casual, it's drama-free, and other than the occasions on which you and Vivienne decide to gang up on me, it's eminently enjoyable. As far as I'm concerned, we could keep this up forever."

Jaccob took a sip of Scotch and sighed. "I like some of those words better than others, but this level of honesty is refreshing."

"And there it is. My cards are on the table. We can keep doing this or we can stop doing this."

Jaccob set his glass down and smiled at her. "I think I want to keep doing this."

"Good. Because I do, too. So how about you get the lights and let's go to bed?"

CHAPTER TWENTY-EIGHT

Ruby was awake, and she didn't like it. Something was *off*. The food, the wine, the Scotch, and the sex had all been more than satisfactory; her evening should have set her up for a good night's sleep. There was no reason for her to be awake and restless at ... she looked at the clock. It was ten past two.

No reason.

Unless there *was* a reason.

Ruby slipped out of bed and padded to her vanity, where her dressing gown lay draped over the bench. Slipping it over her shoulders, she looked back at Jaccob, sound asleep on his side of her bed, facing the empty space she'd just vacated. He was a deep enough sleeper, he wouldn't notice her absence.

At least for a little while.

She scurried back to her nightstand and slipped one of her modified Starbands onto her wrist. Better to be safe than sorry. If whatever had her hackles up turned out to be a genuine danger, a non-magical defense against mortal weapons and a button to wake up Jaccob would likely come in handy.

Ruby left the room as quickly and quietly as possible, pausing only to grab her phone and slide on her slippers.

There was no telling what was wrong, only that her gut told her *something* was. She made a quick trip along the third-floor hallway, reaching out magical feelers in search of anything that might be amiss. Finding no disordered energies among her sleeping houseguests, Ruby headed downstairs.

It wasn't often her gut had her up nights. And in the few times she could remember it happening, there had always been some danger or discord behind it. She'd come too far and survived too much to ignore it now. The second floor was as silent and sewn up as the third floor had been. She found the ground floor equally quiet.

She had half a mind to chalk this feeling up to the weirdness of having Jaccob in her bed and a house full of capes when it occurred to her to look outside. She was approaching the glass doors between the dining room and the patio when her entire back lawn suddenly lit up bright as day.

Those bulbs Jaccob had installed were really something.

It took a moment for her eyes to adjust, but as they did, Ruby spotted a gleaming edifice on the lawn by the hedge maze. It was the same contraption she'd seen on her helipad the day of the shooting—she was sure of it. She'd never seen a machine like that before, and it wasn't the kind of thing a person was likely to forget. Its transparent sides, silver-chrome seams, colorful lights, and unusual shape were unmistakable in the garish light the security floods provided.

As Ruby crept closer to the door, she spotted them—the same two men who'd emerged from that machine on her helipad. The same two men who'd opened fire on her and her hired capes. Those two men were now standing on her lawn.

They were both armed this time, creeping across the grass slowly with one hand on their holstered weapons like actors in a bad police procedural. There was no need to be slow and sneaky when brightly lit and fully exposed. They'd have done better to run for cover.

But never mind. Their foolishness would be her advantage. They had no idea she was watching, no idea she could see them. Ruby considered her options as she reached for the door handle. Part of her wanted to end them—to put them down right where they stood. But she knew she couldn't. For one thing, there would be no explaining away the two corpses on her lawn, especially not to Jaccob.

Plus, she wanted answers only these fuckers could provide. She needed to know why this was happening, what they wanted from her, and why they'd decided on her and Mike as targets. If she offed them, she'd never find out.

Slowly, she turned the door handle and slipped outside, concealing herself at first in the shadow of one of the topiaries flanking the door. She watched as the two trespassers continued across the lawn. They were headed for the pool shed and the pergola, not toward the house, and she had no idea why.

She could get to them with magic. But she had no idea how effective she'd be. She wasn't at full strength, she knew that, and combat had never been her forte to begin with. Ruby looked down at the shiny tactical accessory she wore on her left hand; Jaccob had told her she could shoot a stun bolt from it. It would more than halfway drain the battery, lowering the efficacy of any shield it raised afterward. But if aimed correctly, it could take both the men out in one fell swoop, and she wouldn't have need of any shield at all.

Ruby waited a moment to make sure the two intruders were looking in another direction before she crept out from behind the planter and dashed to a place on the patio where she'd have a line of sight on both of them without risking her shot clipping the railing or any of her shrubbery.

Damage she could handle, but she only had one shot with this thing, and she had no idea whether it could be deflected or diminished by contact with anything between its point of origin and its intended target.

Ruby held her arm out in front of her, sighting the Starband's emitter the way she'd learned to sight a shotgun as a child, and pressed the button to fire. The bolt flung itself forward—a tight-but-expanding shockwave of visual energy—and hit the ground just in front of the two intruders.

"Damn!" For a moment, she was angry at Jaccob for not warning her she'd need to adjust the sight upward. But she didn't have time to be annoyed. She'd given away her presence and her position.

The taller of the two men had barely been knocked off balance by the stun bolt; he swung his firearm in Ruby's direction and squeezed off two shots in rapid succession. Ruby flung her left arm in front of her in the gesture she understood would activate the forcefield emitter on her Starband. The field sprung to life just in time to send the bullets ricocheting back toward the man who'd fired them. However much battery that stun bolt had spared had at least been enough to stop a pair of bullets.

The shooter's accomplice yelled something Ruby had a hard time hearing over the unexpected noise of the Starband's power supply. He was pointing his weapon at her, too. Ruby was no expert on handguns, but she knew they tended to be made of metal.

Metal, she knew a thing or two about.

Ruby swatted the toggle on the Starband Jaccob had assured her would set off his alarm. She'd been woken more than once in the middle of the night by the sound of the thing on her far nightstand. It was loud enough it could possibly wake the rest of the house, but she couldn't be fussed to care. She'd meant it when she'd said she'd gladly let Stardust take all the bullets going forward. As much as the field generated by her Starband was doing an admirable job thus far, she was well aware its batteries were not unlimited, and its capacity to protect her could give out at any moment.

When there's a superhero asleep upstairs, the best policy was to call him down to deal with the shooters. And if the alarm accidentally woke a second superhero—a naturally bulletproof superhero—she would not be complaining about the extra help.

But in the meantime, she could try and deal with the guns. Cold iron was perhaps the most magic-resistant material on the planet, but guns were made of steel, and steel she could handle. Unfortunately, she'd need to see the guns to affect them. Magic under normal circumstances was hard enough without line of sight, but in her currently diminished state, she knew better than to try.

She sent a bolt of loud, stinging magic at the one who'd fired his weapon. He turned toward her and fired again, her still-active Starband taking care of that bullet without her further intervention. Which was precisely what she needed. In the split second the weapon was trained on her, Ruby imbued it with intention, scrambling the carbon, nickel, and manganese in the pistol to a searing heat that soon infected the iron alongside it, turning the thing red hot in the intruder's hand.

The gunman screamed, dropping the pistol and grabbing his burned hand with his other one.

Ruby's heart was pounding. That was more work than it should have been, but it did the trick, and she was pretty sure she had another one in her. She shot off another stinging bang, this time chasing the injured gunman toward his partner.

The other man did precisely as Ruby predicted, raising his gun to cover his partner's flight, giving Ruby the opportunity to repeat her magic with the second pistol. The second man dropped his weapon even faster than the first one had.

They were finally both disarmed, and close together—close enough a single casting could take them both out if only she could make one happen. But the magic she'd used to distract and disarm them was already sapping her strength. She was sure she heard Stardust incoming from somewhere on the far side of the property, a sensory experience that made no sense, as he should be coming from the bedroom balcony and not from the front of the house.

Was there something she didn't know? Another contraption? Additional intruders? If that was the case, she would absolutely need to handle these two herself.

Falling back on an old standby, and the one thing she was confident wouldn't fail in the moment, Ruby strode quickly toward them. As she did, she extended her right hand in front of her, curling her fingers slowly and deliberately, taking as she did the men's abilities to move and to breathe.

She had only just gained control over them when Stardust approached at speed. Whatever had him around the front of the house had either been satisfied or deemed of lesser importance. Ruby looked up at him, gesturing to the pair of immobilized criminals with a grin.

She could only just make out Stardust's expression as he slowed his approach; he looked stricken, and Ruby tried not to think too hard about it. It was one thing to say in the quiet of the bedroom that he wanted to be with her, magic and all, but it was something else to see her power up close. She turned her attention back to the intruders.

"You know nothing," she said softly. "You remember nothing. And you will say nothing. Nothing, until I tell you otherwise."

The men's faces went blank as the familiar spice of her own magic at work replaced the bitter taste of adrenaline in Ruby's mouth. The casting exhausted her, but it would be worth it in the long run. She would be the first to have answers—whenever that opportunity presented itself.

She wasn't thrilled about the need to wait, but she'd long understood the virtue of patience. She did the work then to return their breath to them, but nothing else. She'd keep them immobile until Stardust could take over.

He came in for a landing beside her. "You called," he said, smiling broadly as though his visible upset of just a moment ago had never happened.

"You gave me a button," she said.

"Are you all right? You look tired, but—"

"Yeah, I'm okay. The Starband did most of the heavy lifting. Got something you can hold them with? They're not being still of their own volition, you know. If I could let this spell go, it might do wonders for my pallor. But I don't want to let *them* go if I can help it."

"Oh. Sure. Yeah." With a flick of his wrist, a length of cable extended itself from the cuff of Stardust's suit, wrapping itself tightly around the two trespassers at the shoulders until their faces reflected their increased discomfort.

A whirl of vines appeared then, flower-spotted and thorny, snaking their way up and around the two men's ankles, causing one of them to cry out when a briar pricked his calf.

With a deep breath and a gentle shake of her head and shoulders, Ruby let go of the magic she'd bound them with. She turned to acknowledge Friday's effort and saw then that the avatar of Freya wasn't alone. Yumi stood alongside her, crimson sword crackling with energy, while Angel hovered just above their shoulders, arms crossed and scowling. Somehow the three of them managed to look powerful and menacing despite having appeared on the lawn in their pajamas.

"I thought I heard shooting." Stardust tightened the bindings around the intruders.

"I definitely heard shooting," Angel added, still not bothering to land.

"That you did." Ruby wrapped her right hand around the Starband on her left arm. "I'm starting to see the appeal of a super suit."

"I like the sound of that," Stardust said to her. "This is them, isn't it? The men from the roof of the Tower? The ones who tried to kill you before?"

"It's them. I'm guessing you recognize them from the security footage? Rumor has it you watched it enough times—"

The floodlights were bright enough Ruby could see Stardust's blush even through the tinted visor of his suit. He really was adorably demure sometimes.

"Yeah, I did. And I do."

"Oh, it's for sure them," Yumi told Stardust.

"Absolutely," Friday added, tightening her bramble around the two men's legs just enough to poke the one who wasn't already bleeding.

Ruby looked the men over again and then away, to where the machine they'd arrived in still stood. It was dark and dormant now, not at all the trim she'd observed through the patio doors when it first appeared. She wanted to see it up close, and if the distant howl of police sirens was any indication, she didn't have much time to do so. They'd surround the thing with crime scene tape and eventually cart it off to someplace she might never know.

If she was ever going to have the chance to try and understand the thing, this was her moment. Glancing once more over her shoulder to make sure the team of heroes had the two intruders in hand, she started toward the machine.

Ruby had barely taken three steps before she was suddenly overcome. She felt all at once unbearably lightheaded and nauseated, with an intense throbbing behind her eyes. It was as though the most intense hangover was mingling with the most exquisite migraine, and it took everything she had not to fall to her knees from the force of it. She inhaled sharply, pressing the heels of her hands into her temples and trying her best not to hyperventilate as she kept walking toward the contraption. Her steps were weak and unsteady, and she had to consciously work to remain upright.

"Miss K!" Angel was at her side in an instant, catching her by the shoulders before she managed to collapse. "Are you okay?"

Ruby waved her away.

Angel let go but stayed put as Ruby continued across the lawn.

She needed to touch that machine. She needed to feel what energies were within it. Psychometry had never been among her gifts, but she'd studied it enough to understand the basics. It was the best chance she had of finding out anything useful, and she was determined to do what she could while the damned thing was sitting on her lawn.

The sirens in the distance were getting closer; the police would be here any minute. This was going to be her only chance. Answers from the intruders would come in time. She hadn't scrubbed their memories, just locked them up tight. They'd be babbling nonsense to the police until she had a chance to question them herself, but if there were answers to be found tonight, they'd be found in the machine.

Ruby hadn't managed another step toward the thing when it suddenly vanished from sight. With a flicker from beneath, it was gone, as though it had fallen through a portal to nowhere. And in a moment, her discomfort was gone as well, replaced with a bone-level weariness she recognized as extreme drain and a whiff of cinnamon and vanilla on the night wind.

Ruby stood up straighter.

She turned her head just in time to see the first of the police officers running full speed into her back yard. Response time in this neighborhood was no joke.

She turned around fully then, moving away from the scorched grass left by the vanished machine to meet the police where the perpetrators were detained. It appeared Stardust had added a forcefield to the task of keeping the two men still. In response, Yumi had put away her sword, and Friday had let her vines begin to wilt, but the two of them were still very obviously on alert, as was Angel, who hovered a few feet off the ground behind them.

"Miss Killingsworth," a broad-shouldered lieutenant who looked far too young to have been elevated to such a rank addressed her as he approached. "Are you hurt?"

"I'm not. Thank you. These men are trespassing." She gestured to the two confused-looking strangers straining against Stardust's forcefield. "And they're armed. Or, rather, they were. I can also say without reservation, these are the same two men who appeared on my penthouse terrace and proceeded to open fire on me and my employees eleven days ago. These two young women can also attest to that fact, as can two others who are currently asleep inside the house. And, in case eyewitness testimony is deemed inadequate for prosecution, I'll have my office share the security footage."

"They're armed?" the lieutenant asked her. "Did either of them fire a weapon tonight?" More police were pouring through the back gate. In Kevlar vests and riot gear, with their sidearms drawn and ready, they streamed onto the lawn like a tactical army out of a bad television drama.

Ruby hated it.

"They were. And they did. Look, could ... could you please call off the invasion?" She gestured vaguely to the swarm of officers taking up positions around her pool and pergola. "They've been disarmed. They're detained. It's only been the two of them. Please. This many guns pointed in my general direction ... it's not good for my nerves. Send someone looking for a pair of pistols in the grass between the pool and the pergola and tell the rest of your fellows to cool it? Please?"

"Yes, ma'am." The lieutenant nodded as he reached up to the radio microphone on his shoulder, keying it on before giving an order for the others to fall back and stand down. "But you're sure you're not hurt?"

"Indeed." She held up the Starband clasped to her left wrist. "As a certain gentleman of my acquaintance provided me with the means to protect myself."

"Mr. Stardust, sir." The lieutenant turned his head to address the hero standing beside Ruby.

Stardust turned his head just enough to catch the officer's gaze and give a single nod in acknowledgement.

The police lieutenant said something else unintelligible into his radio before turning his attention back to Ruby. "I know you said it's just the two of them, but I'd like to have my people sweep the perimeter just in case. They'll be quiet, I promise."

"Do what you need to. And tell me the truth. Is there any chance we'll be able to keep this out of the papers? Preferably off the internet as well?"

"You know, I don't know, ma'am. I can put in a call to Public Information if you'd like, and I'll do what I can to keep whatever goes on the blotter as vague as possible."

"I'd appreciate that," Ruby said, as she watched a group of four officers approach the detained trespassers.

"We'll take them from here," one of the newcomers said to Stardust.

Stardust released the forcefield he'd put around his two captives, but waited until both of the men were cuffed and in hand before reeling in his cable. He watched as the four officers walked the intruders out from the pile of wilting brambles and ostensibly toward their waiting police cruisers.

Other officers were interviewing the capes. Yumi was sharing a detailed and very animated version of the whole ordeal, while Friday gave mostly terse, one-word answers. Ruby was pretty sure the officer talking to Angel was trying to flirt, and equally certain Angel had no idea that was going on.

Ruby, jittery and anxious and aching to investigate what she was convinced had just happened, took a shaky step toward Stardust. As soon as she was near enough, she reached out with her right hand and set it on the arm of his suit.

He turned to face her and closed the rest of the distance between them.

"Can you—" She was breathing hard, and she let herself lean against him a little as her gaze found his. "Can you handle the rest of this for me? See the police out, wrap things up, lock the perimeter back down? I need to go inside. I just—"

"Yeah," he replied immediately. "Yeah, go inside. I'll meet you upstairs."

Ruby took a deep breath and squeezed his hand firmly enough she was sure he would feel it through the gauntlets of his suit. She was tired, spent, and drained from the combination of powerful magic and being out of bed at nearly three o'clock in the morning. Letting that show was, she knew for certain, enough to activate Jaccob's insatiable urge to take care of her. She'd been sure before she asked that he'd agree to handle the wrap-up.

"Thank you." She made a point not to hurry too visibly across the lawn to the back door.

Sneaking through the downstairs to the basement door had never been this easy. She had no idea whether the sounds of gunshots or of police sirens had woken any of the other occupants of the house, but there were no lights shining on the ground floor, so she could at least be confident no one was between her and where she was trying to go.

The basement door was just off the kitchen.

Ruby moved as quietly as possible across the tile floor and into the alcove, through the door and down the stairs, switching on the light at the bottom before passing through the mundane and utilitarian areas of her basement. Her exhaustion turned to a quivering buzz as she pressed her palms against the door to her magical sanctum. She keyed in the code and waited for the first tumblers to unlock. Taking a deep breath, she reached out with magic to unpin the two bolt locks on the inside.

The bolts clicked into place, and Ruby turned the knob.

Passing through the ward felt like being wrapped in a warm fleece blanket. The outer chamber of her sanctum was a comforting place warded with magic spun from her fingers at every stage of her various acquisitions of power and surrounded by enough solid earth that in the unlikely event her wards failed, her secrets would remain safe from even the nosiest of arcane snoopers.

But her inner sanctum was something else entirely. The small, innermost room of the subterranean space was lined in lead and tiled in salt, in addition to being safely ensconced in solid earth. And her instincts told her she needed to look inside. Ruby approached the door, traced the runes on the brass of the handle, and waited for it to come ajar.

She pushed open the door and gasped as the motion-sensitive lamp lit up the room.

She couldn't decide whether or not she was surprised when she saw the machine standing there. She'd been right. Out on the lawn, she'd sensed a powerful occurrence of her own magic. But she hadn't cast it. She'd been right to guess this was what had become of the contraption they'd been chasing all this time.

Ruby approached the machine slowly, not entirely sure how much magic might be clinging to it, nor what it might do to her to touch it.

She reached out gingerly and ran her fingers along the smooth metal and cool glass of the machine's exterior, not daring to open it for further exploration while Jaccob was waiting for her upstairs. She'd have time to learn its secrets. She'd have all the time in the world. Because it was hers now.

It all made sense now that she thought about it.

At whatever point in the future, she must have found herself in want of this machine and having some difficulty getting control of it. The best way to be sure she'd win in the end? Come back to a time when she could garner unlimited superhero assistance in service of the goal.

It was obvious to her now that she'd borrowed some future kiddypop cover of Mike's song to get her own hackles up and send her running straight to Jaccob's doorstep. She must have found out about Simon Floyd around the same time. She'd figured out in Texas that a man with both ties to her company and a history with Stardust was unlikely to have been brought to their attention by coincidence.

She'd done the whole thing to herself. *For* herself.

As impossible as it seemed, it was the only answer.

That's why those men had come to do her harm; they weren't the ones who set this episode in motion, but rather they were somehow charged with stopping it from happening. She was glad, too, that she'd listened to her intuition when it told her to cloud their minds before Stardust or the police had a chance to question them. Maybe the day would come when she'd get answers out of them and maybe it wouldn't.

But no one else would, either. They wouldn't be able to implicate her in whatever future crimes had them chasing her through time to begin with. She had the only answers she truly needed; having the machine in her possession was the thing that mattered, even if she couldn't see why or wherefore at the moment.

There were mysteries still to be solved, but for right now, she was satisfied.

CHAPTER TWENTY-NINE

Ruby had no idea what time it was nor how long she'd been in the basement. She knew Stardust had plenty to deal with getting the police to wrap things up, but she also knew he was an old pro at dealing with law enforcement, and he'd be worried enough about her general well-being to hurry them along. She didn't want to have to explain her absence when he came looking if she could help it.

She tiptoed away from the contraption, out of her sanctum, and through the door at the bottom of the stairs, pausing briefly to seal it with a rune traced on the knob before hurrying back up to the ground floor.

The light was on in the kitchen when she got there. Ruby wasn't sure who might have turned it on, but she didn't care enough to bother going all the way to the front stairs. She wasn't surprised to find the rest of her houseguests sitting around the island, watching Stardust round up the last of the police through the pane glass of the patio doors.

"Hi," Lisa said, as Ruby came into the room. "What's ... Kara said there was another spike on the Ometer. They came back, huh?"

For a moment, Ruby could only nod. She took a deep breath as she looked around at the group of them of them.

"It's over." Her voice was quiet, but certain.

"Are you sure?" Kara asked.

"I'm sure those are the men who fired at us on the helipad," Ruby replied. "Yumi and Friday recognized them, too. So unless there was more than one faction of time-traveling miscreants out to damage my artists and my business, then I'd say we're done."

"The machine?" Kara asked.

"Vanished," Ruby replied, enough magic behind the lie that she was sure all in earshot would believe her. "I have no idea how or why, but one minute it was there, leaving scorch marks in my lawn, and the next it was nowhere at all."

"And you were worried about Dad scuffing your pergola," Mike said.

Ruby chuckled. "Indeed. But the lawn can be mended. It's hardly a concern. What I am concerned with is how we wrap this episode up. It's after midnight, which makes it Sunday. I'll pay the five of you through the end of this week. You'll have until then to be out of the Tower. Mike, that includes you, but Angel, you're welcome to stay a while. I can get you in a room with artist development, and we'll see what shakes out."

"Oh, thank you!" Angel said, clapping her hands over her mouth in excited surprise.

"Miss Sparx," Ruby continued, "I would appreciate whatever you're able to do in service of getting the Professor's equipment shut down and packed away for its return to the University."

"Yeah," Kara said, "I can do that."

"And you can tell Cassidy Sweet her check will be mailed."

"Ma'am—?"

"I'm sure you don't take me for the kind of fool who wouldn't have a tail on you," Ruby said, "both to assure your safety and as a bit of insurance against being double-crossed. It's no surprise to me Jaccob called Cassidy, although I'll admit to being a little shocked she agreed to help. I've known for sure of her involvement since the bunch of you got tangled in a bar fight you conveniently neglected to mention. I don't know exactly what Cassidy's role was in all of this, nor do I care to. What I do know is that you must have found her assistance valuable and that you all managed to keep her engaged without any one of you violating the terms of your NDA. Now, I'm no more a fan of hers than she is of mine, but if she's done work for me, she deserves to be fairly compensated. However, I needn't break that news myself. So—"

"Yes, ma'am." Kara nodded, her eyes a little wider than usual.

Ruby decided not to comment on that.

"Along similar lines," she said to the group, "I'll have my accountant in touch with each of you about your bonus, as you may wish to finesse the payout a bit. Lump sums of cash aren't always the best way to take payments, thanks to this country's asinine tax code. I'd prefer you all see as much of that money as possible, and the Prather administration as little as we can manage."

"Thanks," Friday said, nodding. Ruby could tell she was trying not to let on how unbelievable she found it that she was about to come into that kind of money, tax bill notwithstanding.

"Now, Miss Yamamoto," Ruby said, turning to face Lisa where she sat at the counter, "consider our informal freelance agreement extended until November's election. After that, we'll schedule a proper orientation and onboarding, at which time we'll get you a key card and assign you an office and a parking space. If you'd like to put that off until after you graduate, the offer won't expire."

"Yes, ma'am," Lisa said, smiling over her mug. "Thank you."

"And as for you, young man," Ruby said to Mike, "you're back to work on Monday morning. Do you want to let your producers know, or should I?"

"I can tell them." Mike looked down at Katy and smiled. "I think we're all ready to get back to it."

"You'd better be. Now, Miss Jones," Ruby said, turning to look at Friday, "in doing my due diligence in the early days of your employment, I came across a piece of your research."

"You ... you did?" Friday asked, shaking her head.

"I think the work you're doing, particularly around seed maximization and high-yield food crops, is fascinating. And I also think it's important. I don't make a habit of giving money away, but I do make investments. And I'm happy to invest in good science. When you're ready to strike out on your own, you let me know. The funds will be there."

Friday froze, her mouth slightly agape. She nodded at Ruby but said nothing.

Yumi and Lisa jumped in the air and hugged her from either side.

"Miss Kujikawa," Ruby said. "I understand you're also due to finish your undergraduate studies here presently. I don't know what your post-graduation plans are, but if you're interested, I'd be glad to have you in the office as well. We can make allowances for your athletic schedule if that's a consideration; Goblin Media would be delighted to have another Olympian in our employ. But regardless of whether or not that offer is of interest, you should know that as long as you and Miss Yamamoto continue to cohabitate, she's welcome to add you, and anyone else who happens to share your address, to her benefits."

"Benefits?" Lisa asked.

"Benefits," Ruby said. "Medical. Dental. Vision. Retirement. Education reimbursement—"

"Really?" Yumi asked.

"It would be asinine and hypocritical for me to try and enforce hetero-monogamy," Ruby said. "Capitalism writ large may say I'm doing it wrong, but my profit margin doesn't lie. I'll warn you; I've heard the paperwork's exhaustive—something about making sure we're not processing insurance for every one night stand our interns have—but once it's done, we won't take it back, not unless the qualifying employee quits or is fired."

"Or, like, dies?" Angel added.

"No," Ruby replied. "No. If an employee dies, their dependent partners, children, and other family members can keep their coverage free of charge."

"That's ... that's really generous," Friday finally managed to say.

"Nonsense," Ruby said. "It leads to employee retention and a good public image, and if there are two things an entertainment empire needs to operate, they're institutional knowledge and good PR."

"Yeah," Angel said. "That makes sense."

"And there you have it," Ruby said. "It makes sense. Take tomorrow ... today ... you know what I mean—Sunday—to do whatever the hell you want. Stick around here, use the pool, eat everything in the kitchen if you want to. Or head back to town, start moving your things out and getting back to your usual lives. Or, hell, take advantage of the fact I won't be closing your expense account for another week and go bananas at the skymall. I honestly don't care, as long as you're doing what you want to do and taking the day off. That includes you, Miss Yamamoto. We're well enough into this project that you having a Sunday to yourself isn't going to set us back."

"Yes, ma'am," Lisa replied.

"Now," Ruby said. "You're all adults and you have tomorrow off, so I have no business telling you not to be up this late. But I am exhausted and cranky, and I am going to bed. So I'll ask that you please keep the noise down."

"Yes, ma'am," Lisa said again.

"Good night," Ruby said, moving away from the island and toward the back stairs.

"Good night," the others said in near unison.

~

Ruby seldom chose to take the back stairs, partially because she was so rarely in the kitchen, but mostly owing to a series of run-ins with scurrying staff members when she'd first bought the house, back at the beginning of her tenure in the Goblin Records C-suite. She'd quickly gotten the impression her staff didn't appreciate the lady of the house using what was ostensibly their staircase, and she'd made a point to avoid it ever since.

But there was little chance of running into an employee at quarter past three in the morning. The staff rooms were, thankfully, well enough insulated that the few members of her overnight complement should have been able to sleep soundly through the ruckus. Add to that the fact that the back stairs were narrow enough for her to hold both rails at once, and she was willing to run the negligible risk.

When she reached her bedroom on the third floor, the floodlights from her back yard were still shining brightly enough there was no way she would be getting to sleep even with the curtains drawn. She understood intellectually why bright-as-day floodlights made sense as part of the after-dark trespasser protocol, and she even understood Jaccob having put them on heat sensors, so they'd stay on as long as anyone was outside. What she didn't understand was why they hadn't turned off yet. How were the police not done out there by now?

The danger had passed. The intruders were in handcuffs and well on their way to someplace where they couldn't bother her again. And Stardust was seeing the last of the law enforcement personnel off her property and locking the gate behind them.

So why the hell were the godsdamned lights still on? How long could it possibly take to find two red hot guns in the well-lit grass, pack them up, and get out?

Running her fingers through her surely-too-tousled hair, Ruby pulled aside the heavy drape over the balcony door and pushed it open. She stepped out onto her bedroom terrace, leaving the door ajar behind her as she moved to sit on the wrought iron chaise facing the pool. If she couldn't collapse into slumber, she could at least survey the goings on in her back yard.

It looked as though things were truly finishing up. There was no evidence of anyone on the lawn or the pool deck, and there were a scant few flashes of red and blue light reflecting off the white columns of the pergola.

She'd barely gotten herself settled on the chaise when the flood lights finally shut off. The police were leaving; the flashes of red and blue dwindled until there was nothing. For a moment, Ruby entertained the notion of going back inside but decided against it. Her mind was too addled to fall asleep; she'd only drive herself mad trying to. Best to sit here and try to center herself until Jaccob came up. With him in bed beside her, she'd be more able to keep her mind occupied until she was able to drift off.

She leaned back against the cushion of the chaise, pulling her feet beneath her as she listened to the last of the cars leave her driveway and the distant clanking of the gate at the bottom of her driveway. All was quiet for a moment, then she heard a soft creak from the bedroom door followed by the familiar whirring of the Stardust suit as it removed itself from Jaccob's body.

"I'm out here," she called, hoping Jaccob would see the gap in the drapes and figure out that she'd gone to sit on the balcony. The only other night he'd ever spent in this house had been in a guest room; she wasn't sure whether he even knew this balcony was here.

It was only a moment before he poked his head through the doorway. His face was hard to make out in the dim moonlight, but she could see he had a drink in his hand. His chest and feet were bare, and he wore the loose silk pajama pants he'd had on when she'd left him sleeping while she investigated her unease.

"I brought you a drink," he said, approaching slowly; visibly working not to spill the contents of the mug in his hand.

"Warm milk?"

"Whisky toddy."

"Good man."

"How are you?" he asked, as he sat beside her and passed the steaming mug into her hands. "That looked ... intense, looked like a lot."

"I'm okay," she answered, taking a strong whiff of the steam coming off the drink. "The Starband did most of the work. I barely had to exert myself at all."

"So you're all right, then?"

"I'm probably feeling it more than I should be," Ruby said. "I think I'll take tomorrow off."

"It's Sunday," Jaccob reminded her.

"That's why it's possible," she replied.

"Right."

"I figure I'll sleep in, sit by the pool in the afternoon. Drink sangria, eat ceviche, and just let myself be glad this is over."

"That sounds like a great plan."

"I'll be all right."

"I think you will."

"Are you going to be here?"

"Only if you want me."

"I do," she assured him. "But it's all right if you'd rather not."

"Of course I want to be here," he said, sliding closer and placing his hand gently on her knee. "Why would you think I wouldn't?"

"Because I saw the look on your face when I was ... dealing with the trespassers. The way you were looking at me; you're not comfortable with this. With me."

"I'm sorry you saw that. And you're right. I'm not comfortable with magic. I might never be. But I want to try. I want to get to know every part of you—even the parts that scare me."

"Okay." Ruby nodded, sipping at her warm drink with her eyes closed. "Okay." She looked up at Jaccob then and sighed. "I'm not in the habit of giving people second chances, Jaccob. This is uncharted territory for me."

"Hey, me too. But I mean it. I'm not the coward I used to be. I'm not going to turn and run. I won't leave unless you ask me to."

"So you're saying I'm stuck with that abomination in my driveway?"

"I'll get Mike to drive it home tomorrow."

"I can drive us back to the city on Monday."

"Ooh, can we put the top down? Maybe ... maybe swing by the Keep, so I can check on a certain urn that's supposed to be in secure storage?"

"Yes." Ruby chuckled, closing her eyes as she shook her head. Of all the silly things that might make him happy ... "We can do that."

She didn't mention how sure she was the vessel for Simon Floyd's mortal remains would be where it belonged. It likely wouldn't be long before some future version of herself scooped the good Mr. Floyd back up out of Texas and returned him to the place and time where his original murder was once again inevitable.

It was the only way to make sure everything else happened as needed.

"Good. And I think we should plan a dinner out with Mike and Katy this week."

"What? Like a double date?" She was still laughing a little, but even though the idea felt a bit absurd, she wasn't opposed.

"Something like that," Jaccob replied, flashing her the smile that made his eyes crinkle at the corners and her heart flutter in a way she'd never admit to anyone. "But more like a proper way to mark a new beginning. Plus, you still know them both better than I do, and I want us all to get closer."

"I think that would be very nice. As long as we're not going to Icons."

Both of them were laughing then. The threat of a night out with Stardust at the city's hero-themed restaurant had been a running joke between them for the entirety of their prior relationship. If they were really starting over, she wanted it clear that interdiction was still in place.

"I don't know. I think Katy really needs to see what she's gotten herself into."

"She's only lived here since January. She deserves at least a year to ease into things before you show her the full extent of what it means to be Stardust-adjacent."

"Yeah, okay," he agreed, scooting still closer. He leaned in then and kissed her gently on her bare shoulder where her dressing gown had fallen away. "We can pick a restaurant tomorrow while we sit by the pool and drink sangria."

"I like that idea."

"But right now, we should go to bed."

"Are you trying to get me to sleep? Or ... something else?"

"I could be persuaded either way. It's just that it's almost four in the morning, and it's not doing anyone any good for us to be up right now."

"All right," she agreed, reaching out her hand to take hold of his as she got to her feet. "I'll follow your lead. C'mon, let's go inside."

ABOUT THE AUTHOR

Amanda Cherry is a Seattle-area queer, disabled nerd who still can't believe people pay her to write stories. She is the author of five published novels, as well as TTRPGs, screenplays, and short fiction, and a cast member in the Dungeon Scrawlers GREYMANTLE game on Twitch. Her non-fiction writing has been featured on ToscheStation.net, ElevenThirtyEight.com, and StarTrek.com.

Amanda is a member of SAG-AFTRA, SFWA, and Broad Universe.

Follow Amanda's geekery on Twitter, BlueSky, and TikTok @MandaTheGinger or visit thegingervillain.com.